Heartwarm ... *and true love!*

A TASTE OF HONEY
DeWanna Pace

Toya and Betina have been friends forever. But can their friendship survive the rugged Texas prairie, and Toya's arranged marriage—to a man Betina secretly loves?

WHERE THE HEART IS
Sheridon Smythe

Orphans Natalie and Marla were like sisters. And now as adults, when the orphanage is destined to be sold from under Natalie, Marla has plans—to match her up with the orphanage owner!

LONG WAY HOME
Wendy Corsi Staub

Cira Valentino and her best friend, Lucia, are desperate to reach America. But when disaster strikes, can a handsome American heir save Cira, and make her and Lucia's dreams come true?

Long Way Home

Wendy Corsi Staub

JOVE BOOKS, NEW YORK

FRIENDS is a trademark of Penguin Putnam Inc.

LONG WAY HOME

A Jove Book / published by arrangement with
the author

PRINTING HISTORY
Jove edition / July 1999

All rights reserved.
Copyright © 1999 by Wendy Corsi Staub.
This book may not be reproduced in whole or in part,
by mimeograph or other means, without permission.
For information address: The Berkley Publishing Group,
a division of Penguin Putnam Inc.,
375 Hudson Street, New York, New York 10014.

The Penguin Putnam Inc. World Wide Web site address is
http://www.penguinputnam.com

ISBN: 0-515-12440-0

A JOVE BOOK ®
Jove Books are published
by The Berkley Publishing Group,
a division of Penguin Putnam Inc.,
375 Hudson Street, New York, New York 10014.
JOVE and the "J"design
are trademarks belonging to Penguin Putnam Inc.

PRINTED IN THE UNITED STATES OF AMERICA

10 9 8 7 6 5 4 3 2 1

My grandfather, Pasquale Corsi, was a prolific storyteller. After finishing a big plate of spaghetti on Sunday afternoons, he would lean back, light a cigarette, and pour himself a glass of wine. Then, with all of us gathered around him, he would sip and smoke and talk—about people he had known, and places he had been. He had a growl of a voice, and a quirky way of phrasing things. He persisted in calling *grapes* by the singular: *grape*; calling the Thanksgiving turkey, *the bird* ... and always, always he called me *doll*, and his *numero uno* (his firstborn grandchild). I'll never see my grandfather's brown eyes twinkling at me, or hear him say "Hi, doll," again. He died on November 17, 1998, and the loss is still fresh as I write this.

Long Way Home is based on the true tale he often told about his sister, Loretta. Like Cira, she was heartsick over leaving her sweetheart behind in Italy. Like Cira, she was turned away at Ellis Island because the immigration officials suspected trachoma. And like Cira, Loretta was finally admitted to the United States. But her story had a tragic ending. Not long after arriving in America, she fell victim to the Spanish Influenza epidemic. Loretta Corsi died at the age of nineteen. Her memory, and my grandfather's legacy, will live on. Like him, I am a storyteller.

Ti amo, Grandpa.

Long Way Home

Prologue

"*C*ira! Lucia! *Aspettare!*"

Cira Valentino glanced over her shoulder and saw Renzo Passerella hurrying toward them along the winding, dusty road leading from town.

Her heart seemed to leap and flutter in her ribs before falling with a plunk into the pit of her stomach as reality set in. "No, let's not wait for him," Cira said to Lucia Torrio, quickening her pace.

"Why not?" Lucia grabbed Cira's arm and held her back, turning and calling to Renzo, "We'll wait . . . *Faccia presto!* Hurry!" She whispered again to Cira, "Why don't you want to wait for him?"

Cira sighed. "Never mind. It's all right. We will."

How could she tell Lucia that every time she saw him lately, she was beseiged by unsettling, improper thoughts? Not just thoughts—urges. Urges that frightened her in their intensity.

No, she could do nothing but stand here beside her friend, whose round face beamed at the sight of the boy they had known their whole lives, the boy who seemed, to Cira, to have turned overnight into a stranger . . . into a man.

And then Renzo was upon them, his light brown curls damp and his thin cotton shirt soaked with sweat. The summer sun was directly overhead in the blue Sicilian sky, shimmering off the vast fields on either side of the road. Renzo had unbuttoned his shirt nearly to his waist, and where the fabric gapped, his chest and torso were visible—chiseled ripples of bronzed flesh that made Cira's fingers, hidden in the folds of her apron, clench with the ache to touch him.

She couldn't touch him. Not with Lucia standing beside her, staring unabashedly, just as she was, at Renzo's bare skin. Cira had long known that Lucia—just like every other girl in Fiorenza—had a crush on their childhood friend. She herself had been immune to his charms until most recently.

Now she found herself waking before dawn, straining to see out the window of the cramped bedroom she shared with her brothers and sisters, knowing Renzo would be coming out of his house next door to draw the morning water from the well. And she would lie awake in her bed at night, listening for the sound of his footsteps in the gravel of the small dirt courtyard as he returned home from wherever it was that he and his friends went in town. Renzo's parents didn't like his gallavanting, and lately, neither did Cira. Once, not so long ago, she had found his antics amusing. Now she couldn't stand to imagine him talking and flirting and doing who knew what else with other girls.

She caught him casting her a sideways glance as Lucia chattered about the upcoming Saint Joseph's feast at the church. Renzo's green eyes twinkled at Cira, and she quickly looked away, wondering what it meant.

Nothing! she told herself sternly. Renzo's eyes had twinkled at her hundreds of times, thousands of times, in the long years that they had been friends. Her whole life, practically. It meant nothing . . .

And yet lately . . .

Lately, Cira had sensed that there was something more between them than the teasing comraderie they had always shared. That if they were alone together, if Lucia wasn't with them, something might happen.

Which was exactly why she must take care never to find herself alone with Renzo.

Lucia broke off her steady stream of conversation to inquire, "Are you all right, Cira? You look pale."

"I'm fine," she said quickly.

"You don't look fine," Renzo said, and she thought she heard a hint of pleasure in his words. She struggled not to glance up at him again, but couldn't help herself. She found him still watching her, his eyes burning into hers.

"It's just the heat," she said succinctly, determined not to flinch under his gaze.

"Yes, heat can make a woman crazy," Renzo murmured, furrowing his sandy brows at her.

She knew he wasn't talking about the blazing August sun.

She felt herself quiver with anticipation, despite her resolve not to fall for Renzo. She knew him too well, knew she could never compete with the scads of other girls who threw themselves at him, knew that even if he did miraculously want her, there was always Lucia.

Lucia was infatuated with Renzo and had been since they were mere children.

Then again, what did that really mean? Lucia might regale Cira with a lustful cataloguing of his broad shoul-

ders, his quick grin, and his muscular arms, but Renzo
had never shown the slightest bit of interest in Lucia.
And surely Lucia couldn't hold it against Cira if she
agreed, at long last, with her glowing appraisal of their
friend?

They had almost reached the familiar cluster of low
stone houses where all three of them lived. From here
they could see that Mr. Torrio was waiting in the doorway for Lucia, glowering as usual.

"I'd better hurry—I'm late again," she muttered to
Cira and Renzo, and broke into a run.

Left alone with Renzo, Cira quickened her steps, then
felt his hand on her arm.

"What's your hurry?" he asked lazily.

"Mama is waiting." Her heart pounded so loudly she
felt certain he must hear it.

Renzo shrugged. "Let her wait a little longer."

"I can't. I have chores to do, Renzo . . ."

"Cira, don't pretend that you don't feel something
happening between us."

"I—I don't know what you're talking about. We're
friends, Renzo, we've always been friends."

"You want more than friendship from me. Admit it."

"I won't admit any such thing." Reluctantly, she
pulled her arm from his grasp, longing for him to take
hold of her again, to pull her closer.

"You won't admit it yet," he said thoughtfully, shov-
ing both hands into his pockets and rocking back on his
heels. "But you will, Cira. Very soon, you will . . ."

1

"*C*ira, stop rubbing your eyes. Please, please, stop," Cira's younger sister, Giulia, whispered in Italian.

"I can't help it." Cira dabbed at her swollen, itchy eyes with a corner of the shawl that covered her head and tied beneath her chin.

"Here, take this." Giulia offered Cira a crumpled white cotton handkerchief with scalloped edges that had been hand-embroidered by Mama in pale green thread.

Cira accepted the handkerchief mutely and wiped her streaming nose and eyes. Her head ached and she couldn't seem to stop sneezing and clearing her throat.

Hay fever. It had struck her with a vengeance every spring back home.

At sea she had been safe. But in the few hours since her feet had first touched American soil here on Ellis Island, she had been suffering terribly.

It didn't help that her eyes were already red and sore from the tears she had shed on and off through the voyage, particularly today, when the great steel Cunard ship had sailed into New York Harbor.

Other steerage passengers had cried, too, from the moment the towering Statue of Liberty had come into view. But their tears had been joyful. They were celebrating. Some of them had cheered, and others had bent to kiss the soil as they disembarked.

Not Cira.

She was utterly miserable, and had been throughout the two and a half weeks since they had left Palermo aboard the *Princess Irena* to sail for America. Ever since she had said goodbye to Renzo that last morning in the courtyard of the small home where she had grown up . . .

This isn't goodbye, Cira. I will come to America to find you, Renzo had said, wiping gently at the tears trickling down her cheeks, and then swiping his sleeve at those glistening in his own big green eyes. His face, perpetually ruddy from working in the sun-baked fields of Sicily, had somehow looked almost pale that day.

You will never find me, she had protested on a sob, burying her face in his broad chest, knowing she was soaking his thin cotton work shirt, but certain he wouldn't care.

He caressed her hair with gentle care, rather than tangling his fingers in it as he liked to do. He couldn't; today, in preparation for the ocean journey, Mama had coiled the long black tresses and pinned them at the back of her head. And she was wearing her good dress, a navy blue brocade with a skirt that she had lengthened with extra fabric so that it touched the tips of her shoes. It had been made over from one of Mama's old dresses, and Mama had cleverly concealed the worn patches of fabric with braided trim in some spots, pleats in others.

When Renzo had laid eyes on her that last morning, he had gasped and told her she looked like a grown woman, no longer a girl.

Yet, despite the womanly hairstyle and clothing, Cira had never, in all her nineteen years, felt more childlike and afraid.

America is a huge place, she had told him in desperation. *You'll never find me. I'll be lost there. . . . We'll never see each other again. . . .*

You will write to me, he told her hoarsely, trailing a work-roughened finger down her wet cheek. *You will write and tell me where you are. I will work hard, and I will save for my passage, and you and I will get married just as soon as—*

"You're thinking of him again, aren't you," Giulia accused in a low voice. She fiddled with the white rectangular inspection tag pinned just below her shoulder, craning her shawl-covered head as if trying to read what it said. Her attempt would be futile, Cira knew; not only were the words upside down, but they were written in another language, undoubtedly English.

Cira, too, had tried repeatedly to read her own card, feeling resentful at being tagged like a piece of merchandise. They all wore them; the officials had handed them out before allowing the steerage passengers to leave the ship.

"No, I'm not thinking of Renzo," Cira lied to her sister as they shuffled a few steps closer to the head of the endless line.

Lines.

That, it seemed, was what life in America was all about.

After waiting on the ship for several days until there was room for them on the island, they had to stand in line to disembark onto the barge that would bring them across New York Harbor to the processing station at Ellis Island.

Stand in line to get into the building, to the baggage room, and another line before they even reached the long staircase that led from there to the vast second-floor registry room.

Cira dabbed her eyes again with the handkerchief and imagined what she would tell Renzo about this scene. About the throng of people crowding the island, most of whom spoke in strange languages. Some wore queer costumes—elaborate headdresses or wooden shoes. And the smell . . .

She tried not to breathe too deeply, lest she begin to feel faint. It had been worse on the ship, she supposed—particularly on rainy, stormy days, when the unwashed steerage passengers had jammed the cramped quarters belowdecks. Some were seasick, and the stench of vomit had mingled with the rest of it until Cira had thought she would never again take a breath of fresh air without feeling deep appreciation.

"Cira, move," her younger brother Paolo said, nudging her forward.

She advanced a step, then another, as the vast throng inched closer to the foot of the stairs. Beside her, little Flavio, her ten-year-old brother, stumbled. Cira reached out to steady him, and he turned to flash her a lopsided grin.

"His leg," Mama said worriedly, casting a nervous glance to see if any of the immigration officers keeping watch at the top of the stairs had noticed the stumble. "He's getting tired from standing for so long."

"I'm fine, Mama," Flavio protested gamely, straightening his posture. "See?"

But he wasn't fine, and hadn't been in the two months since he'd fallen from a tree in the orchard back at home.

Before he'd left for America last year, Papa had constantly warned the daredevil Flavio not to climb so high. "You're not a little monkey," he had said more than once, his tone serious despite the twinkle in his dark eyes.

And mischievous Flavio, who particularly enjoyed dangling upside down by his knees from high branches, had tried his best to behave.

But once Papa was gone, he had gone back to taking risks. And Mama, who had her hands full with five other children and her elderly parents to care for, hadn't been able to keep an eye on him.

After the fall the doctor had warned Mama that Flavio might never walk again—and that if he did, it would be with a cane or crutch.

Cira, who had been praying for something to happen to thwart the plan to leave Sicily and Renzo behind, had felt terribly guilty over Flavio's accident. She had begun praying fervently at daily mass for her little brother to recover fully, no matter what the cost to her.

And he *had* recovered . . . almost.

His limp was barely discernible most of the time. Only when he grew fatigued did it appear. And he was fatigued now.

Cira and Giulia recognized the distress in Mama's voice and exchanged glances. They knew what she was thinking. Flavio might not pass inspection at Ellis Island. And if he didn't get in, they wouldn't be able to join Papa in America.

Cira wondered how much longer it would be until they reached the head of the line, where doctors were giving brief medical examinations.

Not that she was anxious to begin her new life . . .

Not at all.

She desperately longed for the one she had left behind—for Renzo.

They had grown up together, childhood friends long
before they had fallen in love.

The two of them, together with their friend Lucia, had
roamed the countryside in childish pursuits, climbing
trees, splashing in streams, playing hide-and-seek in
caves. Even later, when they were too old for such
games, they had remained a threesome, sharing jokes and
confidences.

Lucia, a merry, happy-go-lucky sort, had been the one
who brought out Renzo's teasing side. With Cira, he had
always been quieter, more subdued.

For a time, when they were in their early teens, Lucia
had had a secret crush on Renzo. She would rhapsodize
about his charms to Cira, who could never understand
what the big attraction was.

"He's like a brother to us, Lucia," she used to say,
bewildered. "How can you think of him romantically?"

"How can you *not*?" Lucia would reply with a
dreamy sigh.

But then three years ago, maybe four, Cira had noticed
that Renzo's cocky boyhood arrogance had been trans-
formed to a dashing, manly charm. He was terribly handsome, with perfect features and the sandy hair and green
eyes typical of many Sicilians.

Renzo was outgoing and confident, the kind of boy
who was friendly to everyone—little children, elderly
people . . . and girls. Lots of girls flocked around him.
Cira had always found that amusing, until she began to
notice his appeal. Then she became jealous, which
amused Renzo—and beguiled him.

Overnight, they went from being pals to lovers—
though not, of course, in the true physical sense. Cira

adored kissing Renzo, even allowing her hands to roam over the strange, muscular contours of his upper body. But that was where it ended. It had to, she told him every time he pressed her passionately for more. It had to end in chaste restraint. At least, for now.

They had been talking of marriage for months—but secretly, of course. Tradition demanded that Mama and Papa would choose a husband for her. But they liked Renzo, and Renzo's family liked Cira. There had been no question that the adults would find them a suitable match . . .

Until fate made that impossible.

When Papa had first gone to America last March, it was to have been a temporary thing. As an agriculturalist, he had had an increasingly difficult time finding work at the *latifondo*, the great estates scattered throughout southern Italy. The population was burgeoning, and there were simply too many people looking for work. The competition, combined with recent droughts, had made it necessary for Papa to supplement his meager income and feed the family by fishing in the coastal waters. Even that wasn't enough to get by.

Finally, with a sixth child on the way and no prospects for work, Papa had reluctantly decided to look abroad, as many Southern Italian peasants were doing. Almost overnight an Italian contractor, a *padróne*, had arranged a job for him in America; he would work for a year on a rail line that was being built in the legendary New York City.

Other men had left Fiorenza for America, and some of them came back with tales of the fabulous opportunities and great riches that awaited anyone willing to work hard—but not even as hard as they worked in Sicily during a typical harvest. Some men who had gone overseas never came back, and occasionally Cira would hear of someone who had died there, or someone who had abandoned his Italian wife and family for whatever reason. She couldn't help worrying about Papa. She couldn't imagine that he would ever willingly forget all of them, but what if something happened to him there? What if they never saw him again?

Cira would never forget the day they had all traveled to Palermo together to see Papa off. Mama, her belly swollen in pregnancy, had done nothing but sob as they stood there on the bustling pier. Her brothers, of course, had been enchanted by the enormous ship Papa would board. Her grandparents, Nonna and Nonno, looked shriveled and lost amidst the crowds and noise. Meanwhile, Papa had put one arm around Cira and the other around Giulia, and told them to be good girls and look after Mama and the little children.

"I'll be home in no time, you'll see," Papa had said before scurrying off to join the line of people—mostly men—walking up the gangplank.

But Cira had thought, back then, that a year might as well be forever.

How she wished now that she were only leaving Sicily for a year. That in twelve months' time, she would be going home to Renzo.

A year.

A year was nothing.

Funny how perspective could change so swiftly.

Anyway, Papa hadn't been as nonchalant about going so far away as he wanted them to believe.

The money he sent home was accompanied by letters he had dictated to a friend who could read and write. Papa, a peasant all his life, was illiterate, though Mama and the children had all been to school.

At first his brief letters were filled with bitter homesickness.

But as the months passed, his tone changed. Papa spoke in increasingly glowing terms of America, of the opportunity there.

Finally he wrote to tell Mama that instead of returning to Europe, he was sending enough money for all of them to travel across the ocean to join him in New York.

When Cira came into the house that day in January to find her mother clutching a letter and sobbing as Nonna rubbed her daughter's back and murmured in consolation, she had been instantly filled with dread, assuming someone had written to say that something had happened to Papa; that he was dead.

When she learned the truth, instead of being relieved, she, too, had burst into tears.

"But . . . we *can't* leave, Mama!" she had protested, even as Nonna had shot her a warning expression. "We can't move away, across the ocean. What about our home? What about Nonna and Nonno? What about Lucia? What about . . ."

Renzo.

"Your father has made the decision, Cira," her mother said sternly, straightening her posture and shrugging Nonna's hand from her back. "We must do as he says."

She had nodded miserably, knowing it was useless to argue. Just as her mother knew better than to question her husband's decision.

Now Cira glanced at Donatella Valentino. Her mother stood stiffly with her lips pursed, her brown eyes wary. In her arms she carried tiny Aletta, the eight month-old baby Papa had never even seen.

Donatella had done her share of crying back home, at night, when she thought no one could hear her. Cira hadn't been sure whether her mother was anguished over missing her husband or the prospect of leaving the parents and the homeland she would most likely never see again. Probably both.

But by day her mother went about her household work with dry eyes and a grim expression. She would follow her husband no matter what the sacrifices.

Where *was* Papa? Cira wondered as someone passed the wrong way down the staircase and through the crowd, jostling her.

And how long would it be before they were with him again?

Cira longed to be embraced by his lean, yet strong arms, to feel his bushy black mustache tickling her cheek, to hear him call her his *pèscalina* . . . little peach. The sweetest fruit in all the orchard, he always said.

Fresh tears welled in Cira's eyes, and she looked blindly up at the broad staircase that loomed ahead. She couldn't help being frightened of the immigration officers standing at the top. She had learned long ago, back in Sicily, never to trust anyone in a uniform.

Before they saw Papa at last, they would be confronted by those officials, and they would have to pass inspection. Rumors had flown among the steerage passengers during the interminable journey—about how the men would try to find excuses to keep the newcomers out of their country.

America beckons: Americans repel went the saying.

The rumors were horrifying.

The immigrants would be forced into cages like cattle, went the gossip. They would be required to strip naked in front of strangers. They would be probed with fingers and buttonhooks. They would be compelled to answer rapid-fire, inscrutable questions. . . .

And after all that, combined with the hellish journey across the storm-tossed sea, they might not be allowed into the country.

Some optimistically claimed that the tales had been generated by the Italian middle class, who were reluctant to lose their cheap peasant laborers to America and did their best to discourage the mass exodus. But most of the travelers had heard enough, first-hand, from others who had made the journey, to be leery about what would happen once they reached their destination.

Cira knew how her mother had been dreading what lay ahead; knew that Mama's worst nightmare would be if one of the children didn't pass inspection. Flavio with his leg, or seven year-old Antonio, who had been coughing for a week now . . .

Cira hated to see the worried, fearful look in her mother's eyes . . .

And she hated herself for secretly hoping that something *would* happen to keep them from entering into America.

Despite her lingering guilt over Flavio's accident, she knew she would be elated if the inspection officers said, "Sorry, you'll all have to go back to Sicily. . . ."

Then they would find Papa, and he would get back on the boat with them, and they would all go home where they belonged.

She smiled faintly, imagining the look on Renzo's face when she showed up in the spot where they had met every morning, in a corner of the cluttered courtyard between their homes.

You're back, Cira. . . . I must be dreaming. . . .

No, Renzo, I'm really here. . . .

How I've missed you, my darling Cira. Come here, into my arms. . . .

"Move, Cira," Giulia said, elbowing her in the ribs.

She realized that the line had edged forward again, and that she had finally reached the bottom of the steps. She found space to put her foot on it and pulled herself up, careful not to let the jostling crowd send her off balance.

One step closer to America.

One step farther from home.

She sneezed, cleared her throat, and rubbed her eyes, feeling tears welling up once again.

The high, tiled, Guastavino vaulted ceiling gave the registry room an aura of immense space, and so did the many arched windows and immense, brightly lit chandeliers. Yet several stories below, in the shadows, every inch of floor space was jammed. The line coming up the stairs had now been funneled into several lanes separated by shoulder-high metal bars and what looked like chicken wire.

Cira decided it really did give one the illusion of being in a cage. Why did anyone want to come to a country where a human being was first tagged like an object, then herded like an animal?

The din was incredible; thousands of voices echoing in the vast room, speaking what sounded like thousands of different languages. Every now and then Cira picked out a snatch of Italian, but even then, not always in the familiar Sicilian dialect.

She shifted her weight from one aching foot to the other as she stood anxiously with her family just outside the main part of the room, just steps away from the doctor who was giving medical exams.

"Cira . . . I'm scared," Giulia whispered, grabbing her hand.

Cira squeezed her sister's fingers, then shifted her gaze

to the doctor, who was using something that did, indeed, look like a buttonhook, brandishing it toward the eyes of the woman at the head of the line.

"It'll be all right," Cira assured her little sister, wincing and looking away.

"But . . ." Giulia's gaze moved to the white chalk squiggle on the shoulder of Cira's dress.

It had been placed there by an officer who had been standing at the top of the stairs as she passed by. She had looked up just before reaching the upper level to see him gazing intently at her. He barely nodded as he reached toward her, and she flinched, thinking he was going to strike her, or grab her. Instead, all he did was scribble on her with the chalk.

But she knew what that meant.

And it wasn't good.

On the ship, stories had circulated about the men with the chalk. They used coded markings to single out immigrants who showed signs of potential problems—physical or mental defects.

Flavio, too, had been marked, moments after Cira. His wasn't a squiggle; it was more like a right angle—or the letter *L*.

Mama had grown frantic when she first realized that two of her children had been singled out with chalk marks. And Cira, who just moments before had been hoping something would go awry, had found herself filled with trepidation.

What could they possibly think was wrong with her? And what were they going to do about it?

"It looks like the number three, only it's backward," Paolo observed, staring at the mark on her dress.

"Hush, Paolo," Giulia admonished. "It does not."

"It does look like a backward three," he said matter-of-factly, then turned to Mama. "I'm so hungry, Mama. Please, can't we eat now?"

Cira and Giulia exchanged glances. The younger children didn't seem to grasp what was happening here. They kept asking for food, or to see Papa, and they wanted to go back outside to play in the grass beside the water outside the mammoth main building.

The man in front of Cira stepped forward to have his turn with the doctor, and she felt her knees wobble. She would be next.

She turned to look at Mama, and the expression she saw on her mother's olive-skinned face caused a lump to rise painfully in her throat.

"Don't cry, Cira," her mother murmured as she felt hot tears welling up. "It's going to be all right."

Cira nodded and rubbed at her swollen, aching eyes. It felt like someone had poured boiling water into them, then scraped the lids with sandpaper. Her head throbbed, her throat itched, and her nose was raw from blowing it.

This was a nightmare, and—

"Next," barked the doctor at the head of the line, having dismissed the man.

Suddenly overcome by a surge of panic, Cira fought the instinct to turn and run away. Her heart beat wildly in her chest and her breath seemed to have caught in her throat.

Giulia gave her a little push forward, and she found herself standing face to face with the uniformed stranger. He nodded, and she saw that although he regarded her intently, he didn't look cruel or leering, the way some on the boat had described. Yet his expression wasn't kind and sympathetic, either. He was more . . . detached. Businesslike.

As his thorough pale blue eyes took in the chalk mark

on her shoulder, she saw a flicker of—*something* in them.

Something that terrified her, filled her with an awful foreboding . . .

He reached toward her and she saw something gleam in his hand. It was a buttonhook. Before she could react, he was using his left hand to raise her eyelid and his right to slip the instrument beneath the tender fold of skin, flipping it.

The pain was excruciating.

Cira struggled not to cry out, biting her tongue so harshly that she instantly tasted the metallic flavor of blood in her mouth.

"Hmmm . . ." The man made a thoughtful sound and released her eyelid.

She gulped and started to reach up and touch her violated flesh, but then he was grabbing the other eye, using the same torturous method to examine it.

He looked for a long time, then turned to a uniformed officer who stood by, waiting. He said something in English; something Cira didn't understand but for one word.

Trachoma.

She knew what trachoma was. The dreaded, contagious eye disease could cause blindness. It was also the most common reason immigrants failed the medical exam and were deported.

Trachoma?

She didn't have trachoma. Her eyes were fine, except . . .

"I've had hay fever," she told the man in Italian, gesturing wildly at her eyes to show him that there was nothing wrong. "It's the pollen outside—I'm not ill. My eyes are fine."

He merely shrugged and motioned for her to step aside, where the other officer beckoned.

Behind her, Cira heard Mama's anguished cry.

She turned and saw that her mother and Giulia were sobbing, and the other children, even tiny Aletta, looked terrified. The doctor was gesturing impatiently for Flavio to step forward to be examined.

"Mama," Cira called frantically as the officer took her arm gently but firmly. "No, no! Please don't let them take me away, Mama! Help me!"

Her mother tried to rush forward, but another officer stopped her. He spoke to her in Italian, and Cira heard snatches of what he was saying.

They suspected a problem with her eyes and were taking her to another examining room nearby for further scrutiny. Nobody needed to panic. Everything was going to be fine.

Maybe everything really is going to be fine, Cira tried to tell herself as she was led briskly toward a row of doors lining the perimeter of the Great Hall.

If they thought she had trachoma, she would be deported. That meant they would find Papa, and they would all be sent home to Sicily. She and Renzo would be together again, and everything would be back to normal, just as she had prayed.

Mama was hysterical.

She sobbed and screeched and shouted at the men who had summoned her for a discussion of Cira's condition.

The children were herded behind her: the boys, Flavio and Paolo and Antonio, with their faces somber beneath their dark visor caps, and a weeping Giulia, who held in her arms the blissfully slumbering Aletta.

These officers spoke in Italian, and their voices firm and reasonable. But nothing they said could calm Mama down.

Cira was suspected of having trachoma, and she would have to be deported back to Italy.

"It's all right, Mama," Cira kept saying, wondering why her mother was acting as though someone had died. "We'll find Papa, and we'll all go back together. Nonna and Nonno will be so glad to have us home, and Lucia . . ."

Finally her mother spun toward her and wailed, "*Noooo,*" in a high-pitched voice, clutching her head in desolation.

And that was when someone—later, she wasn't sure who it had been—informed Cira of the horrible truth.

Yes, she would be going home. The shipping company was legally bound to pay for her passage back over the ocean, since she had failed the medical exam. But . . .

The others had passed—even Flavio with his lame leg and Paolo with his hacking cough. So the company wouldn't pay for any of them to go with her.

Mama had spent nearly every cent Papa had sent on the fares for all seven of them to come to America. There was no money for seven fares back home.

Cira would be separated from Mama and Papa, from her brothers and sisters.

She would be forced to board the ship and travel across the vast ocean, forced to return to Sicily . . .

Alone.

2

*T*he *Princess Irena* reached the port of Palermo early one morning in the first week of May, in the midst of a warm, drenching downpour. Springtime in Sicily was generally arid, and the peasant farmers were undoubtedly rejoicing at the unexpected rain.

Cira disembarked the great ship hesitantly, clutching the small, battered satchel that held her few belongings, feeling dazed as she looked out among the eager faces of the throng awaiting the ship's arrival.

Somehow, she kept expecting to see Renzo, or Lucia, or even Nonna and Nonno.

But no one was there to meet her.

How could they be?

No one had known she was coming. Even if Mama had written a letter to alert Cira's grandparents or Lucia and her family, the mail wouldn't have reached Sicily before Cira had.

She would have to find her way up into the hills above Palermo, to her home village of Fiorenza, on her own.

Before she had left, Mama, who had been nearly delirious with grief, had pressed some lira into her hand. It wasn't much, but it was all she had. On board the ship Cira had painstakingly sewn most of the money into the seam of her skirt for safekeeping.

Over two weeks had passed since she had bid that heart-wrenching farewell to her family. Because the steerage decks were no longer overcrowded, the trip home was far more comfortable than the other journey had been. She was able to wash herself regularly, and even laundered her clothes using a sliver of bar soap borrowed from a sympathetic stranger.

Yet Cira felt even more desolate and shed far more tears than she had on the way to America, if that were possible.

Yes, she was going home to Fiorenza, home to Renzo and Lucia, just as she had hoped. But this wasn't the way she wanted it to be. She didn't want to be alone in Sicily, without Mama and Papa, without Giulia and Flavio and the others.

Where would she stay once she reached home? The small house where she had grown up had been sold to strangers.

And she couldn't stay with Lucia and her father. Ever since he'd lost his wife five years earlier, Mr. Torrio had become a sullen man who drank too much. He didn't even seem to like having Lucia and her brother around, so he wouldn't take kindly to a houseguest.

Nonna and Nonno had gone to live with her mother's sister, Aunt Roma, in a neighboring village. And Aunt Roma, a perpetually disgruntled widow with ten children, barely had room for her aging parents. She had grumbled about taking them in, wanting to know why they couldn't go to America with her sister's family—as if two elderly people needed or wanted to make that hellish journey and start a new life now.

Mama had told Cira to go to Aunt Roma anyway, to tell her that she would help with her cousins and the chores, that she only needed a place to stay temporarily, until Mama and Papa could send for her.

And they would, she knew. Mama had tearfully promised to send her the money for passage back to America as soon as Papa could scrape it together.

"Next time you won't cry so much that they think you have trachoma," Flavio had said, patting her on the arm.

Cira wasn't sure how to answer that. She didn't know that there would be a next time. She had never wanted to come to America in the first place.

In the weeks that followed, as she stood at the ship's rail staring out at the churning, greenish-gray sea, she had grown increasingly torn.

Part of her was convinced she belonged back in Sicily, the only home she had ever known. She belonged with Renzo. They could marry right away, live with his parents, start a family. . . .

But another part of her wasn't ready for all that. Not yet. She missed Renzo desperately, but she half-longed to remain a child in her own parents' home, whether that home was in Fiorenza or in the foreign New York City.

She had never felt so lonely in all her life as she did during these past seventeen days on the ship.

She almost found herself yearning for the overcrowded steerage quarters of the earlier journey, even with the constant din and overpowering stench. There had been a mood of gaiety then, as people danced and joked and sang to pass the time.

Now, the few people making the return trip with her, having been deported as Cira had been, seemed only to sit and brood, or wandered morosely along the fog-shrouded deck.

There was no one to talk to, no one who would listen, no one to disturb the muddled thoughts that ran through her mind in those melancholy days and gloomy nights at sea.

But the journey was behind her at last.

She was home . . . almost.

She picked her way through the muddy gravel and puddles by the water and looked for the marketplace. There, she knew, she would find farmers from neighboring villages selling their produce and wares. One of them might be willing to transport her back to Fiorenza, for a fee.

She left the waterfront behind and crossed a mucky street, barely aware of the rain pouring down around her, soaking her dress and her hair through the shawl that covered it.

She was too busy convincing herself that there was nothing to fear. She was a grown woman . . . well, practically.

If Mama could travel alone with six children all the way across the ocean, Cira could surely find her way home from Palermo. It was only a few hours' ride in a horse and cart—she would be there in no time. All she had to do was find someone who would be willing to help a young girl on her own for the first time.

She held her head high as she moved along the street, past a group of haggard, unshaven men who had gathered beneath the shelter of an overhang in front of a shop. They reeked of liquor even at this hour of the morning. One of them made a crude comment as she went by, and the others laughed.

For a moment Cira feared that they were going to come after her, but they didn't.

Renzo, she thought longingly, blinking back the tears that sprang to her eyes. *I need you so. . . .*

Once she was back in his arms, everything would be fine. He would take care of her, protect her. She would no longer be alone. Not ever again.

The two of them would go to America together, she thought optimistically. If they were married right away, Papa and Mama might find a way to pay for Renzo's passage as well as hers. After all, he would be family. And they could send for Lucia later. She had been envious when Cira had left, saying she longed to go to America, to find a fresh start. . . .

Cira had reached the marketplace. Despite the rain, it was teeming with activity. Peasants unloaded crates of fruits and vegetables and shouted the praises of their ripe, succulent merchandise, attempting to lure both browsing customers and passersby on the perimeter of the square.

Cira wandered among the stalls, munching on a wedge of fresh coconut she had purchased from one of the vendors, and seeking a familiar face. She knew several of the local peasants who regularly ventured to Palermo; perhaps she could find someone she knew who would take her back to Fiorenza.

But after an hour of searching, she realized she was among strangers. She would have to approach someone who looked friendly and hope he would be willing to help her.

The scream that pierced the air was chillingly close by, so shrill and urgent that it woke Thatcher Montgomery from a sound sleep.

He sat upright in the backseat of the open carriage and

glanced at the driver, a ruddy-faced local he had hired back in Palermo. The man had slowed the horses on the muddy country road. The surrounding area was lined with wild rose brambles, flowering vines, and trees, everything shiny from the rain that had just ended. Droplets glistened in the dappled midday sun that peeked through the leaves.

The only sounds were the steady *drip, drip* of the water falling from the trees, the rattle of the wagon wheels, and the birds that chirped merrily overhead.

"Did you hear that noise? A scream?" Thatcher asked the driver in English. Then, remembering where he was, he repeated the question in flawless Italian.

The man merely shrugged and craned his head to look behind them.

Thatcher did the same, seeing nothing out of the ordinary in the silent Sicilian countryside.

After a few moments Thatcher gave up and nodded at the driver to continue. He leaned back against the seat to return to his nap as they moved forward once again.

Three months of European travel had been both exhilarating and exhausting. He had arrived in England just after the new year, accompanied by several friends from his Harvard graduating class whose parents, like the Montgomerys, were treating them to a European tour as a graduation gift. The young men had caroused their way from London to Paris, from Brussels to Amsterdam. They had spent drunken nights in the beer gardens of Munich, learned to ski in Switzerland, and ridden in the gondolas of Venice.

Of course, Thatcher was no stranger to Europe. He had been abroad several times growing up, with his parents and sisters.

His father, Stoddard Montgomery III, had inherited his

fortune from his grandfather, a prominent financier. Like
the Astors and the Vanderbilts, the Montgomerys were
fixtures on the Social Register and had built mansions in
New York and Newport.

Yet, as if to compensate for their great wealth, life had
dealt several blows to Thatcher's family. His father's parents and only sister had been killed in a fire when Stoddard III was still a boy, away at boarding school.

At twenty, with his fortune on somewhat shaky
ground, Stoddard had married Thatcher's mother,
Eleanor, the daughter of a railroad baron. It was whispered that he married her to save his financial empire,
and that may have been the truth, as far as Thatcher was
concerned. His debonair, fun-loving father seemed to
have little but breeding in common with his prim mother,
and Thatcher had long pitied the man. Growing up, he
had noticed that his father didn't spend much time with
the family, and though he missed his presence, frankly,
he didn't entirely blame him.

Thatcher had always assumed that things would have
been different if his parents' firstborn, Stoddard IV, had
lived. But his older brother had drowned as a child in a
yachting accident in Newport. Thatcher, too, was on the
boat, and vaguely remembered his brother heroically
pushing him to safety before the water swept him away
forever. He had never gotten over the feeling that if he
hadn't been there, his brother would have been able to
save himself. He wouldn't have died.

Their parents had never been the same after that. Stoddard had begun spending as much time as possible away
from home. Eleanor, who had doted on her firstborn, had
never smiled again.

That was what his sisters liked to say, anyway. That
Mother had never smiled again.

Thatcher supposed they had a point, since he couldn't really remember her features ever displaying an expression other than sober-eyed resignation.

But it wasn't as though he had spent much time with her. He had been at boarding school from the time he was five, and at Harvard after that. Summers were spent at the Newport ''cottage''—a three-story granite monstrosity on Bellevue Avenue—but that was hardly family time. Stoddard only came on weekends from the city, and spent those few days playing tennis and sailing. Eleanor and the girls had their social whirlwind and charity events.

Meanwhile, Thatcher was busy with his friends and, increasingly, with the willing and blue-blooded female population of the summer resort. He was handsome and flirtatious, and girls had always found him appealing.

While his mother and sisters were virtual strangers, Thatcher did manage to build a relationship with Stoddard over the years. As his father's only surviving son and heir to the family business, he was the apple of Stoddard's eye. There was nothing his father wouldn't do for him.

That was why Stoddard had pulled strings and called in favors in order to see that Thatcher got accepted to, and finally graduated from, Harvard. It couldn't have been easy. Thatcher's drinking and carousing didn't allow much time for academic concerns, and it had taken him seven years to get through college.

Now that Harvard and his post-graduation trip were history, he would be expected to fulfill his destiny when he returned to New York. It was time to settle into an office in his father's building—and, at twenty-six, begin searching for a suitable wife.

It wasn't that he had a better plan. After all, one could

hardly argue that becoming a married multimillionaire was a horrible fate.

But lately, Thatcher had felt strangely stifled by the idea. Stifled, and . . . restless.

Oh, well.

There was no need to worry about the future now, on a lazy May afternoon in southern Italy.

The carriage rounded a bend, and Thatcher's eyes were just drooping closed again when he glimpsed a horse and wagon at the side of the road up ahead. The horse was tied to a tree and there was no one in sight.

"Stop!" Thatcher called to his driver, who seemed to hesitate before slowing the horses.

They pulled up alongside the wagon, and the horse whinnied and strained at the rope, agitated.

Maybe, Thatcher realized, it wasn't just the presence of strangers that had provoked the animal. Tossed carelessly on the ground beside the wagon, there was a dark-colored lump of fabric that looked suspiciously like a woman's shawl.

Thatcher unfolded his long legs and jumped out of the carriage. An overhanging branch nearly knocked his rounded bowler hat from his head, and he reached up to straighten it before calling, "Hallo . . . is anyone here?"

The only response was a scuffling, rustling sound from a thicket beyond the edge of the road.

Someone was hiding there.

The driver, his dark eyes wide with trepidation, called out to Thatcher in rapid-fire Italian. Though he was fluent in the native tongue, Thatcher had no idea what he'd said. The Sicilian dialect could at times sound like another language entirely. Still, he assumed the driver had called out a warning. He had heard chilling stories about the gangsters—the violent *Cosa Nostra*—who roamed the hills of Sicily.

Still, he was certain he had heard a woman scream earlier, and that meant she must be in trouble, whoever she was.

"Come back!" the driver called to him in urgent Sicilian.

Thatcher Montgomery, who never had been the cautious type, kept going.

A faint frown crossed his dark, handsome features as he took several steps to the edge of the road, not caring that his black leather shoes and the hems of his charcoal tweed trousers were mired in muck.

"Is anyone there?" he called into the undergrowth.

There was more rustling, as though an animal—or a human—lurked just beyond his sight. Then came the unmistakable sound of a muffled female whimper, followed by a sharp slapping noise and a harsh, whispered, foreign curse.

Thatcher waited, listening.

He heard another stifled cry, another slap.

Yes, a woman was definitely in jeopardy, in the clutches of some assailant who held her prisoner. Though he couldn't see her, he could sense her fear.

He had to save her.

His mind whirled for a plan.

Abruptly he called loudly back to the driver in perfectly enunciated Italian, "There's nothing here. Let's go."

As he spoke he saw the frightened driver's shoulders slump in relief.

But Thatcher shook his head to show that his words were only a ruse, and held a finger to his lips to motion the man to be quiet.

He walked back to the carriage and whispered, "You ride on up the road a little ways and wait for me."

The man started to protest, and Thatcher reached inside his coat to his vest pocket. He took out some bills and stuffed them into the man's hand. "Wait for me," he said again.

The driver nodded and promptly called to the horses. Within moments, the carriage was trundling away, around a bend, the rattle of the wheels fading into the distance.

Thatcher wondered momentarily if the man really would wait for him.

If not, he would have to walk the remaining distance to Fiorenza, and he knew he'd be lucky to get there before nightfall—if he found his way at all. He had no idea where the town was located from here, and no map to guide him.

That, however, was the least of his worries.

He glanced back at the bushes as the rustling began again.

This time there was no mistaking the sounds of a woman's screams. She cried out, in an unmistakable but understandable Sicilian dialect, "No! Stop it! You're hurting me!"

A man's voice chuckled and replied, "Yes, and you're hurting me, you feisty little *puttana*. Stop your squirming. See how swollen I am, how I ache with need for you? Now lie still. . . ."

"No!"

"Shut up!"

"No!"

Thatcher crept silently through the tangle of vines and shrubs, moving in the direction of their voices.

Then he saw them, on the ground in a small clearing.

The man, who appeared to be a middle-aged Sicilian peasant, straddled an ebony-haired woman who lay writhing on the ground. He was naked from the waist down, his rapacious intent obvious as he struggled to raise her long skirt.

Bastard, Thatcher thought, hearing the woman's anguished cries for help. He glanced around and spotted a sturdy fallen branch on the ground nearby. Swiftly and silently, he seized it in his hand and edged his way closer to the struggling couple.

Finally he stood just a few feet from the man's back and saw that the monster had succeeded in wrenching the woman's skirt up around her hips. Now he had taken hold of one of her long black stockings and was yanking at it.

As Thatcher raised the branch above his head, he saw the woman suddenly jerk her knee up, making sharp contact with the peasant's exposed genitals. The man gasped, a long, violent intake of air, then let out a keening, high-pitched howl as he fell onto his side like a wounded animal, his body doubled over on the ground.

The woman began to scramble to her feet, caught sight of Thatcher, and froze.

Her dark eyes were startled as they gazed into his.

His first thought was, *She isn't a woman at all. She's just a girl.*

His second thought was, again, *I have to save her.*

Thatcher hesitated only an instant before he brought the tree limb down with all his might on the peasant's head. The man gave a weak moan as his movements stilled and his body went limp with unconsciousness.

Thatcher turned to the peasant girl and found her staring at him, the remnants of fear clear in her eyes.

"Are you all right?" he asked her gently.

She only looked at him, visibly trembling, and then he realized he had spoken in English. He swiftly repeated the question in Italian.

Still, she said nothing.

Belatedly he remembered his breeding and removed his black brimmed hat in a polite gesture, then asked her, "Did he hurt you?"

She faltered, then shook her head, glancing at the man who lay unconscious on the muddy ground.

Thatcher watched her, thinking she was the most beautiful thing he had ever seen, though not in a conventional way.

Her features were hardly delicate. Her red lips were so full they almost appeared swollen, as if from a lover's fervent kisses. Her nose was straight and sharp, her cheekbones high and pronounced. Her skin was olive, with a golden flush—courtesy of both her Mediterranean heritage and the hot Sicilian sun. And her eyes . . . they were enormous, and dark, and fringed with lush black lashes.

He noted that her black hair was loose, a thick, silken tangle tumbling down her back, seeming to beckon his fingers to comb through it, to smooth the errant strands back from her face.

Something glinted in the sunshine, and he saw that her ears were pierced with tiny gold earrings.

She looked up then and their gazes collided.

He quickly shifted his sight downward, and found his eyes traveling the length of her lithe young body. She wasn't slender, the way his mother and sisters were. And yet she wasn't plump, either. Her body was contoured with ripe curves that were plainly visible beneath her thin cotton dress. The fabric had to be damp from the rain, the way it clung to her breasts above the slightly rounded slope of her belly. . . .

"I'm Thatcher Montgomery," he said hastily, because he had to say something.

He couldn't just stand here, staring at this strange girl's luscious body and thinking lustful thoughts. That would make him no better than the scum on the ground who had attacked her.

"Thatcher?" she repeated tentatively, and he smiled at the sound of his name on her lips, in her sweet, soft accent.

He nodded. "I'm from New York, but I've been traveling in Europe for several months now. I'm on my way to Fiorenza—"

"Fiorenza?" she echoed, looking startled. "That's where I live."

"I'll take you there, then," he said, and the grateful expression on her face conjured a warm glow within him. "What's your name?"

"Cira," she replied shyly. "Cira Valentino."

Cira could hardly believe that one moment she had feared for her very life, and the next she was riding along the bumpy, rutted road beside a man who was so worldly, so handsome, so refined, that he made her feel young and shabby and hopelessly ignorant.

When it came right down to it, she supposed Thatcher Montgomery wasn't so much older than she was, now that she saw him up close. Back in the trees he had appeared to be a mature gentleman in his fashionable three-piece suit and hat, with that faint growth of stubble on his cheeks.

But now she saw that his clear green eyes were unlined, and his hat was tilted at a roguish angle. There was

a youthful arrogance about the way he lounged his lanky
body in the seat, his long legs askew, his elbow propped
on the back of the seat, and his head resting on his hand.

He spoke to her a few times, mostly to ask whether
she was all right. He spoke the proper and stilted Italian
of a foreign tourist, though his accent was flawless.

Cira spent much of the drive, when she wasn't pon-
dering the stranger beside her, reflecting on what might
have been her fate if he hadn't come along to save her.

Back in Palermo she had thought herself incredibly
fortunate to have found someone willing to take her to
Fiorenza without even asking to be paid.

She simply hadn't stopped to consider that the man
might not have good intentions. He had seemed so pleasant, at first.

She had only begun to get an ominous feeling as they
left the town behind and she caught him staring blatantly
at her, leering at her body so lasciviously that she felt
naked despite her clothing. The rain had made the fabric
of her dress cling uncomfortably to her, and she did her
best to cover herself with her shawl.

But about an hour into the journey, the man had suddenly pulled the wagon to the side of the deserted road
and yanked the shawl from her hands, telling her abruptly
to stop hiding herself behind it.

Though his voice betrayed not a hint of cruelty, Cira
had instinctively known enough to jump out and run.

He had caught her, of course, and told her in great
detail how he planned to punish her. His full, fleshy features had suddenly seemed frightening, and so had his
tone.

If this handsome stranger, this Thatcher Montgomery,
hadn't miraculously come to her rescue, she had no doubt

that she would have been lucky to escape the peasant only after having been brutally violated.

In fact . . .

He might very well have killed her.

She swallowed hard at the very thought.

When she told Renzo what had happened, she knew he would want to track the attacker down, and make him pay.

That was how Renzo was. Possessive, and with a violent temper.

Once, when he had caught her laughing at another boy's joke, he had been so overcome with jealousy that he'd started a fight right there in the school yard.

At the time Cira had been flattered to know that he cared so much about her.

Now, though, she realized she would have to caution Renzo not to react rashly to the news that she had been attacked by a peasant from a neighboring town. He might get hurt in his quest for vengeance, and she couldn't bear that.

"Are we almost there?" the stranger's voice asked beside her as the road curved and sloped through a muddy orchard.

"Almost," she said, recognizing the spot. "The town is up ahead a little ways."

He nodded. "I've heard it's beautiful."

"It is, but . . . is that why you're coming to Fiorenza? Because it's beautiful?" Her remote village was hardly a popular destination for American tourists.

He chuckled, revealing straight white teeth. "No, that's not why, Cira. I'm here to pick something up for my parents."

"What?"

"A sculpture."

"A sculpture?"

He nodded. "My father collects art. And a sculptor who lives just outside your town is well-known in America for creating exquisite carvings."

"Dante Gasperetti."

"You know him?"

"Everyone knows him." Cira smiled. "My father says he's crazy."

"Uh-oh. I'd better watch my step then." Thatcher smiled back at her.

She shrugged. "Dante isn't really crazy. He's just old, and a lot of old people seem crazy. Besides, Papa worries about everything." She paused, then decided to ask the question that had been on her mind the whole trip. "How old are you?"

He burst out laughing. "Younger than Dante, I should hope. Too young to be considered crazy."

Embarrassed, she said, "I didn't mean—I didn't think *you* were old, *or* crazy. I just . . ." She trailed off, feeling foolish.

"Twenty-six," he said, rescuing her. "I'm twenty-six. How about you?"

"Nineteen. I'll be twenty next month."

He nodded. "I thought you were young."

Young? After what she had been through lately, she hardly felt young, she thought indignantly. She lifted her chin, about to retort.

But Thatcher continued, "Can I ask you . . . what were you doing with that old man?"

For a moment she had no idea what he meant. Then she realized he was referring to the peasant who had attacked her.

"I didn't know him," she said hastily. "I met him at

the marketplace, and he said he was heading in this direction. I asked him to drive me home.''

''What were you doing in the city alone, without a
way back?''

She saw him eye the satchel she held on her lap. She
had retrieved it from the wagon before they'd walked up
the road to the waiting carriage.

''Cira?'' Thatcher prodded. ''Have you been traveling?''

She shrugged, shutting out mental images of the
round-trip journey across the ocean, not wanting to
dredge up any more emotion now, especially in front of
this stranger.

As though he had sensed that she wasn't going to reply, Thatcher commented on the village they could now
see lying in the distance. As they drew closer, Cira told
him that he could drop her in the town square. From
there, she would walk the short distance to Renzo's
home.

''Are you sure you'll be all right?'' Thatcher asked,
looking faintly concerned.

''Of course I will be,'' she assured him. She didn't
know what made her add, ''My fiancé is waiting for
me.''

''Oh.''

Something in his tone, and in his expression, made
Cira feel vaguely uneasy. It was as though he had suddenly grown distant, though he was mere inches from
her.

She tore her gaze from his and stared out over the low-
lying buildings ahead, forcing her thoughts back where
they belonged. Back to Renzo.

He would be so shocked when he saw her.

So overjoyed.

She could hardly wait to see the look on his face.

"You're certain you'll be all right?" Thatcher found himself asking as he reached up to help Cira Valentino down from the carriage in the bustling square at the center of town.

"I'll be fine," she said once again, sounding rather impatient, he thought. He bristled, imagining that she was eager to be rid of him, to rush off to her fiancé.

Then he realized that they were attracting curious stares from the villagers in the square. People fell silent and gaped. Now several townsfolk called Cira's name, looking startled, Thatcher thought, to see her.

Was it because she was accompanied by an outsider, a foreigner?

Or was it something else?

Was her fiancé among those watching? Did he think something was going on between Thatcher and Cira?

Because, of course, there was nothing.

Nothing, he told himself, more than a shade wistfully.

Clutching her satchel in one hand, he clasped her fingers in the other and helped her step down. Her hand was sun-golden and her grasp was sturdy; so different from the pale, fragile hands of the women back home.

"Thank you," she said, her dark eyes meeting and holding his. "For everything. If you hadn't come along . . ."

"But I did," he said easily, with a smile. "If you need anything else, you know where to find me—at least, for the time being. I won't be heading back to Palermo until morning."

"I hope you find your sculpture," Cira told him.

He nodded, telling himself that he would never see this beauty again, and it was a shame.

Then she looked down, and he realized that he still held her warm, surprisingly strong hand in his. Reluctantly he gave it a squeeze, then released his hold on her, and handed over her battered satchel.

"Goodbye, Cira," Thatcher said, tipping his hat to her.

"Goodbye." She scurried away without a backward glance.

"Don't forget . . . if you need anything . . ." he felt compelled to call, then trailed off.

She was already gone.

3

*I*n another moment Cira would be in Renzo's arms.

There, a few paces ahead, was her home—rather, the small stone house that had been home until a short time ago. Now it was inhabited by strangers. That was evident from the unfamiliar clothing that was draped over the branches of the tree by the door. She felt a pang at the sight of someone else's things lying so casually at the entrance of the only home she had ever known, knowing that those clothes belonged there; those people belonged there—and she no longer did.

But Cira wouldn't dwell on that now.

No, all she wanted was to see Renzo. Then everything would be all right. *Then* she would be home.

She quickened her steps as she darted along the side wall of her former house, running into the small overgrown courtyard that separated it from Renzo's house. Dusk had fallen, casting long shadows across the weed-choked stone path beneath her feet. How many nights had she and Renzo met here at twilight, embracing right over there beneath the branches of the olive tree, in the protected alcove near the statue of the Blessed Mother. . . .

Suddenly she stopped, seeing movement in that very shadowy nook.

What . . . ?

Her ears picked up muffled sounds.

A soft giggle.

A low groan . . .

A *passionate* groan.

And it was familiar.

She had heard that groan many times—uttered from Renzo's throat. It was how he sounded when he was aroused; how he sounded when he had her in his arms and his hands were fumbling with her clothing, trying to probe the forbidden regions of her body.

And whenever he groaned that way, Cira would realize that he was losing control, that it was time to reign in the passion; time to pull away from his searching caresses and his dizzying kisses. Otherwise, there would be no turning back from where they were headed.

It was never easy, but she would force herself to stop. She would grasp both of his hands in her own, and she would take a deep breath, and she would look up into his smoldering eyes full of decadent promise, and she would say, gently, *No, Renzo. No.*

"Oh, Renzo . . . yes . . . yes . . ."

The hushed words carried clearly to Cira's ears in the still evening air. There was no mistaking the name— *Renzo*—or that it was spoken by a woman in the throes of passion.

Cira's stomach lurched and she squeezed her eyes shut even as she took a step, and then another, toward the private spot where two lovers embraced. She didn't want to see, couldn't bear to see, and yet she had to . . .

No. *No!*

It was all a mistake; it must be a mistake.

She wouldn't find Renzo there, not her Renzo, not in *their* special, private place, with another woman.

It had to be somebody else, somebody whose name was the same and whose groan was the same and who happened to have stumbled across this secluded courtyard behind Renzo's house. . . .

Because her Renzo was . . . well, he was *her* Renzo. He was waiting for her, waiting to come to America and marry her, and he would never—

No, he would *never* betray her.

Not after what she had been through. Not after she had been forced to return here, alone. He was all she had left, her only hope. . . .

Cira's foot struck a stone and sent it skittering across the path.

There was a rustle in the shadows as the female voice whispered, ''What was that?''

''Nothing . . . it was nothing . . . don't move . . . let me . . .'' murmured her companion.

And as that unmistakable voice slammed into her, Cira's eyes jerked open and she faced the truth in one shattering instant.

There, in front of her, was her beloved Renzo. His sandy hair was mussed and his cheeks were flushed and his mouth was on another woman's bare throat, one hand moving inside her unbuttoned bodice. The woman leaned against the wall and he stood between her parted legs, and his hand had rucked up her skirt and was caressing her thigh. There was no mistaking the intimate posture as their bodies pressed together.

Cira gasped and clapped her hands to her mouth in horror. This couldn't be happening.

At the sound Renzo lifted his head abruptly and his eyes met hers.

She saw the way his expression went from startled to shocked to dismayed.

"Cira!" he exclaimed, jerking his hand from the bare breasts and thigh of the woman before him and hastily stepping back from her. "Cira, what are you—"

Never before had she uttered the curse word that escaped her lips. Never before had she felt anything like the wave of rage and grief that swept over her. She could do nothing for a moment but stand there, frozen, her mind racing incoherently. She saw Renzo moving toward her, saw the bewildered young blonde behind him, saw both of them looking at her, their lips moving, but she couldn't hear anything either of them was saying. . . .

Then she burst into motion, turning and running with all her might, knowing only that she had to get away.

Thatcher accepted the glass from Dante Gasperetti and took a cautious sip. The red wine was far stronger than he was used to, and it burned going down. But he drank more, hoping to block out the disturbing memory of the young woman he had met on his journey to Fiorenza. Ever since he had said goodbye to Cira Valentino less than a few hours ago, he had seen her troubled face before his eyes and heard echoes of the tortured screams that had come from the woods at the side of the road.

Thank God he had come along when he had. He might very well have saved her life.

He sipped more wine from the filmy, grease-smudged glass Gasperetti had given him, wrinkling his nose in vague distaste, and he wondered what Cira was doing now. Was she safely in the arms of her fiancé?

For some reason, the idea bothered him almost as

much as the thought that she might find herself in trouble again, and this time he wouldn't be there to step in.

Why should he care whether a total stranger—a Sicilian peasant girl, for heaven's sake—was engaged to somebody else? Because she was beautiful?

Thatcher had encountered hundreds, thousands of beautiful women in the months he'd spent abroad. His thoughts wandered back over the refined Englishwomen with their clipped accents and the flaxen-haired, blue-eyed Scandinavians, some of them taller than he was. In Germany he had spent several lustful nights in the company of a quick-witted, uninhibited baroness, and in Spain there had been that fiery-tempered dancer. . . .

And what about the women back home? The dozens of American beauties whose social standings were equal to his; women who would make suitable candidates for his bride, when the time came to pick one.

And the time was coming soon.

As soon as he got back home, he would have to concentrate on finding a wife and settling down. The knowledge had been in the back of his mind ever since he'd sailed for Europe several months ago.

Perhaps that was why he felt so strangely restless now; why he couldn't seem to forget the big-eyed, golden-skinned peasant girl with whom he had spent but a few intense hours.

He couldn't help thinking that if things were different—if they had met under more pleasant circumstances, and if she weren't engaged—they might have spent some time together. He might have found out what it was like to kiss those lush, swollen lips of hers and run his hands over curves that would be considered unfashionable back home. . . .

Back home the women he knew wore starched-front,

high-collared shirtwaists with billowing leg-o'-mutton
sleeves, and long straight skirts in somber colors. They
wore their hair in the style popularly referred to as *à la
Concierge*, swept in a pompadour to the tops of their
heads and pinned it in a snug knot, or in a marcel wave,
with stiff curling-iron waves carefully arranged around
their heads.

Cira had been dressed in a simple cotton dress that
hugged her rounded breasts and fell in soft gathers from
her nipped waist over her shapely hips. And her hair had
been long and loose beneath the shawl that was knotted
under her chin—dark, shining hair that begged a man to
tangle his fingers in the silken tresses. . . .

Thatcher swallowed more wine, hard, and shifted his
gaze from the glass to the elderly man who had taken the
opposite seat at the small battered table before the fireplace. Dante Gasperetti was a wizened old character with
a shock of white hair and florid cheeks that betrayed his
apparent affection for his potent homemade wine. He had
greeted Thatcher warmly and welcomed him into the
cramped hillside dwelling that was little more than a
shack, really, and littered with plaster and sculpting tools
and works of art in various stages of development. There
was no evidence, in his modest surroundings, of the vast
amounts of money wealthy foreigners paid for his sculp-
tures. Here, amidst the poverty of rural Sicily, he lived
much as his less fortunate neighbors did, though his
hands were roughened from a different kind of work and
his face wasn't nearly as sun-baked as the faces of the
laborers who spent their days in the vast dry fields.

The old man had eagerly unveiled the piece Thatcher's
parents had commissioned—a bust of a young child, a
boy with curly hair and faintly smiling lips. The immortal
image of the son, the golden boy whom the Montgomerys

had lost so many years ago. When Thatcher got it home, it would be reverently placed on the waiting pedestal in the well-lit domed alcove in the great front hall of the Fifth Avenue mansion, an alcove that had recently been constructed specifically to accommodate the bust.

"More wine?" Gasperetti asked over the rim of the half-empty bottle, tilting it toward Thatcher.

"Please," Thatcher said, nodding and sliding his glass across the table.

Already, he was feeling a telltale, numbing warmth spreading through his gut, and thankfully, the images of Cira Valentino were beginning to dissolve.

Cira pounded on the door frantically, hearing Renzo's footsteps pounding through the dark someplace nearby, behind her, as he called her name.

She pounded again, knowing that somebody was home because lamplight spilled from the windows. After another moment she heard footsteps inside, and then the door was thrown open and a haggard, dark-complected man stood glowering at her, his mouth a thin, pursed line beneath his full black whiskers.

"What do you want?" he demanded.

"It's me, Mr. Torrio," she said desperately, as if he somehow hadn't recognized her and if he did, he might change his demeanor. "It's Cira Valentino. I'm—"

"I know who you are. What do you want?"

She swallowed hard. Lucia's father was as belligerent as ever, and there was no sign of her friend on the premises. If Lucia were here, she would have come running at the first knock on the door, the way she always had. It was as though she was always waiting for some kind of distraction from her burdensome existence as the only daughter of a man who had never let her forget that her mother—the wife he had adored—had died because of her, giving birth to her.

"Is . . . is Lucia at home?" Cira managed to inquire, standing her ground hopefully.

"No," came the terse reply.

"Do you know when she'll be—"

"Lucia is gone," the man said, and Cira saw something flicker in his eyes. It wasn't his trademark anger or impatience; it was more like . . . pain.

"She's gone?" Cira echoed. "But . . . where?"

"Palermo. She left a few weeks ago. Got a job as a chamber maid at some hotel by the waterfront," he said with a shrug. Now there was no sign of the fleeting emotion she'd just glimpsed, only a familiar irritation and disdain.

"But . . . why did she do that?" Cira asked, her mind reeling. If Lucia was gone, there was no one . . . no one to help her.

The man threw up his hands in disgust and said, "Why? Because she's *pazza*, that one."

Cira flinched. Lucia's father was always calling her crazy, and she knew how much it hurt her friend to be described that way.

Lucia had been trying for as long as Cira could remember to win her father's respect, but no matter what she did, he treated her as though she were an imbecile. Apparently, she had finally given up on him and gone away.

Just when Cira needed her most.

"But why would she go to Palermo alone?" Cira asked hesitantly, trying to picture her petite, gullible friend on her own in the bustling port city.

"She thinks she's going to earn passage to America. Thinks her brother wants her to join him there." He snorted, as though that was the most unlikely thing he could imagine.

But even as he said it, it made sense to Cira. Lucia's idolized older brother, Carlo, had left Fiorenza for New York City a few years ago, and Lucia had missed him desperately ever since. Her brother was the only person in the world who mattered to Lucia—besides Cira, of course.

Lucia had been devastated when her handsome, soft-spoken brother deserted her to seek his fortune in America. And after Cira, too, had left Fiorenza, Lucia must have felt utterly abandoned. Enough so to strike out on her own, something Cira had never imagined the un-worldly Lucia doing.

But apparently, she had. Was she already on a ship to the new country? Had Cira actually crossed her path somewhere in the Atlantic Ocean? Or was she still nearby, in Palermo—and if so, could Cira somehow find her?

"Do you know where she is—I mean, which hotel?" Cira asked Mr. Torrio.

"No," he said curtly, and reached for the door.

"Wait," Cira said plaintively. "I have to find her. Isn't there any way you can—"

"As far as I'm concerned, my daughter is no longer my business," the man told her before slamming the door in her face.

Cira stood dazed for a moment, wondering what to do now.

Then she heard a voice behind her.

"Cira . . . I'm sorry."

She turned and saw Renzo standing in the dim light that spilled from the window of the house. The sight of him sent a surge of emotion through her, and she fought the urge to throw herself at him and let him hold her close and tell her everything was going to be all right, that she wasn't alone.

"Come here," he said, opening his arms as though he'd read her mind. "Cira, come here. . . . How I've missed you. . . ."

"You've missed me?" she echoed incredulously, something snapping inside of her as she remembered, with a sickening feeling, the sight of him groping at that woman back in the courtyard, kissing her neck, pressing himself against her . . .

"Cira," he said again, more frantically, as though sensing her sudden revulsion. He took a step closer, reaching toward her. "Cira, come—"

"Don't touch me." Her eyes narrowed at him as she uttered the low, grim warning. She saw him raise his brows as if in surprise, and then he flashed that familiar grin of his, the one that had always been so reassuring.

"Cira . . ." His hand reached out, about to settle on her arm.

"Don't you dare," she said, barely controlled, taking a step back. "If you touch me, I'll . . . scream. I swear. I'll scream."

"Why? Cira, it's me. It's Renzo," he said, his tone soothing, his expression cajoling. "Have you forgotten—"

"Have *you*?" she shot back at him, temper blazing. "Have you forgotten those promises you made when I left? How you were going to wait for me, to come to America, to marry me?"

"Of course I haven't forgotten. I love you, Cira."

She gave a bitter laugh, feeling nothing but disgust as she stared into the face of the man she had loved so deeply. "You don't love me. If you did, you wouldn't have had your hands all over that . . . that . . . who is she?''

"She's nothing," he said with an offhand wave of his hand. "Just a *puttana* who knew I was vulnerable and lonely. I did my best to resist her, Cira, but it was just too much—"

"You make me sick." She spat the words at him, hating him even as her aching heart longed to believe him.

"I'm sorry," he said, hanging his head like a guilty young boy caught skipping school. "It was wrong, what I did. But it won't happen again. Because you're back . . . Cira, why are you back? This is like a miracle—"

"Don't," she cut in. "Don't pretend you're glad to see me. Don't pretend I didn't interrupt your fun. I may have trusted you, but I'm not stupid."

"Why are you back?" he repeated, as though she hadn't spoken. "Did you realize you couldn't leave me behind? That we belong together?"

She stared at him, marveling that his ego allowed him such assumptions, and yet, why not? When they parted she had been head over heels in love with him, apparently enough so to be blinded by his true character. She would gladly have come back home just for his sake if she had come up with a way to do so.

Now it gave her great satisfaction to inform him that he wasn't the reason she had left America.

"I was forced to come back here because I failed the health inspection in New York," she informed him evenly. "My hay fever made my eyes swollen, and they thought I had trachoma. As soon as I can, I'm going back. For good."

"But, Cira—"

"Goodbye, Renzo," she said, turning on her heel and walking away from him.

"Where are you going?"

Where are *you going?* she asked herself, even as she strode purposefully toward the dark road leading away from the cluster of houses that had once been her safe haven.

Now that Renzo had betrayed her, and Lucia was gone, there was nothing left for her in Fiorenza. Nothing at all.

She thought longingly of her family back in America and realized that she belonged with them. Even if they were in a strange land. Mama and Papa and her sisters and brothers . . . even Lucia, she realized, would be there soon.

Lucia . . .

She remembered what Mr. Torrio had said. About Lucia going to Palermo to work in some hotel by the waterfront. She had only left a few weeks ago. Surely that wasn't enough time for her to have earned passage to America. Surely she was still here in Sicily.

I have to find her, Cira realized. *I have to go back to Palermo and find her. She and I can go to America together.*

All she had to do was get to Palermo, and everything would be all right.

But night had fallen, and she was alone, with no way to make the long journey back to the city, and no one to turn to for help.

Unless . . .

If you need anything else, you know where to find me. . . . I won't be heading back to Palermo until morning.

Thatcher Montgomery's words rang in her ears.

He was a stranger, a foreigner . . .

And yet, he had helped her once. Saved her life, really. Still . . .

How could she turn to him again?

Then again . . .

What other choice did she have?

With a heavy sigh, her mind made up, she headed along the dark road leading toward Dante Gasperetti's home on the distant hill above town.

Thatcher had just drifted off to sleep when he heard it.

That voice.

Her voice.

It was somewhere nearby, hushed yet familiar, engaged in a conversation with someone else; a man whose voice also sounded familiar.

He realized he was dreaming. He must be, he thought fuzzily. He turned his long frame on the narrow, slightly musty-smelling bed, and pulled the blanket up to his chin.

"Signor Montgomery?"

He sighed, smiling at the sound of his name in her gentle Sicilian accent. He could hear her, but where was she? He wanted to see her. In his dream. Because he had already resigned himself to the knowledge that he would never be able to see her again, so at least—

"*Signor* Montgomery?" It was louder this time, closer, and he realized with a start that he wasn't dreaming.

She was here. . . .

But how could that be?

No, it must be a dream. . . .

He opened his eyes and saw Cira Valentino standing over his bed.

Incredulous, he blinked.

She was still there.

Behind her, Dante Gasperetti stood in his nightclothes. Cira turned back to him, and the two conversed again in

Italian, too rapid-fire for Thatcher to decipher. Then Gasperetti retreated to the next room, and Thatcher was left alone with Cira.

She was even more lovely than he remembered. In his earlier alcohol-induced fog, he had nearly managed to forget her face. But now that she was in front of him again, he knew that he would never forget those haunting features again. She was exquisite. . . .

"M'aiuti, per favore."

Please help me.

Her words slammed into him and struck some part of him that stirred to immediate attention. She needed help. She needed him. His help.

"What is it, Cira?" he asked, sitting up. He forgot to hold the blanket, and it dropped to his waist, exposing his naked chest.

He saw the way her eyes darted downward, scanning his body before abruptly jerking up to meet his gaze again. She looked flustered, and despite the dimly lit room, he could see the faint tinge of rosy color that slowly stained her cheeks.

He felt something stirring in the lower regions of his body, beneath the blanket, and he realized that he was aroused—and so was she. It was unmistakable; the attraction was there in her eyes for him to see.

But that wasn't why she was here. It wasn't because she desired him. That was beside the point. Cira was different from the brazen Spanish dancer or the coy German baroness who had come to him in his bed and told him exactly what she wanted him to do to her.

Cira would never be here if she didn't need help . . .

His help.

She needs me, he told himself.

And that was all that mattered.

At least, right now.

"What do you need?" he asked gently.

"Are you still going back to Palermo in the morning?"

He nodded.

"If I may . . . I'd like to go with you. I have some money, and I can pay—"

"No," he interrupted. "There's no need to pay. I'm going anyway, and I'd like the company. We'll leave first thing."

She nodded, hesitant, and he sensed that there was something else.

"Cira," he said quietly. "Do you have someplace to stay tonight?"

She cast her eyes downward and shook her head.

And he knew, then, that there was no fiancé. Maybe there had been, and something had happened in the few hours since he had left her. And maybe there was no one at all; maybe she had made it up for some reason

Whatever the case, he didn't question her about it. He simply rose from the bed, careful to wrap the blanket around him, and said, "You sleep here. I'm sure Dante won't mind. I'll stretch out in the next room, on the floor."

"Oh, no . . . I couldn't take your bed—"

"It isn't my bed. I was only borrowing it." He grinned reassuringly at her. "And now it's your turn."

"But—"

"It's all right," he told her as he walked toward the curtain that separated this room from the next. "Get some sleep. And in the morning I'll bring you back to Palermo."

"*Mólte grazie*," she said in a voice he could barely hear.

He smiled but didn't turn around. "You're very welcome,'' he told her, and then left her alone.

Later, as he listened to Gasperetti's hearty snoring from the big bed several feet away from where he lay, he found that he couldn't fall back to sleep. He was too conscious of Cira there, beyond the curtain; too curious about what had happened to her in the few hours they had been apart.

He had thought he would never see her again. Now he would spend the better part of tomorrow with her as they journeyed back to Palermo.

Would she open up to him then? Or would she remain an enigma?

And why on earth did he care? He would be meeting his friends at the elegant Hotel Fortunato for another day or two of fun before they would head back to Naples to sail home. There was no reason to get caught up in the problems of this petite Sicilian peasant.

And yet . . .

Something in her haunted dark eyes beckoned to him. Never before had he met someone who seemed as utterly alone in the world as she did. Why had she spent such a short time here in Fiorenza? Where had she planned to spend the night before circumstances had sent her to find him at Gasperetti's?

What was she going to do in Palermo? The thought of her alone in the bustling port city made him vaguely uneasy. She was too trusting, too innocent. Look what had happened to her yesterday, when that bastard had tried to rape her.

It's not your concern, Thatcher reminded himself. *And she's not a girl, she only looks like one. She's a grown woman.*

A woman who had gazed at his bare chest with undisguised longing. In that fleeting instant a glimmer of pure sexual attraction had sizzled between them. And under other circumstances he might have reached out for her, to see where it would lead.

But he couldn't. She had come to him for help. And after what she had been through that afternoon, with that boorish farmer who had attacked her . . .

He wouldn't blame her if she never trusted another man to touch her.

Thatcher sighed and closed his eyes, determined to get some sleep. The dusty wooden floor beneath his back was hardly comfortable, but he was bone-weary, and he had a long journey ahead tomorrow.

He heard a sound, then, from behind the curtain.

She was awake.

And she was crying.

Very softly, so softly that he could barely hear her, but there it was.

Part of him wanted to go to her, to take her into his arms and comfort her, somehow make her pain go away.

But a voice inside his head warned him to leave her alone.

There's nothing you can do for her. And she's practically a stranger. It isn't any of your business.

After a long time the quiet sobs waned, and the house was quiet except for the sound of Gasperetti's snoring. But Thatcher sensed that Cira was still awake in the next room, and that she, like he, didn't get a moment's sleep for the remainder of the night.

4

"Are you hungry?" Thatcher asked after they had ridden quite awhile in silence.

Cira glanced up at him, startled by the sound of his voice. She had been lost in thought. But the interruption was welcome, because she had been thinking about Renzo and what he had done. And if she allowed herself to dwell on it any longer, she might break down crying. And that was the last thing she wanted to do, particularly in front of Thatcher Montgomery.

"I am a little hungry," she admitted to him.

"I thought you might be. You barely touched your breakfast."

She shrugged. Before they left, Dante had fried eggs with onions and potatoes for them, but she hadn't been able to eat. It was far too uncomfortable, sitting at the small table with two strange men so early in the morning, knowing that they were both wondering why she was there, alone.

"Would you like an orange?" he asked, pulling two

of them from the valise at his feet on the floor of the
carriage.

"Grazie." His fingers brushed hers as she accepted the
fruit, and she held it in her lap, suddenly feeling shy.

She couldn't help feeling a flicker of attraction for the
man sitting there beside her, just as she had last night,
when his blanket had fallen away to reveal that sculpted,
masculine chest. Despite her uncertainty over her future
and the heart-wrenching day she had suffered, she had
found herself wondering what it would be like to reach
out and run her fingertips over his lean, bare flesh, or to
rest her cheek against it and listen to his heartbeat.

He was so different from Renzo, and Renzo was the
only one she had ever touched, ever kissed. But Renzo
was little more than a boy, a boy she had known her
whole life, while Thatcher Montgomery was undoubtedly
a man. . . .

"Would you like me to peel that for you?"

His voice startled Cira from her wanton thoughts, and
she felt her face grow hot as she imagined what would
happen if he knew what she was thinking. Would he
laugh at her? Or consider her a fool for even daring to
imagine a man like him wanting anything to do with a
girl like her?

Woman, she corrected with a stubborn stab of pride.
*You're a grown woman, on your own in the world, with
no one to answer to. No one at all.*

Not her parents.

And not Renzo.

Tears sprang to her eyes as she realized that there was
no one to look out for her now. Until she got back to
America and the safety of her parents' new home, there
was no one to care what happened to her.

"Here . . . let me." Thatcher Montgomery gently took

the orange from her hand and began to peel it. As he did so, he tossed the curls of peel out of the carriage in a cavalier manner, and Cira was reminded again that he was a man of the world, wealthy and confident.

Suddenly she longed to tell him her whole sad story and ask him if he would help her.

But he's already helping you, she reminded herself. *He's been kind enough to bring you back to Palermo with him.*

Yes. And what if he could somehow bring her back to America when he went? What if she asked him if he would loan her the money for her passage?

She wouldn't even consider such a thing if she hadn't been present when he had paid Dante Gasperetti for the artwork he had commissioned. She had seen the thick wad of paper money Thatcher had pulled from his pocket, had watched him count out the bills into Dante's waiting hand. And she had realized that even after he was done paying the sculptor, Thatcher Montgomery had pocketed as much money as her Papa had ever made in a whole year's work. Probably more than that, even.

And this carriage and driver he had hired for the round-trip journey from Palermo must have cost a small fortune, as well.

But she got the impression that when it came to money, Thatcher Montgomery had no worries.

Meanwhile, money was the key to her well-being. Money would get her back to New York, and her family, where she belonged. Her hay fever had all but disappeared, and there would be no tears to swell her eyes on this journey. No tears for Renzo. No regret in leaving him behind, now that she knew what he really was.

"There you are," Thatcher said, and handed Cira the peeled orange.

"Grazie."

"Prego," he replied politely.

She pulled away a section of orange and popped it into her mouth. Some tart juice dribbled from the corner of her lip, and she quickly dabbed at it, then glanced at him to see if he had noticed.

He was watching her, and his eyes were twinkling.

"Delicious, isn't it?" he asked. "The oranges we get back in New York are nothing like these. But then, they're grown right here."

She nodded and swallowed the fruit, noticing the pale amber flecks in his green eyes. The sunlight made them lighter than they had seemed before, a translucent gold with greenish depths, like the sea on a warm summer day.

"What are you planning to do in Palermo, Cira?"

His direct question caught her off-guard, and she fumbled for an answer.

Finally she said, "I . . . I'm going to be staying with a friend. She's working at a hotel there."

"Which hotel?"

Again, she hesitated, turning the orange around and around in her hands. "I'm not sure," she finally admitted, looking out at the trees lining the side of the road. "It's on the waterfront."

"How are you going to find her if you don't know where she's staying? Palermo's a big city. There must be dozens of hotels there."

She lifted her chin. "Then I'll just check them all until I find her."

"And what if you don't?"

"Then I'll find another place to stay. Not that it's any of your concern," she couldn't help adding.

He seemed to ignore that last comment. "Cira," he

said, looking earnest, "I'm going to be at the Hotel Fortunato for the next two nights. If you run into trouble, please find me there."

She shrugged and popped another piece of orange into her mouth.

"Will you promise to let me help you if you run into trouble, Cira?"

She wanted to tell him that yes, he could help her. That he could help her by loaning her enough money to get back across the ocean to her family. But her pride wouldn't let her do that, so she merely offered him a noncommittal nod.

She felt his eyes on her and pretended to concentrate on the orange, eating it methodically, piece by piece, until her hand was empty and her fingers sticky from the juice. She found a handkerchief in her satchel; the white cotton one with Mama's pale green hand-embroidered scalloped edging.

Giulia had given it to her when they were in line at Ellis Island.

As she wiped her sticky fingers on the familiar handkerchief, she was stung by a sudden longing for her sister, for the rest of her family. They were so very far away; they must be so worried about her. . . .

She had to get back to them.

She turned impulsively to Thatcher and, before she could stop herself, was blurting, "I wonder if there's any way you could—"

Then she stopped short, realizing, in horror, what she had been about to do.

Ask him for money.

As though she were a beggar on the street.

And that's where you might end up if you don't get

back to Papa and Mama as soon as possible, she told herself.

Still, she wasn't that desperate. Not yet.

"Is there any way I could . . . what?" Thatcher was asking.

She shook her head, waving him off with her hand. "Nothing. Never mind."

She didn't need his money, or his help.

No, she still had someone else to turn to.

Lucia Torrio's dancing black eyes twinkled at her in her mind, and she could hear her friend's voice saying warmly, "Cira! What are you doing here?"

She imagined how overjoyed Lucia would be when she told her that she would be sailing to America with her. The two of them, together. . . .

It was a comforting thought.

Suddenly she was anxious to reach Palermo and find her friend. She could imagine what Lucia would say when she told her all that had happened since they had parted so many weeks ago. About failing the inspection at Ellis Island, and sailing home alone, and being attacked by that farmer . . . had that been only yesterday?

It seemed a lifetime ago.

A lifetime ago since she had gone hurrying home to Renzo, filled with anticipation and excitement over seeing him again. Had she really believed that it would be so easy? That she would show up and he would be there, waiting? That he would take care of her?

Somehow, she knew that nothing would ever be that easy. Not ever again.

But if she could just find Lucia—if Lucia hadn't yet sailed for America—things would start looking up.

Cira settled back in the seat, turning her head away from Thatcher. She was exhausted, having lain awake all last night in the unfamiliar bed, haunted by the day's traumas. Her body ached from having fought off the farmer's attack, and her heart ached with the reality of Renzo's betrayal.

Before long, the rhythmic rattle of the carriage wheels over the rutted, hilly road lulled her to sleep.

Thatcher awakened slowly, feeling something tickling his cheek.

His eyes popped open and he realized that it was a tendril of Cira's dark hair. She was leaning against him, breathing evenly, every exhale the merest whisper of a sweet sigh. He didn't move, reluctant to wake her.

The carriage was moving down a steep hill on the narrow road that opened up to fragrant orange and almond groves on either side. The sun was directly overhead, blazing down on them, and he judged that it must be around noon. If that was the case, then another hour or so, and they would be at their destination.

He fought the urge to brush Cira's hair away, choosing instead to let it tickle his skin lightly, like the soft flutter of a downy wing. Somehow he wanted her close to him, knowing that it would soon be time to say goodbye to her forever.

Her head was only inches from his shoulder against the leather seat, and he longed to reach out and urge it downward, so that it rested on him. As it was, the warm, flesh-cushioned length of her left side was against him, arm-to-arm, thigh-to-thigh, and he found himself wondering what it would be like to hold her—really hold her, in his arms, awake and willing. What would it be like to press his mouth against her lips, those plush red lips that now were slightly parted in slumber?

Everything about her was so . . . soft.

Her hair, and her voice, and the curve of her hip
against his side . . .

And he was crazy to be thinking this way, he reminded
himself sternly.

It must be the heat of the day, or the exotic thrill of
being in a wild, beautiful foreign land.

He could see the Tyrrhenian Sea now, below, in the
distance; a glistening strip of brilliant blue on the horizon. And beside it, the sprawling clusters of ancient
domed buildings and rooftops that marked the city of
Palermo.

His friends were waiting there. Rupert Wentworth and
Harry Eldridge and Carson Adams, all of them comfortably settled into suites in the elegant hotel, undoubtedly
game for a night of revelry. Carousing with that bunch
would surely rid him of any lingering memories of Cira.
By morning he would probably be looking forward to the
sail home.

Back to the real world . . .

He lifted his hat slightly and wiped at a trickle of sweat
on his forehead, beneath the brim.

Back to the stone mansion on Fifth Avenue and the
office that waited in his father's building on lower Broadway.

Yes, and in a few weeks, the house in Newport would
be open, and he would spend lazy summer weekends
there. He would find someone suitable to court; someone
whose background and family wealth matched that of the
Montgomerys.

She would have to be attractive, too, he mused.

Attractive, and pleasant-tempered.

Otherwise, he wouldn't do it, he told himself resolutely. No, he wouldn't marry anyone who went around

cross all day, and he wouldn't have a wife who wasn't pleasing to the eye.

He glanced down again at the sleeping Cira, wishing he could see her face, but it was hidden from this angle. He tried to picture her all done up like a Manhattan socialite, in a fine velvet gown with real jewels hanging at her throat and ears, her hair coiled on top of her head in that popular Gibson girl style and her skin fashionably pale.

But he couldn't do it. Try as he might, his mind's eye only saw the reality—the simple cotton dress, the tiny gold earrings, the loose tumble of black hair, the sun-kissed complexion.

And he knew, with a pang, that he could never court a woman like her.

Of course he couldn't!

What was he thinking?

Surely he wasn't imagining falling in love with Cira Valentino and bringing her back home with him! He could just imagine the looks on his mother's and sisters' faces.

And while his father—who had a keen eye for beautiful women—might even privately tell him that Cira was indeed appealing, he would probably remind Thatcher that a man in his position couldn't marry a woman like her.

Marry Cira?

Never. He couldn't. He wasn't even considering such a preposterous notion. They had nothing in common.

And in a short time he would be bidding her farewell, and they would go their separate ways.

Again.

This time, for good.

As though his thought had somehow been transmitted

to her unconscious mind, Cira stirred in her sleep. Her
hair moved away from his cheek, and her body no longer
rested against the length of his.

Just as well, Thatcher thought, trying to ignore a
twinge of regret.

"This is fine. Right here," Cira said, her eyes scanning
the crowded, narrow street. It was bustling with pedes-
trians and festive carts that were pulled by horses be-
decked in traditional Sicilian fashion: splashy red
harnesses, plumes, and tassels. The air was filled with the
sound of peddlers' cries and rattling wheels and the
horses' jangling bells.

"You want to be left right here?" Thatcher echoed.
"But there's no hotel here. I thought you were going to
a hotel."

"This is fine," Cira repeated, this time to the driver
as she leaned forward in the seat and touched his shoulder.

The man nodded and slowed the horse, and Cira
looked around, trying to get her bearings. Which was
useless, because she knew little about Palermo. She was
completely lost. But she could smell the salty sea on the
warm breeze, and there were gulls circling overhead, so
they must be fairly close to the waterfront. All she had
to do was walk toward it, and check every hotel she came
across, until she found Lucia.

And what if Lucia has already left for America?

"If you don't find your friend," Thatcher said, as
though he had read her mind, "then please look for me
at the Hotel Fortunato."

"Why?" Cira asked, turning to look at him. She immediately wished she hadn't. He was much too dashing,
sitting beside her, his lanky, lean form draped casually

over the seat and clad in an impeccably tailored suit. On
his feet he wore the most unusual shoes she had ever
seen, with the bottoms made of patent leather and the
tops of soft, buttoned-up kid. She had no doubt that they
were the latest fashion back in New York City and had
cost him a tidy sum.

Again, she thought wistfully that the one-way steerage
passage across the Atlantic would be but a drop in the
bucket to a man like him.

"Why look for me?" he was asking. "Because I don't
want to see anything happen to you. A young girl alone
in the city—"

"Woman," she corrected him promptly, indignantly.

His eyes slid over her in swift appraisal that raised
goose bumps on her flesh despite the heat of the sun.

He nodded. "I beg your pardon. *Woman.*"

And there was something in his tone that made her
squirm slightly on the seat as she felt a familiar sensation
take hold deep in her belly. It was the way she had felt
back in that courtyard at home, with Renzo, when he held
her against his hard male body and kissed her. . . .

Only Thatcher wasn't holding her or kissing her now.
He wasn't even touching her. All he had done was look,
and she felt as though his gaze had set her body on fire.
She realized, with shame, that she desired this man she
barely knew. A mere twenty-four hours ago a vile
stranger had attempted to violate her chastity, and last
night she had caught her fiancé making love to another
woman.

Yet despite all that, here she sat wondering what it
would be like to be held in Thatcher's arms, to have him
kiss her passionately.

"Are you all right?" he asked, concern edging into his
eyes.

"I . . . I'm fine," she said, and cleared her throat. She deftly pulled her dark blue triangle of a scarf over her hair and knotted the corners under her chin.

"But you're all flushed. It must be the heat; it's getting to you."

The heat *was* getting to her—but its source wasn't the glaring Sicilian sun. She fought the urge to shift again on the seat, lest he realize what was happening inside of her.

"You need to rest, have something cold to drink, Cira. Let me—"

"I'm fine. Please stop here," she called to the driver. "Right here is where I must get out."

As the carriage drew to a stop, she swung her legs off to the side to hop down. Thatcher's hand on her shoulder stopped her short.

"Wait," he said, his voice a gentle yet forceful command. "Let me."

She would never know why she sat there and waited for him to climb down and cross around to her side, or why, when he held out a beckoning hand, she placed her fingers in his grasp.

Perhaps it was simply the knowledge that this was the way to behave when you were a lady in the company of a gentleman in the city.

Or perhaps it was just the fierce need to touch him— even if it was merely to place her hand in his.

Was it her imagination, or did he cling to her hand a moment longer than was necessary after she had landed securely on the dusty street?

She felt a pang of regret when he let go and reached up behind her to collect the shabby bundle that was all she had in the world. He handed it to her, then reached into his pocket.

"As I told you, Cira, if you don't find your friend—"

"I'll find her."

"But if you don't, you know where to find me. For the next two days I'll be here in Palermo. Then I leave for Naples, and sail home from there midweek."

She nodded. "Have a pleasant journey."

"I'd like to give you some money, Cira, just in case you—"

"No," she blurted, pushing away his hand that was clutching a fine leather billfold. "I don't need your money."

Even as she heard herself uttering the words, she cursed herself a fool. What was she thinking? She was alone, nearly destitute. She should take whatever he was offering.

But pride wouldn't let her.

He hesitated, then put the billfold away. "All right," he said with a nod.

"I . . . I must be going."

"Good luck."

She nodded, trying to think of something to say. Then she realized that even if the proper words had come readily to her tongue, she would be unable to utter them. An enormous lump had suddenly lodged in her throat, and it was all she could do to swallow past it.

"*Arrivederci*, Cira," Thatcher said softly, tipping his hat to her.

She could only nod, then turn and hurry away.

A moment later she realized, belatedly, that she had forgotten to thank him for all he had done.

She turned to call after him, but he was already on his way, the wheels of the carriage stirring a cloud of dust that swallowed him from her sight.

5

*N*ight had fallen by the time Cira reached the shabby, poorly lit vestibule of the Paradiso, an ironic misnomer if ever there was one.

The run-down inn was as far from paradise as you could get, she thought, wrinkling her nose at the faint odor of rotting fish that permeated the place. It was located around the corner from a large dockfront seafood market.

If Lucia wasn't here, she didn't know what she'd do.

She was worried and exhausted, having spent the last eight hours trudging the city streets, inquiring about her friend at every hotel and inn she came upon. This one was tucked into an unpleasant, narrow side street, more of an alley, really, and she had almost walked right past it. But the weathered, hand-painted sign that said LOCANDA PARADISO had caught her eye, and she had hurried toward the entrance, despite her aching feet and the fierce hunger pain in her side.

Past the vestibule was a narrow room containing only a tall, battered desk and, behind it, an elderly woman who immediately looked up from the needlework in her lap and eyed Cira with suspicion.

Cira's spirits plunked even lower.

She couldn't imagine finding Lucia in a place like this.

She would have to give up her search and find a place to stay for the night. She thought of the lira she had sewn into the hem of her skirt, and then of the money Thatcher Montgomery had started to offer.

Why, oh why, hadn't she taken it? At least with whatever he could give her, she might be able to afford a room for the night—even in a place as dingy as this one. Anything was better than spending the night huddled on the street.

But that was what she would have to do. She couldn't spend the last of the money Mama had given her on a hotel. It was all she had to put toward her passage to America, and the sooner she got on a ship, the better.

She remembered the night they had come to Palermo before their departure for America. They had spent the night, along with hundreds of other emigrants, camped out beside the wharf, all of them trying to get comfortable with their heads propped on satchels and trunks. Her younger brothers had thought it an adventure, but Cira recalled feeling frightened by the unfamiliar city noises and the strangers huddled nearby.

At least then she had been surrounded by her family. Now she was alone. And it couldn't be safe for a woman to sleep alone on the street in a place like this.

If only she had found Lucia. If only—

"Che cosa e?" the old woman asked bluntly, watching her.

I could find Thatcher, Cira reminded herself. *He said to look for him if I couldn't find a place to stay. I could borrow money . . . and pay him back once I get to Amer-*

*ica. He said he lived in New York. I could get a job
as soon as I arrive, and pay him back as soon as possible. . . .*

"What is it?" the woman repeated.

"I'm looking for someone," Cira said, tearing her
thoughts from Thatcher and launching into her now-
familiar, yet so far futile, spiel. "A friend. Her name is
Lucia Torrio, and she's working—"

"Ah, Lucia," the woman echoed, nodding. "Lucia
Torrio."

Cira's heart leaped. "You know her?"

"She is my chambermaid."

Cira gasped, her eyes suddenly swimming in tears of
elation. She hardly dared ask . . .

"Is she here now?"

The old woman nodded. "She's in her room."

Cira's legs felt weak with relief. "May I see her?"

The woman shrugged and gestured toward the staircase. "Top floor. Last door."

Cira flew toward the stairs and mounted them two at
a time. By the time she had completed the third flight,
she was winded but driven by pure determination.

"Lucia?" she couldn't keep from calling out as she
dashed down the drab corridor. "Lucia, it's me!"

She arrived at the door and pounded eagerly, calling
her friend's name.

It was thrown open immediately, and there stood Lucia, wearing a bewildered expression

Cira burst into tears and threw herself at her friend.

"Cira? Cira?" Lucia, sounding dazed, kept repeating
her name, asking what she was doing there.

Finally Cira calmed down enough to speak coherently.
"May I come in?"

"Of course . . . of course. Oh, Cira, I can't believe my eyes."

"Nor can I. I've searched everywhere in this city for you, Lucia."

She stepped into the tiny room, barely noticing the meager furnishings or the clutter of her friend's belongings strewn about. She turned back to Lucia, who was closing the door, and realized, with a start, that her dear old friend looked different than she had the last time they had met.

Lucia's full face lacked the perpetually jolly expression Cira remembered. Her brown eyes were sunken and lined with worry, and her cheeks were no longer rosy, but sallow. Her dark hair, once her crowning glory, was pinned back in a severe braid and coiled at the back of her head. Perhaps that was why her eyes stood out, and why her body appeared rounder than ever. She wore an unfamiliar, ill-fitting black dress that looked uncomfortably snug and too warm for the stuffy room.

"I don't understand, Cira. Why are you here? Why aren't you in America?" Lucia asked, gesturing for Cira to sit on the narrow bed. "Is everything all right? What happened?"

"It's a long story," Cira told her, perching on the edge of the lumpy mattress.

"Tell me," Lucia urged, sitting next to her. She reached out and squeezed Cira's hand. "Tell me everything."

Cira nodded and, before she began speaking, offered a silent prayer of thanks. She had found Lucia, her dearest and oldest friend in the world.

Surely now everything would be all right. . . .

• • •

"What the devil's going on with you, Montgomery?" Carson Adams asked, setting his nearly empty wine goblet on the tablecloth and eyeing Thatcher through his silver-rimmed spectacles.

The restaurant around them was crowded, mostly with foreign tourists, and they were nearly finished with a delicious evening meal that had included seafood, pasta, fruit, and cheese as well as meat for the main course.

"What's going on with me?" Thatcher asked, blinking at his friend. "What are you talking about?"

"You're a thousand miles away," Rupert Wentworth commented from the seat to his right, his fork, laden with a chunk of veal, poised in front of his mouth.

"You've been utterly distracted since you returned this afternoon," Harry Eldridge put in from the opposite side of the table. "What the devil happened to you in that godforsaken little town, Montgomery?"

"Nothing happened to me," Thatcher murmured, spearing a succulent slice of roasted potato flavored with olive oil and oregano. "I'm simply tired, that's all."

"Well, don't plan on turning in too early on us tonight, old friend," Carson advised. "We've planned an evening at the opera with several gals we met while you were out of town."

"They're abroad from Philadelphia, and one of them knows your eldest sister from boarding school," Rupert added. "Her name is Carpenter—her father's fortune came from textiles—and dare I say she's eager to make your acquaintance."

Thatcher nodded, his thoughts drifting back to Cira Valentino, as they had all evening. What was she doing at this moment? Had she found the friend she intended to meet?

He couldn't deny that he had been relieved to hear her

say the friend was a female—not that it made any difference now. He would never see her again.

Just as well. The sooner he put her out of his mind,
the better.

This Carpenter woman of the Philadelphia textile fortune was just the sort of woman he needed to meet. The
kind of woman he could seriously consider settling down
with.

The prospect had been a topic of conversation among
his friends the duration of the journey. All four of them
realized that upon their return to the States, they would
be expected to find a wife and take up the family business. There had been much groaning and teasing each
other about the impending loss of freedom, but Thatcher
didn't sense much genuine reluctance among his friends
when it came to marriage.

Rupert had, after all, been courting a young woman
from Boston for more than a year, and Harry would undoubtedly propose in the near future to Larina Bates, the
comely daughter of his father's business partner, who had
long ago set her cap for him. Carson, meanwhile, was
the type who had scads of willing females at his beck
and call, and there was no doubt that he would soon settle
upon one of them as a wife.

Thatcher had vaguely supposed that he, like Carson,
would simply choose from among the many eligible
women already in his acquaintance. But now, for some
reason, he wasn't so certain.

It just couldn't be that simple to choose the person
with whom you would spend the rest of your life. There
had to be more to it than simply sharing social and financial status and being pleasantly compatible.

Leaning back in his seat, Thatcher reached for his goblet of dry red wine and took a long swallow.

With any luck, he would find a woman to whom he was attracted—a woman who would make his blood race with yearning the way a certain Sicilian peasant had. And all she had done was look at him. . . .

He sighed inwardly and thrust his thoughts back to the conversation at hand, lest he find himself longing again for what would never be remotely possible.

"The rat!" Lucia exclaimed, her dark eyes blazing. "How dare he cross you that way, Cira! I can't believe that he— Who was this woman?"

"I don't know," Cira replied, taking comfort in her friend's loyal outrage. "She was blond, and voluptuous, and now that I think of it, she appeared a bit older than Renzo."

"It's just as well that you're rid of him, Cira. Better to discover his true nature now than after you were already married."

Cira nodded, knowing Lucia was right. But speaking of Renzo and remembering his betrayal had left her feeling strangely hollow.

Just yesterday she had been madly in love, certain of her destiny—to become his wife, and bear his children . . .

Now her heart had been broken by the only man she had ever loved.

And yet, she had so soon afterward found herself drawn to another man, a man whose path had happened to cross hers at the lowest moment of her life. How could that be? What was wrong with her, that she could find herself imagining another man's kisses when the wounds the first had caused were still so fresh?

She would be wise never to trust another man again, as long as she lived. Perhaps she should enter a convent, as her cousin Maria had recently done—or at the very least, resign herself to spinsterhood.

"Did Renzo at least try to explain himself?" Lucia wanted to know, her mouth set grimly.

"He tried, but I refused to listen. What could he have said that would have made it any better? So I simply ran away and warned him not to come after me."

She stopped herself there, not wanting to provide any more details of what had transpired the night before.

She had already almost told Lucia about Thatcher Montgomery, but had hesitated at the last moment. For some reason, that was something she needed to keep to herself. So she had merely told her friend that she had managed to escape the farmer's attack by fighting back and running away.

Lucia hadn't questioned how she had gotten back to Fiorenza afterward, or how she had gotten from Fiorenza to Palermo today.

Despite her concern and sympathy, she had seemed almost . . . preoccupied. As though she had worries of her own. She hadn't shown a hint of her usual wicked sense of humor or sunny optimism. Cira found herself wondering what had happened to change her friend so drastically in the past few months and was about to ask when Lucia spoke again.

"Does Renzo know you were coming to find me?" Lucia toyed with a fold on her white apron.

"No. I didn't tell him where I was going, or that I even knew where you were. Did you say goodbye to him before you left Fiorenza?"

"I . . . no. I left so suddenly . . ." Lucia trailed off and shook her head. "There was no time to go around making proper farewells."

"What happened to send you away so quickly, Lucia?'' Cira asked, studying her friend's face.

Lucia averted her gaze and waved away the question with a work-roughened hand. "Oh, Cira, you know how it has been for me at home, with my father and all," she murmured. "I had to leave sooner or later. And with Carlo already in America . . . and you as well . . . it seemed the thing to do."

"But . . . you came to Palermo alone? With no job and no money? Hoping to earn enough to sail for America?"

"Just as you did," Lucia said pointedly. "And in another few weeks I'll have enough saved to go. Only now we'll go together."

"First I have to find a job and earn my passage."

"It shouldn't be a problem," Lucia assured her. "You'll find that there is honest work available for strong, willing young women here. Cleaning, or cooking, or doing laundry . . . go make the rounds tomorrow. Start with the hotels. This is the busy season. You might very well find something."

"I will start with the hotels," Cira said, remembering that Thatcher had said he was staying at the Hotel Fortunato. Surely a big, elegant, busy hotel such as that would be a likely place to start looking for employment.

Not that she was hoping to run into Thatcher there. No, she was simply planning to do whatever was necessary to find work.

"Don't worry, Cira. Everything will be all right," Lucia said.

"I know it will. Now that I've found you. Before, I felt so alone."

"And so did I," Lucia agreed. "But now we have each other. We'll go to America and find your family and my brother, and we'll start a new life there."

Cira smiled at Lucia and her friend squeezed her hand and smiled back, then stifled a yawn.

"I'm sorry," she said, covering her mouth. "I've been working so hard lately, I'm just exhausted."

"It's all right. You should get some sleep. I'm exhausted myself, anyway."

"You can have the bed," Lucia said with her usual generosity. "I'll sleep on the floor."

Cira tried to argue, but her friend insisted. Before long, they were settled comfortably in the dark, and Lucia's even breathing told Cira that she had fallen asleep immediately.

The Hotel Fortunato was a formidable Spanish Baroque structure located on Fortunato Square in the heart of Palermo, near the Via della Liberta. The sprawling palazzo was surrounded by lush palms and citrus trees, and fronted by a circular fountain surrounded by exquisite statues and an open-air café that, even in the midafternoon heat, was bustling with activity.

Cira had already inquired about jobs within and had been told that there was nothing available today, but to come back toward the end of the week. Rather than make her way to another establishment immediately, she perched nearby on a low stone wall in the shade of a beech tree, to rest for a while. It had been a long day for her already, having traveled about the city on foot, looking for work. So far, no luck anywhere.

Telling herself that she had no ulterior motive, she sat for nearly an hour, until the aching in her feet had subsided and her face no longer felt damp with sweat from the relentless sun. There was no breeze despite the water's proximity, and as she rose to be on her way again, she glanced longingly at the café. At a table near the street side a couple sipped icy beverages from tall glasses, laughing into each other's eyes.

Cira wondered what it would be like to sit at such an elegant café with a refreshing drink and a man who adored her. She sighed and told herself that most likely, she would never know.

"Cira? Is it you?"

Stunned by the sound of her name spoken in that telltale American accent, she spun around and found herself face to face with Thatcher Montgomery.

A surge of triumph welled inside her, though she immediately did her best to squelch it. She hadn't been lingering here in the hopes of meeting him again. Truly, she hadn't.

And yet, she couldn't keep a sudden grin from widening her mouth as she greeted Thatcher with an almost exuberant *"Buon giorno."*

He looked just as pleased to see her. "What are you doing here?" he asked.

"I was just passing by," she hedged, hoping he hadn't seen her sitting on the wall up until a few moments ago. The last thing she wanted was for him to realize—no, to *assume*, she hastily amended—that she was looking for him.

"Did you find your friend yesterday?"

"Of course," she told him, as though she had never doubted that she would. "I'm staying with her at her hotel."

He smiled. "Good. I was worried about you."

"About me? Why?"

He shrugged. "I don't know. I guess I can't help feeling a bit protective after all we've been through together."

She wanted to appear indignant at his words, but for

the life of her, she couldn't do it. She was pleased that he had thought about her; pleased that she had found him again and he was so clearly glad to see her.

As she gazed up at him, she found herself noting the merest details about his appearance: the rugged line of his clean-shaven jaw, the faint dimple in his left cheek, the telltale ruddy color on his skin that revealed he'd spent at least part of the day in the sun. He wore a fashionable, light-colored suit with a bow tie, and white shoes and gloves that appeared to be made of soft kid. On his head was a flat-topped white hat, its brim surrounded by a wide navy ribbon. He looked every inch the wealthy tourist.

"Are you enjoying your visit to Palermo?" she asked him, hoping he hadn't noticed her unabashed scrutiny.

"Very much. I've just come from a visit to the Church of San Giovanni degli Eremiti, and before that, I saw the Palatine Chapel. Have you ever been there?"

"No, I . . . I haven't had a chance," she said, realizing how different her life was from what he must assume. She had traveled so very little in her nineteen years, and certainly never for pleasure.

Meanwhile, here he was, a foreigner, taking in the sights of a homeland she had scarcely seen. It seemed unfair, and she should resent him, but she couldn't. Today she felt only a strange camaraderie with this man—as though they shared a secret.

And they did.

He alone had witnessed her struggle when her virtue had nearly been violated on that mountain road to Fiorenza. He had come to her rescue not once, but twice, and if nothing else, she owed him her gratitude.

But now that she had found Lucia, she no longer felt as utterly dependent on him as she had. She was free to look him in the eye and say, belatedly, "I wanted to thank you, yesterday, for all you've done for me, Signor Montgomery. I don't know how I can ever repay you—"

"But you can," he cut in.

Startled, she clamped her mouth shut and looked up at him.

Please, she thought, her heart sinking. *Please, don't let him turn out to be a* ratto. *Don't let him try to take advantage of me. Please . . . I thought I could trust him. . . .*

"You can repay me," Thatcher said, smiling down at her, "by having dinner with me on my last evening in Palermo."

She just looked at him, wondering what he meant by "dinner"—whether he expected something more than her company.

And why on earth would this dashing, older American want the company of a Sicilian peasant girl who had caused him so much trouble?

Why, indeed?

An image of the farmer's leering, twisted grin flashed through Cira's mind, and her stomach churned.

Surely Thatcher didn't expect her to—

No, he couldn't have any intention of forcing her to—

The thought was so chilling that she found herself taking a step backward, away from him.

"Cira?" his voice was puzzled, and he appeared taken aback by her wary, silent response to his invitation. "Is something wrong?"

"No," she said firmly. "Nothing is wrong. But I can't have dinner with you. . . ."

His smile faded. "Why not? Do you have other plans?"

"I'm not that kind of girl, Signor Montgomery."

"Please call me Thatcher," he interjected.

She went on, without missing a beat, "And I don't repay favors by—"

"By dining with me in Palermo's finest restaurant? Because that's all I had in mind, Cira. Really."

He sounded earnest, she realized. And the concern in his green-gold eyes seemed genuine.

Still, she hesitated. Hadn't she learned the hard way that strangers weren't to be trusted? That even people you thought you knew and loved couldn't be trusted?

An image of Renzo embracing that other woman filled her mind, and she winced and tried to push it away.

It was men, she decided resolutely. Men couldn't be trusted. They only wanted one thing from women.

"I know what you're thinking, Cira," Thatcher said, taking a step toward her, again closing the distance between them. "I would never hurt you. I would never expect anything more from you than the pleasure of your company. I promise."

She didn't want to look into those eyes, but she couldn't help it. And what she saw there was the same sincerity she heard in his voice.

Don't trust him, warned a voice in her mind.

But it was overcome by a stronger urge, an instinct to believe in this man, to believe in what he was saying.

He'd had the opportunity to take advantage of her already, if he was going to. And he had been a perfect gentleman, concerned for her welfare.

There *had* been that moment, though—in the small, darkened bedroom at Dante Gasperetti's house on the hillside two nights ago . . .

The moment when he had lowered the blanket that covered his bare chest, and something unmistakably primal had sparked between them.

But it wasn't just him, she reminded herself, feeling the familiar twinge of shame that had dogged her every time she thought of that incident—and she had thought of it often. *It was me, too. I wanted to know what it would be like to touch his bare skin. If he had reached out and taken me into his arms, I wouldn't have protested. It wouldn't have been against my will. . . .*

"Cira," Thatcher said again, "after all you've been through, I can see why you'd be reluctant to believe that my offer is innocent. But I give you my word that unlike other men you have had the misfortune to encounter, I mean you no harm."

She realized that he was referring only to the attack on the roadside, for he knew nothing of Renzo's treachery.

But there were other ways a man could harm a woman. Not physically so much as emotionally.

Renzo couldn't have meant to cause her any harm, either. She knew, somehow, that he had cared for her in his way. She told herself that if she had never left Fiorenza, he would probably never have betrayed her with another woman. But he was a passionate man, and after so many weeks of abstinence, he had been unable to resist temptation.

Cira looked at Thatcher, wondering what would happen if, despite his good intentions, his masculine desires got the best of him. What if he lost control and wanted more from her than an innocent evening?

To her dismay, she felt a stirring deep inside, in the same intimate place that had been awakened by that mere glimpse of his bare skin.

She did her best to quell it, transferring her thoughts to her other concern—that, in spending an evening with Thatcher, she might be opening herself up to pain that had nothing to do with a struggle to preserve her virtue.

What if they dined together and she found herself—

No, not falling in love with him. That could only happen over time, when two people knew each other very, very well.

But what if she started to care for him?

He was leaving the country in the morning. She would never see him again. What would be the point of spending time with him before he left? Nothing positive could come of it.

But you're going to New York, reminded a little voice. *You will soon be living in the same place. . . .*

Yes, and it might as well be a world apart, came the nagging reality. Thatcher was obviously an upper-class gentleman, while she would be a poor immigrant. That wouldn't change, no matter what happened between them tonight.

Still . . .

He reached into his breast pocket and pulled out a pocket watch on a chain. It was, she saw even with her untrained eye, a magnificent timepiece, the polished gold surface glittering in the sun; yet another reminder that he was staggeringly rich and she was hopelessly poor.

"Listen," he said, "I'm late meeting a friend of mine . . ."

"Go ahead, then," she told him, fighting the irrational urge to ask who the friend was; whether it was a woman.

"Will you have dinner with me tonight? Please, Cira. I would be so disappointed if you refused."

"But why?" she heard herself asking. "Why do you want to dine with me?"

"Because I find you charming," he said simply, and her heart soared despite her apprehension.

"And," he added, "because I'm lonely."

"I thought you were traveling with friends."

He rolled his eyes. "I've spent several months with these chaps. Their company is wearing rather thin at this point, and we still have the long ocean journey ahead. I would much rather spend my last night in this country with a beautiful local woman."

"All right, then," she found herself saying. "I accept your invitation."

He broke into a grin that made the dimple in his left cheek far more pronounced. "That's wonderful. Where shall I call for you?"

"I'll meet you here," she said hastily, not wanting him to see the shabby Paradiso. "Or wherever you want me to meet you."

"But—"

"I'll meet you here," she insisted, "or not at all."

"Very well. I'll look for you beside that fountain at . . . eight o'clock?"

She nodded. "I'll be there."

"I'm looking forward to it, Cira." He tipped his hat to her, then strode away, toward the hotel.

She looked after him, wondering what on earth she had done.

She didn't even have anything to wear to dinner at a fine restaurant . . .

Or did she?

There was her good dress, the navy brocade she had lengthened with the extra fabric so that it touched her shoe-tops. It was simple, hardly elegant, but if she wore her hair up . . .

A shimmer of excitement darted through her, as she remembered the way Renzo had reacted when he'd seen her in that dress, with her hair done up like a real lady.

Would Thatcher's eyes widen when he saw her? Would he be drawn to her . . . ?

Even if he is, she reminded herself, nothing can come of it. *It's dinner, that's all. Just one night. Nothing more.*

Still, she couldn't quite keep her feet from dancing lightly over the cobblestones as she scurried back to the hotel to get ready, all thoughts of finding work today having flown right out of her head.

6

Thatcher almost didn't recognize Cira when he saw her by the fountain at eight o'clock that evening. His eyes had twice searched the area, looking for that familiar tumble of long, dark hair.

Then he noticed the young woman in the navy blue dress, standing off to one side. She happened to look up, and when her eyes met his, he realized that it was she.

He hurried toward her, taking in the simple garment that was longer than the dress he had previously seen her in, and the way her hair was twisted and pinned to reveal a face that was more angular than he had originally thought. Her cheekbones were more pronounced, and her eyes were enormous.

"Cira," he said, reaching her and extending a hand. "You look lovely."

There was no mistaking the flicker of delight in her expression, though she merely said, *"Grazie,"* in that soft voice of hers.

He studied her hair and noted that although it was more grown-up than her usual style, she still exhibited an unconscious, refreshing lack of conformity to current fashion. This wasn't a Gibson girl coif, or a pompadour *à la Concierge* that was so popular back home. There appeared to be no method to the cascade of ebony tresses piled on her head, and he noted the stray wisps that had escaped to softly frame her face and neck.

Her only jewelry was the pair of tiny gold studs that pierced her ears and a delicate cross hanging from a chain around her neck. Simple, modest adornment that was more a statement of her heritage than of fashion.

And her dress . . . it was homemade, he could tell, cut in no particular style. The bodice was more fitted than what she had worn previously, the plain brocade fabric snugly hugging her tantalizing curves, then falling away to graze the tops of her faintly scuffed black shoes.

He realized that it was a fine dress by her standards, though it would never pass muster back home. He pictured his mother and sisters in their well-cut silks and velvets, and he remembered the diaphanous, supremely elegant gown that had been worn the previous evening by Evangeline Carpenter of the Philadelphia textile fortune, whose breeding and appearance had been impeccable, but whose conversation was frightfully dull.

He couldn't help comparing her to Cira, contrasting Miss Carpenter's perpetually pursed expression to Cira's shy smile and dancing brown eyes.

It was with almost a sense of relief that he took Cira's arm and said, "I've been looking forward to this evening since I left you this afternoon."

"So have I," she said, with no attempt to hide her enthusiasm.

He smiled, charmed by her lack of pretense, and steered her toward the street, where the carriage he had hired was waiting to transport them to the restaurant. He

saw the driver raise an eyebrow when he caught sight of
Cira, and knew what the man was thinking. He was surprised to see Thatcher escorting a local girl, and a young
one at that. It was the same man who had driven him the
night before, when Thatcher had been accompanied by
his friends and the young women from Philadelphia, all
of them done up in the latest American fashions and perfectly accustomed to being transported in style.

Cira, on the other hand, appeared quite obviously im-
pressed by the gleaming carriage and fine horses. It was
clear to Thatcher, just as it must be to the driver, that she
had no experience with such sophisticated trappings.

Still, the driver doffed his hat to her and greeted her
as though she were as grand a lady as he had ever seen.

And he'd better, Thatcher thought with a sudden stab
of a fiercely protective instinct toward Cira. She might
not have money or breeding, but she had more integrity
and charm than any woman he had ever known.

She smiled at him as they settled themselves in the
plush seat and the carriage moved forward with a gentle
lurch.

"It's a beautiful evening, isn't it?" he asked her.

She frowned and looked at him blankly, and he realized, with a start, that he had spoken to her in English.
As he repeated the question in Italian, he wondered what
his momentary lapse meant.

Had he subconsciously willed himself to forget that
Cira was Sicilian—part of an exotic foreign world that
could never meld with his own?

He couldn't afford to do that. Drawn to her as he might
be, he had to remember that she belonged in her world,
and he in his.

And after this evening, that was just where they would
be.

• • •

Cira was both slightly irritated and relieved when
Thatcher ordered the wine and their dinner without consulting her. She realized that his take-charge attitude was
gallant; that a gentleman should make such decisions for
a lady. And she would have had no idea what to order,
so it was just as well that he took over.

Still, having him tell the waiter what they would eat
and drink made her feel as though he thought she was
young and naive. Which she was. She just didn't want
him to know it, because she knew he was used to being
with women who were his equal—at least in terms of
their social background.

Had he seen the shock in her eyes when he swept her
through the elegant dining room, with its gilt chairs and
seemingly a hundred glittering crystal chandeliers? Had
he noticed her panic when the first course was deposited
on the table in front of her and she had no idea which
fork to use?

Fortunately, she had followed Thatcher's lead, and if
he had noticed that she faltered, he didn't let on.

He simply talked to her about the things he had seen
in his travels through Italy. She didn't tell him that she
had never seen her country's mainland, or even been off
the island until she went to America. In fact, he didn't
even know that she had been to America—although of-
ficially, only to Ellis Island, and she wasn't sure that it
counted.

Somehow, she couldn't bring herself to tell him about
the nightmare of being branded with a disease she didn't
have and separated from her family to sail back to Sicily
alone. She didn't want him seeing her as any more vulnerable than she must already seem to him.

So she listened as he spoke, and she did her best not

to gape at the generous portions of sumptuous food that were delivered to their table, and when he poured wine into her glass, she didn't protest.

She realized only belatedly that while indulging in wine with a meal was second-nature for Italians, it wasn't necessarily so in America. She remembered that she had heard, somewhere along the journey to New York, that respectable women in America didn't drink alcoholic beverages; not even wine.

Now she wondered what Thatcher must think of her, and she made every effort not to touch the glass of dark red liquid he had poured.

But soon she found herself reaching for it unconsciously. The fruity, familiar flavor was somehow reassuring, and before long her glass was nearly empty and Thatcher was refilling it, and then his own, from the bottle on the table.

She was beginning to feel more relaxed, and when he asked her the first personal question of the evening— about her family—she told him that her parents and brothers and sisters had all gone to America.

"Without you?" Thatcher asked, looking startled.

She realized that she had opened the door to spilling the whole tragic story. There was no way to avoid telling him unless she lied, and she couldn't do that.

"I went with them," she confessed reluctantly. "But I failed to pass the health inspection at Ellis Island."

"Why is that?"

"Because they thought I had trachoma. And I didn't," she added hastily. "It only appeared that I did because my eyes were red and swollen from my hay fever, and from—"

She caught herself before the word *crying* rolled off her inexplicably loosened tongue. The last thing she wanted to do was tell him anything about Renzo.

He seemed not to notice her omission. Instead, he was shaking his head incredulously, his eyes filled with something close to pity.

Cira bristled. She didn't want him feeling sorry for her. She lifted her chin and said with as much stubborn confidence as she could muster, "But I'm going back there soon. . . ."

"You're going to America? To live?" She couldn't read the expression in his eyes, but she saw his right hand tighten around the handle of his fork.

She nodded, "I have to join my family there."

"Where are they?"

"In New York . . ." She hesitated. "I mean, that was their plan. I don't even know if Papa came to meet them at Immigration, or where they're living. Mama was supposed to contact me through my aunt . . . she doesn't know that I'm not staying with her."

"Why aren't you?"

"Because . . . I'm just not," she evaded, not wanting to talk any more about her personal mishaps. "I'm sure I'll find my family when I go back to New York."

"Have you any idea how big a city it is?" Thatcher asked dubiously. "When do you plan to return?"

"I'm not sure," she said, her pride not allowing her to reveal to him that she didn't have the money for her passage. "In the near future."

"Cira, you shouldn't be traveling alone."

"I won't be." She wanted to resent his assumption that she was incapable of taking care of herself, but she found his concern oddly comforting.

"Oh." He reached for his glass. "You'll be going with your fiancé, then?"

"I have no fiancé," she heard herself admit. "I'll be

traveling with my friend Lucia. I'm staying with her here in Palermo.''

"I see." Was that relief she saw in his eyes? She couldn't be sure, and it would be presumptuous of her to assume that he cared whether she was engaged to another man.

"So you made that up . . . about having a fiancé?" Thatcher asked.

"No! I wouldn't lie about such a thing. I was engaged to marry someone when I told you that . . .''

"And a few hours later, when I saw you again, something had happened to change that.''

"Yes."

"What happened?"

"I'd rather not say."

She almost expected him to pry, but he simply nodded, and she was grateful.

She tried to concentrate on the succulent cut of veal on her plate, carefully cutting a piece and putting it into her mouth, but she found that she had no appetite. It was ridiculous of her, really. This was the finest meal she had ever eaten—and, truth be told, the finest she was ever likely to eat. Yet it might as well be a mouthful of dry day-old bread.

What was wrong with her?

She happened to glance up and find Thatcher's green gaze fastened on her, and her heart skipped a beat.

He was what was wrong with her.

The man was a distraction. Every time she thought he was going to do something or say something to give her a reason not to like him, he proved that he was everything he appeared to be. Kind, and trustworthy, and respectful . . .

And handsome. So devastatingly handsome that it was

impossible to keep her eyes off him. And she wasn't the only one. She was sure she'd noticed other women in the restaurant sneaking furtive glances in his direction.

How was it possible that she, Cira Valentino, found herself in such a place, in the company of such a man?

And how could she keep from losing track of her earlier intention not to be swayed by his looks and his charm and his wealth?

She had already told him things she had no intention of revealing. There was something about the earnest manner in which he asked those personal questions, as though he really cared about her answers.

And how could he?

He was only being polite, only making conversation the way a gentleman did when he dined with a lady.

And I'm not even a lady, Cira thought incredulously. *I feel like an inexperienced, hopelessly unsophisticated girl. Especially when I look at him and am so utterly helpless to fight the improper sensations he causes. . . .*

She was ashamed, and embarrassed, by the intense longing she felt for this man she barely knew.

Yet he had seemed oblivious, all evening, to her reaction to him.

And of course he was, for how could he know of the tiny tremors that shook her insides when she noticed how incredibly broad his shoulders were beneath his black suitcoat, or the naughty thoughts that darted through her mind when he merely touched her hand to help her out of the carriage?

She told herself that it didn't matter; the meal was drawing to an end, and in no time she would bid him farewell—again—but this time for the last time.

As though he had sensed her thoughts, he looked up

at her and commented, "I suppose we won't see each
other again after this, will we?"

"Well, no," she said, taken aback by the question.
"How could we? You're leaving Palermo in the morning,
aren't you?"

"Yes," he admitted, "but you said you would be coming to New York. I live there, you know."

"I know. . . ." Heat flamed on her cheeks at the very
thought of meeting him again, in New York City. "But
surely you don't think . . ."

"That you would see me again?"

He sounded half curious, half amused, and she darted
a glance to see him waiting for an answer.

Didn't he know that it was the other way around? That
she knew better than to believe he would see her again
once he got back home?

"I thought perhaps you might need a friend in the big
city," he said. "I've lived there my whole life, and I
know my way around. You don't know where your parents are—"

"But I'll find them."

"I could help," he said, and added hastily, "if you
need help. I could look for them, so that you wouldn't
be coming alone, with no one to meet you."

"I already told you I wouldn't be coming alone," she
reminded him. "I'll be with Lucia."

"Ah, your friend. You did say that. Still, two young
women alone in a place like New York, neither of you
speaking the language . . . I don't like the idea."

"You don't have to like the idea," she retorted, again
perturbed by his assumption that she needed him to take
care of her. "Lucia and I have our plans, and they don't
involve you."

Too late, she realized how rude she sounded. She

clapped a hand over her mouth and waited for him to shoot back a suitably insulted comment, but none came. And when she snuck a peek at him, she saw that his expression was once again faintly amused.

"I don't suppose your plans do involve me," he admitted with a shrug. "I was only trying to be helpful— didn't mean to poke my nose into your business, Cira. But I seem to have a way of doing that, don't I?"

"You mean well," she told him.

"Do I?"

Startled, she glanced into his eyes and saw a fleeting impossible-to-read expression before he smiled at her and said, "Of course I mean well. As I assured you earlier, my intentions toward you are entirely honorable, Cira. I can't help feeling a bit protective of you, that's all."

"I understand that. But really, I'm quite capable of taking care of myself."

"I can see that." He lifted his wineglass and said, "Here's to you, and your fresh start in America."

She smiled and lifted her glass. As the swallow of marsala warmed its way down her throat, she wondered why she had once again been so quick to tell him she didn't need his help.

Perhaps tonight wouldn't have had to mean a permanent farewell. She could have seen him again, in New York. . . .

And why?

Because he pities you? The poor, ignorant immigrant?

But somehow, she had sensed, however briefly, that there might just be more to it than that.

"Must you get right back to your hotel?" Thatcher asked as the carriage transported them once again through the bustling streets of Palermo.

Cira considered the question, uncertain how to answer. Lucia didn't even know where she was—she hadn't been in the room when Cira returned this afternoon, and Cira knew she would be working until evening, so she hadn't been there to witness her preparations for her dinner with Thatcher. It was just as well. Cira hadn't told her friend about him and wasn't prepared to. She knew that Lucia would probably only worry. After all, he was so much older and more worldly, and a foreigner at that.

Cira wondered briefly whether Lucia had returned by now, and if she was worried about Cira's absence. She would probably assume she had found a job or was still out looking.

"If you'd like," Thatcher was saying, "we could take a stroll along the boulevard. It's such a warm evening, and there's a cooling breeze off the water."

It sounded so positively lovely—a moonlight stroll along the water—that Cira's mind was made up instantly. "I'd enjoy that," she told him. "And no, I don't have to be back at any particular time."

He looked pleased and had the driver drop them at his hotel.

"I'll see you back to wherever you're staying later," he told Cira, after paying the man and watching the carriage drive away.

She nodded, not wanting even to think about going back to her hotel, to the reality of her world. She didn't want the evening to come to an end.

Thatcher put his arm around her waist, escorting her across the street that fronted the square, and she found herself quivering at the slight touch. There were several layers of fabric between his hand and her bare flesh, but it was as if she could feel the heat of his fingers, and she fought back the images of more intimate contact that threatened to burst into her consciousness.

He glanced down at her. "You can't possibly be chilled," he said, and she realized he had felt her tremble.

She shook her head mutely, knowing that it would be useless to blame the quivering on the weather, which was quite warm even with the sea breeze.

To change the subject, she asked, "What will you do when you arrive back in New York?"

"Do you mean, for a living?"

She wasn't sure what she had meant, and supposed his interpretation was as good as any, so she nodded.

"I'll join my father's business, I suppose."

"You don't sound very enthusiastic. What does your father do?"

"He's a financier," Thatcher responded briefly.

That meant nothing to her, but she nodded as if it were significant. "Is his business large?"

"Very large. And successful."

"Then you're quite fortunate, aren't you."

He looked at her. "I am, yes. It's just . . ."

He trailed off, and she didn't feel comfortable prodding him.

They were strolling along the wide avenue now, past an ancient chapel fronted by a famed Byzantine mosaic portraying the Nativity in lush, vibrant colors. They stopped and Cira just stared at it, moved by its ancient beauty.

"Did you ever see anything so lovely?" she asked, turning to Thatcher.

"Yes," he said quietly.

Only he wasn't looking at the mosaic. He was looking at her, and the expression in his eyes caused those same odd quivers deep inside of her. Only this time he hadn't even touched her.

"Cira," he murmured, and glanced around.

There was no one nearby; they were alone in the tree-shielded grotto in front of the chapel.

Cira drew in a sharp breath, knowing, before he made a move, what was about to happen.

He reached out and took her into his arms, just as she had imagined he would from the moment she had met him. She gasped, then sighed as he lowered his head and his lips grazed hers softly, the merest whisper of a kiss.

They stood poised that way, breathless, his mouth hovering just above hers, for a long moment as she searched his eyes, needing to know what this meant.

But there were no answers in his gaze, only desire. And seeing it there, so raw and so urgent, gave her a jolt of daring.

She was the one who strained upward on her tiptoes to press her lips tentatively against his.

The instant she made contact he tightened his hold on her and returned her kiss with unbridled passion, his mouth velvety and wet and hungry, igniting the flame of need within her. Muttering her name, he tore his lips away from hers and skimmed hot breath along her neck, burying his face in her throat as she threw her head back. She reached up and stroked his hair just above his starched collar, finding it thick and silky at once. When she inhaled, her lungs were filled with the intoxicating scents of wine and a musky masculinity that mingled with the warm salt breeze.

She heard herself utter his first name for the first time, and it felt natural on her tongue. He pulled back and looked down at her, and said softly, "I'm sorry,

Cira. . . ." Then, seeming to peer more intently into her eyes, he asked, "Should I be sorry?"

She found that she couldn't speak, but shook her head and reached up with a hesitant fingertip to touch his clean-shaven cheek.

"But I promised you that all I wanted tonight was your company," he told her. "And now look at us. Look what I've done."

"I don't care," she said, filled with a sudden wanton recklessness.

"You don't?"

She shook her head, and he dipped his head again, kissing her more deeply. Her mouth opened against his and his tongue slid inside. The brazen intimacy left her weak and curiously longing for more. It was as though, the closer he got, the more she realized that it wasn't close enough.

Never before had she experienced such a fierce yearning. She clung to him as he kissed her again, and again.

He moaned faintly and pulled her against him so that she could feel the hard evidence of his lust. And she knew, somewhere in her passion-clouded mind, that she should put a stop to this now, that he was reaching the point of no return. Yet so, incredibly, was she. She felt powerless to pull away from his embrace, powerless to interrupt the seductive kisses and caresses.

Until this moment she had already felt as though everything about tonight was magical; a fantasy. Now the remaining shreds of reality fell away, and she wasn't a peasant and he wasn't a wealthy foreigner and this wasn't their first embrace—or their last.

For a brief, stolen interlude nothing mattered.

All too soon, though, the rattling wheels of a passing cart in the street nearby shattered their hushed seclusion.

As Thatcher released his hold on Cira, she let out a small, shuddering sigh of protest, though she couldn't deny that it had to end.

They could hardly take things further—not here, and not now. She knew it, and so, by the look on his face, did he.

"I should take you back now," he told her.

She wanted to object, but of course she didn't. What could she say?

It was over, and even now, when her mouth still stung from the pressure of his kisses and her breath was still coming in rapid little gusts, she found herself wondering if it had even happened at all.

Thatcher stood with Cira in front of the entrance to the dismal Hotel Paradiso, knowing he could stall no longer. It was time to say goodbye . . . for good.

Yes, she was coming to America—to New York, even. But he wasn't fool enough to believe that there could be a repeat of what had happened between them tonight. He had been away from home for three months; he was in an exotic, romantic place, and he had gotten carried away and kissed a local girl.

So what?

He tried to tell himself that it was to be expected of a young man enjoying his last night abroad before returning home to settle down.

And if, in his heart, he knew that it had been something more than that . . .

Well, he didn't *want* to know.

So he pushed his nagging doubts aside as he looked down at Cira and said, "Take good care of yourself, all right, then?"

"I will." Her reply was barely audible, and her eyes didn't meet his.

It was just as well. He didn't want to see the blatant longing that had been there earlier . . . or a new flash of anger, which was just as likely now.

After all, before she agreed to come with him tonight, she had made him promise that he wouldn't try to take advantage of her. And what had he done? He had pulled her into a dark corner and kissed her the first chance he got.

He told himself that it was as much for her sake as for his own that he wouldn't be seeing her again. She was too young, too innocent, and if she ever knew what lecherous thoughts had been running through his mind . . .

"Have a safe journey to America, when you come over," he said lamely.

She nodded. "The same to you. When do you sail?"

"On Wednesday, from Naples. On the Red Star line's *Stella Oceano,*" he added, not because the name of the ship would mean anything to her, but because the conversation had suddenly grown awkward, and he needed to keep talking.

Even though there was nothing more to say.

Except . . .

"Remember, Cira," he said, "if you get to New York and you have trouble locating your family, I can help you."

He waited for her to lift her chin and narrow her eyes and tell him, as she had before, that she didn't need his help.

"But . . . how would I find you?" she asked instead.

He paused, realizing that if he gave her his address she might very well show up there, standing on the doorstep of the Fifth Avenue mansion, speaking not a word of

English. How would he explain that to his mother?

Why does it matter what Mother thinks? he asked himself, though he knew very well that it did matter. He hated his own mixed feelings, and yet couldn't help the way he was. He had been raised to believe that he was headed for a certain destiny, and it didn't include an Italian immigrant, not matter how lovely she was or how much he wanted to believe that she needed his protection.

He realized she was waiting for his reply, so he said, "If you ever need me, you can find me through my father's business." His father wouldn't be thrilled if she showed up, either, but he was likely to be more understanding of the situation than Mother would ever be. He added, "It's the Montgomery building, on the corner of Broadway at Seventeenth Street, just above Union Square."

Shame darted through him as he realized that by the time she finally arrived in New York, she could easily have forgotten the address—and that maybe that was his intention.

But hadn't he genuinely offered her his assistance several times in the past few days, and hadn't she seemed to resent it? Hadn't she made it perfectly clear that she didn't quite trust him, and that she could take care of herself?

She had . . .

But that was before he had held her in his arms, felt her heart beating against his own, felt her supple flesh against his aching male need.

Before he had been rattled to the core at the realization that never in his twenty-six years had he been so deeply moved by a couple of kisses in the moonlight.

He looked at her, wanting to touch her again, just this last time. But somehow he knew that it wouldn't be. If he allowed himself to hold her again, it wouldn't be enough. He wouldn't be able to let go for good. And that was the right thing to do.

So he reached up to lift his hat from his head and bowed to her in a gesture that seemed ridiculously formal after all they had been through. He said, "It has been a pleasure knowing you, Cira. I wish you well."

She frowned, a look of incomprehension crossing her lovely features, and he realized that he had once again lapsed into English. And he knew then that in his mind, he was already back at home.

He repeated his farewell in Italian and was answered by an equally formal, "I wish the same to you, Signor Montgomery."

And as she turned and swept into the drab vestibule, he noted that he was no longer "Thatcher" to her.

Just as well, he thought, burying his hands deeply into his pockets as he walked along the dingy alley.

The room was dark when Cira slipped in, but Lucia's voice immediately said, "Cira? Is that you?"

"It's me."

She heard Lucia rustling about, then saw the tattered curtains at the window being parted so that a shaft of moonlight spilled through. It provided just enough illumination for her to make out the silhouette of her friend across the room.

"Where have you been?" Lucia asked.

Cira hesitated, not yet ready to talk about Thatcher. Her heart was heavy and her eyes still stung from the tears that had threatened to fall the moment she had turned her back on him and walked away. Somehow, she had kept her composure, but now all she wanted was to be left alone with her thoughts.

"Cira?" Lucia prodded. "Are you all right?"

She opened her mouth to speak and a sob choked out.

"Oh, Cira . . ." Lucia crossed the room and hugged her. "What happened? Did something terrible happen to you?"

For a moment she couldn't speak. Then she managed, "Yes, something happened to me. But it wasn't terrible . . . at least, not all so."

"What was it? Why are you crying?"

"Because he's gone, and I won't ever see him again." It spilled out of her in a plaintive little wail, and tears rolled down her cheeks.

"Renzo?"

"No," she sniffed, "not Renzo."

There was a moment of silence before Lucia asked slowly, "But if not Renzo . . . then who?"

And of course she had to tell Lucia. She could no longer keep everything bottled up inside.

"His name is Thatcher Montgomery. He's an American. He took me to dinner, Lucia—in a fine restaurant. And afterward he kissed me. . . ." She trailed off, touching her fingers to a mouth that felt as if it were burning as she recalled the fiery intensity of those kisses.

"You just met him today?"

"No, I . . . I met him a few days ago," she confessed, then found herself spilling the whole story—how Thatcher had saved her from the stranger's attack, and how he had brought her back here to Palermo, and how she had "happened" to run into him again this afternoon.

"But just last night you were distraught over Renzo," Lucia reminded her. "Now he's forgotten?"

"Not forgotten," Cira said. "It's just that Thatcher came along and made me feel things I've never felt before . . . not even with Renzo. And now he's gone."

"He left you?"

"Not in the way Renzo did. He just—he has to return to America. He's leaving Palermo in the morning. I won't be seeing him again."

"But, Cira, you'll be going to America, too. You can find him there."

"I only wish."

"What's the matter?"

"It isn't so simple. Thatcher Montgomery is very wealthy, Lucia. An American aristocrat from what I gather. He isn't the kind of man who courts a poor peasant girl, a foreigner."

"But he did court you, didn't he?" Lucia pointed out. "He took you to dinner, and he kissed you—"

"And then he said goodbye. And we both knew it was forever," she said flatly.

"Oh, Cira . . ." Lucia patted her shoulder and sighed. "Men are so very difficult, aren't they? They seem to cause only heartache."

Cira frowned slightly. "You sound as if you speak from experience, Lucia. Did something happen to you since I left Fiorenza?"

"I was speaking about your experience—not my own," Lucia responded, and then fell silent.

After a moment Cira asked, "How much money have you saved for your passage to America?"

"In another two weeks I'll have enough. Did you find work?"

"Not yet. But I will. Tomorrow morning the first thing I plan to do is find a job. I don't want to hold you back, Lucia, but even with the money Mama gave me, it will take me quite some time before I'm able to afford the fare."

"How much time?"

"That will depend on how much money I can make."

She waited for Lucia to tell her that there was no hurry; that she didn't mind waiting as long as she had to so that she and Cira could make the ocean journey together.

Instead, Lucia said, "I had hoped to leave by the first of June, at the latest."

Cira's heart sank. "I won't be able to go by then."

"Perhaps you will, Cira. You never know how much money you'll be able to make, if you work hard."

Cira sensed some kind of tension in Lucia's voice, and she wondered what her friend wasn't telling her. Why was she so anxious to get to America as soon as possible? It wasn't like Lucia to be so restless.

In the old days Cira would have just asked her about it. That was the kind of friendship they had always had. They kept no secrets from each other.

But too much had changed in the few short months since they had parted. Life had been so much simpler back in Fiorenza, Cira thought wistfully. Lucia had always seemed so easygoing, and she herself had been carefree.

"If you must leave without me," Cira told Lucia, "then go ahead."

"Oh, Cira, I don't want to do that."

And I don't want you to, Cira thought desolately. *I don't want to be abandoned again.*

"Well, as soon as I find work, we'll know, won't we?" she said aloud.

"Yes, I suppose we will." Lucia yawned loudly. "And now, if you don't mind, I really am exhausted."

"Please sleep in the bed tonight," Cira told her with a stab of guilt. "It's only right. I won't mind the floor."

"Oh, but you will," Lucia said. "You've always been the squeamish type. There are bugs, and mice . . ."

"I got used to that during the ocean voyage. Just wait until you see the conditions onboard the ship." She sighed. "Wouldn't it be wonderful not to have to travel in steerage, Lucia?"

"I would dearly love to be able to afford second class," Lucia admitted. "Can you imagine?"

"Or first class," Cira said, thinking of Thatcher Montgomery, who would undoubtedly make his upcoming crossing in the utmost comfort of a grand stateroom.

"Well, I don't suppose you or I will ever know what *that*'s like," Lucia told her.

"No," Cira agreed with a wistful sigh, "I don't suppose we will."

Thatcher stood at the rail of the vast Red Star steamship the *Stella Oceano*, looking out over the blue water. The morning sun had set the port of Naples aglow in pink and gold; it was a marvelous day to begin a journey, and his friends had been in high spirits as they boarded the great ship a few hours earlier. Only Thatcher was quiet.

At this point the others had stopped questioning his moods; they had apparently grown used to his introspection in the days since they had left Palermo. If any of them suspected that Thatcher was brooding over a woman, they didn't bring up the matter, and for that, he was grateful.

Meanwhile, thoughts of Cira continued to haunt him, and he wasn't quite sure why. It wasn't as though she was the first woman he had ever been attracted to, or kissed, or said goodbye to.

But somehow, in the brief time he had known her, she had managed to touch him profoundly, and he couldn't forget her. He found himself lying awake at night, remembering how it had felt to cradle her in his arms and feel her responding to his kisses—and longing for just one more chance to hold her . . .

Even though once more would never be enough.

If only she were some wealthy, refined New York socialite he could court and maybe even marry.

If only he hadn't suffered the dubious privilege of being born into the illustrious Montgomery family, where his future was not only secure, but neatly mapped out for him. From the time he had been born, he'd had the best of everything: from the nursemaids who pushed his pram through the park to the quality of linens on his four-poster bed to the Connecticut boarding school where he had spent so many challenging but ultimately rewarding years, followed by Harvard.

He'd had no say in any of it, but then, he was used to that. Stoddard and Eleanor made any necessary decisions, and he obediently lived his life according to their grand plan.

He couldn't even blame his parents for their high expectations of him. Fate had determined his destiny the day his elder brother tragically drowned in the gray Atlantic off Newport.

He was certain that things would have been different if Stoddard had lived. Then Thatcher wouldn't be the sole heir to the family business; the one who was duty-bound to settled down, marry well, and provide a new generation to carry on the Montgomery name.

The irony was, Stoddard IV probably wouldn't have minded the high expectations or the restrictions that went with the family name. He had always been cooperative and eager to please, with impeccable manners and an easygoing yet dignified demeanor that made people like and trust him.

By now Stoddard would have had an office next to Father's and a lovely, well-bred wife, and probably a whole batch of healthy little Montgomerys as well.

And Thatcher would have been left—well, if not to fend for himself, exactly, then to make more decisions about the direction his life would take.

Oh, who was he kidding?

If Stoddard were alive, Thatcher still wouldn't be able to strike up a relationship with a poor Sicilian immigrant. Someone like Cira would never feel at home in his world, even if she were welcome.

The truth, of course, was that she wouldn't be.

And maybe that was why he found her so captivating.

It wasn't a pleasant thought, but one he had been mulling over all morning as he settled into his relatively large, comfortable first-class cabin and tried to focus on the upcoming voyage home.

Perhaps he only wanted Cira because he couldn't have her. Was she his way of rebelling against everything that waited back home?

"Pardon me . . ."

Thatcher started at the sound of a female voice directly behind him. He turned and found a breathtakingly lovely young woman standing there. She was tall and slender, blue-eyed and fair. She wore a smart gray dress, and her hair was neatly done up in a marcel wave. She held a light-colored parasol to keep the sun off her fair skin.

Something about her was familiar.

"Yes?" he asked, trying to place her.

"I'm so very sorry to disturb you, sir, but I was just wondering if perhaps you had the time?"

So he didn't know her. Why did she seem familiar?

"Certainly," he told her, reaching into his breast

pocket. He took out his gold pocket watch, a family heirloom handed down from his grandfather to his father.

This, too, would have belonged to Stoddard, had he lived, Thatcher found himself thinking as he flipped open the case and checked the time.

"Nearly half past ten o'clock," he told the young woman.

"Thank you. I thought it was close to the time we are to embark, but then, I'm so anxious to sail, I couldn't be certain." She spoke in the same fluid accent he'd grown up hearing, an accent that betrayed not only where she was from, but the fact that she belonged to the upper class—*his* class.

"Are you going home to New York?" he asked.

She raised her eyebrows. "Yes . . ."

"And you've had an extended visit abroad?"

"How did you know?"

"A lucky guess. And anyway, I'm doing the same."

"I've been all over Europe these past few months with my aunt, and it's been quite a thrill, but now I can't deny that I'm longing for home, Mr. . . ."

"Montgomery," he supplied. "And you are Miss . . . ?"

"Johnson."

It was a common name; one that meant nothing to him. "It's a pleasure to make your acquaintance."

"Likewise," she said with a smile.

He smiled back and realized why this stranger seemed so familiar. She was so very much like the women he knew back home, with her fine clothes and her modulated speaking voice and her docile confidence. He would be willing to bet that she was heiress to some fortune or other, had attended all the right schools, and had grown up within blocks of his parents' home.

They're all so much alike, he told himself and sighed inwardly.

He was certain that he would marry somebody just like her, some pale, upstanding beauty, and for the rest of his life she would make him a good wife. He would know just what to expect from her—and what not to expect.

So different from Cira, who had, in those few fleeting days, startled him at every turn with her uncanny way of turning up when he least expected her. She was strong where he anticipated weakness, and yet surprisingly vulnerable in some ways, too.

And then there was the passion.

When he made the first tentative move to kiss her that last night, he had presumed she would resist. Instead, he had found her flashing to life in his arms, astounding him with the intensity of her response.

It would have been so much easier if she had slapped him and stormed away, a scenario he had found far more likely than the unbridled sensuality that met his embrace.

The young woman standing beside him at the rail cleared her throat and twirled her parasol, and he glanced at her to find her watching him with the coy, interested expression of a genteel woman who wouldn't be so bold as to ask him where his thoughts had wandered.

He smiled at her and she smiled back, and in a sudden burst of clarity, he knew that she hadn't really needed to know the time; she had merely wanted to strike up a conversation with him.

She was so right for him, this perfect American creature, from the carefully arranged waves on her head to the unscuffed leather at the tips of her fashionably pointed shoes. It would be dreadfully easy to engage her in some idle talk about life back home, or people they both knew—and he was sure there would be many. He could invite her to dine at his table this evening, and he could spend the next week strolling with her on the ship's wide decks, waltzing with her in the ballroom, amusing her with his flirtatious chatter.

Back in New York he would introduce her to his family, and they would be pleased. His parents would meet her parents, though their paths had probably already crossed at one society function or another. And then, after a suitable period of time—perhaps six months or a year— he and the fair Miss Johnson would become engaged.

He swallowed hard, suddenly feeling as though he was being strangled.

"Mr. Montgomery?" she asked, watching him carefully.

He cleared his throat and said, "Would you mind if I excused myself? I'm feeling a bit . . . ah, seasick."

"Seasick?" She was inquisitive. "But we haven't even left port yet."

"I'm afraid I'm very sensitive," he blurted, and hurried away, wondering if she believed him and not caring whether she did.

He simply had to escape her, before it was too late.

Cira slipped into the tiny, stuffy hotel room she had now lived in for the better part of a week, and at first thought it was deserted. Though the late-afternoon sun blazed brightly as ever outside, the light was always dim in here, thanks to a single small window that faced the narrow alley below.

She rubbed her aching back as she closed the door behind her, then froze as heard a low moan.

"Lucia!" she exclaimed, turning to see her friend curled up on the bed. "What's the matter?"

"Nothing," Lucia said unconvincingly. Cira saw that

her face was pale and she was huddled on her side, her
arms wrapped around her ample middle.

"It's so stifling in here . . . why don't you open the
window?" She started across the room to do just that.

"No!" Lucia stopped her. "Please, Cira, leave it
closed. I can't abide the stench of rotting fish right now."

"Is it your stomach? Are you ill?"

"I just . . . it's probably something I ate."

Cira sat beside her and put a hand against Lucia's forehead. She found it cool despite the warm room, and said,
"You don't seem feverish."

"I'm not. I told you, I must have eaten something that
didn't agree with me."

"But you haven't looked well at all lately, ever since
I returned," Cira said worriedly. "You should see a doctor."

"I can't do that. How would I pay him?"

"You have the money you've saved toward your passage," Cira reminded her. "You can use some of that."

"I couldn't. It would take too long to save it again."

Cira was silent for a moment, looking into her friend's
dark, troubled eyes. "So it would take a bit longer to
leave Sicily," she said. "So what? We can go together,
as soon as I—"

"I don't want to wait," Lucia interrupted. "You know
that, Cira. I must go."

"But why?"

Lucia turned away and rolled onto her other side, fac-
ing the wall. "I just have to go. I can't stay here any
longer than is absolutely necessary. And anyway, I've
already booked passage on the *Bella Donna*. It leaves in
less than two weeks."

Cira stared at her friend's back, certain that there was
something that Lucia wasn't telling her.

She had been kind enough to give Cira a place to stay, and had offered encouragement in these past difficult days as Cira adjusted to life in Palermo and her grueling work in the fields of a farm just outside the city. But Cira couldn't help noticing that despite her loyalty and support, Lucia had seemed strangely withdrawn. Clearly, something was bothering her—and just as clearly, she didn't want to talk about it. Every time Cira attempted to turn a conversation from her own troubles to Lucia's, her friend found a way to change the subject right back again.

"Lucia," Cira said quietly now, "I'm worried about you."

"Don't worry about me," came the prompt response. "I'll be fine. I just need to rest a bit. It was a terribly long day and I'm exhausted."

"You're working too hard. You should—"

"What should I do? There's nothing else I can do, Cira. I have to work. I have to earn money. I almost have enough. . . ."

"But look at you. You're making yourself ill. You won't be well enough to travel so soon even if you've already booked your passage. You can't get on a ship in your condition. You have no idea what it's like to spend endless days in steerage. You think the stench is bad here, with the rotting fish . . ." Cira shuddered at the memory. "You have no idea how it is during a crossing. All those people, some of them seasick, in such close quarters—"

"Cira," Lucia said evenly, turning back and fixing her with an unwavering gaze, "I understand all that. And I'll be fine for the crossing. I'm just having a bad day because I ate something that upset my stomach. That's all."

Now leave me alone and get out of here.

She didn't say that last part, but Cira read the message in her eyes. With a sigh she rose and walked back over to the door.

"If you need anything—"

"I just need to rest," Lucia cut in.

"That's fine. Rest." Cira walked out, closing the door behind her and leaning against the other side, feeling utterly depressed—and alone.

She thought of Mama and Papa and her sisters and brothers, all of them halfway across the world. Had they forgotten all about her? Did they assume she was lost to them forever?

What if she was? What if she somehow managed to get back to New York, and she couldn't find them?

She remembered the fleeting glimpse she'd had of lower Manhattan from the harbor. It was a cluttered maze of towering gray buildings, all crowded on the narrow tip of a concrete island.

Thatcher's warning echoed ominously in her ears. New York was an enormous place, and it wouldn't be easy to locate her family. If Lucia refused to wait for her and she had to make the crossing alone, what would she do when she arrived, with no one to greet her? Who would she turn to if she couldn't find Mama and Papa?

Not Thatcher Montgomery—that was for certain.

In the days that had passed since his departure, she had gone over every detail of their last meeting. Yes, he had seemed to care about her. Yes, he had kissed her passionately.

But his offer to help her had been hollow, and his goodbye had sounded final.

She had resigned herself to the fact that she would never see him again. And why should that matter? He was someone she had known only a few short days.

Meanwhile, she had spent a lifetime knowing Renzo, yet she thought of him with far less regret than she did Thatcher. Why was that?

True, Renzo's behavior had been blatantly traitorous. Every time Cira recalled the image of his hands on that blond stranger, she felt a burst of shock and rage bubbling up inside. But she knew that whatever she and Renzo had once had was over before she caught him with the other woman. Her future didn't lie in Fiorenza, and it no longer included him. That wouldn't change even if Renzo magically appeared here in Palermo and begged her forgiveness, promising his lifelong fidelity.

Not that she would believe him if he did, she thought darkly. He couldn't be trusted.

Men couldn't be trusted—that was what Lucia said.

Again, Cira pictured the haunted—even ravaged—expression she'd seen on Lucia's face lately, and she wondered if some man had been the cause of the drastic change in her friend's demeanor.

Had Lucia fallen in love with someone, only to be spurned? Was that why she was so anxious to leave Sicily—because she wanted to escape the memory of some bitter heartache?

If so, why wouldn't she tell Cira what had happened?

Could I have possibly done something to upset her? Cira speculated.

Lucia *had* been distraught when she'd left Fiorenza . . . but she had known it wasn't Cira's choice. Surely she wasn't holding that against her.

And anyway, she wants to leave me behind here in Palermo, rather than wait until I'm ready to travel with her, Cira thought with a mild twinge of irritation. *I'm the one who should feel resentment, if anyone should.*

But somehow, she couldn't muster much indignation.

She was too worried about Lucia, and deep down, she knew her friend would never deliberately do anything to hurt her.

If Lucia could wait, she would.

But something—or someone—had made her want to flee this place as fast as she possibly could.

Cira thought wistfully of the old days when the two of them could say anything to each other; when Lucia had been full of mischief and ideas . . . full of *life*. It wasn't so long ago that they had romped and giggled in the lush vine-covered courtyard between their houses, carefree and unaware that the happy days were numbered.

Where are we headed now? Cira wondered, folding her arms against her stomach and hugging herself as if to ward off the uncertainty. *And what's going to happen to us when we get there?*

Three more days had passed, days consumed by backbreaking labor in the blazing heat and hot, dry wind of a vast field of grain. Cira had seen little of Lucia, who was already gone when she left the room in the mornings, and so sound asleep when she returned at night that she didn't even stir when Cira readied herself for bed.

Cira herself collapsed each night and went right to sleep, relieved not to be tormented by restless thoughts of her family, or Renzo, or Thatcher Montgomery—all of whom filled her mind in waking hours. She was so exhausted from her work that there were no nightmares, or even dreams, to disrupt her deep slumber.

Then, on a sunny, arid day that dawned just like any other, her grueling, monotonous routine was broken abruptly by news that shattered her to the core.

She was standing on a busy Palermo street corner,

waiting for the farm wagon that would shuttle her and a dozen other workers to the field south of town, when the urgent cries of a newsboy reached her ears above the other din.

"Attenzióne! Attenzióne!" he shouted, waving a copy of the latest paper in the air above his head. "Disaster at sea! Red Star ship sinks in the Atlantic! All lives feared lost! Disaster at sea! Disaster at sea!"

Cira's stomach flipped over. Thatcher Montgomery was on a Red Star ship, wasn't he? She thought back to what he had told her when he'd left. She was certain he'd mentioned Red Star. But what was the name of the ship?

"Attenzióne! Attenzióne! Disaster at sea!"

Pushing her way through the crowd, she rushed over to the newsboy and grabbed his shoulder so roughly that his dark cap was jostled from his head.

He turned toward her and glared, muttering a curse before bending to scoop up his cap from the dusty street.

"Tell me . . . which ship?" Cira asked breathlessly, eyeing the paper he was waving around. "Which ship sank?"

"Buy the paper and find out," the boy retorted, holding it out of her reach.

"I have no money with me."

The newsboy shrugged and turned away, resuming his chant.

Panic sliced through Cira. She had to know whether it was Thatcher's ship. Oh, what if it was his ship?

She automatically began to pray, murmuring the Our Father under her breath as she glanced around wildly, uncertain what to do next. She spotted a man walking away with a paper tucked beneath his arm. She ran after him, overtaking him just before he entered a small tailor shop at the end of the block.

"Excuse me, signore," she called. "Please, signore, if you could just tell me . . ."

"Yes?" He turned and looked her over, his eyes puzzled beneath the brim of his dark hat.

"Which ship was it that sank? Which Red Star ship?" She gestured at the paper beneath his arm.

"Which ship? The *Stella Oceano.*"

"No!"

It took her a moment to realize the screeching protest had spilled from her own lips. She clasped a hand over her mouth and shook her head in despair.

"Are you certain?" she asked the man when she recovered her voice.

"The *Stella Oceano,*" he repeated, nodding and handing her the paper. She scanned the chilling, bold black headline, then the brief article beneath, but it told her nothing other than that this man was correct.

Thatcher Montgomery's ship had been lost at sea.

"I'm sorry, signorina," the man said and folded the paper again. "Did you have a friend on board?"

"Yes," she said blankly, staring off into space, picturing Thatcher's handsome face. "A friend . . ."

She turned and walked away, trembling so violently that she had to wrap her arms around herself. It couldn't be. . . . it just couldn't be!

He was gone forever. She would never see him again. *But you never expected to,* she reminded herself.

Or had she?

In her heart, hadn't she believed that somehow, somewhere, their paths would cross again? That even if she didn't go looking for him when she arrived in New York, there would be a day when she would hear her name uttered in that telltale American accent, and she would look up, and there he would be.

Now that wouldn't happen.

He had been lost at sea.

Perhaps not, she thought with a flicker of hope. *Perhaps he was saved, somehow.*

"*Attenzióne!* Disaster at sea! All lives feared lost!" bellowed the newsboy from down the block.

Forgetting all about work and the waiting farm wagon, Cira walked desolately back to the inn, grieving for the man she had known for so short a time, but who had somehow managed to affect her so deeply. She realized that she had been clinging not only to the dream of seeing Thatcher again, but to the fantasy of falling in love with him . . . and him loving her back. Marrying him. Bearing his children.

It was all an impossible dream, and she knew it. He was little more than a stranger. So why did she feel such an acute sense of loss—a loss even more profound than when she had realized that her future with Renzo would never materialize?

"Cira? Are you awake?"

Cira lifted her head from the pillow and looked up to see Lucia in the doorway. She had been so lost in thought she hadn't even heard the door open.

"I'm awake," she said dully.

"Have you been in bed all day?"

"No," she replied, thinking back over the endless hours. "I went to mass this morning. And after that I looked for work."

"I don't suppose you had anything to eat."

"No, but—"

"I brought you this," Lucia said, holding up a crusty roll.

Cira regarded it with disinterest and shook her head. "No, thank you."

"You have to eat something. Take it." Lucia crossed over to the bed and picked up Cira's hand, forcing the bread into it.

Cira sat up and looked at it. There was a bit of green mold starting at one edge, and she broke it away, making a face in distaste.

"Eat it," Lucia urged.

Cira made herself bite off a small piece. It was dry, and she thought longingly of the fresh, fragrant rolls dipped in olive oil that she and Thatcher had eaten the night they dined together. As always, the thought of him brought a hollow ache, and swallowing the mouthful of bread did nothing to ease it.

"Did you hear any more about survivors?" she asked Lucia, who sat next to her on the bed and bent to unlace her dusty shoes.

She knew by her friend's silence that there had been more news, and that it wasn't good. Her fingers clenched the roll, crumbling a piece of crust into her lap.

"There was an updated list just posted at the shipping office down by the water," Lucia told her, sounding reluctant. "I stopped to check it."

Cira's heart pounded. "Were there any more than the sixty originally listed?"

"A few more. Women and children, mostly. Cira, he wasn't on it."

The news came as no surprise, and yet her stomach lurched, threatening to eject the bit of stale bread she had just eaten.

It had been three days since word had come of the disaster; three days of praying and wishing, and struggling not to let hope fade as the reports grew increasingly grim. In dense fog the *Stella Oceano* had collided with another steamer. The other had managed to stay afloat, but the *Stella Oceano* had gone down so quickly that few passengers could board lifeboats. Those who did manage to survive were mainly crewmen, women, and children, although a handful of first-class men had reportedly made it as well.

Cira had fervently looked for Thatcher's name among those that had been posted down by the wharf yesterday, and when it wasn't there, she told herself it was because the list wasn't complete. The Red Star line itself admitted that they were still working to update it, and that more information would be forthcoming as soon as possible.

Now she had it, and still, no Thatcher.

"Will another list be published tomorrow?" Cira asked Lucia, careful not to look at her friend. She didn't want to face the somber sympathy she knew she would find in Lucia's brown eyes. She had seen it enough in the days that had passed.

"There won't be another list," Lucia replied after a moment. "The Red Star line says that all survivors have been accounted for now. There's no one else."

Cira fought back a sob that suddenly threatened to spill out. Her shoulders shuddered with the effort, and when she felt Lucia's arms closing around her, she could stand it no longer. She found herself breaking down, wailing pitifully over the loss of a man she had barely known, but who had somehow mattered so much to her.

"It's all right," Lucia murmured, holding her and rocking her the way Mama would have done, and Cira was swept by a fierce wave of homesickness that only intensified her grief.

How she longed for her mother, and her father, she realized suddenly, and her sisters and brothers. How very far away they were now, so far away that it seemed as though she would never see them again.

"I need to go," she heard herself say, her voice ravaged. She lifted her chin resolutely and wiped at her tears.

"What? Where do you need to go?" Lucia asked, looking bewildered.

"To New York. I need my family. . . . I can't be alone any longer," Cira whimpered. "I just can't do it."

"You aren't alone, Cira," Lucia said, tightening her hold. "I'm here with you."

And Cira realized that although her friend's words were true, it hadn't really seemed as though Lucia had been there in the weeks since they'd met in Palermo. The emotional distance her friend had been keeping had built a wall between them, and Cira had felt utterly alone, even during these past few days, when Lucia had made an effort to support her after the news about the shipwreck.

But Cira couldn't quite bring herself to accuse her friend of not being there for her. Not when it was so obvious that Lucia, too, was suffering—even if it was from some private heartache that she refused to share with Cira.

Instead, Cira said softly, "But you won't be here with me for much longer, Lucia. You'll be leaving on the next ship that sails for New York. You said so yourself."

"Next week," Lucia agreed, nodding. "If only you could come with me, Cira. I don't want to leave you. How much money do you have?"

"Not even half the steerage fare." She sighed, thinking about how she had lost her job after she'd failed to show up the day she'd found out about Thatcher. She had contemplated trying to explain the situation to the furious foreman, but what was there to say? It wasn't as

though she had lost a family member, or even a close
friend.

"I might as well face the truth," she said dismally
now. "I might never see Mama and Papa again."

Lucia hesitated, watching her. "Of course you will.
You'll find another job, Cira."

"I spent all day looking, Lucia. There was nothing.
Nothing."

"So you'll look again tomorrow."

"But even if I find work, I won't be able to save toward my fare. As soon as you leave, I'll need to find a
place to stay. I'm so grateful," she added quickly, "that
you've shared your room with me until now, Lucia."

"It's all right. I'm not paying for it anyway." Lucia's
small room had been furnished as part of her job working
for the inn.

A flicker of hope surged in Cira as something occurred
to her. She wondered why she hadn't thought of it before.
"I can take over your job when you leave, Lucia," she
said, brightening. "That way, I'll be able to—"

"No," Lucia interrupted, shaking her head. "Signora
Giamatti said she doesn't plan to replace me. She can't
afford to. The inn hasn't been doing well. She's going to
take over the work herself."

"Oh." Cira's spirits plunked even lower. "What am
I going to do, Lucia? I'll be on the streets. There's no
one for me to turn to."

She searched her friend's eyes for a long moment, for
the first time feeling as though she and Lucia were really
connecting again. In Lucia's eyes she read how deeply
her friend cared about her, how desperately she wanted
to help. And Cira finally felt a little less alone . . . but
that didn't change the fact that Lucia would be leaving
in a matter of days.

"Take my ticket, then," Lucia said abruptly, breaking the silence.

For a moment Cira didn't understand. Then she gasped and protested, "Lucia, no. I couldn't do that. You've been saving . . . and waiting . . ."

"But I have someplace I can go," Lucia told her. "I can go back . . . *home*." The word was spoken awkwardly, and Cira realized that the small house in Fiorenza had long since ceased being a home for Lucia. Still, her friend repeated it as if in an attempt to make it true. "Back home to Papa. I can at least do that. But you . . . you have no one left here in Sicily."

"No," Cira said, shaking her head. "You can't do that. You were so anxious to get away. You have to, Lucia."

"I'll get there eventually, Cira. Or . . . I'll tell you what. You can go to America and find a wonderful job making loads of money, and you can send me the fare. You'll have earned it in no time." There was a telltale strain in Lucia's voice despite her effort to sound upbeat.

"I can't do that," Cira told her. "I won't let you go back to Fiorenza." Somehow she sensed that despite her friend's confident words about returning to her father, Lucia dreaded doing that. She remembered Signore Torrio's icy eyes and the chill in his voice when he spoke of his daughter, and she knew she could never allow Lucia to go crawling back to him.

For all she knew, he was the very reason Lucia was so impatient to flee Sicily altogether. Again, she wondered what Lucia was keeping from her, and again, she told herself that she couldn't force the truth out of her friend.

"If you don't take my ticket," Lucia said, "what will you do here alone?"

"I'll . . . I'll find work," Cira said, trying to sound confident.

"Here in Palermo? What if you can't?"

"I'll go back to Fiorenza."

"And where will you stay? Your grandparents are gone. And Renzo—"

"Maybe Renzo will want to reconcile." The words were out before Cira could stop to consider them.

Yet she realized, as the idea spilled out so readily, that it must have been in the back of her mind all along. That she must have been thinking of going back to Renzo if he would have her, because he was all she had left in her homeland.

It didn't mean she had forgiven him, or even that she was in love with him anymore. But she was alone and she needed help, and he was a decent human being. . . .

What kind of decent human being makes love to another woman when he's supposedly pining away for you? a bitter voice demanded.

All right then, she admitted. So he wasn't trustworthy or loyal. But surely he was too decent to turn her away from his doorstep. He would ask his parents to take her in, and they would. They had always liked her, had wanted her to marry him.

And maybe she would, she thought, trying to ignore the churning in her gut at the very thought.

Maybe she would find the strength to overlook his betrayal and maybe things would go according to her original plan—she and Renzo, married, in America together . . .

"You've lost your mind. Are you completely *pazza*?" Lucia asked incredulously, releasing her grasp on Cira's shoulders. "You can't go back to Renzo, Cira. Not after what he did to you. How can you even suggest such a thing?''

''Maybe I shouldn't judge him based on what I saw that one night, Lucia. The fact that he slipped up once doesn't make him a scoundrel.''

''How do you know that it was only once?''

''How do I know that it wasn't?''

Lucia stared at her, her mouth opening and then closing again, as though she wanted to say more. Instead, she merely threw her hands up in the air as if to say she wanted nothing more to do with this topic of conversation.

''I'm not saying it's the perfect solution, Lucia,'' Cira told her. ''But it's a better one than for you to give me your money and return to your father. And you can never convince me to allow you to do that, so don't even suggest it again.''

''All right then,'' Lucia said with a shrug. ''I have another plan.''

''What is it?''

''You can stow away on the *Bella Donna*.''

Stunned, Cira stared at Lucia. ''I can't do that.''

''Of course you can. People do it all the time. Only it's mostly men, mostly shady characters.'' Lucia spoke with the authority of one who had become very worldly in the past few months. ''But, Cira, no one would suspect a young woman.''

''How do you know any of this?''

''I've been in Palermo longer than you have. I've been working among strangers; all sorts of characters. I hear things. I see things.''

''But, Lucia—''

''We'll come up with a plan to get you on board the ship when it sails, Cira. I'm not leaving you behind.''

"But . . . it would be committing a sin," Cira protested weakly. Lucia knew as well as she did that such a crime was against their religion.

"God forgives sins," Lucia said with such shocking disregard that Cira wondered what on earth had happened to make her loosen her staunch Catholic upbringing. Had living in Palermo, being on her own, corrupted her so quickly?

"It isn't that simple, Lucia, and you know it."

"It is simple. You'll find a church and make your confession the moment you get to New York."

"But aside from being a sin . . . it's illegal," Cira went on, disconcerted. "What if I get caught?"

"You won't."

"What if I do?"

"What if you don't?" There was a challenge in Lucia's expression, a spark of the old Lucia who seemed to have vanished of late.

"If I don't get caught," Cira said slowly, "I'll be in New York, with my family, in just a few weeks."

"Exactly. You can't stay here in Palermo alone, Cira. And you can't go back to Renzo. It's your only option. There's no where else to turn."

Cira thought longingly of Thatcher, of how he had come to her rescue and offered to help her so many times in the few precious days she had known him. If he had lived . . .

If he had lived, he would be back in New York by now, she reminded herself, *with no intention of ever seeing you again.*

She looked Lucia in the eye and said firmly, "I'll do it. I'll go as a stowaway. You're right. It's the only choice I have."

8

Cira crossed herself with holy water and hurried out of the Church of St. Catherine and across the bustling, sun-drenched Piazza Bellini, wondering what in the world she was doing. Here she was, a pious Catholic coming from morning mass, and in less than twenty-four hours she would be a stowaway on a steamship bound for New York City.

She felt sick inside whenever she thought about the plan she and Lucia had concocted, so she did her best to push the thought from her mind now.

But it wouldn't budge.

She couldn't help dwelling on the scenario they had devised, going over and over it in her mind, as though familiarity would take away her apprehension.

She was to hide inside of a large trunk she and Lucia had purchased with a portion of the money Cira had been saving toward her passage. She had been reluctant to part with the precious lira, but as Lucia pointed out, it would cost her far more than that to buy a legitimate ticket for the voyage.

The trunk was bulky and ugly and cheaply constructed, but Cira was able to contort her small frame enough to fit inside. She had nearly panicked when Lucia shut and locked the lid during their practice session, and her friend's muffled reassurances from outside did little to calm her. The air inside the trunk was hot and close despite the small breathing holes Lucia had poked into the thin wood, and Cira was drenched with sweat after only a few moments. She would have to spend long hours concealed there tomorrow, from before Lucia boarded the ship until the coast was clear for Lucia to sneak into the cargo hold to let her out—if that was even possible. Lucia had assured her that it was; that she wouldn't allow Cira to remain locked away a moment longer than was absolutely necessary.

Still, countless worries flitted through Cira's mind at the very idea of being locked into that small space for any amount of time, and she had prayed during mass for the strength to endure what would surely be a torturous experience. She had little confidence that her prayers would be heeded, considering the immoral, illegal aspects of what she was about to do.

As she continued walking toward the hotel, her stomach rumbled and a trickle of perspiration dripped from her forehead. She thought longingly of the luscious ripe fruit and cold drinks being sold by vendors in the square she had just left. But she couldn't afford to spare any more money, not now. She would need every last lira when she got to America, because they wouldn't let you in if you had no money, and anyway there was no telling how long it would take her to locate Mama and Papa.

She sidestepped a group of fair-haired Sicilian children dressed in rags and kicking a ball in her path, and passed a peasant woman in a dirt-smudged apron balancing a bundle on her head.

A familiar face popped into view then, just over the woman's shoulder, and Cira instantly stopped short and gasped.

Thatcher Montgomery!

But how could it be?

Cira turned and looked for the man she had glimpsed, squinting into the midmorning sunlight. But it was hard to make out anything in the dazzling brightness, and all she managed to see was the retreating form of the peasant woman and an elderly farmer leading a laden donkey toward the square.

But he was there . . . I saw him!

The man had been wearing a light-colored three-piece suit and a broad-brimmed hat, and his handsome face . . .

I would know that face anywhere, Cira thought stubbornly.

She turned and breathlessly retraced her steps, hurriedly glancing along the crowded side streets in an effort to spot him again. But there was no sign of anyone remotely fitting the description, and she finally gave up and turned back toward home.

I must have been seeing things, she told herself heavily, plodding along the dusty street. *It couldn't have been Thatcher. He's dead.*

The knowledge brought with it a fresh surge of anguish. She quickened her steps as though she could run from the harsh reality, but there was no escaping it. All she could think about was the brash, dashing American who had died too young.

She found herself wondering grimly whether he had suffered much pain, whether he had known what was happening to him. She couldn't bear to think of him alone, and hurting, and afraid—or of that handsome face, lifeless, and those dark eyes open wide and unseeing. Had his body had been recovered or did it still drift in the choppy waters of the Atlantic?

Oh, Thatcher, she thought, brushing at the tears that stung her eyes, *it should have been different. . . .*

You shouldn't have left, and you shouldn't have died.

She would never forget him. And maybe, when she got to New York, after she got settled, she would set out to find the Montgomery Building on the corner of Broadway and Seventeenth Street, just above Union Square— whatever that was. The address he had given her was burned into her mind, and she knew she would have to visit the place that bore his name.

But what will you do there? she asked herself. *What reason could you possibly have for venturing into his world under any circumstances—especially when he's no longer in it?*

She had no answer. She only knew that now that Thatcher was lost to her forever, it was the only connection she had to him. Her obsession with the man was inexplicable, yet she couldn't seem to rid herself of his presence.

And now your mind is playing tricks on you, and you're seeing him on the street, she thought with disdain, remembering how certain she had been just now that he had been here, in Palermo, strolling past her.

She could just imagine what Lucia would say if she told her what had happened. She would either laugh incredulously or shake her head worriedly, depending on her mood. There was no telling what frame of mind her friend would be in these days. Cira, caught up in her own problems, spent little time speculating about what was going on with Lucia. Still, she was uncharacteristically moody—pensive and brooding one moment, cheerful or high-strung the next. And she still didn't look well.

Is it any wonder? Neither of us has eaten a proper meal in weeks, nor had a full night's sleep.

The cramped room was stuffy and hot, and they took turns sleeping on the floor. Even on the nights when Cira got the bed, she found it difficult to drift off. She was kept awake by Lucia's restless movements on the floor, and by her own dark thoughts about Thatcher and the upcoming voyage.

But tonight would be the last night, she reminded herself. Tomorrow she could put Palermo, and Sicily, and all that had happened since she had returned, behind her for good. It was time for her to make a fresh start at last.

Cira rubbed her wet hair with a thin towel and stared at her reflection in the sliver of cracked mirror she held in her hand. Her face seemed drawn and pale, and her eyes were rimmed with deep circles.

But at least they aren't swollen from hay fever or from crying over Renzo, she thought resolutely, putting the mirror back into her satchel, which lay open on the bed. The tears she had shed over Thatcher had long since dried, and now it was time to look ahead, to the journey she would begin in the morning. Though she dreaded being smuggled on board the ship, and hardly looked forward to the long crossing, she was actually eager to set foot on Ellis Island again. This time she wouldn't allow herself to be intimidated by the immigration officers with their terse, foreign speech and their probing examinations. She would march into America confident and prepared, without a lingering thought of her homeland.

She tossed the towel aside, sat on the edge of the bed,

and reached back into the satchel for her comb. She ran it carefully through the length of her hair, though it was missing a few teeth. She remembered how Mama had washed her hair for her the night before that last journey, and how she had twisted and coiled and pinned it high on Cira's head for the occasion.

I felt so grown up, Cira marveled, *but what did I know then?*

So much had happened since the day she had first set sail for America. So much would be different this time.

Now she would be alone. . . .

Not alone, she amended. *Lucia will be with me. But I'll be a stowaway.*

What if she got caught? What if the air inside the trunk ran out and she smothered? What if Lucia couldn't get to her to let her out?

Stop fretting! It will be fine. It's the only way.

She finished combing her hair and left it to dry naturally, conscious of its damp weight falling down her back. She stood and crossed the small, cluttered room, looking about for her nightdress but hardly eager to put it on. The night air was hot and still, and she was uncomfortably warm even clad in just her white sleeveless cotton undergarments.

A knock at the door caused her to jump, and she hurried over to open it for Lucia, who had gone down to visit with Signore Giamatti and collect her last day's pay.

Throwing the door open, Cira opened her mouth to greet her friend—and froze.

There, standing on the threshold, was Thatcher Montgomery.

Thatcher watched as Cira's jaw dropped and her lovely brown eyes widened at the sight of him. He searched for

the carefully prepared words he had practiced, but came
up with nothing, and stood silently watching the shock
and disbelief registering on her face.

He found himself noticing that she looked far more
mature than he remembered; that her expression had lost
its sparkle and her cheeks weren't quite as rosy as he
remembered. Her damp hair was parted in the middle and
fell past her shoulders in slight waves, with a few drying
tendrils curling toward her cheeks.

And . . .

Good Lord.

She wasn't dressed.

He swallowed hard as he realized that she stood before
him wearing only some sort of white chemise with a
flimsy slip, revealing portions of creamy skin that con-
trasted sharply with her sun-darkened face, neck, and
lower arms. His gaze fell to the pale swell of flesh that
poked above the neckline of her amply filled bodice, and
he could see the faint, rosy peaks of her nipples outlined
beneath the thin fabric.

She made a sound that cut short his breathless appraisal, a strangled little cry of utter surprise, and he hastily and guiltily jerked his eyes back up to her face.

"Cira," he said softly, "it's me. You remember
me . . . ?" he added then, belatedly wondering if he had
been too presumptuous to assume that she would; that he
had meant anything to her at all.

She looked at him blankly, and for a moment he
thought she was trying to place him, and his heart plum-
meted toward his fashionable kid and patent shoes.

Then he realized that he had spoken in English, and
he repeated the question in Italian, watching her face
carefully and nearly sighing with relief when she nodded,
still wide-eyed and staring at him.

"You're alive," she said at last, her voice as melodi-
ous as he remembered. She was clearly filled with wonder, and she raised trembling fingers toward his arm as
though she were about to touch him, to make sure he was
real. He desperately wished that she would, longing to
feel her gentle hand on him, knowing that he would be
compelled to catch it in his own grasp and raise it to his
lips.

But she dropped her hand abruptly, as though she had
suddenly gotten hold of herself, and said only, "I thought
you had died at sea, Signore Montgomery."

"Thatcher. And I would have died," he said somberly,
"if I had stayed on the ship. But I got off shortly before
it sailed."

"Why?"

Because of you.

He desperately wanted to tell her that, but something
wouldn't let him.

He thought back over the nightmare of the past week—
of how he had found himself fleeing the *Stella Oceano*
as though the demons of hell were nipping at his heels.
He had left so impulsively that it wasn't until he was
standing on the dock, watching the liner steam away from
the harbor that he realized what he had done. By then he
had come to his senses.

What was he doing here? He should be on board, sailing toward home, even if it did mean living his life according to his parents' wishes, and marrying a proper girl
like the fair Miss Johnson who had so charmingly made
his acquaintance on the first-class promenade.

He hadn't even stopped to tell his friends what he was
doing, or to retrieve his baggage. No, he had simply gotten off the ship, driven by some vague, wild notion of
saving himself from a fate worse than death.

Ironically, what he had done was save himself from death itself.

But that truth hadn't been apparent right away.

First, he had spent several days wandering around Naples, wondering what to do next. His instinct was to return to Sicily and find Cira, but that notion seemed even more insane than spontaneously disembarking had been. He tried to tell himself that she wasn't the reason he had stayed; that it was far more complicated than that.

It had to be. Worldly, wealthy men like him didn't disrupt their lives for the sake of chasing young, foreign peasants like her. What on earth would his parents say if he told them that he had decided not to return to New York because he had fallen desperately in love with a nineteen-year-old Sicilian girl?

His mother would probably faint on her woven Brussels carpet, and his father would take him aside and tell him that he must come to his senses, that he shouldn't mistake lust for love.

Surely that was what he had done, he came to realize in those oddly quiet days spent reflecting in Naples. Surely he had confused a fierce physical longing for real emotion, had allowed his healthy libido to interfere with his better judgment.

The thing to do, he came to realize, was wire his parents that he had been delayed, without telling them why, and that he would sail on the next ship to New York.

But before he could do that, word had come that the *Stella Oceano* had been lost at sea, along with most of its passengers. So great was his shock and sorrow that for the first few days, Thatcher could only lie in his bed in the hotel suite he'd rented, staring at the ceiling and thinking about his lost friends, whose names hadn't appeared on the scant lists of survivors. Nor had Miss Johnson's, and he found himself chilled at the realization that the perfect blond creature had met so dreadful a fate.

With his anguish and remorse came the knowledge that if he had been on the *Stella Oceano,* he, too, would most certainly have died. There had to be a reason he had gotten off the ship, a reason that went beyond mere skittishness about returning to the world of his parents' expectations and even beyond his reluctance to leave Cira Valentino behind.

He wasn't meant to drown in the treacherous Atlantic the way his friends had, the way his own brother had so many years ago off the coast of Newport. For the second time in his life, Thatcher Montgomery had been spared a watery grave.

Why?

So that he could dutifully return to the path that had been chosen for him?

No.

He had come to realize, in those grim days following the disaster at sea, that he was fortunate to have a life to live, and that he had better start living it. From here on in, he would listen to his instincts the way he had that day on the deck of the ship.

And his instincts had taken him straight back to Palermo.

Straight back to Cira Valentino.

He had arrived early this morning, and had spent hours wandering the streets in search of the shabby hotel where he had dropped her off that last night. He couldn't remember the name, or the exact location.

Finally, after a hot meal and a glass of wine that left him sleepy, he had decided to return to his hotel and call it a night. But on the way he had passed a fish market near the wharf, and all of a sudden it came rushing back.

He quickly located the alley and the run-down Paradiso, and had hesitated only briefly before going in to inquire about Cira.

Now here he was, standing before her, and his heart was beating like mad at the mere sight of her.

"Why did you get off the ship?" she was asking again, and he forced his attention back to the conversation, not allowing his gaze to roam again over her naked arms and exposed cleavage.

"I got off because I had a bad feeling about going back," he said simply, and told himself that it was the truth. Not the whole truth, but he hoped it was enough to satisfy her.

"You had a premonition about what was going to happen?" she asked, looking and sounding incredulous.

He shrugged.

"But . . . you got off in Naples, didn't you? What are you doing back here in Palermo?"

Now there was no denying it. He had to tell her, if she didn't already know. . . .

Yet from the blank, bewildered expression she wore, he realized that no, she didn't know.

"I came back here," he said quietly, watching her face, "because of you."

Her lips parted and a hushed sigh escaped them, as though she had been holding her breath for his reply.

"Cira," he went on, when she said nothing and didn't move, "I needed to see you again. I'm not ready to go back home, not yet. I thought that if I could stay here for a while, if I could be with you . . ."

She was watching him blankly.

What? he demanded of himself, frustrated. *What are you trying to tell her? What is it that you think will hap-*

*pen if you stay here with her? Will all the answers to
your problems fall suddenly into place?*

"But I won't be here," Cira told him softly then, shaking her head. "I'm leaving in the morning, Thatcher."

"Leaving?" How could she be leaving? Now? "But . . .
where are you going?"

"To New York. To find my family."

To New York.

She was going to New York.

He gave a short, brittle laugh.

"What is it?" she asked, looking startled.

"Irony," he told her. "It's irony. I was on my way to
New York, but I came back to find you, only now you're
on your way to New York."

And if he hadn't happened to stumble across her hotel—if he had gone straight back to his room and gone
to sleep as he had planned, waiting until morning to resume his search—he would have missed her.

"But . . ." She faltered, then said, "I didn't even know
you were alive."

"Nobody does."

"Not even . . . what about your family?" she asked,
wide-eyed.

"I haven't gotten in touch with them yet."

"You haven't . . . ? But Thatcher, they must think you
sailed on the ship. That you died in that wreck. They
must be devastated. How can you let them suffer that
way?"

He knew there was no way to explain it to her. He
wasn't even sure that he understood his reasoning himself. He only knew that for the first time in his life, the
pressure was off. Nobody expected anything of him, because nobody knew he existed.

"I'll tell them soon enough," he assured Cira, hating

the accusatory way she was looking at him. "I'll send them a wire. The moment I know when I'm going to sail for home, I'll get in touch with my family."

"Why don't you sail tomorrow morning on the *Bella Donna*?"

"With you?"

She hesitated, then nodded. "Of course, you wouldn't be going steerage class."

He shook his head, not welcoming the image of her crammed into the third-class quarters in the bowels of the ship.

He heard himself say, "Cira, let me upgrade your passage for you."

"What?"

"You would be so much more comfortable going first class . . . you have no idea. It's the least I can do."

She gaped at him, opening her mouth and then closing it. Finally she managed to say, "I couldn't let you do that."

"Why not?"

"Because . . . I don't even have a ticket in the first place."

He frowned. "What are you talking about? You just said that you were sailing—"

"I know, but not as a passenger. As a stowaway."

Horrified, he could only stare at her, sensing the bitter shame that had stolen over her as she made her shocking revelation. Still, she managed to keep her head held high, and after a moment she went on, "It's the only way for me to get back to my family."

"Oh, Cira." For a moment he was at a loss for words. Then he found his voice and said, "Let me help you, all right? Let me get you on board the ship the regular way. As a first-class passenger."

"With you?"

"Not with me. I told you, I'm not ready to go back to New York yet. I'm going to stay here."

Without her? Why do you want to do that? demanded a voice in his head.

She shrugged. "Then I won't let you pay for my passage."

Taken aback, he replied quickly, "You can't do that."

"I can't do what? Refuse to allow you to hide here in Sicily while your family thinks you're dead? I don't know what you're up to, Signore—Thatcher, but I do know that it's wrong not to let them know you survived. You should go back."

Her words sank in. He pictured his mother, who had been so consumed by grief over Stoddard's death so many years ago that she had never smiled again. What must she be going through now, thinking she had lost her only surviving son?

And what about his father, who had been counting on him to join the business and carry on the family name?

"All right," he said, nodding at Cira. "All right. I'll go back."

She smiled briefly, then caught her lower lip in her teeth and looked down at her bare feet.

He wondered what she was thinking, then knew.

If he went back on the ship tomorrow, they would sail together. In first class. Days upon days at sea. Together.

His heart began to pound at the thought. He reached out and slipped a fingertip beneath her chin, tilting her head up and forcing her to meet his gaze.

"Cira," he said, "I don't expect you to share my cabin. You'll have your own."

She said nothing, but he saw the tension in her face. Was she thinking what he was thinking? Was she won-

dering what it would be like if they did share a cabin . . .
and a bed?

He pictured her lying back against fine linen sheets,
wearing nothing more than she wore now, her clean,
damp hair fanned against a feather pillow. He pictured
himself reaching out and slipping first one, then the other
of her camisole straps down past her rounded white
shoulders, bending his head to brush his lips against the
swell of her breasts . . .

As though she had read his thoughts, she suddenly
seemed to realize that she wore only her undergarments.
A deep crimson blush crept swiftly up her neck and over
her face, and she raised her forearms to her bosom in a
futile effort to cover herself.

"I . . . I forgot that I . . ." She stammered and took a
step back, and then another.

"It's all right," he told her, remaining in the doorway.
"Don't be ashamed. You're beautiful, Cira."

"No . . ."

"Yes," he said softly, and moved tentatively forward,
into the room. She stood by the rumpled, narrow bed,
her arms still crossed in front of herself, warily watching
him. He ached to take her into his arms, to caress her
bare skin, to feel those lush curves against him.

"What are you doing?" she asked softly, but there was
no fear in her voice.

"I don't know," he replied truthfully, and returned,
"What are you thinking?"

"That I can't believe you're really here . . ." Her voice
was hushed. "That you're alive."

They stood staring at each other, and then he closed
the short distance between them and reached for her. His
hands closed gently over her upper arms, and he could
feel her trembling.

"It's all right," he whispered. "I won't hurt you."

"I know."

He was surprised by her response, and it was all the encouragement he needed. He trailed the backs of his fingertips from her arm, across the jutting angle of her collarbone just above the neckline of her camisole, and then, ever-so-tenderly, down over her breast.

She gasped softly, and he looked down to see that her nipples had become rigid, straining the pure white cotton chemise. His jaw clenched as he fought to maintain control, and he gently cupped her breast in the palm of his hand. He could feel it rise and fall beneath his fingers, could feel and hear her breathing accelerate. Her head was bent and he was struck by the realization that she was looking at his hand on her, but wasn't protesting. The idea that she accepted, even wanted it there, that he was giving her pleasure, stirred his arousal almost painfully. He felt his own hard flesh straining against the front of his trousers, and he was seized by the impulse to pick her up and lay her on the bed, to rip away her clothing and then his own, and to plunge himself into her waiting, willing flesh.

Instead, he bent his head, and he captured her soft, sweet lips with his own, kissing her deeply, taking his time to let his tongue wander over the soft interior of her mouth, stroking her, tasting her.

And still he grasped her breast, now letting his fingertips flick over her stiffened nipple until she moaned and he needed desperately to find it and take it into his mouth. This time he didn't resist his primal instincts.

Breaking the kiss, he slipped the straps of her garment down first one shoulder and then the other, struggling not to force the fabric away too roughly in his haste to reveal her breasts. He dipped his head in anticipation, then heard someone gasp and felt her tense.

For a moment he thought the sound had come from Cira, and he looked up, confused, to see her staring over his shoulder.

He turned his head and saw, in the doorway, an unfamiliar young woman. She was dark-complected and roly-poly, and wore a stunned expression on her round face.

"Cira?" she asked tentatively. "Are you—"

"Lucia." Cira's voice came out strangled. "I'm all right."

Thatcher had hastily pulled his hands from her body and stepped away from her, but there was no place to go in the tiny room. He hardly wanted to move closer to the newcomer, given the accusatory look on her face.

"Who is this?" Lucia asked.

"It's Thatcher Montgomery."

He heard Lucia gasp again, and knew that Cira had told her about him, that she must be aware that he had presumably been lost at sea. He felt a surge of pleasure at the knowledge that Cira hadn't dismissed him from her thoughts the moment he had left; that he had been on her mind, since she had obviously discussed him with this woman who must be her friend, the one she had mentioned.

"I thought he was dead," Lucia said.

"So did I. But he's not."

"Obviously." Lucia continued to stare at him, her expression softened a bit, but hardly welcoming.

Thatcher cleared his throat, held out his hand to her, and said, "I'm pleased to make your acquaintance, Signora . . ."

"Torrio," Cira supplied. "She's Lucia Torrio, a dear

friend of mine. We grew up together in Fiorenza, and I've been staying with her here since my return.''

"How kind of you," Thatcher told Lucia, still sensing an iciness in her demeanor.

Well, she *had* walked in at an inopportune moment. She must have been shocked to witness their passionate display. Thatcher swallowed hard at the memory of just what Lucia's appearance had interrupted. If she hadn't shown up, where would it have led?

"Lucia is sailing for America tomorrow, too," Cira told him, and turned to her friend. "Signore Montgomery has kindly offered to pay for my passage."

"That was very nice of him, but I'm afraid the steerage class is completely sold out," Lucia informed them, still keeping a wary eye on Thatcher.

"Cira won't be traveling in steerage. She'll be in first class, with me."

He couldn't read the expression in Lucia's eyes but knew she wasn't pleased. She shrugged and said to Cira, "So, your dream has come true after all."

Thatcher glanced at her, and she colored faintly but said nothing. A terrible, preposterous thought struck him. Was Cira interested in him only because of his money?

Why is that so preposterous? he asked himself. *She's a poor Italian peasant. I'm a wealthy American. The difference between us is impossible to ignore. Why wouldn't she be enchanted by the power I have to buy her anything her heart desires?*

And yet, he had certainly encountered his share of gold diggers, both at home and here in Europe, and Cira hadn't struck him as being one of them. He had convinced himself that she cared about him, that she was drawn to him for reasons that went deeper than mere money.

Had he been wrong about her?

He recalled how she had reacted to his intimate advances only moments ago. She had been hesitant, yet willing. He had assumed she was hesitant because of her youth and innocence, yet willing because she was caught up in emotion and passion, just as he was.

But what if she was simply and quite shrewdly prepared to be a rich man's whore?

He turned back to Cira and studied her lovely face intently, searching for a clue to her true nature. He saw nothing to prove that she was a calculating temptress, and yet nothing to convince him otherwise, either. Her expression was carefully neutral, and her eyes were focused on Lucia.

"Isn't it wonderful, Lucia?" she asked her friend. "Now we won't have to go through with our stowaway scheme."

"You *told* him? Cira, how could you? Do you know what would happen to us if anyone found out?"

Cira paled. "No one will find out. Thatcher won't tell anyone . . . will you?"

"Of course not. Why would I do that?"

"Why, indeed?" Lucia asked tartly. "Now that Cira will be joining you in your cabin, you have no reason to cross her."

"That isn't true," Cira protested, and turned to Thatcher. "Tell her what you told me, Thatcher. Tell her that I will have my own cabin."

"Why bother?" Lucia asked. "I saw what the two of you were doing when I walked in. There you were, half-dressed, in his arms. Surely a second cabin will be a waste of Signore Montgomery's money, even if he does have an enormous amount of it."

Thatcher felt an unpleasant rolling in his gut. So Cira

had told her friend that he was wealthy. His earlier pleasure at learning she had discussed him with Lucia had all but dissipated. Now he wondered what she had told her friend. That she had found a rich American willing to wine and dine her in exchange for indulging his raging lust?

"Lucia, I resent what you're implying!" Cira said in a tone Thatcher had never heard her use before. "How dare you hint that Signore Montgomery has been anything but honorable and respectful toward me!"

Lucia didn't reply, merely walked over to the open window and stood looking out, her arms folded across her middle.

"Lucia, what has gotten into you?" Cira asked, softening. "Why are you suddenly so bitter? Aren't you glad that we won't have to take a risk getting me on board the ship? We could have found ourselves in terrible trouble if we had been caught."

"I know. But I was willing to take that chance to help you," Lucia said. "You know that. I wouldn't have left you behind, alone."

"Well, now you don't have to. I'll be sailing with you."

Lucia made a scoffing sound but said nothing, and Thatcher knew what she was thinking. Cira would be in first class; she would be in third. Their paths were hardly likely to cross on the ship.

"You won't be sailing with me," Lucia pointed out. "You'll be sailing with him. You no longer have any use for me."

"Of course I need you. You're my friend. Lucia, I can't believe you're acting this way. What's wrong?"

Thatcher shifted his weight uncomfortably.

"As long as you're going to be traveling with him,"

Lucia said, still not turning away from the window, "you might as well leave with him now. I would like to get a good night's sleep for once, and this room is too small for both of us."

Appearing stricken, Cira said nothing but looked at Thatcher.

"Come on, then," he told her, gesturing toward the door. "I have a room in a hotel not far from the waterfront. You can spend the night with me there."

"But . . ." She was obviously torn. "How can I do that?"

"She just told you she doesn't want you here," Thatcher said reasonably, hating his detached tone but unable to help himself. "And there's plenty of room in my suite for two. So come along."

"But where will I sleep?" Cira asked with such a plaintive note in her voice that he was almost—not entirely, but almost—convinced she really was the naive girl he had assumed her to be all along.

"Where will you sleep?" he echoed. "With me, of course."

Her mouth fell open and her eyes widened. She glanced back at Lucia, who had finally turned away from the window and was watching the two of them.

"Lucia?" she asked, the word almost a plea.

"Go on," Lucia said, her mouth set.

Cira's shoulders slumped and Thatcher impulsively reached out and put an arm around her. He found himself wanting to protect her, yet unwilling to trust her entirely.

"Let's go, Cira," he said resolutely. "Get dressed and get your things."

9

*C*ira stood just inside the doorway of the lavish hotel suite, awestruck by the sight before her. The floor was covered in floral carpeting in shades of rose and sage; the walls in contrasting paper and framed by ornately carved molding. The tall windows were framed by heavy draperies in a rich brocade, and the four-poster bed was covered in a similar fabric. There were countless uphol-stered chairs and small tables and chests of drawers; paintings of Roman ruins on the walls and vases of spring flowers that gave off a delicate scent.

The room was positively sumptuous, and easily ten or even fifteen times the size of the dismal quarters she and Lucia had shared. Larger, even, than the house in Fior-enza where she had grown up. Never in her life had Cira set foot in such a vast, grand room.

"Go ahead," Thatcher said behind her, and she real-ized that she had almost forgotten he was here. "Go on in."

She took another step forward, and then another, and heard him shut the door behind them. Turning, she saw that he had set her small satchel down and was watching her, wearing the same guarded expression she had seen on his face earlier.

She wondered if he felt as fluttery and nervous as she did at the prospect of spending the night together. Not, she hastily amended, that she had the slightest intention of sharing his bed, as he had so brazenly suggested. She would sleep on the floor just as she had with Lucia, and it would all be very proper.

She shoved aside an image of their earlier heated encounter and cleared her throat, doing her best not to look at him.

"I'll just put these"—he brandished the two first-class tickets he had just purchased for tomorrow's sailing of the *Bella Donna*—"into this drawer for safekeeping overnight."

She watched as he opened a polished wooden desk and slipped the tickets into the top drawer. When he closed it and turned back to her, she quickly cast her gaze to the carpet, tracing the swirling floral pattern with unseeing eyes.

"Cira, we should get some sleep. We have to be up before dawn tomorrow."

"All right." What else could she say? Which was more awkward—standing here a few feet away with nothing to say to him, or lying in the dark, knowing he was so close by? More than anything, she wanted to flee, but there was no place to go.

Lucia had made it clear she no longer wanted Cira around. What on earth had gotten into her? Why had she behaved so rudely? The Lucia Torrio Cira had known back in Fiorenza would never have treated Thatcher that way—and she certainly wouldn't have treated Cira as she had.

What did I do to enrage her so? Cira wondered desolately. She knew her friend hadn't been happy to stumble across her kissing Thatcher—anyone would be embarrassed under the circumstances. But why wouldn't Lucia be happy that he was helping her get to America by buying her a ticket? Was she jealous? Disappointed that Cira wouldn't need her help? There was no clear answer. Lucia was simply no longer her sunny, predictable self, and Cira could do nothing more to find out why.

Perhaps we can talk once we're on board the ship, Cira told herself, and her thoughts turned to the adventure that awaited her.

First class!

In all her life she had never dreamed of traveling first class, or sleeping in a first-class hotel suite like this one. Yet here she was, in Palermo's finest hotel, standing on a real woolen carpet in a breathtakingly lovely room that seemed the size of a palace, with a man who had spent more money on her than Papa had earned in his whole life.

She stole a glance at Thatcher and saw that he had removed his gray coat. Beneath it, he wore a long sleeved white shirt and trousers, and a pair of dark suspenders that made his shoulders look impossibly broad. He casually tossed his coat over a chair, and Cira marveled that anyone would treat such a fine garment with such disregard. Mama had taught her to handle her few precious items of clothing carefully, creating as little wear and tear as possible. After all, most of her dresses had already been made over from Mama's wardrobe and would be handed down again, first to Giulia, and then to their younger sister. She couldn't afford to toss things haphazardly around the way Thatcher did, and she found herself resenting the fact that he had no idea what it was like to want for anything.

Then she remembered that he'd said he had left his luggage behind on the *Stella Oceano*, and she impulsively asked, "What about your clothes?"

He looked startled. "What about them?"

"You said you walked off the ship without your bags."

"I did. All I had was the clothing on my back, and the money in my pockets."

The money in his pockets.

Right. She had seen him pull out an enormous wad of cash and peel off several bills to buy their first-class tickets for the *Bella Donna*. She realized that to a man like Thatcher, the loss of a few pieces of luggage and everything in it must mean nothing.

"So you replaced what you lost?" she asked.

"Not nearly. But I did buy enough to wear for quite some time. Why do you ask? Afraid I'll run out of clothes and have to walk around naked?"

The very idea made her feel flushed, and she did her best to banish the provocative image his words had conjured.

"What's the matter, Cira?" He seemed to deliberately shove his suspenders off his shoulders so that they hung against his thighs, then slowly unfastened the top button of his shirt, his gaze focused on her face.

"Nothing," she said resolutely. "Nothing's the matter."

"I promise"—he undid another button, and she looked away—"that I won't walk around naked. Unless you ask me to."

"What! Why would I do such a thing?" She glanced back at him and saw that he was teasing her. His dark eyes twinkled and his mouth was trying not to smile.

"Oh, I don't know." Another button. A full-blown grin. "I just thought that after what happened between us before I left Palermo . . . And again, back there to-night, before your friend interrupted—"

"How dare you!" she erupted. "How dare you make light of that? You have no idea what that meant to me. What you did to me. You have no idea!"

His grin faded. "I'm sorry, Cira. I don't know what's wrong with me."

"I do. You're a spoiled, womanizing cad. You have no idea how your attitude hurts other people, do you?"

He raised his eyebrows.

Even she was startled by the ferocity of her attack. After all, what right did she have to accuse him of hurting other people? She hardly knew him, and only knew that he had hurt her. But that was enough.

"I never meant to hurt you, Cira. . . ."

"But you did." She refused to bend.

"By teasing you about what happened between us?"

"No, Thatcher. By leaving!"

The words were out before she could stop them. They fell into a void of silence.

She stared straight ahead, fidgeting with the bottom of the braid she had hastily formed in her still damp hair before leaving Lucia's room. She wondered what Thatcher was going to say, what he would do. Would he throw her out, the way Lucia had? If he did, she would have no place to go. She would be on the street. And for all the bravado she had managed when she had told Lucia she could take care of herself, she was filled with terror at the very thought.

Then Thatcher said, as though he was choosing his words very carefully, "You're telling me that I hurt you because I left Palermo to go back to New York? Back home?''

''Yes—no. No, that wasn't it.''

It was the way you left. As though you had suddenly remembered who you were, and who I was, and had realized that I didn't belong in your world. You left without a backward glance, without any hint that we would—or should—ever see each other again.

But she couldn't bring herself to tell him all of that.

All she could say was ''It was the way you left, Thatcher. After wining and dining me, and . . . and . . .'' She couldn't think of a delicate way to put it, but he filled in for her.

''And taking you into my arms and kissing you passionately.''

She nodded, aroused at the mere memory, despite her anger.

''But how am I to know what that meant to you? For all I know, you're a jaded young gold digger after my money, plying me with your charms to get what you really want.''

Horrified, she stared at him. ''Is that what you really believe?''

''No. It isn't. But then there's a part of me that asks if I'm being a fool to trust you. Just as you're too wary to trust me,'' he added when she opened her mouth to protest. ''You've said you're angry with me for leaving, Cira. But remember, I came back.''

''You did. You came back.'' She realized the implications of that were sinking in for the first time as the shock of seeing him again gradually wore off. ''You came back to me.''

He nodded.

She became aware of his shirt, half-unbuttoned, revealing a patch of his bare chest beneath. He wasn't wearing an undershirt. A few more buttons, and he would be half naked. She found herself bending her fingers restlessly, then clasping her hands together as though to prevent them from reaching out to touch him—to unfasten those buttons herself.

"Cira, please," he said, coming closer to her.

She swallowed hard and fought the urge to move toward him, right into those strong arms. Instead she stood her ground, waiting to hear what else he had to say.

"Can't we start over?" he asked softly. "Can't we pretend that I never left? Let's start over, Cira. Let's pretend we know nothing about each other and see where that leads us. Allow me to introduce myself. I'm Thatcher Montgomery. And you are . . . ?"

She couldn't help smiling. "Cira Valentino."

"Charmed to make your acquaintance," he said, and reached toward her.

She tensed, but he only took her hand, and raised it to his lips. She felt them brush against her skin only briefly, but the mere contact tempted her to squirm. She held still, trying to ignore the quivery sensation that had started building in her stomach.

"I'm from New York," he went on conversationally, still clasping her fingers in his own. "And you?"

"I'm Sicilian," she told him, playing along, relieved for a distraction from the way his touch made her feel. "A small town not far from here. Fiorenza."

"Ah, I've heard of it. The home of an internationally renowned sculptor."

"Yes. Dante Gasperetti."

"You know him, then?"

"We've met." She couldn't help smiling, then clapped a hand over her mouth as she remembered something.

"What is it?" Thatcher asked.

"The sculpture. The one you got from Signore Gasperetti to bring home to America . . . what happened to it?"

A shadow crossed his features. "It's at the bottom of the Atlantic, I presume."

"That's such a shame . . . you traveled so far to get it, and he worked so hard to create it." And surely, it must have cost him a fortune.

Thatcher shrugged, and she was irked again by his cavalier attitude about his money and possessions until he said, "It was only a thing, Cira. Things can be replaced. There are *people* at the bottom of the Atlantic, too."

"Oh, Thatcher." For the first time it occurred to her that he must have lost his friends in the accident, that he must be grieving for them. This time she didn't hesitate to reach out to him. She laid a gentle hand on his upper arm and said, "I'm so sorry."

"I had three friends," he said slowly, his eyes full of pain. "Three old friends with whom I had spent the past several months here in Europe. And now they're gone. I shudder to think of their horrible deaths. . . ."

Cira remembered how many times she had imagined Thatcher on board that ship, being washed into the sea, the cold water drowning the life out of him. She moved her hand to his face and stroked his cheek. She found it smooth and soft, almost like the skin of a young boy. In the dim lamplight he appeared younger than his twenty-six years, and more vulnerable than he ever had before.

She was drawn to that vulnerability, to the realization that, for the first time, she wasn't the needy one, with him coming to her rescue. No, right now he needed her, and her instinct was to take care of him, to soothe the shadows from his handsome face. She ran her fingertips along his jaw and felt the tension give way as he seemed to realize what she was doing.

"Cira?" he asked, his voice almost a whisper.

"It's all right."

He caught her hand gently in his and said, "Do you know what you're doing? I mean, what you're doing to me? When you touch me?"

"I'm trying to help you to feel better," she responded, and her heart started to pound at the expression she saw in his eyes.

"What I feel when you do that," he said, low, "is wicked temptation."

She couldn't respond, couldn't find her voice.

He let go of her hand.

She raised it again to his face, coyly this time, and touched his cheek, his jaw, and finally, his lips. She found them trembling and heard a faint moan spill from the depths of his throat.

"What are you doing, Cira? Do you realize where you're leading me?"

She nodded, finding it impossible to speak, or to stop what she was doing. She slid the tip of her forefinger along his lower lip, then up to his eyebrows and across his forehead, learning the exquisite contours of his face.

"I don't think you do know where this is leading. I may be an honorable man, a man who has every intention of respecting you, but, Cira . . . I'm only human."

She stopped touching him. Studied his face for a long moment, becoming aware that he was holding his breath, and so was she, waiting to see what would happen next.

She was in control. It was up to her.

She could back away from him, suggest that they both get some sleep.

Or she could touch him again, knowing that there would be no turning back.

She knew precious little about what went on between a man and a woman when they managed to get past the barriers of propriety and morality. All she had to go on was the basic biological knowledge she had giggled about in the schoolyard, those fumbling encounters with Renzo in the grotto, and the fervent need she had experienced with Thatcher.

But, looking into his eyes and seeing his hunger for her, she forgot all about what was proper and moral; forgot to be insecure over her lack of experience. It was as though her conscious thought detached from her physical and emotional self, and all she could do was act, and feel. There would be time for thinking later.

She reached toward him, with both hands this time, and found the next button down on his shirt, slipping it deftly through the buttonhole. She felt him quake and looked up to see that he was watching her, his eyes smoldering with fascination and, perhaps, with disbelief. Fired by the knowledge that she was in charge, that he had no idea what to expect, she lowered her hands to the next button, the last that was visible above his waistband, and she unfastened it. Then she gave a slight tug on the fabric and raised his shirttails from his trousers.

He swallowed audibly.

Only one button remained, and she quickly released it, then pushed the shirt away from his shoulders. He let her, keeping his arms straight at his sides so that the sleeves fell easily past his wrists and the shirt dropped to the floor.

Her breath caught in her throat and she was unabashed in her appraisal of him. She allowed first her eyes, then her hands to roam boldly over the contours of his arms,

his shoulders, his chest, his torso. She marveled at the
firm bulges of his biceps and rippling muscles of his lean
stomach, and at the smooth expanse of his hairless chest,
not quite bold enough, at first, to examine his hardened
nipples. But then curiosity overcame her and she ran her
fingers over the rigid tips, feeling him tense and hearing
him groan softly in response. Still, he didn't move, didn't
take her into his arms or attempt to stop her frank explo-
ration. She stroked his bare chest, his broad shoulders,
his strong arms . . .

And then, daringly, she turned her attention to his
waistband. She longed for more of him to see, to touch,
and she brazenly unfastened the top button of his trousers
before her wrist grazed the unmistakable evidence of his
desire straining urgently against the fabric. Unnerved, she
dropped her gaze and saw that he was fully aroused, and
she faltered.

"Don't stop," he whispered raggedly, and she looked
up to see that his eyes were closed and tiny beads of
sweat had formed on his forehead.

He was waiting for her to go further, but suddenly she
was shy, unwilling and unable to confront the inevitable.
She stood there with her hands still clutching his waistband, and after a moment he opened his eyes and looked
down at her.

"I'll help you," he said, and reached down. He gingerly unfastened his fly and then the trousers, too, fell
away, leaving him in his off-white cotton drawers. He
glanced up at her, as if to ask whether he should stop
then and there.

She held her breath and did nothing, then watched as
he slid the last garment over his hips and stood before
her, finally nude.

She didn't want to stare at him, and yet she couldn't

help herself. She had never before seen a naked man, and though she'd had some idea what to expect, she was stunned by the reality of him. He was glorious, all golden skin and contoured muscles, and so obviously stimulated by what she had done to him. Rather than being frightened, or repelled by the sight of his rigid manhood, as she had once imagined she would be when the time came, she found herself undeniably excited. Yet still she held back, uncertain of what he expected her to do next.

When he put his hands on her shoulders and bent his head, she lifted her face expectantly. He kissed her deeply, stirring the fire that had already ignited inside of her, so that when he finally pulled away, she was weak with need, her legs wobbling beneath her.

As though sensing that she could barely stand, he scooped her into his arms and carried her across the room to the bed. He laid her gently down on her back, and stretched out beside her, capturing her lips again with his own and kissing her tenderly, as though they had all the time in the world.

She marveled that he didn't share the urgency that was building inside of her. Then he lifted his head, and she caught sight of the concentrated effort in his face, and realized he was holding back, taking things slowly for her sake. She was overcome with tenderness for him in that moment and pulled his head back down, kissing him, opening her mouth against his and boldly allowing her tongue to slip past his lips. She wanted more, though, and she pulled him closer to her still, sensing that he was trying not to bring the full length of his body against hers. She desperately wanted to feel him, and when, with a groan, he finally lowered his weight over her, she was gratified by the heady sensation of his masculine hardness sinking against the soft flesh at the apex of her legs, cushioned by the folds of her skirts. She writhed, wanting to be rid of her clothing, wanting more intimate contact.

Still, he held back, kissing her, allowing his hands to roam over the bodice of her dress but not attempting to probe beneath it. Never before had she felt such intense longing, and she splayed her hands on his bare back, holding him to her, needing more.

"Thatcher . . ." His name was a soft, high-pitched cry on her lips. "Please . . . please . . ."

He lifted his head and looked into her eyes. His face was flushed, his breath coming in pants. "Are you sure?"

She could only nod but caught his hands in her own and directed them to the front of her dress. Her eyes drifted closed as he worked the fastenings and carefully pulled first the bodice, then her chemise away, and she sighed in pure pleasure as she felt his warm, wet mouth nuzzling her bare breast. The heat built between her legs, and she writhed beneath him, wanting him to do away with her remaining undergarments so that he could enter her at last.

When he continued to take his time, moving his mouth from one breast to the other, she first reveled in the exquisite sensations he was causing, and then, impatiently, reached down and pushed the last of her clothing away. Belatedly she realized that she was behaving like a wanton *puttana*. She looked up to see his reaction and saw that he was staring at the length of her body, an expression of awe and reverence on his face.

She forgot to be ashamed, or hesitant, and when he ran a tentative hand along her bare waist, over her hip, she sighed in rapture. This was right; there was no doubt in her mind, and no reason, no time to think otherwise. She felt the flutter of his fingers against the tender folds of skin between her legs, and she opened her thighs to give him access. She let out a blissful cry when he stroked her there, and was lost, momentarily, in the ripples of unfamiliar, intense sensation.

Then Thatcher moved on top of her again, and his gaze locked on hers as he hovered over her, seeming to ask her permission to let go, to banish this final restraint.

"Yes," she murmured, clinging to his shoulders. "Oh, yes, Thatcher."

He muttered something in English, and when she looked at him questioningly, he remembered and repeated in Italian, "I don't want to hurt you."

For a moment she didn't comprehend, and then she realized that he meant physically, not emotionally. She shook her head and said, "Don't worry about it, it's all right."

He shifted his weight and let out a ragged breath, and then she felt strange, intense pressure as he sank into her slowly, with painstaking care. She gasped at the piercing sensation, and he froze and looked at her, concerned. "Cira?"

"It's all right," she told him as the pain gave way somewhat to pleasure. She bit down on her lower lip and held his shoulders, and he began to move inside of her. She tried to relax, but there wasn't time before he shuddered and called out her name. Aware that his rhythm had changed, she reached up to stroke his sweat-coated face and felt the molten tremors as he spilled into her.

Then he was quiet, lying on top of her, still inside of her. Bemused, she caressed his head as he lay against her neck, running her fingertips through his dark hair.

"Are you all right?" he asked after a moment or two.

She nodded.

"Cira?"

She realized he thought she hadn't answered, and she

struggled to keep the disappointment out of her voice as she said, "I'm fine."

But she wasn't fine. She hadn't expected the pain that had left her feeling slightly raw, nor had she realized it would be over so quickly. Maybe the ecstasy she had experienced leading up to the moment of truth had led her to expect so much more.

"Good," he said, and settled his head against her again, his breathing gradually becoming slow and even.

She wondered if he had fallen asleep, and what she was supposed to do now.

Suddenly she was positive that she had made a terrible mistake.

She had done the unthinkable; had lost her virginity to a man who wasn't her husband, and never would be.

How could she have gotten so carried away? How could she have behaved the way she had?

Because I care about him, and I believed that he cared about me.

Panic edged its way into her mind as she tried, and failed, to shut out the voice that told her she was a fool. Thatcher Montgomery was a worldly, wealthy American who could have any woman he desired, and she had no business letting him make love to her.

But he came back to you, she reminded herself, wanting desperately to make it all right. *He never had to see you again, yet he got off that ship, and he traveled all the way from Naples back to Palermo.*

Yes, he came back. And now that he's gotten what he wanted, he'll leave again.

Then she remembered that he couldn't leave her behind just yet. He had bought her a ticket to sail with him on the *Bella Donna* tomorrow morning. She had been so swept away by passion that she had forgotten what they were doing here in the first place.

Well, once they had arrived in America, he would be through with her, wouldn't he?

Her mind whirled with uncertainty as she lay staring at the high ceiling above, lit by flickering lamplight. She was awake long after Thatcher had rolled away to lie, snoring peacefully, on his side, his back to her. And when sleep finally came, it was restless punctuated by burning memories of Thatcher's passion, and Lucia's accusing face, and her own regrets.

Thatcher opened his eyes abruptly in the darkened room, coming awake all at once, but unsure of where he was.

Then it came rushing back at him.

Cira.

He felt her weight beside him on the mattress and turned toward her, then listened for the telltale sound of even breathing that would mean she was asleep.

Instead, he heard her breath coming in sharp little bursts, and he heard her jerk her head on the pillow, as though a nightmare was tormenting her.

He started to reach for her, then stopped himself, realizing that she might not take kindly to being awakened, even from a nightmare. He didn't know her well enough to tell how she would react, and that fact made him suddenly uncomfortable. He had made love to her, had lain naked on top of her and inside of her, had slept here beside her, and yet, he didn't know her. Not really.

He turned onto his side, his back to her, and thought about the other women he had shared such intimacies with over the years. He was no rogue, yet there certainly had been a handful. Of course, the women he courted, those whose social station and breeding were similar to his own, never permitted more than a chaste kiss or two. But of those he had bedded, he realized now, all were essentially strangers, a few in the truest sense of the word. Yet he had never stopped to consider the irony that he had only shared the intimate act with women he scarcely knew, nor had he let it bother him.

Until now.

He wanted to know Cira well enough to understand how she felt about him and what they had done, and yet, it was impossible. It wasn't just that there hadn't been time, or that they had alternately kept each other at arm's length. No, they came from two different worlds, and he couldn't expect to truly understand her feelings . . . about anything. Nor could he expect her to understand his.

How could he ever explain to her that he cared about and respected her, and he certainly wasn't ashamed of her, yet he couldn't make her a part of his life?

He thought of his father, of the difficult life he had led after losing his parents and nearly his fortune. For the first time, Thatcher fully realized what he must have sacrificed to save it.

He had married Mother.

He loved his mother, he thought hastily, ashamed. But she was hardly the kind of woman a man like him wanted to marry. She was handsome, but not pretty by any stretch of the imagination. She was a devoted wife and mother, but hardly loving. And Thatcher had never seen her smile or seem to enjoy herself, a fact he had always attributed to his brother's death. But when he really thought about it, he realized that he couldn't remember Eleanor Montgomery as a happy, fun-loving sort before Stoddard IV had drowned. She seemed to have always been a somber, even dour, individual. So unlike his father.

What if there had, at one time, been other women who brought Stoddard III pleasure and happiness? Surely there had been, before he was married. He was a handsome, sharp-witted man who loved to socialize; he must have had his share of girls in his youth. Yet he must have seen that no one could fill the role that Eleanor had so willingly, so expertly taken on.

Even if he had only married her to save his family's fortune, Stoddard must have realized that she would be the ideal wife in many ways. She was a member of the same class, she knew the rules of the game, and she played it well. She was a true society lady, loyal and dutiful, well-connected and well-bred, qualities a man couldn't possibly ignore in a potential bride.

Nor could her son ignore the fact that those qualities were conspicuously lacking in Cira Valentino. She was a foreigner who came from a poverty-stricken family, and though she radiated a quiet charisma no man could be expected to ignore, she could hardly be considered a well-bred lady. She was too naive, too impulsive . . . too vulnerable.

And as for the rest of it, Cira hadn't proven very loyal in her unwillingness to trust Thatcher, and he couldn't call her dutiful by any stretch of the imagination. She was a willful little thing, and though he had found that quality charming, even appealing until now, he seriously wondered how well it would serve her when she married. Cira didn't strike him as the kind of woman who would let any man tell her what to do, not even her husband.

He remembered how she had seduced him earlier; how clear it had been, at first, that she was controlling the pace—or, at least, that she wanted to think so. She hadn't understood that it was he who was maintaining the utmost control, holding back when he wanted to take her from the first moment her hesitant fingertips touched his bare skin. Yet he had allowed her to lead the way, to seduce him more effectively than any other woman ever had—and all of them were infinitely more experienced than Cira.

He had been overwhelmed by tender feelings for her, even after his burst of passion had subsided and he lay sated in her arms. Dangerous feelings, because he didn't want to hurt her again, nor did he want to hurt himself. He had tried to escape the reality of his destiny by returning to Palermo, to Cira . . . and she had managed to force him to confront it.

He was sailing for New York tomorrow.

How could this be?

He hadn't intended to go back for a long time; maybe even never. He supposed that somewhere in the back of his mind, he had been entertaining fantasies about finding Cira again and falling in love with her, perhaps even marrying her and living out his days in the bright Sicilian sunshine.

But that could never have happened. That wouldn't have made him happy, would it? Sooner or later he would have missed the privileged world he had left behind, wouldn't he? At least, he would have been overcome by guilt over allowing his parents to believe he had died at sea.

Yet it wasn't guilt that had caused him to agree to go back. It was Cira, and the realization that he didn't want to stay in Sicily without her. What would be the point?

But what's the point of bringing her back to New York? he asked himself. *Once the ship docks, you will once again be a Montgomery, and she will be a poor immigrant. Can there possibly be a happy ending to such a relationship?*

He didn't want to consider the one logical answer to his question, so he grimly tried to put it out of his mind.

10

Cira stood at the rail of the steamship *Bella Donna,* squinting into the morning sunshine across the blue-gray water as the port of Palermo slid into the distance. She had witnessed this same view once before, had heard before the shouted, repeated warning, *"Chi non e passeggèro, a tèrra!"*—"All ashore that's going ahsore." It had been a mere few months ago, yet that seemed like another lifetime.

Then she had been flanked by her mother, and Giulia, and her younger siblings, and though the ship had been nearly identical to this one, there had been more engine noise then, more crowding at the rail, and a lot less space between the deck and the water.

Now she was alone, and the other passengers who had stood nearby to wave goodbye to the crowd at the wharf had long since dissipated. Most of them were impeccably dressed Americans returning home, along with clusters of upper-class Europeans and a few wealthy Sicilians. And this time she stood on the spacious first-class deck, high above the water line and the grating sounds of the engines below.

After taking one last lingering look at the distant coast of her homeland, she turned away from the rail . . . and gasped.

Thatcher Montgomery stood not ten feet away, leaning against a pole and watching her. His arms were folded casually across his chest, and his eyes were narrowed thoughtfully—or maybe just because of the glaring sun reflected off the water.

Why did he always seem to catch her off-guard? Cira felt her face grow warm under his intent gaze, and she wasn't sure whether to walk past him, or acknowledge him. Things had been awkward between them all morning, although their mad dash to get to the ship on time had helped to diffuse the tension in the beginning.

She hadn't known what to say to him under the circumstances—what did a woman say to a man the morning after she'd lost her virginity to him? Somehow, he seemed more like a stranger to her now than ever before, and by the time they boarded the *Bella Donna,* an awkward silence had grown between them.

She had found herself almost longing to be down in third class with Lucia and the other familiar types, the hordes of poor Sicilians transporting all their worldly possessions to America. Even being smuggled aboard in the steamer trunk seemed a better alternative to this uncomfortable strain between her and Thatcher.

It didn't help that they had been assigned adjoining cabins. Cira was too anxious to fully appreciate the accommodations, which were nowhere near as lavish as last night's hotel room, but a far cry from the overcrowded din and stench of the steerage deck. She had her own small porthole, and a twin bed that looked comfortable enough, and a small wardrobe in which to store her things. There was a bureau with a desktop, and a wingback upholstered chair, and a pitcher and bowl on the washstand, and a chamberpot tucked beneath the bed; everything compact and fitting neatly into its designated place.

After putting her few meager belongings away, she had ventured back out to the deck in time to see the ship set sail. This time there was no one waving to her from the pier; last time Nonna and Nonno had been standing there with tears streaming down their faces.

But it felt like the right thing to do, so she had stood on deck and waved anyway, wondering if Lucia was doing the same two decks below. She had hoped for a glimpse of her as they boarded, but they were rushed, and most of the steerage passengers were already on board by the time they arrived.

"Cira?" Thatcher pushed off the pole with the heel of his polished black shoe and came toward her, looking almost tentative. "Are you all right?"

She shrugged and stopped in front of him, fiddling with the corners of the black shawl she'd draped over her head and tied beneath her chin. She had noticed that none of the other first-class women wore their shawls that way, but Mama had taught her to keep her head covered in the sun, and she had no fine, fashionable plumed hat to wear. She was conscious that she stood out from the others on the deck.

She saw a couple cast a curious glance at her and Thatcher as they strolled by.

She realized what an odd-looking pair they must make; he in his fine tailored clothes and shiny spats; she in her peasant dress and scuffed shoes.

"Why wouldn't I be all right?" she asked in response

to Thatcher's question, turning away from the strangers' probing eyes.

"You've just left Sicily behind, maybe forever. Doesn't that bother you?"

"There's nothing left there for me." She thought briefly of Renzo. Difficult as things were between her and Thatcher, she was grateful that she hadn't been forced to go crawling back to Renzo, the way she had actually considered doing.

"Still, Sicily is your home, Cira," Thatcher pointed out. "Leaving has to have some meaning for you."

"Not anymore."

"You're determined to put it behind you forever and make a fresh start in America, then?"

"Of course. Isn't everyone?"

She expected him to grin at her flippant response, but he only said seriously, "The streets there aren't really paved with gold, you know, Cira."

"They aren't?" She had figured it was just an expression, and yet, one never knew.

"No, they aren't. They're paved with cobblestones and brick. Not gold." He smiled, and she resented him for thinking she was naive enough to have taken the phrase literally.

"I knew that."

He nodded. "I just don't want you to get your hopes up too high. New York is a difficult place, Cira. Especially for an immigrant. And a woman at that."

"How would *you* know?" she asked with a touch of defiance. "Do you make it a habit to associate with immigrant women?"

"Not usually," he admitted, and she thought she saw a flicker of admiration in his eyes. Why? Because she had dared to confront him?

She had nothing to lose. After all, right or wrong, she had already let him see the most intimate side of her.

She felt a surge of shame bubbling up inside of her again at the memory of what they had done together last night. She wondered how he felt about it. He hadn't made any reference to it this morning, even though they had awakened naked in the same bed. He had discreetly and silently turned his back while she was washing and dressing, and she had done the same when it was his turn. There was no hint that they had, only hours earlier, been entwined in each other's arms.

Thatcher asked, "Have you given any thought to what you'll do when you reach New York?"

"Go through Immigration at Ellis Island." *And this time I won't be trembling and afraid, or filled with sorrow over leaving Renzo. Good riddance to him.*

He looked amused. "I meant after you've passed through Immigration."

He made it sound so easy. What if she didn't pass?

You will pass. This time they'll let you in. They have to!

"And," he went on, "you're traveling in first class this time, Cira. You won't have to go through Immigration at Ellis Island. First Class passengers are processed on the ship by individual immigration officials. Didn't you know that?"

"No." She tried to conceal her excitement at that news. There would be no long lines, no crowds of anxious foreigners, no endless waits, no barrage of questions and examinations by countless uniformed officials.

"It's much simpler this way," he said, and she wondered how he could possibly know what a person went through at Ellis Island. "So what will you do after you disembark in New York?"

"Then," she said with outward calm, "I'll find my parents."

"You've had word from them, then? Since I left Palermo the first time?"

"No, but I'm sure they're in New York." There wouldn't have been enough money for the whole family to have returned to Sicily so soon, even if there had been a reason to.

"But where are they? Do you have an address?"

"No. I thought I would ask around, and see if anybody—"

"Cira, you can't just ask around. Do you know how big New York City is? It isn't like one of your quaint Sicilian villages, where you can walk into the town square, mention a name, and be taken straight to the person in question. There is no town square. And there are hundreds of thousands of people in New York."

"And are there poor Sicilian immigrants in every neighborhood? Are there any in *your* neighborhood, Thatcher?"

He colored slightly. "No, but . . . I mean, there certainly are concentrated areas where the immigrants are settling. But even then, Cira . . . there are blocks and blocks of tenements on the Lower East Side alone. Where would you start?"

"If the Lower East Side is where most of the Italian immigrants are, I'll start there," she said with far more confidence than she felt.

"And do what? Go knocking door to door? Where will you sleep at night?"

"If I still haven't found my family?"

"Yes," he said, sounding impatient. "You don't expect to find them in one day, do you?"

"I . . . hadn't really thought about it. But I won't be alone. Lucia—"

"Is terribly upset with you," he reminded her, cutting her off. "So upset that she ordered you out of her room. From the sound of things she has very little intention of maintaining your friendship."

"We're old friends. She'll come around. I intend to speak with her as soon as possible," Cira told him, wondering why she felt so defensive with him, but unable to help herself.

"What if she won't reconcile?"

"She will. And anyway, what business is it of yours? I can take care of myself."

"I've heard that before. And I don't doubt that you can," he added quickly, when she flashed her eyes at him. "I just wonder if you understand what you're getting yourself into, Cira."

She saw that his expression was filled with concern, and though that should have been reassuring, she found that it bothered her. She didn't want him to care about her, because then she would find herself caring about him. Again.

And look where *that* had led. Straight into his arms . . . and trouble.

"If you'll excuse me," she said abruptly, "I'm going to retire to my cabin to get some rest."

"It's a bit early for a nap," he said, reaching into his pocket and flipping open his gold watch on a chain. He examined it and announced, "It's not even ten o'clock yet."

"Well, I didn't sleep very well last night," she retorted, and spun on her heel.

She walked swiftly back toward her cabin, resisting the urge to glance over her shoulder at him. She didn't want him to know how much he mattered to her.

Why, oh why, had she allowed herself to get caught up in his spell again? It would have been better for her if he had never come back, even if it meant believing he was dead. At least then she could have mourned him and gotten on with her life.

Now her mind would be forever branded with the memory of their lovemaking. How could she ever forget that . . . or him?

Cira hesitated in the doorway of the first-class dining salon, suddenly filled with hesitation. The tables were crowded with men and women dressed in the latest fashions. A violin played in the background, and above the sweet classical melody, voices murmured and polished silver clinked against fine china. Cira took a deep breath, inhaling exotic scents: wine, and some kind of roasted meat or fowl, and tobacco, and oil from the flickering oil lamps, and ladies' perfume.

Go ahead. You belong here, she tried to tell herself.

But it wasn't true. She might be sleeping in a first-class cabin, but she wasn't one of *them*. In her cabin she had stood before the looking glass and almost convinced herself that she could pass as one of them, though; that her made-over navy brocade dress was presentable. She had patted her coiled hair dozens of times, banishing imaginary strands from her face, and, realizing she was ghostly pale, had repeatedly pinched her cheeks to give them color. She noted that if she maintained a certain posture while standing still, it was possible to conceal the scuffed tips of her shoes beneath the bottom of her skirt.

She tried to see herself through the eyes of the other first-class passengers, wondering if, when they looked at her, they would know immediately that she was a Sicilian

peasant. And what if they did? It wasn't as though she
had snuck up from the steerage compartment below; she
was traveling first class, and she had every right to be
here, among them.

Finally she had decided that she was ready to venture
from the small quarters where she had spent the better
part of the day sleeping. She had been so certain she
wouldn't be able to get a moment's rest after what had
happened with Thatcher, but she had found the narrow
bed incredibly comfortable—a far cry from the stained,
lumpy mattress or floor in Lucia's room, or the thin mat
she had shared with Giulia back home.

When she awakened, her stomach had felt hollow and
was rumbling audibly. She realized she had no choice
but to get dressed and come to dinner.

Scanning the dining salon now, she saw no sign of
Thatcher. She told herself that that was a positive thing.
She didn't want to see him. No, she wanted nothing more
to do with the man.

Lifting her chin, she took a step forward.

She heard a female voice laugh gaily just behind her.
She turned her head abruptly, certain that the woman had
caught sight of her, in her pauper's dress and worn shoes,
and was making fun.

But all she saw was a lady clinging to the arm of her
gentleman escort, who was apparently in the midst of a
witty tale. Nobody was looking at Cira; she might as well
be invisible.

What should she do? Where should she sit? Who
would she talk to? The tables were filled with society
people making conversation, much of it in English. She
searched the room for somebody who looked as though
they might speak Italian, all the while telling herself that
she did *not* wish that Thatcher was with her to translate.

"You're looking lovely this evening."

The words, spoken in her native tongue and a familiar voice, came from directly behind her. She jumped but didn't turn around. She was afraid that if she did, Thatcher would realize from her expression that she was glad to see him. She didn't want him to see that; she didn't want to feel that, but couldn't help herself.

"I called for you in your cabin, but you had already left." The words were spoken into her ear, his warm breath slightly stirring her hair.

"Did we have plans to meet?" she asked airily, though her heart was pounding at his nearness. "I must have forgotten."

"No, we didn't have plans. You left before I could ask you about it this morning. Still, I assumed we would dine together. After all, you *are* my guest on this ship."

Now she turned to face him, and saw that he was wearing a top hat and a dark coat with tails, along with that familiar rakish smile. She found herself smiling back despite her intentions to remain chilly toward him.

"Shall we?" he asked, offering his arm.

She hesitated for a moment, then decided it was only proper to accompany him to dinner. After all, she *was* his guest. Although, until he had put it that way, she had seen herself more as a charity case upon whom he had taken pity. A "guest" was a much nicer way to think of her situation.

She closed her hand around the soft wool fabric of his sleeve and allowed him to escort her into the room. To her surprise, nobody turned to gape at her made-over dress, and there were no snide whispers as she passed. By the time they reached a small table on the far end of the salon, she almost felt as though she belonged here and found her thoughts turning to food.

Only briefly did she allow herself to wonder whether he had chosen this out-of-the-way spot because he was ashamed to be seen with her. She tried to tell herself that if that were the case, he wouldn't have chosen to dine with her in the first place, but she couldn't help realizing that he was a good-hearted man, and might merely feel sorry for her.

"Are you hungry?" Thatcher asked, pulling a chair out for her and helping her into it as though she were a real lady.

"I'm famished," she replied without thinking, then blushed.

He chuckled and sat across from her. "So am I. It must be the sea air. Did you spend much time on deck this afternoon?"

"None at all."

"What did you do?"

"I rested."

"Did you catch up on all the sleep you missed last night?"

His question brought impromptu images of their decadent encounter in his hotel suite nearly twenty-four hours earlier, and she felt the warmth from her face spreading down, heating her within. She fought the urge to squirm on the upholstered seat, and wondered if he could possibly know what she was thinking—and whether he might even be thinking the same thing. There was something about the way he was looking at her that made her feel as though he could see right into her mind.

"I did sleep, yes," she said, and pretended to be very interested in a potted palm plant standing nearby.

Thatcher changed the subject, chatting about some kind of card game he had played in the gentlemen's lounge. When a waiter appeared and asked if they would

like wine, he looked to her and she shook her head. The
last thing she needed was to indulge in a heady glass of
wine at this point. Thatcher declined as well, then went
back to his story.

She struggled to pay attention to what he was saying.
But though she focused on his face as he spoke, she
found herself remembering what it had felt like to have
those full lips moving over hers, and how surprisingly
soft his skin had been when she stroked his jaw, and how
his eyes had clouded over with the intensity of his passion as he moved above her, and inside of her.

"Are you chilled?"

"Pardon?" Cira realized that Thatcher had interrupted
himself to pose the cryptic question and was watching
her, looking concerned.

"I said, are you chilled? You just shuddered."

"I did?" Embarrassed, she realized she had been re-
living what had happened between them. She was far
from chilled. Her breasts felt hot and heavy and her nipples swollen under the tight-fitting bodice of her dress,
and there was a tingling heat between her legs that didn't
subside when she shifted her weight slightly. "Yes, it is
a bit chilly in here."

"Did you bring a wrap?"

"A wrap?" She shook her head. A wrap. Had he forgotten that she wasn't a first-class lady with an entire
wardrobe at her disposal? All she had was her slightly
tattered black shawl, and she had left it in her cabin.

"Take my coat, then."

Before she could respond, he was out of his chair and
sliding his arms out of the sleeves. He dropped the garment around her shoulders, and his masculine scent
promptly wafted to her nostrils—the same scent she had

breathed last night when she had buried her face in the damp skin between his head and shoulder.

Now, once again, she was enveloped in the essence of him, and she crossed her legs beneath the table, clamping her thighs together to make the unpleasant sensation go away.

Rather, *not* unpleasant. Hardly unpleasant.

But it was hardly proper for her to be feeling this way, particularly here, particularly now. Did he know? Could he tell?

"Is that better?" he asked, settling into his chair again.

"Hmm?"

"My coat? Did it warm you?"

Did it warm me? If you only knew . . .

"Oh . . . yes. Yes, it warmed me. Thank you."

"You're welcome."

He resumed his conversation and she resumed her pretense of listening, but she couldn't seem to keep her mind from wandering back to last night. The memory was sending faint tremors throughout the lower regions of her torso, rather like a nagging itch that needed attention, and she struggled not to shift on her seat again.

When a plate was set before her, she realized that she had lost her appetite—at least, for food. She was now consumed by a hunger that could only be assuaged by Thatcher Montgomery's hands, and his mouth, and—

"Do you like duck?"

"Duck?" she echoed blankly.

"Duck," he repeated, gesturing at the steaming, juicy slab of poultry on her plate. "Cira, are you all right?"

"Yes, I am. I am quite all right, thank you. And I have never tasted duck before, so I didn't realize what it was."

"I see. Well, try it, then. It's really very good. Not quite as gamey as pheasant—"

"I've never tasted pheasant, either," she said a bit sharply, to remind him—and perhaps, more important, herself—that they came from vastly different worlds.

He shrugged and speared a wedge of seasoned potato on the end of his fork, then popped it into his mouth.

She turned her attention back to her plate, sliced off a succulent morsel of the roasted poultry, and tasted it. It was delicious, moist and seasoned with some kind of citrus flavor. Her appetite returned with a vengeance, and for a short time she simply ate, not forgetting Thatcher's presence across from her but not caught up in it, either.

Finally she pushed her plate back and looked up at him, finding him leaning back in his chair, his head tilted slightly, watching her with a hint of amusement. But it wasn't a cruel expression; it wasn't as though he were laughing at her ravenous appetite. Still, as she scanned the people seated nearby, she belatedly wondered if she should have left a portion of her meal untouched, as the women at the next table had delicately done.

"It is so very refreshing," Thatcher said, leaning forward and propping his elbow on the table and his chin in his hand, "to see a woman who isn't afraid to eat."

"I . . . I was hungry, and it was so delicious . . ." she offered lamely, knowing she was blushing again.

"I'm glad. Soon they'll be bringing dessert."

"Dessert?" Though she was full, she couldn't help being tempted at the thought of something sweet.

"Some sort of pastry or cake, no doubt. I see that you're interested."

"I . . . perhaps I'll taste just a bit of whatever it is."

He chuckled. "Don't be embarrassed, Cira."

"I'm not embarrassed," she lied, hating that he could see right through her this way. "Why would I be?"

"There's no need to be. I'm pleased to see you enjoying yourself. After this, perhaps we should go for a stroll on deck.''

"After this,'' she corrected him, ''I plan to go below to find Lucia. I need to see her, to make sure that she's all right.''

"I'll come along, to make sure you find your way.''

"Surely it can't be very difficult. You simply keep going down into the bowels of the ship,'' she said tartly.

If he caught the sarcasm in her tone, he chose to ignore it. ''Well, in any case, I'll escort you.''

"That won't be necessary. I'd rather go alone. I don't think Lucia will be particularly pleased to see you.''

"And will she be pleased to see *you*?''

She narrowed her eyes at him. ''Lucia and I have been friends our entire lives, Thatcher. One disagreement couldn't possibly change that.'' She wished she were as certain about that as she sounded.

"I hope you're right about that'' was all he said before the waiter arrived with two plates filled with some glorious concoction of cake and fruit and custard.

Cira meant only to taste a bit of it, but the dessert was so heavenly that she found herself devouring every bit of it, even using her fork to scrape the remaining crumbs from her plate. Never in her life had she tasted food as delectable as the meal she had just eaten. She thought wistfully of Lucia, knowing that she was, at this very moment, in some crowded, smoky, stench-filled room far below, eating plain bread or bean stew or potatoes.

"Hallo, Montgomery!''

A jovial male voice interrupted Cira's thoughts, and she turned to see a well-dressed, middle-aged man stopping at their table and clapping Thatcher on the back. He was obviously an American, as was the woman on his arm, a beautiful, much-younger creature who eyed

Thatcher with coy interest. Cira found herself bristling, and when the woman turned her curious gaze to Cira, she felt a definite flare of anger. It was clear that she was wondering what a handsome and wealthy man like Thatcher Montgomery was doing with someone of Cira's caliber.

Cira held her head high and allowed her eyes to flash defiantly at this newcomer, conveying a confidence that she hardly felt.

Thatcher and the woman's escort seemed oblivious to what was going on, chatting amiably in English for a few moments before Thatcher turned to Cira and said in Italian, "This is somebody I met in the lounge during the card game this afternoon. He's also from New York and his name is George Clifford."

She nodded politely at the man, who nodded back as Thatcher introduced her in English. Then the man presented the woman he was with. Cira didn't understand his exact words, but grasped enough to know that this was his fiancée, Amy Danforth. The woman all but batted her eyelashes at Thatcher and ignored Cira.

Thatcher said something else in English, and by his gestures Cira realized he had invited this couple to join them. Dismayed, she smiled pleasantly as they sat down, and tolerated a few moments of conversation in rapid-fire, American-accented English. Amy Danforth giggled merrily at something Thatcher said, and Cira pushed back her chair abruptly.

All three of them looked at her.

"What are you doing?" Thatcher inquired in Italian.

"I told you before, I must find Lucia." She took his coat from around her shoulders and thrust it at him.

"Must you go at this very moment?"

"I'm afraid so."

"But—"

"*Buona nòtte,*" she said to the couple seated at their table.

"Good night," the gentleman answered gallantly, while his fiancée merely watched as Cira stood and walked away.

She couldn't help resenting them for the intrusion. Before they had come along, she had, of course, been aware of the differences between herself and Thatcher. But the presence of the two upper-class Americans had served to make it painfully obvious that she didn't fit into his world. She couldn't compete with Amy Danforth's beauty or her fine clothing or her distinct air of wealth and breeding. She couldn't even participate in the conversation. There was nothing for her to do but sit there like a dolt or a servant.

She threw open the door and stepped out into the chilly night air on deck. The sky was clear and starry, and she had a fleeting image of what it would have been like to stroll along with Thatcher in the moonlight.

But that wasn't meant to be. Instead, she had to find her friend. She thought longingly of Lucia, remembering how grateful she had been to find her back in Palermo. Then, as now, she had felt as though she were cast adrift, longing for a familiar face, for a sense of belonging.

She quickened her pace and headed toward a flight of stairs leading below deck.

Thatcher watched Cira until she disappeared through the doors leading out to the deck, then turned back to George Clifford, who was saying something he hadn't been listening to.

"Pardon?" he asked, trying to force his attention back to the conversation.

"I was just saying she seems like a feisty little thing, that's all. Those eyes of hers shot daggers at you before she left."

Thatcher shrugged, uncertain how to reply. It wasn't as though he knew this man. They had gravitated together in the way that men do over poker and cigars, and inviting him and his fiancée to join them had been second nature to Thatcher. It was what you did in polite society. But now he understood that Cira had been threatened by the newcomers, and he berated himself for not realizing that that was sure to happen. She didn't speak English; they didn't speak Italian, and there was more to it than the language barrier. She had seemed distinctly ill-at-ease throughout the meal, and he knew that she must be feeling out of place here. Still, he assumed she was getting over it. And it had given him pleasure to watch her indulge her appetite and to see her eyes widen like a child's at the sight of the rich dessert.

"Is she your maid?"

"Is who my maid?" Thatcher looked over his shoulder, not understanding Amy Danforth's question. He saw nothing but a potted palm behind him.

"That foreign girl. The one at your table."

"Cira?" Thatcher frowned. "Of course she isn't my maid." But even as he said it, he realized he could hardly blame Miss Danforth for drawing such a conclusion. How often did a gentleman of his stature dine with a young immigrant in the first-class dining room?

"Then who is she, Mr. Montgomery?"

"Just . . . a friend. She's a Sicilian, traveling to America to join her family in New York."

"How charitable of you to invite her to join you for dinner."

He loathed the smug look on her beautiful face. Before

he could respond that it wasn't merely charitable, George Clifford elbowed him, winked, and said in a low voice, "I'll bet she'll be joining you for something more a little later, eh, Montgomery?"

That did it. Thatcher pushed back his chair and rose, tipping his hat at them before placing it on his head. "I'm afraid I must ask you to excuse me," he said curtly. "I just remembered a previous engagement."

With that, he strode toward the door, wondering if it was too late to catch up to Cira before she went below. Perhaps she was lingering at the rail, taking in the beauty of the clear night and calm seas.

But there was no sign of her on deck. He stood for a moment, wondering whether he should follow her down to steerage, then asked himself why he would do such a thing. There was little to say to her that he hadn't already said.

Then again, he hadn't said much of anything. There had been no talk of what had happened between them last night. He didn't know what to say about it, because he didn't know how he felt about it.

There had been more to it than merely a release of physical passion—at least, for him. At first. But something in her had shut down when he had actually entered her. He had vaguely realized it, yet had been powerless to stop at that point, to see that she was all right. He had known then that she was a virgin, but that didn't ensure that she wasn't a gold-digging opportunist, did it?

How did he know whether she was interested in him for what he could give her, or whether she really cared? There were moments when he felt certain that she was as honest and naive as he had initially believed her to be, yet at other times, when she seemed to treat him with chilly disregard, he found himself uncertain.

Was she using him?

Then again, was he using her?

He thought of George Clifford's snide implication and told himself that he most certainly was not. He hadn't brought her on board this ship in the hope of sleeping with her. And yet, the mere thought of their lovemaking filled him with restless lust, and he knew that he wanted her in his bed again. Tonight, God help him. He wanted to make love to her; he *ached* to make love to her.

With a dispirited sigh, he turned away from the rail and made his way toward the gentleman's lounge. Perhaps an after-dinner brandy would help to ease his frustration.

"Lucia!" Cira spotted her at last, huddled on a bench on the far side of the crowded, dimly lit room. Filled with relief, Cira hurried toward her friend.

She had been searching for quite some time, wandering through the dank, narrow, bunk-lined sleeping spaces and inquiring about her friend from time to time. Nobody knew who she was talking about, or seemed to care. Many of the women she spoke to had red-rimmed, swollen eyes, and she remembered, with a pang, how she had felt during the last crossing, when she was leaving behind the only home she had ever known.

She had begun to wonder, as she looked for Lucia, whether her friend had boarded the ship after all. But here she was, clearly recognizable though her shawl was draped over her head, and Cira forgot to be leery about approaching her after the argument they had had the night before.

She had to make her way through hordes of people: jovial men who reeked of liquor, and stern-faced, weary-looking women, many of them clutching babies as they struggled to keep watch over throngs of children, some scampering underfoot, others whining and clinging. The din was as deafening as Cira remembered, as was the scent of unwashed clothing and skin, and this was only the first day of the journey. How had she endured these conditions for nearly two full weeks? How would Lucia?

She drew closer to her friend and saw that her face was pale and her eyes staring off into space. Her arms were wrapped around herself as if she were trying to keep warm, but the air here was close and stuffy.

"Lucia?" Cira reached out and touched her shoulder.

Startled, Lucia glanced up. There was a flicker of relief in her eyes before she frowned and asked, "What are *you* doing here?"

"Looking for you." Cira had to raise her voice above the cheerful notes of the accordion someone had started to play nearby.

"Why?"

"Why? Why wouldn't I?"

Don't do this, Lucia, Cira begged silently. Don't alienate me. Please, I need you. I need your friendship. . . .

"Because you're safe in first class, with your lover. There's no reason for you to climb all the way down here to the slums to find me."

Cira wanted to retort that Thatcher wasn't her lover, but she bit her tongue. It would be a lie, wouldn't it? He had been her lover, just last night. But it wasn't as though they were in love. It wasn't as though they were together, a couple with a future, the way George Clifford and Amy Danforth were.

She drew a deep breath and said to Lucia, "I miss you, Lucia. That's all. I wish you weren't so angry at me. And I wish I knew why you acted the way you did last night when you found me with Thatcher.''

She braced herself for an angry retort, but none came.

Lucia was silent for a few moments, then said, "I was angry at you because you were being a fool, Cira."

"A fool? How so?"

"You were trusting that man. How could you?"

Cira stared at her, uncertain how to respond.

"You know that he's merely using you, Cira. A man like that . . . what would he want with a poor peasant girl?"

Coming from anyone else, the words might have stung. But Lucia herself was a poor peasant girl, and Cira knew that she was at least partly right.

What did Thatcher Montgomery see in her? What did he want from her? Wasn't it what Cira had asked herself all along?

To Lucia, she said, "What if he isn't using me? What if he's an honorable man, merely trying to help?"

"I saw his hands on you, Cira. I saw what you two were doing when I walked into the room. He wasn't 'helping' anybody but himself."

Cira wasn't comfortable with such frank talk, but she couldn't shut down now that Lucia was finally opening up a bit to her. She pointed out, "I was willing, Lucia. What he was doing . . . I wanted it, too."

"Of course you did. Because you wanted him, all of him. You thought that was a way of getting him."

"No . . ."

"Yes. You were willing to cheapen yourself, to believe whatever it was that he told you, Cira. . . ."

Anger flared to life and Cira could no longer remain passive. She demanded, "What makes you such an expert on men, Lucia? You have never been passionately involved with one, so you—"

"Oh, yes," Lucia cut in. "I have."

So her suspicions were correct. Somebody had broken Lucia's heart, and her spirit, in Cira's absence from Fiorenza. "Who was it, Lucia?"

"Renzo."

The name was spoken so softly that for a moment, Cira didn't believe she had heard it right. But the tortured look of guilt on Lucia's round face confirmed it.

Speechless, Cira stared at her, waiting for her to say something more.

But Lucia merely cast her eyes downward, at her hands twisting nervously in her lap, and was silent.

"Renzo?" Cira echoed at last. "How . . . when?"

Lucia didn't reply.

"Lucia . . . answer me!"

"It was . . . after you left," Lucia said haltingly. "He came to me one night, Cira. . . . He kissed me before I knew his intentions. He told me—"

She broke off, and Cira demanded, "What? What? He told you what?"

"He told me that he had always been in love with me."

Stung even now at the depth of Renzo's betrayal, Cira could only stare at Lucia and wait for more.

"He didn't love me, of course. It was a lie. But it accomplished what he wanted, Cira. I believed him at the time. And . . . well, you know how I felt about him. Before the two of you ever got together, I mean. You know that I always felt attracted to him."

Cira nodded, her mind whirling. She had known, but she had written Lucia's feelings off as an innocent childhood crush. By the time she herself had fallen in love with Renzo, she had forgotten all about Lucia's infatuation with him, or perhaps had merely assumed it had died long ago.

Now, horrified at what she was hearing, she asked, "Were you . . . in love with him the whole time I was with him?"

"I couldn't help it, Cira. I tried to get over him. Honestly, I did. But he was always on my mind. Always."

How you must have resented me, Cira thought sadly, marveling that she had never realized her friend's true feelings. *How you must have wished that I would just disappear so that you could have him all to yourself. And finally I did.*

She clenched her hands tightly in her lap and listened as Lucia's story spilled out, wishing she had never brought it up, wishing she didn't have to hear this confession that changed everything.

"He was so handsome, so witty, so romantic. And when he came to me, and he said those things, and he kissed me the way he did . . . I couldn't help myself."

"Didn't you think about me?" Cira demanded, unable to fathom how Lucia had done what she had done.

"No." The word was quietly, reluctantly spoken. "I'm sorry to say that I didn't, Cira. Not then, at the time. Not until it was too late. The damage had been done. He was the first man who ever looked at me, spoke to me, wanted me that way. . . ."

"And I don't doubt that you were one of dozens of women for him." Cira couldn't help herself; she wanted to hurt Lucia for what she had done.

And Renzo! How could he? How dare he? Even after seeing him with that other woman, after coming to grips with the fact that he was a spineless, selfish cad, she felt renewed shock and outrage at his behavior. To go after

Lucia, her best friend . . . what on earth had he been thinking?

"I don't doubt that you're right," Lucia agreed, catching her by surprise. "I'm not proud of what I did, Cira. In fact, I've hated myself for it ever since it happened. You've no idea—" She broke off, looking off into space, hugging herself again.

"Then why did you do it?"

"I told you. I was helpless. He was so charming, and the things that he said . . . I believed them. Every last word." She gave a soft, humorless laugh.

"And you have the nerve to call *me* a fool?" Cira asked her. "Because I have fallen in love with Thatcher Montgomery, a man who happens to be wealthy, and an American? At least I'm not stealing him away from somebody else. From my best friend."

"Cira, I'm so sorry—"

"You should be, Lucia."

"Believe me, I would take it back if I could. I would never have done what I did with him. . . ."

"Just what was it that you did?" Cira watched Lucia, fearing the worst, realizing when her friend cast her eyes downward that it was true. "Did you let him make love to you? Did you?" she demanded, stunned.

Lucia only nodded silently.

Cira spun on her heel and pushed her way back through the people who were jammed into the room, fumbling for the steep ladder that led up out of the crowded, stinking steerage class.

It wasn't until she was on deck, clinging to the railing for support and inhaling deep gulps of fresh sea air, that she allowed herself to acknowledge her own words.

I have fallen in love with Thatcher Montgomery.

How could she have said such a thing? It was hardly

true. She wasn't in love with him. She barely knew him. . . .

She blinked away a memory of lying naked in his arms.

She barely knew him. He had been generous with her, had repeatedly rescued her from difficult situations, had made her laugh, had shown concern. . . .

Yet how could she love him?

She couldn't.

She didn't.

It was just something that had spilled from her lips in her agitated state. She had been so furious at Lucia.

And she had every right to be. Her best friend had betrayed her. The knowledge hurt even more profoundly than it had to discover Renzo's unfaithfulness. No wonder Lucia had been so cagey, so remote. No wonder she had fled Fiorenza. . . .

Had Renzo broken her heart? Had he cast her aside for somebody else? Had Lucia actually believed that he wouldn't?

Cira turned from the rail and walked slowly back to her cabin. As she passed Thatcher's closed door in the dimly lit, dank-smelling corridor, she glanced longingly at it. Was he inside right now? What would he do if she knocked? Would he invite her in?

And if he did, what would happen between them? Would she land in his arms again? Would she lose control of herself and allow him to do to her what he had done last night?

Who are you fooling? she asked herself. *He didn't do anything to you. You were as much a part of it as he was.*

More so, even, she realized, remembering the way he

had lain back, allowing her to explore his body, to seduce him . . .

She had wanted him so desperately. She hadn't stopped to wonder what it meant to him, or to care.

With a sigh she opened the door to her cabin and stepped inside, pulling it securely closed behind her.

11

Thatcher woke to the unmistakable sound of rain and wind pounding against the small porthole above his head. He opened his eyes and saw that the room was dim, with little gloomy gray light filtering in.

He lay awake, feeling the swaying of the ship, suddenly struck by haunting images of the *Stella Oceano*, and what had happened to it. He thought of his friends, of Rupert and Carson and Harry, wondering what they felt as the cold water closed over them, choking the life out of them. Had they struggled? Been knocked unconscious? Had they realized what was happening?

It could have been me. It could have been me.

He stared morosely at the ceiling and tried to shut the dark thoughts out of his mind, but they wouldn't go. Tears sprang to the corners of his eyes, and he blinked them away, telling himself that he had done his mourning in those hollow, lonely days in Naples after he'd heard the news.

He thought of his parents, and his sisters, and he remembered Cira's horror when she found out he hadn't bothered to let them know he was alive. He knew that he was wrong not to have contacted them, yet he could change what he had done. Cira would never understand how desperately he craved an escape from the life he was expected to lead, or how hopeless the chances of that had seemed. The tragedy had provided him with the opportunity, fleeting though it might be, to live his life according to his wishes.

Yet here he was, steaming toward New York at this very moment. If it hadn't been for Cira, he wouldn't be here.

Oh, he had known he would go back eventually. Just not yet. Not until he had experienced whatever it was that he needed to experience.

He rolled onto his side and stared into space, thinking about Cira. If it hadn't been for her, he wouldn't be heading for home, and yet if it hadn't been for her, he would have stayed on board the *Stella Oceano* and sailed to his doom.

He heard a faint thump and realized it had come from her cabin on the other side of the wall. So she was awake. What was she doing? How would she react if he knocked on her door and invited her to eat breakfast with him?

He wouldn't know unless he tried.

Thatcher threw back the covers without pausing for further speculation and hurriedly got dressed in the damp morning air.

Cira retrieved the shoe she'd dropped onto the floor and thrust her foot into it, noticing that the sole had started to pull loose from the toe. In no time there would be a gaping hole there. Would it last until she got to New York? It certainly wouldn't do to wander the city streets barefoot.

She finished lacing first one black shoe, and then the other, then stood and examined her reflection in the glass. She had braided her hair this morning and left it hanging in a single tail down her back. She wore her cotton everyday dress, drab and threadbare as could be, and found herself thinking wistfully of the fine gowns she had seen on the other women in the dining salon last night. What would it be like to wear something you were proud to be seen in, rather than something that made you ashamed?

What would Thatcher Montgomery think of her if he saw her in a beautiful silk dress, her hair done up properly, with real jewels at her ears and throat instead of the crucifix she wore and the tiny gold earrings that, rather than providing adornment, only seemed to enhance her ethnicity?

It didn't matter. Thatcher would never see her that way, because that wasn't who she was. She could never be a fine lady like that horrid woman she had met last night, Amy something-or-other—nor would she want to trade places with her. The woman looked half the age of her fiancé, and the two of them had scarcely seemed to look at each other. Cira wondered why they were marrying at all.

Then again, wasn't it obvious? A wealthy, older man; a beautiful, younger woman. He wanted a pretty ornament for his arm, and she wanted his money.

But you don't know that for certain, Cira scolded herself, ashamed at what she was thinking. *It isn't fair to judge strangers by appearances*.

Besides, was that what people assumed when they saw her with Thatcher Montgomery? That she was after his wealth, and he merely wanted a young plaything to keep him amused during the crossing?

Was it true? Was that how he saw her? Was Lucia right about him?

She didn't want to believe it. Lucia was merely angry about the way Renzo had treated her, and she was taking that anger out on any man who crossed her path.

A knock at the door startled Cira, and she turned toward it expectantly, her heart thumping in her chest.

Only one person on this ship would knock at her door.

No, that wasn't true. It might be a cabin steward, or some other member of the crew . . . or even Lucia.

No, not Lucia. She wouldn't be allowed in first class, even if she did swallow her pride and come up to find Cira.

She approached the door slowly, telling herself that it couldn't be Thatcher, either. But when she opened the door, there he was. He looked dapper as always in a light-colored jacket and trousers, a matching hat tilted rakishly on top of his head.

"Good morning," he said, tipping his hat to her and giving a slight bow. "Did you sleep well?"

"Yes . . . thank you." Of course, it wasn't true. She had been tormented by images of Lucia and Renzo. She had thought that she was over him, but this new realization at the depth of his betrayal had filled her with resentment and hurt. Beyond that, there was her shock that Lucia, whom she had once trusted more than anyone else, could have done such a thing behind her back. She tried to tell herself that her friend had been a victim of Renzo's sweet-talking charm; that she was naive and inexperienced when it came to men, and could hardly be blamed.

But was that any excuse for what Lucia had done?

"It's a shame that the weather is so grim this morning, isn't it?" Thatcher asked, cutting into her thoughts.

Wondering what he wanted, she eyed him warily. He seemed cheerful enough, considering that she had rather rudely walked away from him after dinner the night before.

"Have you eaten breakfast yet?" he asked.

"Oh . . . no, I haven't."

"Would you care to join me?"

She studied his face. He was smiling at her, and once more, she couldn't seem to keep from smiling back.

"That would be nice," she told him at last. Then, belatedly, she remembered her simple cotton dress. She looked down at herself, knowing she couldn't possibly enter the first-class dining salon dressed this way.

"You look lovely this morning," Thatcher said, as though he were reading her mind. And then, as though he hadn't seen this dress on her before, he added, "That's a nice color on you."

She looked up at him, feeling a sudden lump in her throat. He was kind. No matter what she tried to tell herself about him, she couldn't quite make herself believe that he wasn't a good man, a man who meant well.

"I . . . I don't have anything else to wear," she confessed.

"You don't need anything else to wear, Cira. As I said, that dress suits you very well."

"But the other ladies—"

"Will be green with envy when they see you. Shall we?" He offered his arm.

She hesitated only a moment before taking it. And as they strolled down the narrow corridor, she found herself feeling, if not lighthearted, at least contented.

"What shall we do now?" Thatcher asked Cira, finishing the last sip of his strong coffee and leaning back in his chair to look at her.

She had finished every last bit of the hearty breakfast
the steward had set before her—the eggs and potatoes
and sausages and bread and butter and stewed prunes,
along with a cup of tea and a large glass of milk.

It thrilled him to see her indulge, knowing that she had
been poverty-stricken her whole life. Most women he
knew ate like finicky children, delicately nudging the
food on their plates as though they thought it impolite to
actually eat it.

"What is there to do?" Cira responded to his question,
glancing toward the window overlooking the deck.

He followed her gaze and saw that it was still raining
outside, with storm clouds stretching to the horizon so
that the water and the sky were the same blue-black
color, and it was impossible to tell where one left off and
the other began.

"Have you ever played checkers?"

"Checkers?" She repeated the strange, foreign word
and shook her head. "What is that?"

"A game. It's great fun. I saw that they had several
boards set up in the lounge. I'll teach you if you like."

"Oh . . . that's all right. You don't have to—"

"I'd like to. Besides, what else is there to do?"

She shrugged, then nodded. "All right. I'll play . . .
checkers . . . with you."

He smiled at the way she pronounced the word in her
heavy Italian accent. He was becoming used to her Sicilian dialect, although there were times when he had to
pause and mentally decipher things that she said. He
wondered if she knew any English at all, and whether
she was willing to learn.

But he was leery of asking. He sensed how defensive
she was, particularly in this setting. He didn't want her
to think that he was criticizing her.

"Shall we go now?" she asked, glancing around the dining salon, which was still crowded with other first-class passengers lingering over breakfast.

He noticed that her fingers fluttered self-consciously to the neckline of her dress, and she fidgeted with it, as she had done throughout the meal. He knew she was uncomfortable in the simple, threadbare garment, and his heart went out to her. He would like nothing more than to take her to a skilled seamstress and buy her a dozen custom-made gowns. Perhaps when they arrived in New York . . .

But he didn't want to think about what would happen then. She would set out to find her family, and he would go back to his family.

And never the twain shall meet, he added with bitter irony, mentally quoting a line from Rudyard Kipling's "Ballad of East and West."

"Thatcher?"

The still-unfamiliar ring of his name on Cira's lips warmed him, and he glanced up at her.

"Shall we?" she asked, a bit timidly.

"If you're ready, we can go," he agreed, rising and escorting her from the dining room. He was conscious of people glancing in their direction as they passed, and heard a snicker or two that he knew was directed at Cira. He felt her stiffen at his side as they walked and thought that he would do anything to spare her the indignity. He knew how difficult this was for her, but there was nothing he could do about it.

This is what it would be like, only thousands of times worse, in New York, he reminded himself. If he were to bring her into his world, she would be the object of constant gossip and speculation, and worse than that, her clothing and her accent and her lack of proper breeding would be criticized and laughed about.

He wouldn't subject her to that. It wouldn't be fair to her.

But deep down, he knew that his intentions weren't entirely noble. Sparing Cira the ordeal of mingling in New York's elite society wasn't the only reason he wouldn't let their relationship progress.

He couldn't possibly expect to court a poor Sicilian peasant when he was expected to carry out his destiny as the only Montgomery male: to find a proper wife and take over his father's business. It always came down to that.

With a sigh he ushered Cira into the lounge and looked about for a checkerboard. He could certainly use a few hours of mindless amusement.

"That was such fun!" Cira exclaimed as they left the lounge several hours later.

"We can play again tomorrow, if you like," Thatcher promised.

"I would love to."

They passed a stairway leading down to steerage as they walked along the narrow corridor, and she was instantly reminded of Lucia. She hadn't thought of her at all since she and Thatcher had gotten so engrossed in one checkers game after another. But now she felt the familiar dark heaviness return, and she fought back a sigh.

As though he had sensed the shift in her mood, Thatcher looked down at her and asked, "Is everything all right?"

"Yes, everything is fine."

"You suddenly seem disturbed by something. Is it your friend, Lucia?"

Her eyes widened and she asked, "How could you possibly know that?"

"Because we just passed the stairs leading to steerage, and I wondered if you had tracked her down last night. Did you?"

"Yes . . ."

"And you had more words with her."

"Yes," she admitted again. "But I'd rather not talk about it now."

She half-expected him to push her, but he didn't. Instead, he changed the subject to lunch which was now being served. Tantilizing aromas floated through the hall, and Cira felt her stomach rumbling in anticipation of another delicious meal. But the thought of returning to that dining room, and the probing stares of countless wealthy strangers, filled her with dread.

"I believe I'll skip this meal," she told Thatcher. "I'm not very hungry."

"Of course you're hungry," he responded. "You must be. I'm starved."

"You go ahead," she said, coming to a halt where the corridor branched off toward the dining salon. "I believe I'll go to my room and lie down for a bit."

She felt his eyes on her face, studying her, and refused to meet his gaze. She didn't want him trying to talk her into something she really didn't want to do. He couldn't possibly understand how it felt to walk into that crowded room and know that you didn't belong, that you never would, and that everyone knew it.

"Thank you for teaching me the game," she said politely to Thatcher. "I enjoyed it."

"You're welcome."

"Then . . . I'll be going," she said, and scurried off down the hall before he could stop her.

In her room she stood once more in front of the mirror and examined her reflection hopefully. She thought that

perhaps she would see that she didn't look as out of place
as she felt; that her dress wasn't quite as shabby as she
imagined. But she saw a girl who clearly belonged in
third class; a girl whose olive skin and dark features
shouted to the world that she was an Italian, an immigrant.

Swallowing hard over the lump that rose in her throat,
she told herself that she should be proud of who she was.
Hadn't Papa always told her that?

But Papa wasn't here. And Papa couldn't know what
it was like to travel in first class, rubbing shoulders with
people who would never dream of giving a poor Italian
peasant the time of day.

Cira laid down on the bed and stared at the ceiling,
listening to the rain outside and hoping that the gentle
rocking motion of the ship would put her to sleep.

She didn't know how long she stayed like that before
she heard a knock on her cabin door. Startled, she sat up.
It couldn't be Thatcher. He would still be in the dining
room, eating his lunch.

Lucia?

She doubted it.

She went to the door, opened it, and for the second
time that day found Thatcher Montgomery grinning at
her. He was also carrying a tray, and on it were several
covered platters, silverware, two empty plates and two
stemmed glasses filled with water, and a crimson rose in
a vase.

"If you won't come to lunch," he told her, "lunch
will come to you."

She only stared, too startled to respond.

"May I come in?" he asked gently. "I'm awfully hungry."

"Oh . . . of course. But how did you . . . ?"

He shrugged. "It was no problem. The staff is always willing to help out a passenger in need, Cira. And I figured you needed to eat. Besides, so do I."

"But you didn't have to—"

"I wanted to. It's no fun dining alone."

He set the tray down on the bureau and lifted a lid with a flourish. Steam seeped out, along with a savory scent.

"Now then," he said grandly, "let's see what we have here. Ah, some sort of baked fish. And here"—he peered under a second lid—"are potatoes au gratin. Do you like them?"

"I've never had them."

"You'll adore them. I promise."

He went on, describing each dish, then filling two plates with generous servings of everything. He motioned for Cira to sit in the armchair while he perched on the end of the bed, his plate balanced in his lap.

He chatted as they ate, but later, she didn't remember what it was about. She only knew that she was touched by his incredibly sweet gesture, and that as long as she lived, she would never forget what he had done for her. All of it. Someday, somehow, she would repay him for his kindness.

When they had both finished, he stacked the empty plates and used silver back on the tray and she fully expected him to leave. Instead, he returned to the bed, sat down, and looked at her expectantly.

After a moment she asked tentatively, "What is it?"

"You've been awfully quiet, Cira. Do you mind if I ask what you're thinking?"

"I'm thinking," she said softly, "that nobody has ever done for me what you have. And you and I are really strangers."

"Strangers?" He shook his head. "No. Too much has passed between us for you to consider us strangers, Cira."

"Then . . . what are we?" She found herself meeting his level gaze head-on, resisting the urge to turn her head away.

"Friends?" It was more of a question than a definitive reply, and he seemed to be waiting for her to response.

"Friends," she echoed. "Yes . . ."

"More than that?" He stood and crossed the room to where she was, picking up both of her hands in his own. She welcomed his warm grasp and allowed him to pull her to her feet. She didn't know where he was leading, and for once, she didn't care. She was weary, suddenly, of the emotional tug-of-war that had been going on in her head. For once, she wanted simply to feel, instead of think and think and think. . . .

"Cira," Thatcher said in a low voice, "I've tried to stay away from you. But it's impossible."

"Why?"

"I don't know. I find myself drawn to you, over and over again. . . ."

"I know. I feel the same way."

"What are you doing to me?" He traced a fingertip along her lip, and she felt herself trembling so that she couldn't reply.

It wasn't necessary, anyway. He was lowering his head, and then his mouth captured hers hungrily, and she was swept away in a kiss that seemed to go on endlessly. She didn't want it to stop; she clung to his jacket and didn't want to let go, not ever.

He lifted his head and told her breathlessly, "I can't help myself, Cira. If you want me to stop, say so now, because—"

"No," she said raggedly. "No, please don't stop, Thatcher."

He bent his head again, and this time his lips seared the sensitive skin just below her ear. He slid hot kisses along her throat, and his hands moved from her shoulders to her waist as he held her firmly to him. There was no question where this was leading. She felt his hard arousal against her stomach, and she strained upward on her toes, longing to feel him pressing into a lower, more intimate part of her.

As if sensing that, he pulled her backward to the bed and laid her gently on the blanket, then stretched out next to her. He began kissing her again, his tongue swirling sensually into her mouth, and she moaned and pulled him closer. He rolled fully onto her, and she gasped in pure pleasure as she felt him at last, swollen and prodding into her.

But their clothes were in the way, and when he began fumbling with her skirt, she didn't stop him. He gathered it up around her hips, and she felt him easing her stockings down, and then her drawers. She shivered, but not from the cool air hitting her bare skin.

He had slid down so that his head was positioned somewhere beyond her vision, and she felt him touching her, stroking the folds of tender skin between her legs.

"Oh . . . Thatcher . . ." She writhed on the bed and realized that he was holding her thighs firmly in place, then understood that he was using his mouth on her, not his fingers as she had assumed. She whimpered and grasped his head. His wet tongue probed into her and flames licked at her core. She thought that if he stopped she would die right then and there, but he didn't; he kept up the rhythmic strokes until she felt an urgent pressure building deep inside of her. Uncertain of what was hap-

pening, she gasped, suddenly, inexplicably frightened of
what was happening . . . of what was going to happen.
But still he didn't stop, and she was powerless to fight
the sensations sweeping through her. A moment later she
was plunged into a dizzying series of spasms, her body
quaking uncontrollably as she cried out, over and over,
calling his name.

When the intense throbbing finally ebbed, she opened
her eyes and saw that he had moved back up on the bed
and was watching her. She knew vaguely that she should
have been embarrassed, but somehow, she wasn't. She
found herself reaching for him, kissing him, sliding her
hands beneath his clothes, awkwardly fumbling for his
bare skin.

"Please," she whispered, and as though he understood, he quickly shed his clothes, tossing them haphazardly to the floor around the bed. Then he helped her out
of her dress and chemise, and lay beside her again, both
of them naked at last.

This time his movements were languid. He kissed her
mouth, and then her breasts, and suckled her there as she
threw her head back and closed her eyes. She felt his
hands everywhere, and she arched her back, straining toward him, wanting still more of him.

At last he was on top of her, poised against her, holding his weight up on his elbows as he looked down into
her eyes. She saw the question there and nodded, too
overcome to speak. But he didn't need to hear a reply.
He reached down and guided himself into her, and she
braced herself for the inevitable pain, but it didn't come.
She was ready for him, and she felt only a warm, delicious pressure as he entered her and began moving.

She clung to his shoulders and stared into his eyes,
marveling at his nearness. He was a part of her now, and

when she reached up and wiped the sweat from his brow, he kissed her fingertips, then her lips. She felt those same quivering sensations again, rising from her core, and this time she didn't fight it, but let herself ride with it. In no time she was once again borne away on wave after wave of euphoria. She knew that he had been swept along with her when she heard him groan. She felt his strokes grow more fervent, spilling wet heat into her as her name tumbled from his lips.

When it was over, he rolled onto his back and held her. As he petted her hair and his breathing slowed, she closed her eyes and, completely sated, drifted off to sleep.

12

Thatcher lay in bed, watching Cira brush her hair at the mirror. She was naked and her back was to him, affording a view of her pale, shapely legs and rounded bottom that was just visible beneath the length of silken black waves. He thought idly that he would be quite content doing just this, all day long.

But too soon she set the brush aside, pulled on his maroon silk robe, and turned to him. "And what are you doing, *Signore Pigro*?"

"Don't call me lazy," he protested with a laugh. "I was just resting."

"Resting? It's the middle of the day, and you've been in bed for the past three hours."

"With you. That's why I need the rest," he said, grinning at the memory of this most recent passionate encounter.

It had been three days since they had fallen into each other's arms in her cabin. Since then they had scarcely emerged on deck, choosing instead to spend the long days and nights behind closed doors. Thatcher had discovered that his shy Sicilian beauty had an insatiable appetite for lovemaking, and he had been most willing to indulge her desires. Still, he supposed she was right. He couldn't spend all day, every day, in bed with her.

"Shall we go for a stroll on deck?" he suggested.

She seemed to consider that, then shook her head.

"Why not? The sun is shining and we could both use some fresh air. Soon enough we'll be in New York, and there's precious little of that in the city."

Her eyes clouded over. "Don't talk about New York, Thatcher. Please."

He understood how she felt about that. He felt the same way. In the three days they had been together, they had spoken of everything but the real world that drew closer every minute. He had told her about his travels in Europe, and she had talked of her childhood in Sicily. But she hadn't mentioned Lucia, and he hadn't mentioned his family.

"You know that we're more than halfway there, Cira," he pointed out now, realizing they couldn't avoid the subject of their destination forever.

"I know." She sat heavily on the bed beside him. "But let's not talk about it. I don't want this to end."

"I don't, either."

"And it will have to end, once we reach New York," she said flatly. Yet she turned to him and looked into his eyes, as though searching for a contradiction to her words.

He wanted more than anything to give her one.

But he said nothing, and shifted his gaze to the porthole over her shoulder.

"That's it, then," she said. "Isn't it? You have no intention of seeing me again after we arrive in New York."

"I didn't say that!" he protested. "Of course I'll see you again. I already offered to help you find your parents. I don't want you wandering alone through the city for God knows how long before you locate them."

"So you would look with me?"

"I would help you, yes. And I would find you a place to stay, temporarily."

"With you?" She seemed to brighten.

"With me? Well, no," he admitted reluctantly. "I live with my parents."

"And there isn't room for an overnight guest in their house, is that it?"

He didn't miss the caustic note in her voice, and he wasn't sure how to respond. He couldn't lie . . . and yet, the truth was too painful.

"Cira," he began at last, and waited for her to cut him off the way she often did.

She didn't. She only sat waiting for whatever it was that he was going to say. He wished he knew.

He drew a deep breath. "I would be happy to get you a hotel room someplace. . . . There are some very grand hotels in New York, did you know that?"

"I'm sure that there are. So you would hide me away in some hotel, is that it?"

"I—I can't bring you home to my parents' house, Cira. Not . . . not after what I've put them through. They think I'm dead. If I show up—"

"Won't they be overjoyed?"

"Of course they will. But they'll need some time to recover from the shock."

"And giving them another shock wouldn't be very wise, would it?" She stood and paced across the room. "You don't want to show up with your lover, who happens to be a poor foreign immigrant who speaks not a word of English. *That* would upset them more than the idea that you had drowned in that steamship accident, wouldn't it?"

"Of course it wouldn't," he protested lamely.

"You're lying."

"Cira, I have no control over my parents. I can't help what they think, or how they feel."

"Nor can you defy them."

"I have a responsibility to live up to. I owe them that. If you could just understand—" He broke off, wanting to tell her about his brother's death, and his father's expectations, but realizing that wouldn't make any difference. She was right. He couldn't change the way things were.

"I know that you have no intention of ever seeing me again, Thatcher," she said after a long moment. "What we've had—these past few days—this is all there can ever be, isn't it?"

He didn't respond. He couldn't.

Tears were glistening in her eyes when he looked up at her, and she quickly turned away. She began to gather articles of clothing from around the room, pulling on her undergarments and then her plain cotton dress, and finally sitting gingerly on the edge of the chair opposite the bed to lace up her shoes.

"What are you doing?" he asked, though it was more than clear.

"I'm leaving. I don't belong here."

"We still have several days—"

"We have nothing," she cut in, leveling her dark gaze at him. "We both know that. We have *nothing*, Thatcher."

With that, she rose and walked to the door, disappearing into the corridor without another word, then slamming it behind her.

The tears didn't fall until Cira reached the deck. She wiped angrily at her eyes and told herself that she should have gone back to her cabin, where she would have had some privacy. But she didn't belong in a first-class cabin any more than she belonged in Thatcher Montgomery's arms. She should have known better than to pretend otherwise.

How had she let things go this far?

She walked miserably to the rail and stood looking out over the vast expanse of sparkling ripples of seawater. The sun was warm on her face, and a balmy breeze lifted her hair, letting it tickle her cheeks.

She took a deep breath, filling her lungs with salt air, thinking it might help to clear her muddled thoughts. But still her mind whirled with questions and denials and futile wishes.

She stood for a long time at the rail, her hands gripping the chilly steel pipe; she needed something to steady her. Finally she decided to return to her cabin. But as she turned toward the doorway, two thoughts stopped her.

The first was a familiar one: that she didn't belong in first class, that here, she stuck out like an accordion solo in a chamber music concert.

The second was that if she went back to her cabin, Thatcher would know where to find her, and he would. He was too gentlemanly to let her go without trying to explain himself further, and there was nothing he could say that would change the basic fact that their relationship was doomed.

But if he came to her, if she found herself alone with him again in such close quarters, she wasn't entirely sure that she could stay away from him. Didn't she always seem to land in his arms? And now that she knew the forbidden pleasures that lurked there, it would be more tempting than ever.

Despite her resolve, she felt her body tingling with the memory of every exquisite sensation he had caused over these past few days. She remembered the feel of his hands on her, and the taste of his skin, and the scent of him . . .

She closed her eyes and prayed for the strength to resist him somehow.

Then she realized that she wouldn't have to resist him if she never saw him again. All she had to do was avoid him for the rest of the journey, and it would be over. She could get off the ship in New York and disappear into the crowd. He would never find her . . .

Nor would he try.

Not then. Not when his own world was beckoning him back.

Her mind made up, Cira turned and walked quickly toward the stairwell leading to the depths of the ship. She could get lost in steerage.

She thought of Lucia as she descended the steep stairs into the dampness. She realized she hadn't given her friend much thought in the past few days. She had been too busy concentrating on Thatcher.

Now she wondered why she had been so angry at her friend. She didn't care about Renzo. He was long ago and far away, a part of another lifetime. He was a boy, while Thatcher was a man. . . .

No. Stop thinking of Thatcher. He isn't what this is about.

Lucia. Yes, she had betrayed Cira by getting caught up with Renzo.

But suddenly Cira understood what it must have been like for her. She had been infatuated with Renzo, unable to resist his charms or the ache of desire in her own body . . .

Just as Cira had been unable to resist Thatcher.

And maybe Lucia had been right to warn her about Thatcher. Her friend's cynicism suddenly seemed to ring true, and Cira found herself not only forgiving Lucia but wishing she had heeded her warnings. If she had, she wouldn't have allowed herself to fall so easily into Thatcher's arms, and his bed. It would have been far easier to walk away from him if she didn't know the physical pleasures he could bring her, and if she didn't have to battle the barrage of emotions he had inspired.

Cira quickened her pace, suddenly eager to find Lucia and tell her that she was forgiven . . . and that she had been right all along.

Thatcher lifted the crystal snifter of brandy to his lips and took a long sip, swallowing it hard and feeling it burn its way down to his stomach. He leaned back in the leather chair and stared unseeingly across the gentleman's lounge, wondering where Cira had gone.

He had been looking for her all evening. She wasn't on deck, or in any of the public rooms, or, presumably, in her cabin. He had returned to it repeatedly, knocking at the door and calling her name, to no avail. If she was there, she wasn't answering him, and he wouldn't put that past her. However, there was a hollow feeling hovering about the place, and he was almost positive the cabin was vacant.

Yet where else could she be?

Steerage.

It was the only possible answer. Rather, the only one

he wanted to consider. He had, more than once, gone to stand at the rail and stare down into the foaming sea below. She wouldn't have—couldn't have—jumped overboard.

Of course she hadn't.

His instincts told him that Cira wouldn't do that. She was too feisty; she had seemed more filled with anger than despair. She didn't strike him as one who would give up without a fight.

Yet wasn't that what he wanted her to do, in the long run? Didn't he want her to forget everything that had happened between them, so that he could quietly slink back to his life and do what was expected of him?

Shame darted through him, and he downed another swallow of brandy, unwilling to face the harsh truth about himself.

He inadvertently slammed the glass down on the polished mahogany tabletop, and a group playing poker at the next table turned curious glances toward him. He recognized George Clifford and a few others who had joined him at cards that first day, and swiftly turned away, not wanting to invite companionship. He would much rather be alone with his melancholy thoughts.

He motioned to the bartender to refill his glass, thinking of Cira and wondering if he should venture down to the steerage compartment to find her. Clearly, she didn't want to see him. Perhaps tomorrow, after her ire had had a chance to die down . . .

But why would it?

She had every right to resent him.

And he had every right to put her out of his life. He had never promised her anything more; had never let her believe that there was a future for them. It wasn't as though he had told her he loved her . . .

No, but he had thought it. The words had come bubbling up countless times these past few days. How often had he stopped himself from saying it?

Ti amo, Cira. *Ti amo.*

He had told himself it was just passion speaking; just the incredible things that were happening between them in bed. He couldn't possibly be in love with her. If he was, wouldn't he be willing to give up everything for her?

No.

It wasn't that simple. He didn't just have himself to think of. His parents . . . they had their expectations. They had every right. He was their only living son; he couldn't let them down.

The bartender set another glass filled with amber liquid in front of him, and he nodded his thanks, then lifted it resolutely to his lips.

"Is that better?" Cira asked Lucia, replacing the damp rag on her forehead with a new one she had just soaked in cold water.

Lucia nodded, her eyes glassy, and made a move to sit up.

"No," Cira said, laying gentle hands on her shoulders, keeping her down on the thin straw mattress of her bunk. "Rest. You need to rest."

"I've done nothing *but* rest," Lucia told her.

"Not according to her." Cira motioned at the elderly Tuscan woman who was sitting on a bunk across the narrow patch of floor. The woman's head was bent in prayer, and she moved her rosary beads expertly in her fingers as she muttered aloud.

"What does she know?" Lucia asked, a hint of disdain in her weak voice. "She's a stranger."

"Maybe, but she's been keeping an eye on you since the ship left port. You should be grateful."

It had been the old woman who told Cira that Lucia had been sick since the journey began. Concern had filled her eyes as she described how Lucia had been throwing up for days, and restlessly thrashing about at night. She had asked if Cira was a friend, and had urged her to take care of Lucia.

Lucia, of course, had denied being ill, though she had seemed glad to see Cira. Neither of them had made mention of what had happened between them a few days ago, when Lucia had confessed to her affair with Renzo.

"Why don't you try some fruit now?" Cira asked, producing an apple from the pocket of her dress. Its skin was thin and slightly wrinkled with age and there were several worm holes, but it was all she had been able to scrounge for Lucia; she had paid a young peasant boy for it.

The only food available to steerage passengers was salt herring and potatoes, but Lucia had turned down offers of both, saying they had made her sick.

Cira thought longingly of the sumptuous spread of food they would be serving in the first-class dining salon right about now, and wished she could venture there to get something for Lucia. But she didn't want to risk running into Thatcher, and besides, she doubted that she would be allowed to remove a meal from the dining room. He had told her that he'd bribed a waiter for the privilege of bringing her lunch to her cabin that day. She didn't have the means to do that, she realized, resenting how easily things came to those who had money.

Lucia turned her head away from the fruit Cira offered. "I'm not hungry. Please, take it away."

"You have to eat something, Lucia," Cira protested.

"You didn't even keep down the water I brought you before."

"I can't help it. I'm seasick."

Cira nodded. The ocean was a little rough today, and the rocking motion was intensified here in steerage, well below the waterline. Besides, there was no ventilation here. The air was damp and stale, reeking of body odor and mildew and tobacco. It was enough to make Cira a little queasy herself.

But as she stared at Lucia's drawn face, she wondered if it could be more than the dreadful conditions on board the *Bella Donna*. Her friend had been sick back in Palermo, and that had nothing to do with the sea. What if there was something seriously wrong with Lucia?

"I wonder if there's a doctor on board the ship?" she asked Lucia, who shook her head so violently that the cloth slipped off.

Cira retrieved it from the floor and settled it back over her brow before saying, "There isn't one? Did you already check?"

"No . . . I just . . . I don't need a doctor, Cira. It's just the motion of the boat, that's all. It's making me ill. As soon as we reach land, I'll be fine."

Cira looked at her doubtfully, then shrugged.

"Why are you here?" Lucia asked her.

It wasn't the first time, but Cira had managed to avoid answering before, pretending to be too caught up in nursing Lucia to reply. She had gotten a basin of water and gently sponged her friend's sweaty face, then combed the tangles from her matted hair.

She had offered to help her change into a clean nightgown, too, and even borrowed one from a kind woman in a neighboring bunk. The garment Lucia was wearing was soiled and reeked of vomit. But Lucia refused to

allow Cira to remove it, saying that she would do it herself, later, when she felt strong enough to rise and dress.

"I'm here," Cira said, wishing there was something
to do other than sit here beside Lucia on the bunk, "because I was worried about you."

"No, you aren't. You didn't know I wasn't well before
you came down here to see me." Lucia was watching
her intently.

Cira shrugged. "That doesn't mean I wasn't concerned
about how you were weathering the journey, Lucia. I'm
your friend. You've been on my mind."

"Where is Thatcher Montgomery?"

"How should I know?"

Cira realized she had responded too quickly and flip-
pantly to escape Lucia's scrutiny. Her friend raised an
eyebrow and asked, "What did he do to you, Cira? What
did he do to send you running back to me?"

"I told you, I came here—"

"You came here because he hurt you."

Cira shifted her gaze, looking up vacantly at the sag-
ging, stained straw mattress of the bunk on the tier above
them.

"I was right about him, wasn't I?" Lucia asked quietly.

Cira evaded that question, merely answering, "I won't
be seeing him again."

"Why not?" Lucia pressed.

She took a deep breath and looked her friend in the
eye. "Because I'm not worthy of him, Lucia. He's a
wealthy American. I'm a poor immigrant. I don't belong
in his world . . . unless it's as a servant."

Lucia breathed in sharply. "Did he tell you that?"

"He didn't have to say the words. We both knew it—I

as well as he. There's no place for me in his life, Lucia."
She swallowed miserably over the lump that seemed to
have taken up permanent residence in her throat lately,
bringing an ache that mirrored the one in her heart.

"I know how difficult this is for you, Cira," Lucia
said sympathetically, reaching out and laying a clammy
hand over Cira's wrist.

"You can't possibly know," Cira started to protest.

And then she remembered Renzo, and she smiled rue-
fully. "Or maybe you do, Lucia."

"I'm so sorry, Cira . . . about what I did. I never meant
to hurt you. I was just weak where he was concerned . . .
I wasn't myself."

"It's all right," Cira told her, and she realized that she
meant it. "You were right about him. He was a rat."

"He was," Lucia agreed, and Cira saw tears shining
in her eyes. "He was a rat. And I . . . I hate him, Cira."

"He really hurt you, didn't he?"

Lucia nodded mutely.

"Well, you've left him behind, Lucia," Cira told her,
squeezing her hand. "Don't worry. You will never have
to see him again, and neither will I."

"And you will never have to see Thatcher Montgomery again, either. You can stay here with me . . . if you
don't mind exchanging your first-class cabin for this narrow bunk, that is."

Cira smiled. "I don't mind at all."

"If I move over a little," Lucia said, pulling her body
toward the wall, "there will be room for you to lie down,
Cira. Right here." She patted the mattress beside her and
motioned for Cira to recline.

"Thank you, Lucia. I don't know what I'd do without
you."

"We'll stick together," Lucia told her. "It will be all right. You'll see."

But Cira couldn't help noticing a hollow note in her resolute words.

13

The *Bella Donna* reached New York Harbor on a bright May day. Warm sun glinted off the Statue of Liberty as she stood proudly against the cloudless azure sky. Now, as before, the passengers on the steerage deck erupted as she came into view. Some people cried, others prayed, still others danced an impromptu tarantella.

Cira and Lucia stood beside the railing, each of them silent and staring at the majestic statue, lost in thought, as the ship glided past.

Cira's mind was on Thatcher.

She had done her best to forget him these past few days, but it was useless. She couldn't help wondering what he was doing; what he was thinking. She had half-expected him to come looking for her in third class; he must have known that was where she had gone. But there had been no sign of him.

She had returned to her cabin at one point, just to get her things. She went late at night, when she assumed Thatcher would be asleep in his cabin next door. As she quickly gathered her few belongings and bundled them into her tattered satchel, she found herself listening for footsteps in the hallway outside her door, for a knock and the sound of his familiar voice calling, "Cira?"

But there was nothing, not a sound.

She had told herself that she should be grateful she hadn't run into him, but deep down, she couldn't deny that she was disappointed. Not that anything could have come of such an encounter. They both knew nothing would change. It was best just to let it be; she knew that.

Her time in steerage had been consumed with taking care of Lucia, who had grown progressively weak during the crossing. She couldn't keep much of anything down, and her complexion was sickly and pale. Thankfully, she hadn't lost any weight, although she was decidedly frail, and Cira promised her that as soon as she was on dry land, breathing fresh air, her usual energy would come right back. But inwardly she wasn't so sure. She couldn't help feeling that there was something seriously wrong with her friend.

And though Lucia said she was certain it was only seasickness, she had grown increasingly quiet and brooding. Cira wondered if she was thinking about Renzo, and asked Lucia about him a few times. Lucia denied it, but it was clear something was bothering her.

Now, as the ship drew to a stop at last, with the familiar buildings of Ellis Island looming a short distance across the harbor, Cira felt a familiar twinge of worry. She knew what was waiting: crowds, and noise, and endless lines, and men in uniforms who would ask probing questions and scrutinize her every answer, her every move.

Wistfully she remembered what Thatcher had told her—that in first class, the immigration officials boarded the ship and quickly and efficiently processed passengers right in their cabins. It was tempting to consider returning to her cabin several decks above, just for the inspection process.

But she couldn't leave Lucia. Not now.

"Are you all right?" she asked her friend, looking at her and seeing that she wore the wan, faraway expression that had grown so familiar over the past few days.

"I'm all right," Lucia said. "Just anxious to pass through immigration and find my brother. He'll be waiting for me."

Lucia had sent word to Carlo weeks ago that she would be sailing on the *Bella Donna*, and that he should meet her at Ellis Island. She promised Cira that she could stay at his apartment with them until she had located her parents.

"Maybe Carlo already knows where they are," Lucia had said hopefully.

"Maybe," Cira agreed, but she doubted it. Thatcher had told her that New York was enormous. It wouldn't be like Fiorenza, where everybody knew everybody else and you could easily locate a person simply by asking around.

She was grateful that she would have a place to stay once they landed, along with both Lucia and Carlo's help finding her family. It meant she wouldn't need Thatcher Montgomery for anything.

And it's time you stopped thinking of him, she reminded herself. There was no way, now, that she would ever see him again.

Thatcher stepped out of the dim interior of the horse-drawn buggy and blinked into the midday sun. The broad expanse of Fifth Avenue was teeming with activity, as it always seemed to be. The sidewalk was inhabited by briskly scurrying businessmen in dark suits and hats, strolling ladies with parasols over their shoulders, peddlers pushing their wares, and aproned French and Irish nursemaids, most of them dressed in gray uniforms, pushing children in wicker carriages with spoked wheels.

Oblivious to the crowds, Thatcher stared up at the familiar brownstone and brick box of a building looming above the street. Three imposing stories of tall leaded windows, with a massive oak door at the base, flanked by pillars and fronted by a wide flight of steps leading up from the street.

The place, sitting proudly in the midst of the mile-and-a-half row of millionaires' homes on Fifth Avenue, was as grand as he remembered. And as welcoming as a prison cell, he couldn't help thinking bitterly.

Turning back to the driver, he paid him for the trip up from Battery Park and nodded briefly as the man expressed his pleasure over the generous tip.

"Shall I bring your bags inside for you, then, sir?"

"No," Thatcher said, reaching for them himself. "I'll take care of it, thank you."

"Good day, sir."

Thatcher nodded again, then turned his attention back to the house. He set his bags down at his feet and stood there motionless on the sidewalk long after the carriage had rattled off down the avenue. He was vaguely aware of passersby who shot curious stares in his direction, but didn't acknowledge them.

He was thinking of Cira, realizing that she was at Ellis Island this very moment, enduring the exhausting immigration process. She had told him about it one night, as they lay entwined in each other's arms in the dark. He remembered how her voice had trembled when she described how a doctor had jabbed at her eyelids with a buttonhook, and he winced now at the memory, wanting to spare her the ordeal.

But there was nothing more that he could do for her. She could have returned to her cabin and been examined in a brief, civilized fashion there by the doctor and immigration official who boarded in the harbor. He had almost expected to see her this morning; in fact, he had waited outside of her cabin for nearly an hour, prolonging his own departure.

But there had been no sign of her. Finally he had bribed a passing steward to unlock her door. That was when he discovered that her room was empty; she had obviously crept back without his knowledge to retrieve her belongings.

He sighed, telling himself it was just as well. There would be no heart-wrenching final goodbyes. She was gone, and he was back where he belonged, ready to resume the life he had left behind—and managed to escape, if only for a short while.

A faint smile touched his lips at the memory of those fleeting days spent with Cira, when he had almost forgotten the reality that lay ahead.

Then, setting his jaw grimly, he picked up his bags and walked toward the wide stairway that waited.

Cira felt Lucia falter at her side as they reached the entrance to the vast Registration Hall. She turned to look at her and saw that Lucia's face was ashen and she was staring at the throng of strangers choking the entrance.

"It's all right," she assured her. "Come on, Lucia. We should get in line quickly before another crowd arrives."

"I . . . I'm not feeling well," Lucia said, hanging back. Her satchel began to slip from her arms.

Cira caught it and struggled to balance it with her own bag. She hurriedly glanced around to see if there were any uniformed officials nearby. She fervently hoped not. The last thing she wanted was for one of them to notice Lucia's weakened state and pull her out of the line, marking her shoulder with chalk.

She spotted an immigration officer several yards away, but he was caught up in an argument with a man who had just arrived, laden with baggage and surrounded by fair-haired children dressed in rags. The two men were speaking what Cira recognized as German—the officer haltingly, the newcomer in rapid-fire fluency. Both sounded frustrated and angry.

"Lucia, please try to make it until we get through the inspection and find Carlo," Cira said, turning back to her friend. Her heart sank as she noticed that Lucia was panting, as though under an incredible strain. "Please, Lucia . . . you must try very hard to hang on. You can rest as soon as we're through."

"I'm trying. . . ." Lucia wiped at her sweat-slicked forehead, then pressed a hand to her bosom.

"If they notice that you're ill, they won't let you through. They might send you back." She had warned Lucia about that several times already, but she knew there wasn't much her friend could do. Anyone would be able to tell just by looking at her that she wasn't at all well.

"I know. I know. I promise I'll try not to let them see that I'm sick," Lucia promised shakily. "I can take my satchel back. . . ."

"No, I've got it—"

"But—"

"I've got it. Just . . . breathe some fresh air," Cira advised as they inched forward toward the clogged doorway. "We won't be outside again until much later."

She tilted her own head back and inhaled deeply, gulping the salty tang of the sea breeze. It was a relief to breathe freely again after so many days spent in the stench of the windowless, stuffy steerage accommodations. Everyone around them seemed relieved as well that the journey was over. Still, there was an air of tension at what lay ahead once they passed through the doors into the registration hall.

Cira remembered her own ordeal of a few months ago and bit her lower lip, trying to steel her nerves.

This time, she promised herself, everything would be fine. Her hay fever was gone and she hadn't been crying, although she could have wept over Thatcher if she had allowed herself. She had nothing to worry about this time. . . .

Nothing but Lucia.

She glanced at her friend and was dismayed to see that she was leaning weakly against the pillar beside them, her eyes closed.

"Lucia?" she asked, filled with trepidation. "Are you—"

She was unable to get the rest of the sentence out before her friend's legs crumpled beneath her, and she fell to the ground, unconscious.

"Has she come around yet? Will she be all right?" Thatcher asked anxiously.

"She's had quite a shock. But yes, she'll be all right. She needs to rest. You can see her later and reassure her that you really are here, that you didn't die after all." Smiling wryly, Stoddard Montgomery III carefully closed the door to his wife's bedroom and gestured for his son to follow him down the hall.

Thatcher fell into step beside his tall, gray-haired fa-

ther, thinking about his mother's reaction when she had
spotted him standing in the entrance hall a short time ago.
She had fainted dead away, dropping promptly to the
marble floor in a graceful swirl of rustling black silk.

Guiltily he wondered what he could have done differ-
ently. He realized that there was nothing, short of wiring
from Europe, as he should have done in the first place,
to let them know he was alive. But he simply couldn't
do that at the time. And he supposed he would have to
tell his father why.

"I'm sorry I just popped up this way, Father," he told
Stoddard.

"Yes, well, I'm so wildly happy to see you that I can't
quite see fit to accept an apology for the way you sprang
the news on us. At least, not yet," the older man said as
he led the way along the wide, carpeted second floor
corridor to his own suite of rooms at the end of the hall.

The Montgomerys had always lived in separate bed-
rooms, a fact Thatcher had never questioned until now.
He remembered how glorious it had been to fall asleep
with Cira in his arms and wake with her beside him those
few nights they had spent together, and found himself
wondering what it was that had driven a wedge between
his parents. Had they ever shared a bed? Clearly they
had, at least briefly, in order to conceive five children.
But had they ever been passionately in love or known
what it was like to drift off to sleep in each other's arms?

Now there seemed little more than a cool detachment
between them, evidenced when his father had ordered the
butler, Emerson, to carry his unconscious wife up to her
room, rather than doing it himself.

Inside the familiar study adjoining Stoddard's large
bedroom, Thatcher sat in a Chippendale chair beside the
fireplace and looked around at the familiar yachting tro-

phies on the marble mantel, the rows of books behind
the glass doors of the built-in bookcases, the collection
of crystal decanters and glasses on a low table beneath
the wide window overlooking the avenue. The room was
decorated in deep shades of burgundy and blue, the
grandfather clock ticked rhythmically in the background,
and the air was tinged with masculine scents of tobacco,
hair tonic, and leather. This was his father's world, a
comforting, yet distant place that Thatcher had never
quite considered before now.

Now he wondered what it would be like to be the
master of a grand house, to be in charge of great wealth
as Stoddard was. To know what was expected of you
each day and to meet those expectations; to have a proper
wife down the hall, a wife who had stood by you without
question for thirty-five years.

"Would you like to join me in a drink?" Stoddard
asked, taking off his dark suitcoat, tossing it over a chair,
and then crossing to the window and reaching for a half-
filled decanter.

"Yes, thank you, Father." Thatcher watched him pour
generous amounts of the golden liquor into two glasses
and accepted his willingly. He had spent the final nights
aboard the ship indulging rather freely in whiskey and
brandy, trying to numb the ache Cira's departure had left
inside him.

Stoddard sat in the chair opposite Thatcher's and took
a long swallow of his drink before saying, "You understand, of course, what a shock it has been, your showing
up here this way, son."

"I understand. You thought I was dead. And why
wouldn't you?"

"How did you make it into a lifeboat? Why weren't
you on any of the lists of survivors?"

"Because I didn't make it into a lifeboat, Father, and I wasn't rescued from the wreck. I wasn't on board the *Stella Oceano* when it left port in Naples."

Stoddard's eyes widened, but he said nothing, waiting for Thatcher to go on.

But Thatcher didn't know what to say. He couldn't confess to his father that he had gotten off the boat because he wasn't ready to return to New York and the life that awaited him . . . the life his parents had created for him. Nor could he tell his father about Cira. There was no point now, anyway.

"Why weren't you on the ship?" Stoddard asked expectantly after a long moment of silence.

"Because I . . . I was late arriving," he improvised. "I had overslept, and by the time I reached the pier, it was too late. The ship had sailed."

"You've always had difficulties with punctuality," Stoddard said, amusement flickering in his blue eyes. He reached over to a table and picked up his pipe and a pouch of tobacco. As he filled it methodically, he asked, "How many times did I criticize you for that in your youth? I even gave you my grandfather's gold pocket watch, hoping it would inspire you to keep an eye on the time. Never did I imagine that your life would be saved by your habit of being chronically late."

"Nor did I," Thatcher said, squirming slightly on his chair and focusing his attention on his glass. He drank another burning sip of the Scotch and willed it to take away some of his uneasiness.

"And the statue of your brother? The one we commissioned from Gasperetti?"

The statue! His father's words slammed into him and he fumbled for an apt reply. "I'm sorry, Father," he said at last. "It went down with the ship. I had delivered it to the pier to be safely stored on board the night before the ship was to sail. I'm sorry."

"It's all right, Thatcher," his father said after a long moment spent lighting the pipe he clenched between his teeth. "It was just a statue. The important thing is that you're safe and you're home."

"Yes . . . that's the important thing."

Everything was going to be all right now, he told himself. He was home. Back where he belonged.

"What I wonder," Stoddard said thoughtfully, puffing on his pipe and watching his son, "is why you didn't wire your mother and me to let us know that you were alive. Surely you must have heard about the wreck. Surely you must have known that we had concluded you were lost at sea. . . ."

"But I *did* wire you, Father," Thatcher said, the lie spilling out courtesy of the liquor, which had relaxed him enough to loosen his tongue and his morals. Surely one lie couldn't hurt. Not when it was meant to spare his father's feelings.

"We didn't receive a wire."

"I realized as much when I saw Emerson's face," Thatcher said, referring to the butler, who had answered his knock earlier. "He looked as though he were seeing a ghost. That was when I knew that the wire hadn't reached you, that you didn't know I was alive, or that I was sailing for home on the *Bella Donna*. These past weeks must have been terribly difficult for you and mother."

"Terribly difficult," his father acknowledged, then cleared his throat with a strangled sound that betrayed his emotion.

Thatcher felt a rush of guilt for the grief he had caused his father. How could he have been so selfish? How could he have allowed this man to believe he had lost a second son in a tragic accident?

He would make it up to his father, he swore. If it took him the rest of his life, he would make it up to him. He would never allow himself a selfish moment again; he would spend every moment living up to the role that had been cast for him as Stoddard Montgomery's only heir.

He lifted his chin and said, "It is good to be back, Father. You have no idea how eager I am to begin working with you."

His father's brows lifted, and he broke into a pleased smile. "You have no idea how glad I will be to have you. When I thought that you were—well, I had assumed that your responsibilities would eventually fall to Harold."

Harold Springer was the husband of Thatcher's eldest sister, Margaret. He was a quiet, intelligent sort who had been working in the family business since his engagement to Margaret.

"I'm certain that Harold would have done a fine job in that capacity, Father," Thatcher said, balancing his nearly empty glass on his knee.

"I don't doubt that he would have been competent," Stoddard agreed.

"You've said all along that he's a hard worker, and dedicated, and that he catches on very quickly," Thatcher pointed out.

"And so he is, and so he does. But he isn't a Montgomery. You, Thatcher, are my only son. You're the future of our business. You always have been."

Unable to speak, Thatcher managed to nod, then raised his glass and drained what was left of the Scotch.

•   •   •

"Signora Valentino?"

"*Si?*" Cira rose from the hard-backed chair she had been given in the tiny, windowless room. She looked expectantly at the man who had emerged from behind the closed door she had been waiting beside for hours. He wore a loose-fitting white coat, and his manner was brisk and detached. Clearly, he was the doctor who had been tending to Lucia since she had been brought here.

The man began speaking in rapid-fire English, and Cira's heart sank. She interrupted him, gesturing and saying futilely, "*Non capisco. Non capisco. Parlo italiano?*"

He shook his head and, looking impatient, motioned for her to wait there. He disappeared into the other room again, then finally returned with a dark-haired woman who introduced herself as an interpreter.

The doctor began to speak to the woman, who listened for what seemed like a long time but was surely only a matter of seconds.

Cira's heart pounded as she wondered what he was saying. Whatever had happened to Lucia? The woman's expression revealed nothing, but the doctor's mood was serious.

Finally the woman turned to Cira and translated, "Dr. Benson tells me that your friend is in grave condition. She is still unconscious and is being tended to now by a nurse in the infirmary. Both she and the baby are in danger."

Cira bit down on her lower lip at the news that Lucia's condition was "grave" . . . then raised her eyebrows, startled, as the woman's last words sunk in.

Both she and the baby are in danger.

"*Ripeta, per favore,*" she requested, thinking that she must have heard wrong.

The woman sighed, then glanced at the doctor and explained that Cira had asked her to repeat what she had said. He nodded and spoke again, too quickly for Cira to pick up on anything.

The woman turned back to Cira and said essentially what she had before. Again, she concluded with "Both she and the baby are in danger."

Cira frowned and shook her head. "Baby? There is no baby. You must have heard the doctor wrong. Please ask him again."

The woman hardly looked pleased at the criticism, but obediently turned back to the doctor and said something in English. The man nodded and replied. Once again, the woman began speaking to Cira in Italian.

"He says that I was not mistaken. There is a baby. Your friend is pregnant, and both her life and that of her child are in danger."

"Lucia? *Incinta?*"

But . . . it simply couldn't be.

Cira's mind whirled as she struggled to absorb the preposterous news.

It made no sense . . . and yet it made perfect sense.

She thought about how exhausted Lucia had been, and how sick to her stomach, even back in Palermo. Just as Mama had always been, every time she was expecting one of Cira's younger brothers or sisters.

Aghast, she had to admit to herself that it was true. It must be. Lucia was pregnant. . . .

But why hadn't she told Cira?

Because of Renzo.

Of course that was the reason.

She remembered now that it had seemed that something was bothering Lucia even after Cira had forgiven

her for her indiscretion. How often her mind had seemed
far away . . .

And how eager she had been to escape Sicily!

It made sense now, the abrupt manner in which Lucia
had departed from Fiorenza to live alone in Palermo, how
adamant she had been about sailing on the *Bella Donna,*
and not waiting until Cira, too, had saved the fare. She
had obviously wanted to have her child in America, far
from Renzo and her disapproving father and the gossip
of the townsfolk.

Oh, Lucia, Cira thought sadly. *How you must have
suffered with your secret. How alone you must have felt.*

Suddenly struck by the urgent need to see her friend,
she turned her attention back to the interpreter and the
doctor, and asked, ''Can I see her?''

To her dismay, she was told that she would eventually
be allowed a visit, but not yet. Not while Lucia's condition was still so precarious.

''She'll be all right, won't she?'' she asked, fear gripping her heart.

Her question was repeated to the doctor, who
shrugged.

''Please,'' Cira said, a sob tearing into her voice,
''please do everything you can for her. Please tell her . . .
tell her I'll wait for her here. I won't go anyplace until
she can come with me.''

''But you have already passed inspection,'' the woman
said, noticing the telltale papers Cira still clutched in her
hand.

She nodded. She *had* passed. They had made her go
through the immigration procedure before bringing her
here to the infirmary. She had been so preoccupied with
worries about Lucia that she had forgotten to be nervous
or intimidated by the uniformed officers and their ques-

tions. Even the buttonhook examination hadn't disturbed her as much as she had anticipated.

In retrospect, it seemed so simple. Answer a few questions, allow yourself to be examined, and you're in.

So, here she was. Free to go on her way, to find her family, to settle into her new life in America.

But she couldn't do it. Not yet. Not without Lucia.

"I'll stay with her," she told the woman again, who passed the information to the doctor.

After a consultation between the two of them and a hastily summoned official, Cira was informed that she would be housed in the detention dormitory, and given instructions on where to go. Feeling numb, she picked up her heavy luggage and started to leave, then turned back to the interpreter, remembering something and doing a quick calculation in her head.

"Will Lucia be required to stay here for seven months, until the baby is due?" she asked. "Or can she leave Ellis Island once her condition is stabilized?"

Her question was again repeated to the doctor, who knit his white brows and shook his head.

The woman passed his response to Cira once again. "He says the baby isn't due in seven months. It's due much sooner than that. Next month."

"Next month?" she echoed. "But . . . that's impossible."

"That's what he says," the woman repeated in a no-nonsense tone that dared Cira to accuse her of misunderstanding again.

Bewildered, Cira simply turned and walked away.

Next month?

That would mean that Lucia had gotten pregnant . . . early last fall.

But she had said that she had slept with Renzo after Cira had left.

Either the child wasn't his . . . or she had lied.

Tears streamed down Cira's face and she stopped in the dimly lit corridor, setting down her bags and leaning against a cold tile wall. She sobbed and hugged herself, rocking back and forth, not wanting to believe any of it. How could Lucia . . . ?

How could you? an inner voice pointed out. *You're no better than she was. You let Thatcher make love to you, and not just once. You, too, could be carrying a child . . .*

Her heart lurched at the very idea, and for a moment, she thought it was because she was frightened and repelled by the notion.

But as she considered it, she realized that somewhere deep inside, she wasn't repelled at all.

On the contrary; some part of her was filled with an inexplicable yet undeniable longing at the thought of Thatcher's baby growing inside of her.

That way she would still have some part of him, something to keep and cherish forever.

But that's ridiculous, she scolded herself. *You can hardly be in your right mind, imagining that you would want to be expecting a child out of wedlock! You would be wise to pray that isn't the case.*

Trembling, she crossed herself and looked heavenward, asking to be forgiven for what she had done, begging not to be punished with an unwanted pregnancy, the way Lucia had been.

She thought again about the doctor's news that the baby was due next month, and wondered again what the circumstances were.

Had Lucia been involved with someone other than Renzo?

Or had she lied? Had she been seduced by him while Cira was still in Fiorenza? Had the two of them sneaked around behind her back, while she, oblivious, had blissfully gone on dreaming of a future as Renzo's wife?

Anger bubbled up inside of her at the thought. Anger at Renzo, and yes, God help her, anger at Lucia.

How could you have done that to me? she demanded, wiping the tears that again stung her eyes. *You were my friend. I trusted you.*

"Signora?" A uniformed official had stopped beside her and was looking questioningly at her.

Cira straightened and picked up her bags, not wanting him to think something was wrong with her and send her back to inspection. Better to let him believe she was lost. She cleared her throat and asked, *"Qual'e la strada per detention dormitory?"*

He gave her instructions, and she set off down the corridor. As she walked, lugging both her own satchel and Lucia's, she thought about how easy it would be to leave this place. Right now. And never look back.

She was free to go. All she had to do was get on a boat bound for the battery, and find her family. . . .

But she had to stay.

For Lucia's sake, she told herself firmly. Regardless of the mistakes Lucia had made, she was Cira's oldest and dearest friend in the world. She had been there for her in Palermo when nobody else was.

I can't, I won't, abandon her now.

Pausing briefly, Cira closed her eyes and offered a brief prayer, asking Jesus to please watch over Lucia, to forgive her and not to judge what she had done.

Then, her heart aching, she added silently, *And please, dear Lord, please help me to do the same thing.*

14

"Cira . . . ?" The voice was feeble and hoarse, barely loud enough to carry from the bed, but still, it was recognizable.

A sob rose in Cira's throat as she realized that her friend was conscious at last, and she clutched a hand to her breast, closing her eyes and silently thanking God for answering her prayers.

"Cira, is that you?"

"Yes, Lucia, it's me." After hesitating only briefly just inside the doorway of the small room crowded with patients, Cira approached the bed nearest the door. It was a familiar spot; she had visited it on several occasions in the past few weeks, as often as the authorities would allow.

But each time she had been met by the disconcerting sight of a pale form huddled beneath the sheet, so frightfully still that Cira had almost convinced herself, more than once, that Lucia had died and nobody had told her.

Today, however, there was no mistaking the sound of

her voice, or the brown eyes that were open and looking expectantly in her direction.

Cira hurried to her and picked up her hand, finding it unexpectedly cold on such a warm June day.

"You're awake," she blurted, unable to think of anything but the obvious to say.

"Yes . . ." Lucia moved her head in a partial nod, and it was clear that even that much effort was painful.

Choking back a lump in her throat, Cira said in a rush, "I've been here, Lucia. . . . I've visited before, but you were never awake. I didn't want you to feel alone. . . ."

"I know. . . . They told me. . . ." Lucia stopped to lick her parched-looking lips, then continued, "I'm sorry, Cira . . . so sorry . . ."

"Sorry for what?" Cira attempted to wave the apology away with an airy hand, but Lucia's haunted expression stopped her in mid-gesture. She paused, longing to be anyplace else, and finally asked, "Is it Renzo's baby, then, Lucia?"

"I'm so sorry. I . . . I couldn't tell you. Not before . . . I wanted to . . . but I just . . . couldn't, Cira . . ."

"Shh . . ." Cira squeezed the cold, limp fingers in her hand. "Shhh, Lucia . . . it's all right."

So now she knew. Lucia and Renzo had made love long before Cira had left Sicily for New York. The knowledge stung even though she had, in the past few weeks, had plenty of time to prepare herself for it. But she forced herself past it, made herself say, "I've forgiven you. And it doesn't matter. Really, Lucia . . ."

"It was only once," Lucia pressed on, her face ravaged by the physical pain of speaking, or the emotional pain of confronting Cira. "I couldn't resist him, Cira. It was just as I said on the ship . . . only you were still in

Fiorenza. And after that time . . . I told him never again. I couldn't hurt you. . . ."

"It's all right," Cira said again. "Shhh . . ."

". . . just want you to know . . . it wasn't . . . I didn't mean to do it . . . just happened . . ." Her words were coming slowly now, the faintly spoken phrases spilling out amidst Lucia's shallow breathing.

"Please rest, Lucia. Don't speak. Please . . . you can tell me later. But it won't change anything. I'm here for you. And . . . for the baby."

Her eyes shifted downward, to the bulge of Lucia's belly protruding beneath the white sheet.

Lucia was silent, her gaze following Cira's, then meeting it. Cira longed to tell her not to worry, that both she and the baby would be all right. But that wouldn't be the truth.

She had spoken with Dr. Benson whenever she could pin him down in the weeks since Lucia had been brought here. Each time he had told her the same thing: that the situation looked grim; that he would do his best to save both the mother and the child, but that he couldn't guarantee anything.

"Carlo . . . ?"

Startled, Cira glanced at Lucia, deciphering the single word she had whispered. Carlo. Lucia's brother. She was looking for him.

"I don't know, Lucia," Cira admitted. "After you were brought here, I checked to see if he was here, waiting for us, the day we arrived. But there was no sign of him. And nobody could offer any help in locating him without an address. Do you have an address?" She had searched Lucia's belongings in hopes of finding some information about her brother's whereabouts, but there had been nothing.

"No . . . Not . . . no. I wrote to him. . . ."

"There's a chance your letter never reached him, Lucia. Or he might have moved before that. It's difficult to find somebody from here without an address."

Actually, it was impossible, she told herself desolately. She had tried not just to locate Carlo, but her family, as well. The officials she had questioned had told her that there was no way they could contact someone without knowing where they lived.

There had been nothing Cira could do but spend the long, lonely days in the detention dormitory, waiting . . . waiting . . .

Like every other lost soul in residence there—the women whose husbands or children were ill or had been detained for some other reason; the children who waited for parents in the infirmary or detention or parents who hadn't showed up to meet them. Cira lived and ate and slept among the haunted people who, like her, could do nothing but wait. . . .

"My baby," Lucia said. "Find Carlo. Give my baby . . . to Carlo. . . . Tell him . . . tell him . . ."

Realizing what she was saying, Cira shook her head and blinked, hoping Lucia hadn't spotted the tears that had sprung to her eyes.

"No, Lucia," she said fervently, "*you* will bring your baby to Carlo. The two of you will take care of it together. And I'll help you. You'll see. And no one will have to know about . . ." She hesitated, looking into Lucia's eyes, knowing her friend understood what she was trying to say. "We'll tell people that you were married, that you lost your husband in Sicily. No one will ever know. . . ."

"Yes . . . that was my plan. . . ." Lucia inhaled deeply,

then winced and gripped Cira's hand with a sudden burst of strength.

Cira realized that she was in pain. "What can I do?" she asked, looking around for a nurse. "Should I get help?"

"No . . . no, don't leave me," Lucia said, loosening her grip again, her contorted features slowly relaxing. "Cira, tell Carlo . . . tell him the truth. About the baby. He'll raise it . . . and if he doesn't . . ."

"Renzo?"

"Renzo? No! No!" Lucia reacted with more strength than Cira thought she possessed. She managed to shake her head vehemently, thrashing on the sweat-soaked pillow. "No! Never give my child to him. When I told him . . ." She trailed off, lying still again, a faraway look in her eyes.

"What? What did he do when you told him, Lucia?"

". . . Laughed . . . said he would deny . . . everything. . . . Called me a liar. . . ."

"Bastardo," Cira muttered, filled with rage. How could she have ever thought she loved a man who would turn his back on his own child—and the woman who carried it?

"Never . . . never give my baby to . . . Renzo," Lucia said again.

"Don't worry. *You* will raise the baby," Cira said again, brushing a tendril of hair from Lucia's clammy forehead.

"No . . ." The look in Lucia's eyes filled Cira with dread. "If Carlo doesn't . . . you will, Cira. . . . You will be its mother. Please . . ."

"No, Lucia! I told you, *you* will be its mother. All you have to—"

"Promise me." Lucia strained to get the words out. "Promise."

"I promise," Cira said feebly, anguish twisting her gut. "Rest, Lucia. You need to rest. You're going to be fine."

Lucia's eyelids fluttered closed, yet her breathing remained labored. Cira sat with her until the nurse came to tell her she had to leave. As she walked slowly back through the dreary halls to the dormitory, she thought about the promise she had made to Lucia.

If anything happened—

Please, God, don't let anything happen to her. . . .

But if it did . . .

Could she take Lucia's child and raise it as her own?

That wouldn't be necessary. She would find Carlo. Carlo would take the child. It would be his own flesh and blood.

She thought of Lucia's older brother. He was good-hearted, and he adored his sister. He would never turn away her child. Cira would go to him and tell him what had happened—

She stopped walking, realizing what she was doing. She was thinking as though something was going to happen to Lucia. As though it already had . . .

No! she thought fiercely. *Stop thinking that way! It's going to be all right. . . .*

But in her heart there had settled a bleakness that she couldn't seem to banish, though she did her best in the days that followed.

Thatcher sat at the desk in the large corner office on the third floor of the Montgomery Building. It was high enough to escape the street noise and afford a view of bustling Union Square, yet low enough so that he could walk up with relative ease if he didn't feel like waiting for the elevator to make its slow descent to the lobby.

He had personally chosen the green and gold carpet and cherry furniture for the office, at his father's insistence, and all of it had been hurriedly ordered and installed despite his protests that there was no rush.

"Of course there's a rush," his father had said, clapping him on the shoulder. "The sooner you're settled in and ready to get down to business, the better."

Now, as he sat behind his polished desk, a pile of reports on the desk in front of him, Thatcher told himself that everything had worked out for the best. This was where he belonged. He was filling the position he had been born to fill. In a few years, when he had learned the business inside and out, his father would retire to the life of leisure he so deserved, and Thatcher would become president of the company.

There would be no more surprises, he thought, trying to take comfort from that fact.

Restless, he rose from the desk and wandered over to the wide window. He stared down at the bustle of Broadway below, then out over the expanse of avenue that stretched beyond Union Square, leading downtown.

Cira might be out there someplace, he thought. Just blocks from here. Someplace on the Lower East Side, in the vicinity of Mulberry Street, where most of the Italian immigrants had settled.

Had she found her parents, her sisters and brothers? Had she found a job, as so many other young immigrants did, working in a factory? Long hours and backbreaking labor . . .

The American dream, Thatcher thought bitterly.

Had she forgotten him yet? Or did she think of him still, struck now and then by a vivid memory, unexpect-

edly recalling some detail or other of the time they had
spent together.

Just this morning, as he made his way to his office, he
had passed an Italian peddler in the street and inhaled
the scent of the freshly baked rolls and bread the man
was selling. Instantly he was carried back to Palermo, to
the restaurant where he and Cira had dined together. He
saw her clearly, with her hair all done up, wearing that
navy brocade, looking jittery and shy as she sneaked
glances at him from across the table.

The haunting memory slammed into him with such
force that he had to stop walking for a moment.

The peddler, mistakenly believing he intended to buy
something, waved a fragrant roll beneath his nose. *"I
panino, eh, signore? Delizióso, eh?"* he asked in
Sicilian-accented Italian.

"No," Thatcher bit out, pushing his hand and the
bread away. "Please. No, thank you."

He moved on blindly, trying to rid himself of the memory, but it wouldn't go. He was filled with an intense
longing for her, a need so profound that he physically
ached, long after he had settled at his desk.

Now, as he stood looking out over the city streets, he
told himself that he couldn't go on thinking of her. She
was gone, and he had moved on.

Tonight, he would be taking a Miss Charlotte Carpenter to the theater. She was a friend of his youngest sister's, the daughter of a respected Manhattan hotelier and
his wife, who was a distant cousin of Queen Victoria.

"You'll adore her, Thatcher," Louisa had promised.
"She's perfectly charming, and quite lovely. I'm certain
you'll find that you're perfectly suited to each other."

"I don't doubt that," he had responded, resigned to

the notion that he must court suitable women if he expected to find a suitable wife.

He turned away from the window with a heavy sigh, returning to his desk and the paperwork that awaited.

"Cira? Cira!"

The hushed sound of her name spoken in a flat American accent startled her from a sound sleep.

She blinked and woke to find that the dormitory was dark, yet the figure of a nurse stood over her. It was Miss Grafton, who tended to Lucia in the infirmary and had befriended Cira in these past long weeks.

She spoke not a word of Italian, but had communicated with sympathetic expressions and gestures.

Now, Cira sat upright, her heart pounding, and asked, *"Che còsa e?"*

"Lucia," came the hurried reply, and it was all Cira needed to hear.

She got out of bed and began fumbling for her clothes.

"No . . . hurry," Miss Grafton urged.

Cira had picked up enough English in the few days she'd spent with Thatcher to understand bits and pieces of the language. She knew that *hurry* meant *"Faccia presto,"* and she realized that it was serious. There was no time to waste dressing.

She grabbed her shawl, threw it over her nightdress, and followed the woman through the dark corridors and through the warm night air to the infirmary. She kept asking about Lucia, but Miss Grafton couldn't understand . . . or wouldn't reply.

Cira hadn't seen her friend in days. She hadn't been allowed. The last time they had spoken was when Lucia had extracted her grim promise to care for the child. Her words had haunted Cira in the long days since.

By the time they reached the familiar door leading to the infirmary, Cira was shivering despite the seasonable temperature. She struggled to force back the panic that had risen in her, even as she tried to prepare herself for the worst.

A figure emerged from the shadows of the hall as they rushed forward, and she saw that it was a doctor in a white coat. Blocking the doorway, he glanced at her, then spoke to Miss Grafton in English, his tone somber. Cira saw him shaking his head sadly and terror welled within her.

"Lucia?" she asked desperately, clutching the nurse's sleeve. "Please . . . where is she?"

The nurse turned to her, and the expression in her eyes told Cira that it was too late.

"No!" she cried out, clasping trembling hands to her mouth and staring in disbelief. "No!"

The doctor patted her on the arm and spoke in English, and she knew that he was offering his condolences. That Lucia had died.

"No!" she cried again, hot tears streaming down her cheeks.

Miss Grafton put her arms around her, holding her as she wept, murmuring words that Cira couldn't understand.

And then, as her sobs subsided and she quieted at last, Cira heard it.

Faintly.

Echoing through the empty corridor.

The unmistakable cry of a newborn infant.

Thatcher cut a piece from the slice of rare roast beef before him, the scraping sound of his knife against the china plate the only sound in the dining room, other than the steady ticking of the mantel clock.

He put the meat into his mouth and chewed methodically, glancing from his mother to his father.

Eleanor Montgomery, dressed in a cranberry-colored dress with her great-grandmother's mother-of-pearl brooch pinned at the high collar, was sipping water from her crystal goblet, her eyes staring into space.

Stoddard Montgomery, wearing a coat and vest despite the heat of the day, had his head bent and his attention focused on his plate as he raised a spoonful of mashed potatoes and gravy to his mouth.

Another delightful Sunday dinner, Thatcher thought wryly, cutting another piece of beef as the maid, hovering at his elbow, refilled his water glass from a Limoges pitcher.

He cleared his throat, and both his parents looked up expectantly.

"I was just . . . clearing my throat," he said lamely, and saw the disappointment in their eyes. He wished that he could think of something to say, but there was nothing.

His mother didn't believe in discussing business at the table, so there was no question of asking his father about the meeting they had scheduled for first thing tomorrow morning. And anyway, there was no reason to ask about it. They had already discussed it in great detail at the office.

As for making mundane, polite conversation about the weather, his mother had already done just that, during the soup course. She had also covered this morning's church service—Weren't the new stained-glass windows exquisite?—and the food—Did anyone else find the creamed peas a bit too salty? She would have to speak to Helga—and yesterday's tea with the governor's niece, and next week's trip to Newport, to oversee preparations for opening the house later in the season.

There was nothing left to say.

Thatcher sighed inwardly and went back to his food, then glanced up when his mother spoke to him.

"And how is Miss Carpenter?"

"Pardon, Mother?"

"Miss Carpenter . . . you did see her again last evening?"

"Oh. Yes, I did," he admitted, setting down his fork and reaching for his water. "She's quite well."

"Did you enjoy the symphony?"

"Yes. It was a fine performance."

"Good." His mother took a ladylike nibble from her buttered roll.

Thatcher went back to his plate.

"What are your intentions, Thatcher, if you'll pardon my asking?"

He looked up at his mother again and found her watching him carefully.

"My intentions?" he echoed. "Well, after I finish this delicious meal, I plan to have a slice of Helga's berry pie, if there's any left. Then I'll go into the study and read the Sunday papers."

"You misunderstood my question."

No, I didn't, Mother, he thought grimly, noticing that a slight smile quirked the corners of his father's mouth.

Aloud, he said to Eleanor, "Oh? What did you mean?"

"I meant, what are your intentions where Miss Carpenter is concerned?"

"And what did you mean by intentions?"

"Thatcher! Are you deliberately being dim with me?

What I'm asking is, do you plan to marry her?''

"Marry her?" he echoed. "Mother, I've known her for scarcely a few weeks—"

"And in that amount of time you should be able to tell whether or not she would make a suitable wife," Eleanor finished for him.

Suitable.

There it was again, he thought distastefully, curling his lip.

His mother turned to his father, but continued to speak to Thatcher. "Your father proposed to me very soon after we began courting," she said resolutely. "There was no hedging, no wondering on either of our parts. We both knew that marriage was the proper course for us."

Proper.

Another word that begged Thatcher's disdain.

He toyed with his fork, listening as his mother went on to recount how she had hand-picked Harold for his sister Margaret, and how his sister Grace's husband, Charles, had been a lifelong friend of the family. And as for Louisa, she was betrothed to her longtime sweetheart Douglas Browning, a young man whose family resided in a mansion on a neighboring block. Suitable, proper matches, every one of them.

"What is it that you don't like about Miss Carpenter?" his mother asked suddenly, catching him off guard.

"Don't like?" he echoed. He glanced at his father, who sat placidly finishing his meal. "There's nothing that I don't like, Mother. . . ."

"Then there's no reason in the world that you shouldn't take this courtship seriously. You need a wife, Thatcher. It's time."

He wanted to ask if she wished him to be in a cold, distant marriage like the one she and his father had endured. He wanted to tell her to stop poking her nose into his business. And he wanted to tell her about Cira, about how she had made him feel warm and comfortable and alive—and not, thankfully, the least bit "proper."

But Cira was gone, and anyway, he couldn't deliberately hurt his mother. Not after the way he had caused her to suffer, believing he had been killed in the wreck of the *Stella Oceano*. He had noticed the telltale lines of grief around her eyes, had seen her dressed from head to toe in mourning black, had heard from his sisters about how she had carried on in the days after his "death."

He owed her his respect, and his cooperation.

So he said obediently, "I shall bear all of that in mind, Mother, and I promise to keep you apprised of the situation with Charlotte."

She looked pleased.

His father glanced up from his plate briefly and offered a fleeting smile.

And Thatcher asked to be excused, having lost his appetite for Helga's berry pie.

Cira held out her arms, trying not to be stiff, and the nurse gingerly placed a small bundle into them. Looking down, she saw a round face peeking solemnly at her from the folds of white blanket.

"*Ciao, bimbo,*" she said softly, cradling Lucia's son close to her bosom at last. She had been forbidden to hold him, or even get close to him, for weeks. The birth that had killed his mother had left him barely clinging to life. But the doctors had cared for him more diligently than Cira had expected, considering the fact that this was a public infirmary, and the child of an immigrant. She had come to realize that there was some truth to the legends about America—that here, everyone had a chance.

"What is his name?" asked the nurse.

And Cira, who had spent the past few weeks trying to learn English, had no answer for her, even though she had understood the question.

She had assumed that it would be Carlo's privilege to name the child, not hers. And now that the baby was well enough to be released from medical care, she would be free to leave the island, find Lucia's brother, and hand over the little one.

The baby made a soft cooing sound, and Cira smiled down at him, grateful that he looked like his mother and not like Renzo. He had Lucia's round, dark eyes and a headful of glossy black hair, and his expression seemed to convey a hint of laughter, despite his young age. Cira hoped that the child would have his mother's merry disposition, and thought wistfully that it had been far too long since she had seen Lucia that way.

She didn't want to remember her friend as the tortured, solemn soul she had been in her last months on earth. She would forever think of the Lucia of her youth— happy-go-lucky and carefree.

And someday, she thought, looking down at the baby in her arms, she would tell him tales of his mother, tales that would make him laugh for real.

But then she realized that it would be up to Carlo, not her, to keep Lucia's memory alive. And even though she knew it was best for the baby to be raised by his uncle, she felt a pang in her heart at the thought of giving him up.

She rocked him and looked expectantly at the nurse, who handed her several documents. The woman tried to explain what they were, but Cira couldn't follow. An interpreter was summoned, and while she waited, Cira sat in a wooden chair by the sun-streamed window and crooned an Italian lullaby to the baby.

The nurse returned with a woman who could translate, and she first spent a few moments exclaiming over the baby's perfect little features and strong grasp on her finger. Cira found herself reacting like a proud, smug new mother, and planted a gentle kiss on the little boy's downy hair in a gesture that came quite naturally.

The woman smiled, then got down to business. "You must name the child before you can process his papers," she informed Cira, after conferring with the nurse.

"But . . . that's not up to me," Cira told her. "I'm going to turn him over to his uncle's custody. He should be the one to name him."

"Where is the uncle?"

"That's the problem. I don't know. I plan to locate him as soon as I leave the island."

The woman consulted the nurse, who shrugged and said something in English.

"That doesn't matter. The baby needs a name. The guardian can always change it later if he must. Have you given it any thought?"

"No . . ." Cira said, knitting her brows and looking down into the sweet face of Lucia's son.

And it came to her then, as perfect a name as she could have imagined if she had taken hours of soul searching. A name that Carlo would never see fit to change—that much, she knew.

"His name will be Luciano," she announced decisively. "Luciano Torrio."

The nurse smiled at her and nodded, then turned her attention to the sheaf of papers.

Cira kissed the baby's head again. "Luciano," she whispered to him. "After your dear mother."

And she felt an ache in her chest at the thought of Lucia, who had never even seen her child. The doctor had told her that her friend had died in childbirth, slipping into unconsciousness before the baby was fully delivered. Her last moments of awareness had been agony, and she had never known that she had borne a son.

Cira had found herself resenting Renzo in the hopeless days after Lucia's death, had found herself vowing to get even with him someday for what he had done to her friend. She even felt resentment for the child Lucia had borne, wondering why he had lived, instead of his mother.

But gradually, the anger and bitterness had subsided, and she had realized that the baby was Lucia's legacy—and her responsibility.

Now, as she clutched his tiny hand, she remembered her promise to Lucia.

If she couldn't find Carlo, she would raise the child as her own—and she would have no qualms over doing so.

I'll be here for you if you need me, she silently promised the little boy. *Just the way your mother was there for me*.

A few hours later she stood with her bags in the registration hall. It was a beautiful June day. Sunlight streamed through the high windows, casting a golden glow over the place that had once seemed so dreary to Cira. The baby was well-wrapped in a blanket and curled against her shoulder as she handed his documents and her own to the immigration officer behind the desk.

He examined her paperwork, then glanced up at her.

She smiled, remembering how intimidated she had once been by anyone in a uniform. It seemed so long ago. . . .

"Who is here to escort you?" the man asked tersely in stilted, American-accented Italian.

Cira blinked. "Escort me?"

"Yes. We cannot permit a single woman with a child to leave Ellis Island unescorted."

"But—"

"Surely you were aware of this restriction."

"No," Cira said feebly. "I wasn't."

And as the man continued to speak, telling her that she would have to go to a detaining area until she could arrange for an escort, she felt her legs begin to wobble beneath her.

There was no one she could ask. She didn't know how to find her parents, or Carlo. Not from here.

There was no one . . .

Except . . .

No! she told herself vehemently. That was out of the question.

"What if I have nobody who will be able to escort me?" she asked the officer.

He shrugged and replied matter-of-factly, "Then you and the child will have to return to Sicily."

Thatcher returned from lunch at a nearby Childs restaurant, where he and Harold had sat at a long table and struggled to make conversation as they dined on bowls of beef stew.

It wasn't that he disliked his brother-in-law. They simply had nothing in common, aside from the business and Margaret—neither of which made for interesting conversation, as far as Thatcher was concerned.

Harold had brought up the dinner party he and Margaret were hosting on Saturday night. They had invited Thatcher to attend with Charlotte, and as he couldn't think of a good reason not to go, he had accepted. Harold wasn't the type to pry into his relationship, as mother had, but he *had* asked whether Thatcher had been seeing a lot of Charlotte, and had mentioned that he had heard that her family had recently built a home on Bellevue Avenue in Newport, just a few doors down from the Montgomerys.

Thatcher was relieved to be back in the office, though not at all eager to resume working on one of the many reports he had been preparing for his father. Still, any thing was better than discussing his relationship with Charlotte. He was coming to resent the poor girl, and she had done nothing to deserve that. She was everything his sister had promised—lovely, and charming, and well-bred.

So whatever is the problem? Thatcher demanded of himself, and not for the first time.

She isn't Cira, came the inevitable reply—which he promptly pushed right out of his head.

At least it was raining out today, he thought, glancing at the dreary scene outside the window as he sat down at his desk. Yesterday had been balmy and beautiful, the kind of day that made it all the more difficult to spend twelve hours indoors, hunched over piles of papers filled with boring statistics.

He reached for his pen, then saw a white envelope sitting on top of the report he had been working on. He picked it up and saw that it had come by messenger, addressed to him. There was no specific street address— just the words *care of Montgomery Building, Broadway at Seventeenth Street.*

It couldn't be, he thought, ripping at the seal with suddenly trembling fingers and pulling out a folded sheet of paper.

And as he read, his heart began to pound.

• • •

Cira stood in the crowded, dimly lit meeting room, the swaddled baby in her arms and her luggage at her feet, keeping an eye on the door.

She bit her lip nervously and wondered, for the hundredth time that hour, whether he was going to show up.

She couldn't even be certain he had gotten her message. The bilingual clerk who had helped her fill out the form had seemed dubious when she had given him the information. At first Cira had assumed it was because she didn't have an exact street address, but that wasn't the reason for his questioning look.

"You're trying to contact Thatcher Montgomery . . . one of *the* Montgomerys?" he had asked. *"Why?"*

"Because he's a friend," she had said curtly, lifting her chin and doing her best to seem confident.

"A friend? Of *yours*? Yes, I'm certain that he is," came the skeptical, sarcastic reply. "And you don't have the street address?"

"No, but he told me that his family owns the building on that corner. . . ."

Now Cira wondered if Thatcher had gotten the message . . . and how he had reacted if he had.

She had kept the request short and to the point, saying that she had been detained on Ellis Island since they had landed, and now needed an escort in order to leave. She hadn't mentioned Lucia, or the baby, afraid that revealing anything more complicated would scare him off.

What if he didn't come?

What if he did?

She let out a long, shaky breath and told herself that if he did show up, she would keep things light and businesslike between them. There would be no emotion. She couldn't afford to go backward. What had happened between them was long over, and she had reached out to him now because she had no other choice.

She simply couldn't return to Sicily with little Luciano. There was nothing for either of them there. She would never find a decent job in Palermo, and even if she did, how would she care for the baby while she worked?

And returning to Fiorenza was out of the question. Renzo was there. The last thing she wanted was for him to lay eyes on his child, his beautiful son, and decide he wanted to keep him.

No matter what he had said to Lucia when he had discovered she was pregnant, Cira couldn't imagine him turning away from an infant as sweet and as beautiful as his baby son. In the twenty-four hours since she had taken responsibility for the child, she had been utterly captivated by him. She was certain that no one in his right mind wouldn't want this child.

A hollow ache consumed more of her soul every time she thought about turning Luciano over to Carlo when she found him. She knew she would do it—she would have no choice—but the very thought of it filled her with a loneliness more desolate than anything she had ever experienced, even in these past few difficult months.

"Signora?" a voice asked at her elbow. She turned to see an elderly man, gesturing at the seat he had just vacated. "You take it. Sit down. My daughter, she is arriving now. I see her through the window."

"*Grazie,*" Cira murmured, and stepped toward the chair, one of only a few in the room. The man had tried to give it to her earlier, but she had refused, too anxious to sit down.

Now, however, as the old man hurried across the room to embrace a tearful middle-aged woman, Cira sank into

the seat gratefully, realizing that she might have a long
wait for Thatcher . . .

If he came at all.

Thatcher stepped off the boat and glanced at the cluster
of buildings ahead. Until now he had seen them only in
passing, from the water, usually while aboard his father's
yacht or from the first-class deck of a steamship bound
for Europe. He had never paid much attention to the
small island. There had been no reason.

Now he thought of the thousands of people who had
taken their first steps on American soil in this very spot;
poverty-stricken, oppressed people who had left everything and everyone they had ever known to endure a
harrowing journey across the ocean, not knowing what
to expect.

Cira had done that, he acknowledged, filled with new
respect for her. She had come all this way, twice. Had
arrived on this small island and been probed and quizzed
and, for some reason, detained here for weeks.

He thought of her, alone and afraid, and needing his
help. His steps quickened as he walked toward the main
building. He had to find her, quickly. Had to tell her that
he had done nothing but think of her during these past
lonely weeks. That he had missed her terribly. That he
wanted to be with her, and that he would figure out a
way . . .

What are you thinking? he asked himself, startled by
his own sudden convictions. *You can't be with her. Nothing has changed. She's summoned you here, yes . . . because she needs an escort. Not because she needs you.*

And even if she did need him . . .

Even if he did need her . . .

Well, there was still the matter of his parents, and his

role in their world. How could he bring an immigrant girl—*woman*, he corrected hastily—home and announce that he planned to marry her?

His father's eyes would bulge and his mother would undoubtedly crumple to the floor once again. They would be horrified, both of them.

And then . . . ?

And then, he told himself, *they would get over it. Sooner or later. They would have to. They might not accept Cira as their daughter-in-law, or welcome her into their world, but they would survive the shock.*

Just as they had survived his "death."

The realization filled him with wonder. He had been so certain that there was no way he could bring her into his world. Now, suddenly, he knew that there was no way he could avoid it. He couldn't live without her.

And there were worse things a man could do than marry beneath him. He thought darkly of his parents' marriage.

Besides, Cira was beautiful, and intelligent—she would learn quickly. He would teach her everything— how to speak his language, and how to dress, and how to fit into the glittering world of New York society. She would do it for him—just as he would do anything for her. Anything.

He strode quickly through the registration hall, barely conscious of the pressing throng of people and the lines and the stench and the din of what seemed like hundreds of different languages.

He hurriedly located a uniformed officer and tapped him on the arm.

"Can you please tell me where I can meet a passenger who has been detained here?" he asked briskly.

The man took in Thatcher's appearance, from his polished spats to his spotless light gray suit to his matching hat. He looked taken aback, but replied, "Go through those doors over there, and the officer will point you in the right direction."

Thatcher nodded, thanked him, and headed off, making his way through the sea of immigrants.

She doesn't belong here, he thought, glancing around in distaste. *I can take her away from this. I can make her a princess. And she can make me the happiest man alive.*

It seemed like hours, but was probably a matter of minutes, before he was shown to a small waiting area crowded with people.

He stood in the doorway and scanned the crowd, searching for her familiar face. Finally he spotted her. She was sitting off in one corner, her head bent, as though she were concentrating on something in her lap.

"Cira!" he called, going into motion, moving forward, jostling people out of the way. "Cira!"

She looked up and her eyes widened.

He was practically running by the time he reached her, his arms open, ready to pull her against his chest and hold her close.

"How I've missed—"

He stopped short then—stopped speaking, stopped moving. Stood still and silent, just feet from her, gaping at the baby she held in her lap.

Cira had thought she was prepared to encounter Thatcher again, had thought she would be able to face him without faltering. But as she sat staring up into his familiar face, she felt light-headed and shaky, and she was grateful that she was sitting down, certain that if she were standing, her legs would be swaying beneath her.

She struggled to regain her composure, then realized

that he, too, was thrown. He stood gawking at her, in fact, as though—

The baby!

She realized that he was staring at the baby, and hastily stood and started to explain.

"This is Luciano, Thatcher. He belongs to Lucia—"

"Lucia?" Relief was evident on his face. He leaned forward and peeked at the baby, even touched his tiny cheek with a large but gentle finger. "Thank goodness. For a moment I thought you were going to say he was yours."

"Mine? No . . ." Something in his tone roused her defenses, and she narrowed her gaze at him. "That is, I didn't bear him. But he is mine."

He stopped stroking Luciano's cheek and glanced from the baby to her face, clearly puzzled—and dismayed. "He is yours? How so? I thought you just said he was Lucia's."

"Lucia died, Thatcher." She said the words stoically, even as she realized that this was the first time she had uttered them aloud.

Lucia died.

Somehow, saying it brought on a fresh wave of grief, almost as though she herself were hearing the news for the first time. She swallowed hard and busied herself tucking the corner of the blanket around the baby's legs, unwilling—unable—to look at Thatcher. She didn't want to see his reaction, afraid that it wouldn't be the one she hoped for—whatever that was.

"I'm sorry," he said finally, quietly.

Still, she didn't look at him. Tears blinded her eyes as she kept her head bent over the little boy in her arms.

"I know how much she meant to you, Cira," Thatcher

went on. "I'm so sorry for the loss. I didn't realize she
was . . . expecting a child."

Nor did I, Cira thought, but couldn't bring herself to
tell him. She merely shrugged and stole a glance at his
face.

His gaze collided with hers and told her nothing. There
was sorrow in his eyes, but there was more than that; an
expression she couldn't read, and she remained wary as
she waited for him to say something else.

When he didn't, she offered haltingly, "Lucia died
giving birth to Luciano. . . . Before that, I had promised
her . . . I promised that I would watch over him if anything happened to her."

Something stopped her from telling Thatcher the rest
of it . . . that she was to find Lucia's brother Carlo and
hand over the baby to him.

"So that means . . . he's yours now. Your child. To
raise."

She nodded, wanting to know what was going through
his mind. Was it disapproval?

What could it matter to him? she wondered, suddenly
filled with ire. It wasn't as though Thatcher Montgomery
had any say over what she did with her life. It wasn't as
though he was a part of it, or had a right to judge her
decisions.

Maybe it was children in general that disturbed him so
much. Maybe he didn't like them. . . .

But she thought of how easily he had reached out to
touch the baby's cheek, and she knew that it wasn't the
gesture of a man who didn't like children. She had been
moved by the sweet gesture of affection; it had struck
something deep in her soul, the very place that had, not
so long ago, wondered what it would be like to carry
Thatcher's child.

"Well," Thatcher said abruptly, glancing around the crowded room as though he had just remembered why he was there. "I suppose we should get your paperwork processed so that you can leave this place at last."

She nodded, filled with disappointment at his sudden all-business attitude.

But what did you expect? she demanded of herself. *He isn't here because he wants to win you back. He is here because you needed a favor. Because he's a decent human being.*

"Let me help you," Thatcher said, as if to prove the very point on her mind. He reached out and took her elbow as she stood, then bent to retrieve the two satchels at her feet—one belonging to her, the other to Lucia— and the small bundle of the baby's things: a bottle, a spare blanket, some diapers, booties, and an extra gown and bonnet, all provided by the infirmary. She had wept at such kindness when the nurse had given her the bundle, unable to fathom that here in America, government officials reached out to help other people.

"You retrieved your things from your cabin," Thatcher said suddenly in a matter-of-fact tone, gazing at her bag.

"Yes," she acknowledged, suddenly awkward, re- membering how they had parted on board the *Bella Donna*. "I came back to get them. . . . I couldn't leave everything behind. It's all I have in the world," she added, a bit defiantly.

He nodded, looking for a moment as though he was going to say something more, but apparently changing his mind.

"Let's go then, shall we?" he asked, and she followed him toward the immigration official, holding the sleeping baby close to her heart.

15

"*O*h!"

Thatcher glanced at Cira, amused by her small outburst, followed by a little gasp, as she stepped out of the Barge Office and into the bright June midday sunshine at Battery Park.

Her eyes were wide and her jaw hung slightly open as she gazed at the bustling scene before them. Strolling New Yorkers and shouting vendors mingled with the newly arrived immigrants, along with patient drivers milling beside carriages, and uniformed transit officials perched in open wagons that waited to transport the throngs of newcomers uptown to Grand Central Station.

"This is New York—at last, Cira," Thatcher said, momentarily forgetting everything that lay between them. Just for now she was someone he cared about, someone who was embarking on the greatest adventure of her life, and he was here to share it with her, to show her the way. He saw the sparkling anticipation in her eyes as she looked around, and it was all he could do not to pull her close in a triumphant hug and shout, "You made it!"

Instead, he smiled at her and said, "Welcome to America. And you, too, little fellow," he added, reaching out to touch the baby's downy head.

Cira watched him do it, and looked at him with such unmasked gratitude that he quickly removed his hand, lest she read more into it than he intended.

When he had seen her sitting there with a newborn baby on her lap, something inside of him had shriveled and died. A split second before, he had been rushing toward her, filled with plans to bring her home with him, to convince her that they could make a go of it, together. That maybe their differences wouldn't matter as much as he had imagined.

But the baby—it shattered everything in an instant.

Bewildered, he had speculated that it belonged to Cira—what other conclusion could he have drawn in those first startled moments? Distraught, he had wondered how she could have hidden her pregnancy from him. Only later, when he learned the truth, did he realize that of course it couldn't have been her child. He had been intimate with her, had seen her naked body, had stroked her soft belly that wasn't flat, but clearly wasn't bulging with a soon-to-be-delivered baby.

But it didn't matter that the little boy belonged to Lucia. Lucia was tragically gone and she would never be coming back. Cira had become his mother—and that changed the blissful dreams he had conjured for their future.

He might very well have been able to bring a beautiful Italian outsider into his world and eventually make her his wife—but not now. Not with a child. People would talk. They would assume the baby was Thatcher's; that it had been born out of wedlock. The scandal would be devastating to his family, perhaps to the business as well.

It could—and most certainly would—destroy everything his parents had worked to build, to hang on to, their entire lives.

He had been numb with disappointment at first but, during the short ferry ride across the harbor, had managed to recover a bit. Now he told himself that he was merely back where he had been before she had contacted him yesterday—and was that so terrible a place to be? He had certainly resigned himself to his fate once before, and he could do it again.

But that didn't mean he couldn't enjoy this time with Cira, fleeting as it might be.

"I must look for Papa and Mama now," she said, touching his sleeve and glancing around as though she half-expected her parents to be peeking out from behind the nearby stand of trees.

He chuckled and said, "Of course you will." He added impulsively. "But first we must find a place for you to stay."

"To stay?"

"Tonight. And for as long as it takes you to find them. We'll get you a hotel room and you can settle in."

"A hotel?" She looked dismayed. "But I can't afford—"

"You don't have to. I'll pay for it, Cira."

"No. I can't allow you to—"

"And I can't allow you to roam the streets of this city alone with a baby. Surely you realize that you have to think of his needs, Cira? You have no choice in the matter."

Wearing a resigned expression, she shrugged and said, "All right. I'll stay in a hotel. But I will pay you back, just as soon as I locate Papa and Mama and find a job. Just as I'll pay you back for the fare."

"There's no need to do that," he told her gently, not wanting to remember the crossing. But his mind was already filled with images of their wanton lovemaking—and those final, lonely days after she had left him. "That was a gift, Cira," he told her, unwilling to betray his sudden emotion.

"No. I will pay you back. It will take me a long time, but—"

"Please," he said quietly, shaking his head. "Let's discuss it later. Right now we should eat, and then we'll find a hotel."

"Eat?" she echoed, and he found himself grinning again, amused at the blatant interest on her face.

"Are you hungry, Cira?"

"Perhaps . . . just a bit."

As if on cue, the infant in her arms lifted his head and wailed loudly.

"It sounds as though Luciano is hungry, too," Thatcher commented.

"He must be. I have to get him some milk. The nurse taught me how to prepare for him, with water and a bit of sugar."

"All right, then. Let's go to lunch," he said, hoisting her bags and leading the way toward the row of carriages for hire.

"This is . . . This is . . ." At a loss for words Cira turned to Thatcher and shrugged helplessly. "Thank you."

"You're welcome." He set her bags on the floor and closed the door. "I thought you would be comfortable here. The Fifth Avenue Hotel is one of the finest in New York, and the biggest in the world."

She clutched the baby, who had fallen asleep again and was purring softly against her shoulder, and she walked around the room, taking it all in—the carpeting, the furnishings, the draperies. She went to the window that overlooked the teeming brick-paved intersection of Fifth Avenue and Twenty-third Street, and she decided she could spend an entire day right here, just watching the people go by.

"Oh, I just realized . . . where will the baby sleep?" Thatcher asked behind her, interrupting her thoughts.

She turned back to him and looked around the room, her gaze following his to the large bed. She wondered if he was remembering, as she was, the passionate night they had spent together in bed in the hotel room in Palermo.

She swallowed and said, "He can sleep with me, in the bed."

"That can't be safe. You need a cradle for him."

"Then I can use one of the bureau drawers," she said.

"A drawer? That's preposterous. He can't sleep in a drawer."

"Why not? That was where my younger brothers and sisters always slept as newborns back in Sicily," she said, lifting her chin and daring him to criticize.

He hesitated, then said carefully, "I don't doubt that it's a good solution when a cradle isn't available—"

"And one isn't available now," she reminded him.

"No, but I can buy one. You'll need it, once you find your parents. They have no idea you'll be bringing a baby. You can't expect them to be prepared. So I'll go out to a store and have the necessary items delivered here."

"No," she said flatly. "I can't allow you to do that, Thatcher."

"Why not?"

"Because . . . can't allow myself and Luciano to be

any more a burden on you than we already have been. You were kind enough to come to Ellis Island for us, and take us to lunch at that lovely place—what was it called?''

"Delmonico's," he supplied with a smile.

"Yes." Her mouth watered at the thought of the incredible meal they had just eaten.

Never in her life had she been in such an elegant place. The round tables were covered in pure white tablecloths and set with delicate china and silver candlesticks and vases of fresh lilies. There were gilt-framed mirrors and softly lit sconces on the walls, floor-to-ceiling windows framed by heavy brocade draperies, and elaborate globed chandeliers suspended from the ornately paneled ceiling. And the people dining alongside them—there were elegant ladies in gowns of silk, accompanied by fine gentlemen.

Cira had felt distinctly out of place in her simple cotton dress, and at first was carried back to those awkward moments in the first-class dining salon on board the ship. Now, too, there was the baby—and though he slept blissfully on her lap once she had fed him the milk mixture from his bottle, she was uncomfortably aware, at first, of the curious stares of the other diners and the waiters.

But Thatcher's nonstop conversation soon took her mind off of her self-consciousness, and she soon found herself talking with him, even laughing with him. He had kept the topic strictly impersonal, sticking to tales of New York City, making the place come alive for her.

"I'm glad you enjoyed Delmonico's, Cira," Thatcher said now. "It was my pleasure to treat you to lunch. But you must allow me to buy whatever the baby needs, as well."

"I can't allow you to do that. I'm already indebted to you—"

"Then let me do it for him," Thatcher interrupted. "It will be my gift to him, to welcome him into the world. You can't argue with that."

"No," she agreed at last, "I don't suppose I can."

"I'll go now, before the stores close for the night. I'll tell them to deliver everything here. Get some rest, in the meantime, Cira."

"But . . . what about my family? I have to find them," she protested, following him to the door. "And Carlo, too," she added without thinking.

He stopped and looked at her. "Carlo?"

"Yes . . ." She faltered, remembering that she had decided not to tell him about Lucia's brother. She said, "Carlo is a friend from Sicily. From Fiorenza. He's living in New York." And that much, she reminded herself, was the truth.

"A friend," Thatcher repeated, hardly looking pleased.

"I'd really like to find him. And my parents, Thatcher."

"I know. And you will. But not today. You've been through so much, and so has Luciano. The two of you should stay here and get a good night's sleep. You must be exhausted."

She realized that he was right. Her eyes burned from too many restless nights, and her back ached from carrying the baby around all day. Still, she couldn't help being frightened at the thought of being alone here overnight with the baby. What if something happened? Who would she call for help? Suddenly she wanted to grab on to Thatcher's coat and beg him not to go, to stay with her.

But she couldn't do that. She had no right. And he had

done so much already. All she could do was ask lamely, "Will you be back?"

"Tonight?" He looked at her, and she could tell by his expression that he hadn't intended to. "I'm afraid that I have a prior engagement, Cira," he said, sounding reluctant. "But I promise I'll be here first thing tomorrow morning—oh."

"What is it?"

"I'll have to come later, as soon as I can get away from the office. I have an important meeting at nine o'clock, and it will probably last all morning."

"That's all right," she said, trying not to sound disappointed. "Luciano and I will be fine."

"Of course you will be," he said, smiling at her. "When I come, we'll head downtown and see what we can find out about your parents. All right?"

"All right," she said, doing her best to smile back at him.

Only when she had closed the door behind him and heard his muffled footsteps retreating down the hall did she let out a shaky sigh and look down at the baby, who gazed back at her solemnly.

"What are we going to do, Luciano?" she asked softly. "What are we going to do?"

The baby had no reply, though she half-expected one, given the strangely knowing look in his newborn blue eyes.

"I'll bet you know what I'm thinking, don't you?" she asked him, stroking his dark hair. "You know how I feel about Thatcher Montgomery, don't you? Well, if you're as wise as you seem, you also know that I've no right to feel this way. The sooner I get him out of my mind, the better."

. . .

Thatcher realized that Charlotte had asked him something, and blinked down at her, hoping she didn't know
how far away from her his thoughts had been.

"I beg your pardon?" he asked, as though he simply
hadn't heard her above the string orchestra that played in
the background.

She frowned slightly, tilting her blond head to one side
so that the tall plumed feather in her jeweled headpiece
swayed gently. "I had merely asked you whether you
enjoyed your meal."

"Oh, yes, I certainly did," he replied. "And you?"

"It was wonderful," she said politely.

He wondered how she knew. She had barely touched
the lamb and rice and vegetables on her plate, toying with
her food as coyly as his mother and sisters would at a
society ball like this one. He thought of Cira, of how she
would heartily tuck into a meal.

But Charlotte had been far more interested in watching
the other couples filling the vast ballroom of Mrs. Hav-
emeyer's Madison Avenue mansion, and in checking her
reflection in the large gilt-framed mirror mounted on the
wall across from their table. She would cast her blue eyes
coyly in its direction, purse her rosy lips, and pat her
upswept hair using subtle gestures that might have eluded
someone else. But Thatcher was on the lookout for such
vanities tonight, battling a growing feeling of resentment
that he was here with this woman, instead of with Cira,
who might need him.

The thought of her alone in the hotel room in a strange
city at night worried him. He hadn't quite managed to
forget the haunted look in her eyes when she'd said goodbye to him at the door, or the way she clutched the baby
protectively to her bosom, as though determined to shield
him, and herself, from the foreign world outside her door.

Nor had he forgotten her mention of "Carlo," whom she had called a friend from Sicily. He hadn't missed the cagey expression in her eyes and suspected that the man was more than a friend. Jealousy had bubbled up inside of him, though he knew that he had no right.

She didn't belong to him. She never would.

He wondered whether the items he had bought at Siegel-Cooper Company had been delivered promptly, and whether he had forgotten anything. He had made a mad dash through the large department store after leaving the hotel, snatching up toys and gowns and blankets for the baby, and ordering a cradle and, as an afterthought, a wicker pram. He had noticed Cira rubbing her back every so often, as though from the strain of carrying the baby, and he wanted to give her the luxury of pushing him about the city streets in a carriage from now on.

Passing through the ladies' dress department on his way back to the street, he had stopped to examine a bolt of rose-colored silk fabric, imagining Cira in a gown of that shade. It would match her full lips and her cheeks, which by the time they had disembarked from the ferry, were rosy from the salty fresh air.

He had almost stopped to order such a dress for her, but, remembering the proud angle of her chin, caught himself and decided against it. She might take such an offering as a criticism from him, a hint that her clothes weren't suitable. The last thing he wanted to do, now that they had reached this guarded level of peace between them, was alienate her.

"I do so love this piece." Charlotte's voice intruded once again upon his thoughts, and he glanced up to see her swaying slightly to the waltz the orchestra had struck up. He took in the diamonds at her ears and dangling at her throat, above the nonexistent cleavage at the neckline of her emerald-colored gown. The folds of silk draped loosely over her slight frame like a sheet tossed over a coatrack, he thought cruelly, unable to help himself.

He couldn't help thinking of Cira's worn cotton dress, a dress he had seen on her several times, a dress that clung to her ripe curves and strained across her full breasts. He thought of her hair, hanging long and unfettered down her back, and compared it to Charlotte's stiffly arranged waves poking around her elegant plumed headdress.

He knew that Charlotte wanted—expected—him to ask her to waltz. And he should. He was, after all, her escort. He had invited her here, had gone through the motions of enjoying himself all evening. It wasn't her fault that his mind was several blocks away, on a woman he had sworn he would put out of his life.

He looked at Charlotte, and he thought of Cira, and he knew what he had to do.

He cleared his throat and said, "Charlotte, I'm afraid I'm not feeling well. Would you mind terribly if I took you home?"

Her eyes widened and disappointment flooded her face, but she kept her composure. Graciously she shook her head and said, "Of course not."

He knew that he should be consumed with guilt for the lie he had told, and for the ladylike way she had accepted it. But all he could think was that he had to get back to Cira. He told himself he merely wanted to see that she was all right, and that the merchandise had arrived safely.

But in his heart, he knew it was more than that, much more, and he ached with forbidden longing.

• • •

Cira stood over the new maple cradle, rocking it gently with her foot, crooning a lullaby to the sleeping baby, her little angel.

How on earth was she going to give him up when she located Carlo? In these past few days the child had become a part of her, and she had become his mother. The thought of turning him over to Lucia's brother filled her with pain.

But she had promised her friend, and she would abide by her wishes.

Tears stung her eyes as she turned away from the cradle, looking toward the bed. She supposed she should climb in and get some rest. She was exhausted, and it was late. Yet for some reason, she didn't feel ready for sleep. Her body was too tense, her mind too preoccupied.

Seeing Thatcher again today had been even more difficult than she had anticipated. She had hoped to find that her attraction for him had waned during the time they had spent apart.

Instead, it seemed to have grown stronger.

Every time she looked into his dark eyes or heard his deep voice say her name in that American accent, she was carried back to those stolen hours she had spent in his arms. Lord help her, but she yearned to be there again.

The sooner she found Mama and Papa, the better, she told herself, crossing to the mirror and picking up her hairbrush.

Just then, a knock sounded on the door.

Startled, she turned toward it, trepidation slicing through her. Who could it be at this hour? She wasn't even dressed; she had already changed into her plain white cotton nightdress, and her feet were bare. She could hardly answer the door in this condition.

What should she do?

She heard another knock, and then Thatcher's voice, calling her name.

Instantly her apprehension gave way to elation, and she hurried over before she could stop to think, unlocking the bolt and throwing the door open.

"Thatcher!" she exclaimed, even as she told herself she shouldn't be so unabashedly pleased to see him. He would think—

Who cared what he thought? She was weary, suddenly, of playing games. She was alone in a strange country, and he was her only friend.

"Did I wake you?" he asked, and she felt his eyes on her, traveling down her body, clad only in the thin nightgown. Something stirred within her, and she felt her nipples grow tight beneath his gaze.

"No," she managed to say, holding the door open. "No, I was just rocking the baby. Please come in."

He hesitated in the doorway. "I was on my way home from—I just wanted to stop and make sure that you were all right."

She noticed that he wore evening clothes and a top hat. He had clearly been out, and she was struck by the realization that he probably hadn't been alone. He'd said earlier that he had an engagement, and a man like Thatcher wouldn't want for female companionship.

Then why is he here? Cira asked herself.

The answer came readily, yet with reluctance. *He just told you why. He wanted to make sure you were all right.*

"I'm fine, thank you," she told him.

"Did you receive the delivery from Siegel-Cooper?"

"Yes, thank you!" she exclaimed belatedly. "You were far too generous. I don't know how I'll ever repay you."

"You don't have to, remember? It was my gift to the baby. Is he comfortable in the cradle?"

"Yes, he's sound asleep. And it's the most beautiful cradle I've ever seen," she told him.

"May I see it?" he asked. "Or will it wake him if I . . . ?"

"No," she said hastily, wanting to prolong the visit despite herself. "He seems to sleep through anything. Come in."

He stepped over the threshold, and she closed the door behind him. The moment she did, she was conscious that they were alone together in a hotel room, with a bed. She should have left the door open. She should have told him he couldn't come in.

"He's so very sweet," Thatcher said, and she looked up to see him standing over the cradle, gazing down at the sleeping baby.

"Yes, he is." She went over to stand beside him, and bent to adjust the new woven blue blanket Thatcher had sent.

When she straightened, she saw that he had shifted his attention from the cradle to her. He was looking at her, wearing an expression that sent quivers through her, and she struggled for something to say.

Before she could open her mouth, he had brought his own down over it and was kissing her. She was lost in a heady release of pent-up passion, clinging to his broad shoulders and allowing his heated tongue entry to her mouth.

Later, she didn't remember how they got to the bed, or when he removed his own clothing and her nightgown. She only knew that it felt right, to be naked in his arms again; that she was powerless to keep this from happening, nor did she want to.

Their joining was infused with the frenzied heat of lovers too long denied. His hands and lips were everywhere, searing her flesh, bearing her along on waves of pure pleasure toward exquisite release. He moved rhythmically within her, and when the time grew near, his gaze locked on hers and she bit down on her mouth to keep from crying out delirious with the thrill of becoming one with him—even if just for now, just for tonight.

When it was over, he held her close, kissing her lips gently, over and over again.

Neither of them spoke. There was nothing to say.

And finally, wrapped in the hushed afterglow, Cira drifted to sleep.

Thatcher woke to the sound of a baby crying and gazed sleepily into the darkness of the unfamiliar room.

"Cira?" he whispered.

"Yes."

He followed the sound of her voice and saw her silhouetted against the window. She wore her white nightdress again and sat holding the baby to her, crooning to him.

"What's the matter with him?" Thatcher asked, propping himself on his elbows.

"He's hungry. I'm trying to give him water. I gave it to him before he went to sleep earlier, but he won't take it now."

"He wants milk," Thatcher guessed, getting out of bed and wrapping a blanket around his waist before padding over to where she sat.

"I'll get milk for him first thing in the morning," she told Thatcher, sounding desolate.

"He doesn't want to wait that long. I'll go get some for him now."

"At this hour? Where—"

"This is New York City, Cira. And a fine hotel. I can find some milk for the little fellow. Don't fret, Luciano," he said, laying a hand on the head of the crying baby. "I'll be back before you know it."

It wasn't quite as easy as he made it sound to Cira, but he did manage to locate a sleepy-looking porter and bribe him to obtain a bottle of milk from the hotel's kitchen. As he hurried back along the long corridor to the room, Thatcher thought about what had happened between him and Cira. About what it meant.

And when he realized that he didn't know, he told himself that it was all right. For a change, he wanted to live in the moment. He wanted to follow his impulses and make love to Cira and take care of the child and tomorrow be damned.

Luciano was still wailing pitifully when he reached the room. Cira was pacing the floor with him, and gratefully asked Thatcher to hold the baby while she prepared the bottle.

There was no time to protest that he had never held a child before she had thrust the sobbing infant into his arms. He held the bundle stiffly, but only for a moment before his instincts took over. Cradling the little boy against his chest, he walked back and forth, talking to him in a low, soothing voice. Though Luciano didn't stop crying, his sobs weren't quite so frantic now.

"I think he likes you," Cira said, coming to him with the bottle ready at last. "Why don't you feed him?"

"Me?"

"It's simple," she told him. "Sit down . . ."

He sat.

"Take the bottle and tip it upside down . . ."

He took the bottle and tipped.

"And pop it into his mouth. That's all there is to it."

He did as she said and was rewarded by an abrupt end to the crying as the baby began to suck hungrily.

"See?" Cira asked softly, perching beside him on the arm of the chair. "There's really nothing to it."

Filled with awe, Thatcher stared down at Luciano, and for the first time he wondered what it would be like to be a father. What if this were his child, his son? What if he were responsible for this little life?

Cira was responsible, he realized, amazed and filled with a new respect for her. And something more.

He was wistful, he realized, when she took the baby from him and put it up on her shoulder to gently pat its back. He wanted to be a part of her life, to be nurtured by her—to take care of her the way she took care of this child. He wanted her to know that she would never be alone or frightened again.

"Cira," he said softly.

She lifted her head toward him expectantly.

He couldn't say it. Any of it. He couldn't make promises he wasn't capable of keeping.

"You have an early meeting in the morning," she told him, when he was silent. "You should go."

"I should. I should go."

"Yes."

He looked up at her, silhouetted in the moonlight spilling in through the window, the baby snuggled against her shoulder. And he thought that his heart would break if he got up and walked out the door.

But he had no choice.

"I'll be by for you in the early afternoon," he promised. "I'll take you downtown, and we'll start looking for your family."

"Thank you, Thatcher."

He fumbled in his pocket and pulled out several bills, tossing them onto a table by the door. "Take this money," he told her, "and in the morning go and buy something to eat for yourself, and more milk for the baby. And don't argue with me," he added, sensing that she was about to.

She was quiet, then said, "I won't. Thank you for everything you've done, Thatcher."

"It's nothing," he said as he walked out the door.

And it was nothing, he told himself as he made his way down the deserted corridor. She deserved more. So much more than he could give her.

Cira pushed Luciano along Mulberry Street in his wicker pram, hoping that he wasn't too warm in the bright morning sunshine. She'd draped a light blanket over him to shield his tender flesh from the golden rays, although back in Sicily, the sun was far stronger. And the air was dry there, unlike here, where an oppressive mugginess tended to settle over the city by midday, radiating from the brick and cement-paved streets in shimmering waves.

Cira wiped a trickle of sweat from her forehead and stopped short, pulling the baby's carriage back as a rag-filled pushcart rattled directly in front of her. She had been in New York nearly a week but was hardly used to it yet. The crowds, the noise, the foreign language, the traffic . . .

She didn't know if it would ever feel like home . . . or whether she wanted it to. She hadn't found her parents yet, or Carlo, though she had spent the better part of every day combing this Lower East Side neighborhood for information about them.

She had also written to Signore Torrio, gently informing him of Lucia's death and inquiring about Carlo's whereabouts. She didn't mention the baby in her letter, feeling that it wasn't her place to give him that particular news. He would be better off hearing it from Carlo when the time came. She didn't expect a reply for weeks or, more likely, months, knowing how slowly the mail moved between America and Sicily.

Thatcher accompanied her on her search when he could, although most days, he had to be at his office from morning until night. But he took her to dinner every evening, and he asked her about her progress, and made suggestions. Last night he had told her that his father's valet had a brother who was a detective, and that Thatcher would hire him to track down Mama and Papa if she hadn't located them by tomorrow, and she hadn't protested. She was growing weary of the search.

And weary under the strain of seeing Thatcher every day.

Neither of them had dared to mention what had happened between them that first night in the hotel. It was as though that brief interlude was meant to be a bittersweet coda to a relationship that never should have gone further than friendship, and both of them knew it.

Still, there were times when Cira caught him watching her with a yearning expression that made her heart skip a beat. But he always looked away quickly, and so did she.

She knew that he wouldn't be out of her life until she found her parents, yet she couldn't take much more of the frustration of seeing him every day, being close enough to touch, yet knowing that any physical contact was off-limits. The sooner he was out of her life, the sooner she could move on and get past the pain of wanting what she would never have.

Cira's feet ached as she pushed the carriage across the

Spring Street intersection. Thatcher had insisted on buying her a new pair of shoes when he had noticed that her old ones were falling apart. These were made of soft leather and had fashionably higher heels. Although she supposed she would get used to them eventually, they still hurt her now, their narrow cut blistering her cramped toes. And they had buttons instead of laces, which meant that she must use a buttonhook to fasten them in the mornings. Every morning when she picked up the pronged instrument, she found herself wincing, remembering the agony of having a buttonhook prodded beneath her eyelids on Ellis Island.

Thank heaven she would never go through that ordeal again.

Unless . . .

What if she never found her parents or Carlo? She couldn't live in the Fifth Avenue Hotel forever. And she couldn't work to support herself with Luciano in her care. What if she had to bring him back to Sicily, to Lucia's father?

Don't be ridiculous. There is nothing for you there. And you promised Lucia that you would raise her son if Carlo couldn't be found—not hand him over to her father.

Lucia would never want that, Cira thought, remembering with a shudder Mr. Torrio's harsh words and mean disposition.

Brushing tendrils of sweat-dampened hair away from her face, she made her way along the block that was filled with commotion as always. Hordes of children romped underfoot, vendors hawked their wares from pushcarts, men gathered in small groups to joke and trade stories, women cradled infants and swept sidewalks and carried bundles on their heads as they had back in Sicily.

The overcrowded atmosphere and the familiar language reminded Cira of home, and she knew that her family had to be here someplace. But how would she ever find them—or Carlo—amidst this mass of other immigrants?

She stopped a passing peddler lugging a basketful of onions and asked him if he knew her parents or Carlo Torrio. The reply was a brisk shake of the head, as usual, and she moved on, keeping her eyes trained on the crowds, hoping to glimpse a familiar, beloved face.

An hour later, thirsty, exhausted, and overheated, she was ready to make her way back uptown. She turned west along Broome Street . . .

And found herself face to face with Carlo Torrio.

It happened so unexpectedly that for a moment she couldn't even react, merely stood staring at him, her jaw hanging open.

He glanced at her, started to look away, and then, his dark eyes lighting in recognition, gasped her name.

"Cira Valentino?"

"Carlo!"

She was in his arms then, sobbing in sheer relief, stunned that her search—at least part of it—was over at last.

Only when he pulled back and glanced down at the baby, sleeping in his wicker pram, did she slam back to reality.

"The baby . . . he is yours?" Carlo asked, looking perplexed.

"No, not mine. Carlo," she said hesitantly, looking into his handsome, cheerful face, into twinkling brown eyes that were identical to Lucia's. "I'm afraid I have some sad news for you."

She told him, then, about his sister. She held him, pat-

ting his shoulder beneath his thin work shirt while he
sobbed openly, there on the street. Finally he pulled himself together and looked again at Luciano, who had awakened and was cooing quietly.

"He looks like her," Carlo said, smiling through his
tears.

"Yes, and he has her lighthearted personality," Cira
told him proudly. "He is so like her, Carlo. You'll see."
She must tell him, right now, that he was to take custody
of the baby. She must. Yet she couldn't summon the
words, so great was her anguish at the thought of giving
him up.

Perhaps, she thought with a sudden burst of hope,
Carlo wouldn't want him. Perhaps he wasn't in a position
to care for a child; maybe there wasn't room in his life
for a motherless nephew.

"Can I . . . hold him?" Carlo asked, turning to her.

"Of course." She scooped the baby into her arms and
deposited him into his uncle's outstretched hands.

Carlo cuddled him and tickled him and made faces,
and Cira realized, with a sinking heart, that there was no
way he wouldn't want this child. It was time to tell him
of Lucia's wishes. She only hoped that Carlo would agree
to let her visit often. . . .

Visit.

It could never be enough.

She opened her mouth to speak and found that she
couldn't. Profound pain over the prospect of losing Luciano had crippled her, had squeezed around her heart
and strangled the breath right out of her.

"Your mama and papa didn't tell me that you were
coming," Carlo commented, oblivious to her suffering,
lifting the baby into the air and watching his feet kick in
delight.

Mama and Papa?

For the second time that day Cira was filled with utter shock.

She managed to find her voice after a moment and asked, "My mama . . . my papa?"

Carlo nodded, bouncing the baby up and down. "I knew that they had tried to send for you, but I thought they were having trouble locating you back in Italy. They didn't mention you would be here so soon."

"Carlo . . . you know where my parents are?"

Looking startled, he nodded, then said slowly, as it dawned on him, *"You don't?"*

"No," she said shakily, clenching her trembling hands to her heart. "No, I haven't been able to find them."

Carlo broke into a slow smile, then turned and, pointing down Broome Street at the row of tenements, said, "But, Cira, they live right over there."

Thatcher sat slumped at his desk, staring into space, so caught up in his dismal thoughts that he didn't hear the door to his office open.

"You're still here?"

Startled, he glanced up and saw that his father stood in the doorway, looking surprised.

Thatcher nodded and vaguely noted the pleased expression that crossed the older man's features. Clearly, his father thought he was so wrapped up in his work that he couldn't bring himself to leave. Thatcher wasn't about to tell him that he had rushed out of here hours earlier, so eager to see Cira and Luciano that he couldn't care less about preparing for tomorrow's board meeting, or anything else.

"I thought I saw light coming from under your door as I passed by. Well, why don't you call it a night now, son? You can ride uptown with me," Stoddard suggested, buttoning his coat and adjusting his tie.

"I still . . . I have a few things to finish up," Thatcher told him. The last place he wanted to be was in that Fifth Avenue mausoleum his parents called home. That was why he'd come back here after seeing Cira. He could think of no other place to go where he could be alone with his thoughts.

"It's after ten o'clock," Stoddard said, after consulting his pocket watch, a watch that was far more ornate and twice as valuable as the heirloom timepiece he had given to Thatcher. "Whatever it is can wait until morning . . . although, it doesn't appear that it's work that has you so absorbed," he said, suddenly seeming to notice the empty desk before Thatcher.

"It's . . . not work, actually, Father." Thatcher sighed and ran a distracted hand through his hair, then rubbed his weary eyes.

"What is it, then?" Stoddard surprised him by coming into the office and sitting on the low sofa across from Thatcher's desk. He removed his hat and peered at his son through the lamplight. "Is everything all right?"

No. Nothing is all right. Nothing will ever be all right again. Not for me.

But as for Cira . . . she had been elated when she had come bounding into the hotel room hours after he had arrived. He had been nearly frantic with worry when he hadn't found her there, and his momentary relief at her arrival was quickly replaced by panic when he saw that Luciano wasn't with her.

"Where's the baby?" he had demanded, his heart racing.

"With my mother!" she had announced, her eyes shining. "I found them, Thatcher. I found my parents. And

Giulia, and Flavio, and Paolo and Antonio and Aletta—
my whole family. I found them at last!''

He wanted to be happy for her. He did. But all he
could think was that she had found her family—and he
had lost her. She no longer needed him.

"What's happened to you, Thatcher?" Stoddard was
asking, leaning forward and watching him warily.

"Nothing . . ."

"You look terribly upset."

"I . . . I am." There was no use denying it, he realized.
Clearly, he was sitting here moping. His father was no
fool. Nor was he the type to let something like this drop,
once he had started to probe.

"Is it Charlotte?"

"Charlotte?" Thatcher echoed blankly.

Then he remembered. Charlotte. The lady he had been
seeing—until Cira popped back into his life. His parents
had no idea that he hadn't been out with Charlotte in a
week that he had no intention of seeing her again.

"No," he told his father, "it isn't Charlotte."

"Then who is she?"

Startled at the old man's perception, Thatcher fumbled
for a reply.

"This is obviously about a woman," his father went
on when he was silent. "At your age, in your position,
nothing else could matter so much."

"It is about a woman," Thatcher said at last, deciding
the time had come to tell the truth.

"Of course. And who is she?"

"Her name is Cira. Cira Valentino."

Stoddard frowned slightly. "Valentino? I've never
heard the name. . . ."

"You wouldn't have. It's Italian. She's Italian, Father.
Sicilian, actually."

There was a pause before his father said, somewhat stiffly, "I see."

"She's a peasant, and I met her in Europe. But she's here now. In New York."

"I see," came the same flat reply.

"And I want to be with her. I know she's not—*suitable*." He came down hard on the word and glared down at the polished, barren desk top as he said it. "But I care a great deal about her. I can't bear the thought of never seeing her again. I know what you think of me for being foolish enough to fall for a woman like her—"

"No, you don't."

His father's interruption caught him off guard. Thatcher glanced up at him in surprise. "What do you mean?" he asked.

"You don't know what I think of you for falling for an unsuitable woman. But I'll tell you what I think." Stoddard leaned back and cleared his throat. "I think that you must be a lot like me."

Whatever Thatcher had been expecting, it hadn't been this. He searched for something to say, but a reply wasn't necessary. His father continued speaking, a distant look in his eyes.

"I, too, fell for a woman who was wrong for me," Stoddard told him. "She wasn't an immigrant. No, it was worse, even, than that. She was a prostitute, Thatcher."

Stunned, Thatcher could only stare.

"I met her in the usual way a gentleman encounters a lady of her profession. It was years ago. I was young and brash. And your mother—well, your mother has never been very . . . affectionate."

Thatcher shifted in his seat, increasingly uncomfortable with his father's candor, yet fascinated just the same.

"Lily made me laugh, Thatcher. She made me happy.

She—'' He cut himself off, inhaled deeply, and looked Thatcher in the eye. "She still does."

"What are you saying, Father?"

"I'm saying that I couldn't let her go. I fell in love with her. I knew that I had to keep her in my life. But there was no place for her there. Your mother—well, Eleanor is my wife. She always will be. She's a good wife, a good mother. I had no desire to destroy a marriage that had always worked for us."

"What about . . . Lily?"

"She lives a few blocks away from here. In a nice apartment with a view of Madison Square Park. An apartment I bought for her, Thatcher. Along with . . . other things. Clothes. Jewelry. Art. She no longer has to . . . work."

Thatcher swallowed audibly, mesmerized by his father's tale, knowing he should be repelled, yet understanding him on some level—and hating that he did.

"Lily will never be my wife," Stoddard said succinctly. "But she will always be my love. There's no reason she has to be both. And neither does your little Valentine."

Thatcher bristled at his father's tone, at the casual mispronunciation of Cira's name.

"Just what is it that you're suggesting, Father?" he asked, unable to keep the chill from his words.

Stoddard didn't seem to notice. "Find her an apartment someplace. Buy her whatever she wants. Spend as much time with her as you want to. But in the meantime, look for a wife. You need a wife, Thatcher."

"But not a wife like Cira. Or your . . . Lily."

"Precisely. That kind of woman doesn't belong in public on the arm of a man like you or me, Thatcher. She belongs behind closed doors, in our beds."

That did it. He slammed his palms down on the desk and stood to face his father, who looked taken aback.

"Don't talk about Cira that way, Father," he growled. "She isn't a prostitute, not like your—You've never even met her. You know nothing about her."

"You just told me—"

"I didn't tell you that she's the most courageous, most loving, most wonderful person I've ever met. I didn't tell you that *I* don't deserve *her*. I didn't tell you that I'm insanely in love with her."

And as the words spilled from his lips, he knew they were true. He was in love with Cira. Irrevocably, helplessly, in love.

And dammit, he was going to do something about it at last.

"I'm leaving, Father," he said, standing abruptly and heading for the door.

"That's fine, Thatcher," Stoddard replied in a mild tone that infuriated him. "You go ahead. Blow off some steam. Find your little—Cira. I'll see you here in the morning and we can—"

"No, Father. You don't understand. I'm leaving. I won't be coming back here tomorrow morning, or ever again. I don't want *this*." He gestured around the tastefully appointed office and shook his head. "This is your life. Not mine."

"It *is* yours. It's your destiny, Thatcher."

"No. It was my brother's destiny. Not mine. He's gone, and I've spent my whole life feeling guilty about that. If it weren't for me, he might be alive. He died saving me. But I can't change that. I can't bring him back. And I can't live his life for him. Not anymore."

"Thatcher—"

"Goodbye, Father."

"Where are you going?"

"To make something of myself," he said, astonished at the clarity with which he suddenly saw his life. How could it have taken him this long to realize what he had to do? "I have to make something of myself so that I can go back to Cira and show her that I'm serious about her. That I want to take care of her. On my own."

With that, he strode out of the office, leaving his father speechless—and not caring.

For the first time in his life he was in charge. And for the first time he knew what he wanted.

Cira as his wife.

And Luciano as his son.

But he didn't deserve them. He had nothing to offer them.

Not now.

Not yet . . .

16

Summer was nearly over, but oppressive ninety-degree temperatures and humidity continued to hover over New York City, as though the brisk days of autumn would never arrive. The September sun beat mercilessly down on Mulberry Street that September afternoon, but there was a yellowish cast to the sky and a heaviness in the air, as though a storm was brewing.

Thatcher Montgomery didn't notice the weather as he made his way along the sidewalk, moving briskly despite the heat. In one hand he held a bouquet of flowers he'd bought from the new refrigerated case at Joseph Fleishman's Florist Shop at 71 Broadway. In the other he clutched a scrap of paper bearing the Broome Street address he had scribbled the last time he had seen Cira, in that room at the Fifth Avenue Hotel nearly three months ago.

And in his coat pocket was a small square jeweler's box. The ring inside was hardly impressive; not by most standards. The plain gold band was adorned with a small setting of diamonds, rubies, and sapphires, some of the stones scarcely larger than grains of sand. But he had bought it himself, with money he had earned from his job at a newly opened automobile showroom.

He had found that he was quite good as a salesman; that he enjoyed mingling with people and was fascinated by the motorcars themselves, which were rapidly gaining in popularity. He was hardly growing rich in his new position, but he was able to afford a two-room flat on the West Side and had, in just a few months, tucked enough money away in the bank to provide a small nest egg.

It was a start.

He knew that he would be much better off a year from now, even six months from now. But he could wait no longer. Every morning he awakened with Cira on his mind, and every night when he climbed into his narrow bed, he dreamed of her. Many times he had vowed that he couldn't let another day pass without seeing her. Yet he held on, unwilling to propose until he had something to offer her.

Now, at last, the day had come.

He rounded the corner onto Broome Street and made his way along the sidewalk, checking the addresses on the tenement houses as he passed. The block was alive with activity—adults chattering in rapid Italian, children romping, babies squawling, dogs barking—even chickens clucking from some nearby pen. Vendors hawked their fresh harvest of fruits and vegetables: apples and tomatoes and corn from Long Island and Jersey farms. The street was jammed with carts and horses and bicycles.

And Cira lived right here, amidst the confusion, Thatcher thought, marveling at the fact that this was her world, and he was about to step back into it at last.

He found the address, a four-story brick tenement with

a group of dark-skinned boys gathered on the stoop, playing catch, using a large squash as a ball.

Thatcher smiled as he stepped past them, aware of their
curious stares, and scanned the little faces beneath the
flat-topped caps, wondering if any of them were Cira's
younger brothers. Any of them could have been; they all
had round, ruddy cheeks and dark hair and eyes.

In the dreary hallway that was infused with the scent
of frying onions and garlic, he saw that there were several
apartments, as well as a stairway leading up to the floors
above. He realized that he didn't know which floor she
lived on, and would have to ask someone. And as he
walked toward the nearest door, which was standing ajar,
a terrible thought struck him.

What if her family had moved from here in the three
months since he had seen her?

What if they had left the city, or even worse, gone
back to Sicily?

He clenched his jaw as he knocked tentatively on the
door, praying that wasn't the case. He couldn't wait any
longer. He *had* to see her.

A woman's voice called something in Italian, the
words obliterated by the sound of a clattering pot lid.
After a moment Thatcher poked his head inside and
called, *"Buon giorno?"*

"Si?" A large middle-aged woman looked up from
the pot she was stirring on a dilapidated stove. The
wooden spoon and her apron were splattered with tomato
sauce. When she saw that he was a stranger, she put
down her spoon and looked at him warily.

Quickly he told her that he was looking for the Valentino family . . . did they still live in the building?

"Valentino . . . ? *Si,*" she said, and he let out an enormous sigh of relief. Eyeing the flowers he clutched with

blatant curiosity, the woman told him they lived on the third floor in the back apartment.

He barely paused to thank her before dashing out the door and up the two steep flights of steps, taking them two at a time.

He stopped to catch his breath outside the closed door, removing his hat and running a hand through his sweat-soaked hair before replacing it. Then, with a trembling hand, he knocked.

Voices carried from the other side of the door and footsteps approached. And then it was thrown open, and he found himself face to face with a young boy who immediately looked intrigued.

"I'm looking for Cira Valentino," he said, even as he spotted her in the background.

There she was, seated at a small table crowded with people.

He had to fight the urge to rush toward her and haul her into his arms, conscious of the startled stares from a mustached man and aproned woman who had to be her parents, a lovely teenaged girl who resembled Cira—her sister Giulia?—and a collection of wide-eyed moppets, the youngest barely a toddler and seated in her mother's lap.

Cira herself looked astounded. She hadn't moved, but sat with her eyes transfixed on his face as though she were seeing a ghost.

"Cira?" he asked tentatively, and took a step forward.

She stood then, and he saw that she had been holding Luciano on her lap. He had grown into a chubby baby, and he, too, stared solemnly at Thatcher, who longed to see recognition in his eyes, but knew it was impossible. The baby was too young to remember him.

But Cira . . .

Why hadn't she come to him?

Why hadn't she said something?

Her mother spoke to her in Sicilian so rapid-fire that Thatcher didn't catch whatever she said, or Cira's answer.

Then Cira was handing Luciano to her sister and coming toward him. He resisted the urge to open his arms to her and busied himself glancing around, vaguely dismayed at the condition of the tiny apartment. The single room was crowded with rickety furniture and an array of odds and ends—cookware and baskets and clothing strewn over bedknobs and draped on nails pounded into the wall. The yellowed wallpaper was water-stained and peeling off in some spots.

And there, tucked into one corner, looking entirely out of place in the shabby surroundings, were the polished wooden cradle and wicker pram he had bought for Luciano.

"Thatcher," Cira said, her voice a mere whisper.

"These are for you," he said shakily, handing her the bouquet.

She took it, then held it as though she didn't know what to do with it.

"I'll take them," said the young boy who had answered the door and still hovered at Thatcher's side. "I'll put them in water."

Cira handed them to him, looking dazed, then said to Thatcher, "Come out into the hall. We can talk there."

He nodded and held the door open for her, aware that her family's inquisitive gazes followed them until he had closed it behind them.

Then he turned to her and reached out to hold her at last.

She allowed him to pull her into his arms, but he realized that her body was stiff, and when he pulled back to look at her, her face wore an expression he couldn't read, an expression that filled him with apprehension.

"You're angry," he said, although he didn't quite think that was the emotion in her eyes. "Angry that I haven't come to you before now."

"No," she said, shaking her head swiftly. He could feel her whole body shaking as he clutched her arms in his hands, and he wanted to pull her close again, to pat her back, to tell her not to be upset.

That everything was going to be all right now.

But as he looked into her eyes he was suddenly uncertain about that.

"Cira," he said softly, "I wanted to come to you sooner. I would have. But I couldn't—"

"It's all right," she interrupted. "It's all right, Thatcher. I've been just fine without you."

He wondered if that could possibly be true—if she had put him into the past and gone on, while he had been haunted every waking moment, even in his sleep, by memories of her.

"Well, I haven't been fine without you," he said raggedly. "I can't live without you, Cira. I came to bring you this."

With that, he reached into his pocket and pulled out the jeweler's box. His hands were shaking so violently that he could barely flip it open. When he did, he heard her gasp and looked up to see utter shock on her face.

"Cira . . . will you marry me?" he asked, finally able to utter the words he had practiced for so long that they had become a constant refrain in his mind.

"Oh, Thatcher . . ." She looked at him, and he realized that she was crying. Tears of joy.

"I love you, Cira," he said, and started to pull her toward him for a kiss.

But she was holding back.

And shaking her head.

And that was when he realized that they weren't tears of joy at all. Her eyes were filled with sorrow and regret.

"I can't marry you, Thatcher," she said on a sob.

I can't marry you.

The words fell between them with a dull thud, and he couldn't believe he was hearing them. Never, in the months that he had practiced his proposal, had he imagined that this would be her reply.

"But . . . why not?" he asked, shattered, bewildered, sickened. "I love you. Don't you love me? You can't tell me you don't love me, Cira. I've . . . I've seen it in the way you look at me. On the ship . . . In the hotel . . . I know. Don't deny it."

"It isn't that," she choked out.

"Then what? Why can't you marry me?"

"Because I'm going to marry somebody else. The wedding . . . it's tomorrow morning."

Cira finished fastening Luciano's clean diaper around his chubby tummy and reached for the off-white cotton gown Mama had sewn for him, a gown edged in lace with a matching bonnet, made especially for this day.

Her wedding day.

Her hands shook as she pulled the garment over his black curls, and when he giggled as his face popped out through the neckline, she found it nearly impossible to smile back at him. Still, she tried. He was just a baby. What did he know about heartache?

"Cira, I can dress him for you," Giulia said, coming up behind her. "You should get ready yourself."

"It's all right. There's plenty of time before we have to leave for the church," Cira told her.

"No, there isn't. And you want to be beautiful for your groom, don't you?"

Cira didn't reply, just went on pulling the gown over the now-squirming baby, gently putting his roly-poly arms into the gathered sleeves. She reached for the booties that lay on the bed beside him, but Giulia snatched them up first and gave her a little shove.

"Go . . . Get dressed," she urged. "I'll finish with Luciano."

"All right . . ."

"Cira?" her sister asked as she turned away.

"Yes?"

"You aren't a happy bride, are you?"

Turning back to her sister, Cira opened her mouth to speak. Instead, to her horror, a sob spilled from her throat.

She clenched her hand to her mouth and fought to speak over the aching lump that had risen, but found that she couldn't.

"What is it?" Giulia asked, putting her arms around her. "Cira, what's wrong?"

She shook her head, her eyes blinded by hot tears that pooled in them.

"It's that man who came yesterday, with the flowers, isn't it? He wasn't just a friend, the way you said, was he? That's why you didn't want to talk about him afterward."

"I . . . I don't want to talk about him now, either," Cira said. "I have to go get dressed."

She moved away, to a corner of the crowded room where Mama had hung her freshly pressed wedding dress. It wasn't white, or fancy, but Mama had made it over from one of her own dresses, and Cira knew the rose-colored fabric was attractive on her, complimenting her complexion.

"Just wait until Carlo sees you in it," Giulia had said wistfully, when Cira had obediently tried it on the night before.

Carlo.

In a matter of hours he would be her husband.

She wanted that knowledge to fill her with joy, or at the very least, contentment. She wanted to be happy about marrying Lucia's brother, who was, after all, a good man, a hardworking and loyal man, a man who would provide and care for her and Luciano.

It was for Luciano's sake that she had said yes when Carlo had proposed a month ago. Cira had been caring for the baby since they had arrived on Broome Street; there was no room in the tiny one-room flat Carlo shared with several other rail workers. But the plan was for Carlo to eventually move, and to take the baby along.

And Cira had known that giving him up would be like ripping out her own heart.

She had already lost Thatcher, a fact that had been inevitible from the moment she said goodbye to him that night at the hotel. Still, in those first few weeks with her family, she had hoped he would come to her—at least just to visit her. She had given him the address, and he had promised that he would.

But as days, and then weeks, passed with no sign of him, she had realized that he was out of her life forever. Just as she had known he would be one day. And she tried to convince herself that it was for the best.

That was why, when Carlo's visits to the Valentino's apartment became clearly more than just checkups on his nephew, she had done her best to go along with it. She had always liked him, so it wasn't hard to laugh at his jokes, or thank him for his compliments.

The day he asked her to marry him, he had kissed her first, and she hadn't protested. She had let him move his lips over hers, had tried to lose herself in the kiss. But her mind was screaming that it was wrong, that he wasn't Thatcher.

And when he had proposed, she had told herself that she shouldn't accept. But then she had thought of Luciano, had realized that if she were Carlo's wife, she would remain Luciano's mother.

And that was enough to make her say yes.

Carlo had been thrilled. Her parents had been thrilled. And she had been swept up in their excitement, relieved that she wouldn't have to give up the child she loved. She had shoved memories of Thatcher to the back of her mind, and it worked during the busy days filled with the confusion and demands of family and childcare and wedding preparations.

But on those sweltering summer nights, as she lay on the thin straw mattress she shared with Giulia, she was too weary to keep thoughts of Thatcher from stealing into her mind. She let herself remember what it had been like with him, how she had felt with him, and she knew that she would never forget.

She told herself that she could endure a marriage to a man like Carlo—a good man, but a man she didn't love—if she could just keep alive in her heart the memories of the man she had loved, and lost.

Now, as she reached for her wedding dress, she told herself again that she was doing the right thing.

It was what Lucia would have wanted—for her to raise Luciano with Carlo, the brother she had adored. They belonged together. He, too, had come from Fiorenza, he shared her background, her ideals, her religion. And, most important, her love for the child whose mother had been her dearest friend on earth.

I'm doing this for you, Cira told her friend silently as she fumbled with the buttons on her dress. *For you, and for your son. Our son.*

The large Roman Catholic church was empty at this hour on a weekday, except for the priest and the cluster of people gathered before the altar.

Cira glanced at them as she stepped into the vestibule on her father's arm, then looked away, down at the Bible she held in both hands before her. Giulia had suggested that she carry the beautiful bouquet of flowers down the aisle, but the very suggestion had made bile rise in Cira's throat. How could she marry Carlo carrying the flowers Thatcher had given her?

How could she marry Carlo at all?

She didn't want to raise her head, couldn't bring herself to look at him, frightened of what she would see on his face. He would be happy, filled with expectations, eager to get the ceremony underway.

And she . . .

She was devastated.

If only Thatcher hadn't come to her yesterday. If only he had waited one more day, until it was too late. Until she was already married to Carlo.

But he hadn't.

And seeing him again, hearing him speak the words she had never dared believe he would utter, had made this marriage all the more difficult. Despite her promise to Lucia. Despite her love for Luciano.

Her father looked at her, squeezed her arm, asked if she was ready.

Too distraught to speak, she merely nodded.

Together, they began to move down the aisle, slowly approaching the group at the altar. The church was silent, except for the occasional babbling of Luciano in Giulia's arms.

Cira's legs wobbled beneath her but she refused to falter.

I'm doing this for you, she told Lucia again. *For you. This is what you would have wanted.*

Finally, she realized, they had reached the front of the church.

It was time.

She could no longer put off looking up. Her father was placing her hand in Carlo's, and he was squeezing it firmly, and she had to raise her eyes to meet the gaze of her groom.

She did.

And she was struck by the sweeping knowledge that it was the wrong face, the wrong groom.

This should be Thatcher.

She should be marrying Thatcher.

She loved Thatcher.

"Carlo," she said, his name spilling from her lips unexpectedly as the priest began to intone in Latin.

The outburst took everyone, even herself by surprise.

The priest stopped speaking. Carlo stared. So did her family and Carlo's friends.

"I need to speak to you," Cira blurted to her groom. "Alone."

She was vaguely aware of the startled murmurs of her parents; of Carlo leading her, at the priest's direction, to a small room at the back of the church.

There, he faced her and asked, with trepidation in his voice, "What is it, Cira? What's the matter?"

"I can't marry you."

"What?"

He was clearly shocked, and yet, Cira wondered, how could he be? Hadn't he realized that she was just going through the motions? Hadn't he realized that they weren't in love? Didn't he know that when you married someone, you should be in love?

"I can't marry you," she repeated calmly, buoyed by the realization that these words felt right, that there was nothing else she could say.

"But . . . why not?"

"Because . . ." She couldn't tell him about Thatcher. Not here. Not now.

Instead, she said gently, "Because we don't love each other."

"Of course we do."

"No, we don't. *I* don't, Carlo," she said at last, wanting to look away from the pain that ravaged his kind face, but unwilling to allow herself that reprieve. She hated hurting him this way, hated that she had to do it, but knew that there was no option.

She loved Thatcher Montgomery. She wanted to marry Thatcher Montgomery.

"But . . ." Carlo wavered, then said, "You will learn to love me, Cira."

"No. I won't."

Stark hurt was evident in his eyes. And something else—pride. As she acknowledged it, she realized that such fierce pride wouldn't let him beg for something she couldn't give. It was going to be all right. He would let her go without a struggle.

He was silent for a long time. Finally he shook his head and said, "But what about Luciano?"

Luciano.

There it was.

She could only hope now that Carlo would understand. He was a reasonable man. A good man. A man who would understand that a baby needed a mother.

"I adore Luciano," she told him carefully. "I've been caring for him since he was a newborn, Carlo. I'm the only mother he's ever known. I want to keep him with me . . . and raise him. I promise that we'll stay right here in New York. And that you will see him whenever you want—"

"No!" Carlo said, silencing her with a fierce glare. "You won't keep Luciano. He's my sister's child. He has my blood in his veins. Not yours!"

"But . . . I'm his mother," Cira protested, unable to believe what she was hearing. How was it possible that she was going to lose the child she adored?

"No," Carlo practically spit the word at her. "You aren't his mother. Not if you aren't my wife."

"But, Carlo—"

"Luciano is a Torrio. He belongs to me. Go," he said, pointing at the door. "Get out of here. And tell your sister to bring Luciano to me right away."

Sobbing, Cira stood her ground, staring at him, shaking her head. "I can't give him up, Carlo. Please . . . Please don't do this."

"I didn't do this, Cira. You did."

Cira's feet tapped loudly across the marble floor as she approached the man seated behind the lobby desk. He looked up from his newspaper and eyed her with bored curiosity.

"Yes?"

"I am looking for Thatcher Montgomery," she said in carefully rehearsed English. "I am a friend."

"Thatcher Montgomery?" The guard narrowed his eyes at her. "You're a friend of his?" There was no mistaking the dubious note in his voice, and Cira fought to keep herself from breaking eye contact with him. She couldn't let him see how uncertain she was.

"I must see him," she said, and searched for more words to make the guard see that this was urgent.

But the man was already shaking his head, saying Thatcher's name and something else she didn't understand. Frustrated, she reached out and grabbed his arm.

"*Per favore* . . . Please," she corrected, remembering the English word. "Please . . . I must see Thatcher."

The guard studied her for a long time, and she willed him to understand that she was desperate, not to turn her away. She had lost the child she loved because of her feelings for Thatcher. This building on Broadway was the only place she knew to look for him, to tell him that she hadn't married Carlo, that she would be his wife after all.

At last the man shrugged and pointed toward the wall behind him.

Cira glanced that way and frowned, seeing an elaborate cagelike door that seemed to lead to an empty alcove, with another man standing before it.

"Go," the guard said. "He will take you up."

She pieced together his instructions and, puzzled, walked toward the man, peering past his shoulder to see if the alcove concealed a stairway. None was evident.

The guard was calling something to the other man, and again she heard Thatcher's name mentioned. The second man cast a doubtful glance in her direction, then reached out and threw a switch on the wall.

She heard a grinding sound from behind the cage and stepped back in trepidation.

The man chuckled and asked her a question she couldn't decipher.

Frustrated, she said, *"Non parlo inglese."*

The man shook his head and said nothing. Moments later, to her astonishment, a small platform was being lowered on mechanical pulleys behind the cage, and the man threw it open as soon as the grinding sound had stopped and the platform was level with the lobby floor.

He motioned for her to step inside.

She hesitated, leery of the peculiar contraption, of these strangers in their matching navy coats with gold buttons. But she reminded herself that this was America, where men in uniform weren't enemies, and that she was here to see Thatcher, and she had to believe that they were taking her to him.

So, mystified, she did as she was told, and the man got into the compartment with her, lowered the cage, and threw a switch on the wall. There was a jerk, and then the contraption began to rise.

Cira cried out, and the man glanced at her, amused, and mumbled words that sounded reassuring.

Finally the platform came to a stop. A second cage was thrown open, and Cira found herself in a vast, carpeted reception area.

For a moment she was too shaken to move.

But then her legs propelled her forward, toward the desk where a gray-haired woman sat studying her with wary eyes.

This was torture.

Where was Thatcher?

She asked for him in a trembling voice, struggling to remember the right phrases and having to repeat them for the skeptical-looking woman. But at last, after motioning for her to wait, the woman stood and walked down a long hallway.

Cira fidgeted with her hands as she waited, telling herself that everything would be fine the moment she saw Thatcher. Nothing else would matter . . .

No. That wasn't true.

There would always be Luciano.

Her empty arms and hollow heart had ached from the moment she had kissed him goodbye yesterday morning at the church, before allowing Giulia to bring him to Carlo. She had wept over him, telling him how very much she loved him and how desperately she wished she could keep him.

He had stared at her with those wise, round brown eyes as though he understood, but she knew that of course he didn't, and that he would soon forget her.

He had started to cry as a weeping Giulia had carried him away, stretching out his chubby little arms in Cira's direction. The sound of his pitiful wails had haunted her for the rest of the day and all through the restless night. Paralyzed by grief, she hadn't been able to summon the energy to explain to her baffled family what had happened between her and Carlo. All she could do was sob, and stare at the wall, and thankfully, they left her alone as much as was possible in the tiny apartment.

And when the sun rose, and there was no hungry Luciano to rouse her from bed, clamoring for his breakfast, she forced herself up anyway. She dried her tears, and she got dressed, and she made her way uptown to find Thatcher.

Now, as she waited nervously for him to appear, she told herself that the seemingly endless journey she had begun months ago back in Sicily was almost over. There would be no more wandering, no more searching for a place to belong. When she saw Thatcher, when he took her into his arms, she would be home again at last.

Footsteps approached, and she drew in a sharp breath in anticipation.

But the man who emerged from the hallway wasn't Thatcher. He had Thatcher's lanky build, and his angular features, but his hair was gray and his eyes were somber.

"Hello," he said cautiously, seeming to look her over from head to toe in one swift movement.

"Hello," she returned in English. "I am looking for Thatcher Montgomery."

"Cira? Cira Valentino?" the man asked.

Startled that he knew her name, for she hadn't given it to the woman, she widened her eyes and nodded.

"My son told me about you."

She was struck by the fact that he spoke to her in fluent Italian; that he was clearly Thatcher's father; that, miraculously, Thatcher had told him about her.

Could he have asked her to marry him with his family's blessings? Somehow, that possibility had never entered her mind. She had assumed that he was defying his parents and his upbringing for her.

She looked at this man, and his eyes weren't unkind. But they contained an expression of melancholy, as though they hadn't smiled in a long time.

He startled her again, then, by asking, "How is my son?"

"How is your son?" she echoed. "Don't you know?"

"Don't I know what?"

"Don't you know how he is?"

Looking puzzled, he shook his head and said, "Cira, Thatcher walked out of here three months ago and never came back. I thought he was with you."

"With me?" Her mind raced. Thatcher was gone?

Where was he? How was she going to find him now?

"He told me about you. He said that he loved you. That he wanted to make you his wife. I assumed that was just what he had done."

"No . . . No," she said, realizing that Thatcher had walked away from this man who clearly loved him, from this palatial building that bore his name, from the privileged world that was the only thing he had ever known. He had done it for her . . .

And she had turned him down, told him she was going to marry another man.

"Signore Montgomery," she said slowly, "I must talk to you."

He nodded and led her down the hall to an immense office and motioned for her to sit down on one of the comfortable-looking chairs before the desk.

She did, perching on the edge of the seat, and began to talk.

She only meant to tell him the bare facts, but she found herself opening up to his father, spilling out the whole story. She had to keep backtracking, taking him back to Sicily, telling him everything except the most intimate details.

And when she was finished, the older man leaned back in his chair and stared up at the ceiling, his fingertips steepled on the desk in front of him.

"You clearly love my son," he said at last. "And he loves you."

"Yes."

"You gave up your child for him."

"Yes."

"And he gave up his family and his fortune for you."

Cira nodded. "I only wish that I knew where he was, Signore Montgomery. I don't know how to find him."

"Nor do I," Thatcher's father said, and her heart sank. She could never track Thatcher down on her own. Not in this vast city. Not with the language barrier. It would be impossible.

"But if I could find him," his father went on, "I would tell him that he was right to do what he did. And I was wrong. About a lot of things. When I thought I had lost him when I heard his ship went down in the Atlantic last spring, I was devastated. Partly because he's my son and I love him, but partly because he's my only heir . . . the future of my business. And I'm ashamed of that."

Cira sat watching the regret play across his wrinkled face, hearing the sorrow in his voice, and realizing that Thatcher's world was a complicated one—more complicated than she she had ever imagined.

"This time, when I lost him, I was devastated as well," the old man went on. "But this time I knew he had left me by his own choice. And that hurt. And this time I was devastated because I love him, and he's my son. The business, all the rest of it, be damned."

Cira held her breath, saying nothing.

"If I ever see him again, Cira, I plan to tell him that. That he doesn't have to live a life he doesn't want to live. That he should marry you, and be happy. He should take chances I should have taken. But I was too much a coward."

They sat in silence for a long time, Cira watching Thatcher's father as he sat with his head buried in his hands. Finally he raised it and looked at her.

"We have to find him, Cira," he said resolutely.

Relief coursed through her, and she nodded. "But how?"

He tapped his desk thoughtfully with his fingertips. "My valet has a brother . . ."

Thatcher sat at his cluttered desk in the small back office of the automobile showroom, munching thoughtfully on the thin sandwich he had brought for his lunch. The roast beef was dry and tasteless and the bread was a few days old, but it didn't matter to him. He had little interest in food these days . . .

Or anything else.

He had merely been going through the motions in the weeks since Cira had turned down his proposal—eating and working and sleeping, but not really *living*. He doubted he would ever really *live* again.

Not without her.

Not knowing that she now belonged to another man, while his heart would always belong to her.

Dully he wondered for the hundredth, or perhaps the thousandth, time, who Cira's husband was. She had wasted no time in finding someone after leaving Thatcher, and that surprised him. It wasn't that he expected her to carry a torch for him forever. But Cira hadn't struck him as a woman who trusted—or fell in love—very easily.

At least, she hadn't with him.

But maybe he'd been mistaken.

Maybe she hadn't loved him after all.

Maybe—

"Thatcher?"

"Yes?" He looked up to see Mr. Spencer, his boss, standing in the doorway, looking bemused.

"There's a lady here. She's been looking at the new touring car."

"A *lady*?" he echoed, startled. Virtually every serious

customer who came into the store was a man, although a handful were accompanied by their wives. But women tended to be leery about automobiles, some even frightened of the newfangled contraptions.

"A lady," his boss confirmed. "A beautiful one, at that. And young. She wants someone to take her for a drive. And she asked for you."

"For me?"

"For you."

Thatcher frowned, setting down his sandwich. "Why me?"

"I asked her. She wouldn't say. Perhaps she's a friend of yours."

Thatcher doubted that. He had no lady friends in his new life. And no one from his old life was aware that he was working here. He supposed it was inevitible that sooner or later somebody he knew would walk in off the street one day and recognize him. But until that happened, he could pretend the old life hadn't existed; that he was Thatcher Smith—the name he had been using since the day he walked out of the Montgomery building and into blessed obscurity.

"You'd better hurry," his boss told him. "This lady seems impatient, and she looks like she has a lot of money."

Obediently Thatcher stood and pulled on his suit coat before making his way to the large room at the front of the building, where the gleaming automobiles were displayed.

The driver's side door of the new touring car, which was alread parked on the street with the motor running, was standing open, waiting for him, and a woman sat in the passenger's seat. She wore an impeccably cut, high-

collared coat and a broad-brimmed motoring hat with a
veil that covered her face.

He glanced at her, surprised to find that she appeared
to be a stranger, and said, "Ma'am? I'm Thatcher
Smith."

She nodded.

He wondered if perhaps she was one of the few ladies
who had come in with her husband, and decided that
must be the case.

He slid into the seat beside her and took the wheel,
pulling the door closed beside him.

As he did, she turned to him and said, "Thatcher . . .
it's me."

That voice jolted him like a runaway train.

She pulled off her veil in one abrupt, impatient movement, and he saw that it was, indeed, Cira. Her hair was
done up in the latest fad beneath the hat, and the dress
that peeked from beneath the stylish coat appeared to be
made of silk. But it was her lovely face, and she was
smiling at him, and he was swept by a rush of emotion
that rendered him momentarily speechless.

Finally he found his voice and asked, "How did you
find me? And . . . where did you get those clothes? Is
your husband . . . is he a wealthy man?"

She shook her head. "I have no husband, Thatcher.
Not yet."

Flabbergasted, he stuttered, then managed, "But you
were getting married."

"I couldn't do it. I couldn't get you out of my mind.
I love you, Thatcher. I want to be your wife."

"You do?" This couldn't be happening. How could
this be happening?

"I do."

"But . . ."

"You don't want to marry me anymore?" she asked, watching him anxiously.

"Oh, yes . . . Cira, of course I do. Of course I do . . ." With that, he took her into his arms at last and captured her lips hungrily with his own. He kissed her until he was breathless and weak with desire, and stroked her cheek in wonder, gazing down at her.

"How did you find me?" he asked again, still dazed.

"Your father's valet has a brother who's a detective . . . remember?" she asked, smiling.

"My father?" Dumbstruck, he could only stare.

And she told him, then, how she had gone to his father's building looking for him. She told him how her father had taken her under his wing, insisting on buying her clothes and finding her family a bigger apartment. She told him how they had searched for him together, with the detective's help, and how elated they had been when he turned up at last. And when, finally, she told him what Stoddard had said about his decision to turn his back on his destiny, he found tears stinging his eyes at the realization that the old man had finally understood him—had given his blessing for Thatcher to marry Cira.

But he hardly dared to ask . . .

"What about my mother?"

"Your mother?" She shook her head. "She doesn't know about me. Not yet. Your father said not to worry, though. He said he would stand by you, and that she would eventually come around."

"I doubt it."

"I think your father does, too," Cira said, amusement mingling with regret on her face. "Is that a problem?"

"No," Thatcher told her, stroking the unnatural waves in her hair. "It's not a problem. I don't need her approval. Not anymore. I've built a life of my own, Cira.

It isn't much . . . but I can take care of you and Luciano."

Her eyes clouded over then, and his heart skipped a beat. "Where is Luciano?" he asked. "Has something happened to him?"

She opened her mouth to speak, but a sob spilled out instead. He held her while she soaked his shirt with her tears, and gradually, the whole story came out. Saddened as he was by the fact that she had lost Luciano, he found himself relieved that it had been Lucia's brother she planned to marry—that it hadn't been some stranger who had swept her off her feet. She had never thought she loved the man; had only agreed to marry him for the child's sake. And that banished the last lingering doubt from his mind. He had never lost her at all. Not even for a moment.

"I'm so sorry, Cira," he said, brushing tears from his eyes at the thought of the pudgy little boy he would never hold again—the boy he had intended to raise as his own son. "I can only promise you that we'll never forget Luciano. And that your arms won't be empty forever. Someday, hopefully soon, you'll have a baby of your own."

She smiled through her tears and he kissed her again. And again.

"I promise," he said, his voice choked with emotion, "that I will stay by your side for the rest of your life, Cira."

"And I promise that I'll be the wife you deserve, Thatcher."

"I know you will," he told her, loving her with all of his heart.

Epilogue

"*C*ira?"

Thatcher's voice came to her faintly, across a vast, misty field.

"Cira?"

She struggled to find her way back to him, conscious of another sound.

It was . . . a baby crying.

Luciano . . .

But Luciano was gone . . .

Wasn't he?

Confused, she tried to unscramble her thoughts, to clear her brain of the woolly clouds that obscured reality.

"Is she all right?" she heard Thatcher ask in the distance then.

"She's fine," came the doctor's voice. "Just exhausted and groggy from the chloroform. She'll come around soon. Just keep an eye on her."

The voices faded and Cira stumbled into blackness again.

Then she heard Thatcher's voice.

"Cira? Please wake up, sweetheart. Please. Wake up. I love you, Cira . . ."

Fuzzily she made her way back to him, opening her eyes to see his dear face wearing an expression of concern, and looming over her.

"What . . . ?" She asked hazily.

"There you are," he said, smiling at her. "I've been trying to wake you for so long. How do you feel?"

She blinked, considering his question, and realizing, as the numbness wore off, that she was sore. Terribly sore. In places that—

"The baby!" she exclaimed, remembering, suddenly, what it was that was happening. "Is the baby almost here?"

"The baby *is* here, Cira," he said, laughing. "You did a wonderful job, sweetheart. You were so strong . . . so brave."

She saw then that there was a bundle in his arms. A bundle wrapped in a white blanket that had once belonged to Luciano.

"Meet your daughter, Cira," Thatcher said, bending over her and showing her the baby's cherubic, bright red face. Her bright blue eyes blinked solemnly at her mother, and Cira felt more of the numbness give away to joy . . . pure joy.

"A daughter?" she echoed, staring at the child she had labored so long to bring into this world. "We have a daughter, Thatcher."

"Yes. A daughter and a son," he agreed. "Although big brother wasn't very happy to meet her. He wanted to know how long she was going to be staying with us."

Cira laughed even though it hurt, and said, "He'll come around. He'll learn to love her."

"Of course he will."

She reached up to take the baby from her husband, then winced.

"Don't," Thatcher said quickly, patting her arm. "You've been through too much. Just rest now, Cira."

She sighed gratefully and smiled, allowing her eyelids to flutter closed.

But she didn't drift off again right away.

Though her body was paralyzed with sheer exhaustion, her heart was spilling over with happiness, and her mind was racing with thoughts of the future—and of the past.

She thought about Thatcher . . .

And about Luciano.

She thanked God for him again, as she had every day since the morning two years ago—not long after she and Thatcher had married—when Carlo had shown up on their doorstep with the crying baby in his arms.

"He's been miserable ever since I took him away from you," he said unhappily. "You were right, Cira. You are his mother. And he needs you. It isn't that I don't love him, but . . . I know Lucia would have wanted you to have him."

"Oh, thank you, Carlo . . . thank you . . ."

And he had smiled at her, and told her that he was glad she had found happiness. He said he was going west to look for better work and that he would stay in touch. "Please tell my nephew that someday I will be back to visit him. And please tell him about my sister," Carlo had said, his voice choked with emotion.

"I will," Cira had promised.

And she had.

She had told her little boy about Lucia, her best friend, and about their happy days in the old country. Luciano was too young to understand, really, but still she told him. She needed to, for her own sake as much as for his.

Lucia had given her a beautiful son . . .

And now Thatcher had given her a daughter.

She lay there contentedly in the big feather bed they shared, listening to her husband in the next room, crooning to the baby, and to their son running and playing with his toys.

And she smiled as she drifted off to sleep, lulled by the sweet sounds of home.

Friends Romance

Can a man come between friends?

__A TASTE OF HONEY
by DeWanna Pace   __ 0-515-12387-0

__WHERE THE HEART IS
by Sheridon Smythe   0-515-12412-5

__LONG WAY HOME
by Wendy Corsi Staub   0-515-12440-0

All books $5.99

Prices slightly higher in Canada